SECRETS IN TIME

SAN FRANCISCO

MERLA ZELLERBACH

firefall ™

First Edition: February 2009

cover illustration by Gladys Perint Palmer

FIREFALL EDITIONS
Canyon California 94516-0189

literary@att.net
www.firefallmedia.com

Printed in the United States of America

ISBN: 0-915090-32-5

Prologue

The House on Jackson Street

A dazzling blonde in a red BMW convertible, open to a San Francisco sunshine, raced through a yellow light and sped north on Laurel, turning left onto Jackson Street. The car came to a sudden stop at the curb of a tall stately mansion. Melanie Morris grabbed her camel's hair coat and jumped out.

How ridiculous to need a wrap on such a warm day, she thought, especially indoors! All because her strong-willed, loveable grandmother, Clara Hayes Stockton, had read about a research team, who had prolonged the lives of laboratory rats by cooling their cages.

Rats were not people, Melanie had pointed out. Nevertheless, Clara insisted they were valid test subjects. Born the year after the 1906 fire and earthquake that ravaged half the city, Clara recalled no personal encounters with such creatures.

The city's extensive trade with the Orient, however, had led to an influx of the pesky rodents in 1900, causing an outbreak of bubonic plague. The Public Health Department issued strong notices, urging residents never to leave any bits of food on the floor, tables, or kitchen counters. By the time the plague ended in 1908, the warnings had triggered a lifelong obsession with cleanliness that Gertrude Hayes passed on to Clara, her only child.

Clara had always had definite ideas about — well, just about everything, including life and death.

As a young girl, and adult also, Clara pooh-poohed the idea of dying, insisting she had no intention of honoring that unpleasant custom, at least not before she reached the century mark. Mindful of that goal (and the lab rats' longevity), she had ordered that the house on Jackson Street be kept unheated all year round. Family, friends, and staff had learned to dress accordingly; shivering visitors often were offered the comfort of a fur throw.

Melanie hurried up the brick walkway, glancing at her watch, and smiling to herself. What an amazing lady her grandmother was at 99, her memory of past events as acute as her memory of recent events was not.

And how lucky they were to have a special bond. Uncle Tim liked to tease that they were as similar as two acorns — and everyone knew that acorns were nuts. Jokes aside, they shared a tendency to be stubborn, a fierce independence, an impatience with bigotry, and a deep loyalty to family and friends. Beneath seemingly tough exteriors, they also shared a generous, loving nature.

One character trait Melanie thanked God she *didn't* inherit, was Clara's compulsive neatness. Every Wednesday after breakfast, Clara would put on a fresh pair of white gloves and test the various moldings and cabinet tops in the house. If the tiniest speck of dust darkened her fingertips, she would instantly point out the "trouble spot" to her long-suffering maid, Kai.

Clara's late husband, James Tyler Stockton, the illustrious newspaper publisher, was far less fastidious, but he'd have approved of Clara's no-heat philosophy. Sixteen years her senior, Grandpa James had welcomed every economy. How many times had Melanie heard the story of the cub reporter who'd had the audacity to call the great publisher "stingy."

Grandpa James had replied that he agreed in principle, but not so semantically; he considered himself "prudent." And the young man, he'd added, could consider himself "released" from his job. And that was long before anyone in San Francisco *thought* about political correctness.

Poor old tightwad Grandpa James. Melanie hadn't known her mother's father; he'd died in 1953, nine years before she was born. Yet Clara spoke of him so often, his character was quite familiar. The masses of pink roses in Steuben vases around the house were a luxury James Stockton would never have permitted. Nor would he have allowed Clara to buy any of the fine antiques she'd acquired from her art expert friends — "extravagances" that had become near-priceless.

"One old relic deserves another," Clara loved to quip, when guests admired her treasures.

The Stockton manor dominated the northwest corner of Jackson Street overlooking Julius Kahn Park and 1,480 acres of the Presidio — the former army base said to be "the best property in town."

In the very early 1900s, Holt and Edith Stockton had commissioned architect Bernard Maybeck to design their handsome Tudor dwelling, a four-story mansion with a typical Alpine exterior of brown timber slats against bright white stucco.

A protective hedge surrounded the front garden, high enough to ensure privacy, but low enough not to seem forbidding. Above it, masses of red geraniums bloomed in a trio of window boxes. As a child, Melanie had often called it her "gingerbread palace," and fantasized that all its occupants were talking cookies.

Using her key, Melanie opened the front door and scurried upstairs to the library. Inside the spacious sitting room with its redwood-beamed ceiling, a giant window looked out on the bay. Nearby stood a carved fireplace that had been imported, stone by stone, from a 16th century English castle. Built-in wall shelves displayed books, mostly about California history, along with her late grandfather's untouched collection of cable car memorabilia.

As expected, the indoor temperature was a cool 50 degrees. Wrapped in cashmere, Clara relaxed on a chaise, apparently enjoying the mid-day view of the Golden Gate Bridge, sparkling in the sunlight.

"Knock, knock. Anyone there?"

The reverie ended abruptly. "You're late, Miss Celebrity!" Clara's voice was raspy, but clear. She spoke in concise sentences, with rarely an extra word. "I almost called the police."

"You did no such thing." Melanie hurried across the room, tossed back her golden mane, and bent to bestow a kiss. Her blue eyes twinkled. Freckles danced across the bridge of her delicate nose. "You've been sitting there dreaming up ways to drop the temperature in this bloody igloo so you can outlive us all. Don't deny it!"

"I deny nothing. And I thank the Lord I never talked back to *my* grandmother. I'd have been spanked and sent to bed."

"Spanking's supposed to be fun, Nonna. Guess I'll have to educate you and bring you into the 21st century."

Struggling not to smile, Clara forced a frown. "You're a wicked child, Melanie Morris. I don't know where you get that perverse sense of humor."

"I wonder."

"And how they tolerate you at that television station…"

"I'm a woman, not a child. And how they 'tolerate' me is no mystery. I'm the best news anchor they have. Besides, after eleven years, I know too many secrets. They wouldn't dare fire me."

Pulling up the collar of her coat, Melanie sank deep into a chair — noting with pleasure that her grandmother, who'd slightly loosened her shawl, looked alert and well.

Clara Hayes Stockton was the quintessential grande dame, elegant in a black wool challis dress — a classic 40-year-old Galanos that had nothing to do with trends. Superbly-matched Mikimoto pearls graced a long, fluid neck that Avedon had once photographed in profile. Her white hair was short and neatly coiffed, her features fine and regal. Vestiges of great beauty remained.

Melanie grinned across the room. "I hate to say this, Nonna, but freezing agrees with you."

"Thank you, my dear." Clara's hands trembled slightly. "We must be serious for a moment."

"Is anything wrong?"

"No. But I asked you here to tell you a rather indelicate story about your grandmother."

"Oh, dear!" Melanie crossed her legs, then quickly uncrossed them. "You're *not* going to discuss the shooting, are you, Nonna? There's no need to dredge that up. I made peace with the matter years ago."

Clara shook her head. "No, my dear, I'm afraid you've simply buried it. Now it's time to clear the air, before I join my ancestors."

"Don't talk that way. You're much too stubborn to die."

A torrent of memories flooded Melanie's brain — painful reminders of all the nights she had tossed in her bed as a child, and later, as a teenager, trying to ponder the tragic death in her grandmother's house — the fatal shooting that no one, not even her mother, would explain.

Now she felt torn; the excitement of finally getting an answer to the questions she had repressed for so many decades, clashed with a desire to spare her grandmother grief.

Footsteps announced the entrance of a petite Chinese woman, who set down a tray of tea and petits fours. "Thank you, Kai. Close the door, please. We mustn't be disturbed."

"Yes, Madame."

The room was silent for several seconds. Melanie fidgeted uncomfortably. Clara had summoned her for a reason, and she knew she had no hope of trying to talk her out of it.

Clasping her hands to stop their shaking, Clara spoke softly. "I've waited years to tell you this, Melanie. When I'm done, you'll see why I couldn't take it to the grave."

"Please don't say that. You're not —"

"Yes, I am. I know I won't make 100, so this chat is way overdue. I'll get right to my story. That fatal night in 1960 actually started in the 1940s. Grandpa James and I had been married eleven years..."

Part I

Peace At Last

Chapter 1

(To understand Clara's story, we must begin in 1945.)

San Francisco was in turmoil — excited turmoil. Delegates from around the world, representing almost two billion people, convened in San Francisco for the launching of the United Nations. The War Memorial Opera House and the Veterans' Building on Van Ness Avenue became the daytime activities centers, while after dark, the city's top hostesses competed to entertain the distinguished visitors.

Thanks to *San Francisco Herald* publisher James Tyler Stockton's political connections, and to the envy of all their friends, he and his wife Clara had the good fortune to snag both feisty President Harry Truman and tall, slender British Foreign Secretary Anthony Eden to be their honored dinner guests.

At the same time, however, accommodations had to be found for 3,000 out-of-towners and 2,500 reporters. Delegates began demanding preferential treatment in hotels and restaurants. Socially prominent Lurline Matson Roth, daughter of Captain William Matson, founder of the Matson Navigation Company, recruited hundreds of Red Cross volunteers to help solve the problems, and somehow, almost miraculously, the city got through it.

On Tuesday, May 8th, shortly before the first UN Charter was signed on June 26th, the *Herald's* headlines reported that Germany had at last surrendered to the Allies, officially ending World War II in Europe.

Two atomic bombs later, on Wednesday, August 15th, Emperor Hirohito had announced Japan's surrender. The welcome news prompted James Stockton to momentarily forget his frugal nature, and to the amazement of his office staff, actually pop open a magnum of champagne.

Thousands of their fellow San Franciscans celebrated V-J (Victory over Japan) Day with spontaneous revelry — waving signs from rooftops and windows, shouting and singing on Union Square and all along Market Street, where servicemen were going wild, grabbing and kissing any woman they could find.

Even the wounded rejoiced. The veterans were proud of their role in assuring a safe future for their children and grandchildren and, despite their disabilities, looked forward to years of peace and good living. They had earned it.

Across town at the Stockton home on Jackson Street, the family was busy planning for a wedding.

"How come you always wear bow ties?"

Timothy Stockton leaned forward in his armchair and turned down the radio. As usual, his 16-year-old half-brother, Will Stockton, had come barging into the library, breaking his concentration. They shared a father, James Tyler Stockton, but had little else in common.

"I wear bow ties because they clip on, Will. They're easy to attach with one arm. I wear loafers for the same reason — so I don't have to tie the laces."

"Tell me what happened?" Will rested his Coke bottle atop the stone fireplace and plopped down on a brown leather couch, setting his muddy shoes on the foot rest. "Please?"

"Take your feet off the stool."

"Okay." He did as instructed. "Please? How'd you lose your arm?"

With a sigh, Tim sat back. Deep furrows around his mouth gave his handsome face a look of maturity greater than his 26 years. Dark brown hair, graying at the sides, bolstered the impression. He stared out the window a few seconds. What looked to be a military transport crossing the bay reminded him that the war was finally, irreversibly, over. "Okay, but this is the last time. I *mean* it."

"I promise." Will sat up and leaned forward eagerly. In sharp contrast to his half-brother's good looks, the boy was pale, almost anemic-looking. Thick glasses seemed too heavy for his face. Signs of acne marred his skin.

"It was November 15, 1943," Tim began in a low voice. His psychiatrist had told him the memories might not diminish for years to come, and it was healthy to air them.

"As you know, Will, our 2nd Marine Division was aboard the *Feland*, a 4300-ton troopship. We'd heard that our destination was Wake Island, in the Pacific, but that morning we learned we were headed for the tiny island of Betio, part of Tarawa atoll in the Gilbert Islands.

"All we knew at the time was that the *Maryland* and the *Colorado* were supposed to bomb the hell out of the Japs, and what they didn't get, the Navy dive bombers would finish. By the time we got ashore, the enemy — supposedly — would've been pretty well cleaned out."

"You mean dead."

"Unfortunately, yes." Tim paused, trying not to react. "Our goal was to take the airstrip. Naval Intelligence said they had 2,800 well-armed men. So there we were, sixteen transports of troops and equipment steaming toward this three-mile-long island. The bombers had done their bombing, but the enemy still returned heavy fire."

"Get to the good part."

"Good?" The boy tried his patience. "At five AM the next day, we — three dozen marines — piled into our square-nosed Higgins LCVP."

"That's when you barfed."

"The sea was rough. My buddy Hart Doyle held onto me and yes, I heaved over the side. Then we got the orders to disembark and wade in to shore. We had to hold our rifles over our heads so they'd stay dry. And we were ordered to spread out so we wouldn't be easy targets."

"They were shootin' at you!"

"They were shooting, Will — you could see the bullets kicking up the water on all sides. Bodies began dropping and there was nothing we could do but move forward…"

"Sort of like those wooden ducks at Playland at the Beach."

"Yes. All of a sudden, I felt the reef give way under my feet. I began to sink into the water, but I had so much gear I got entangled and just couldn't swim back up. I was positive that was the end, until I felt someone tugging at me. It was Hart, my buddy. He cut away my equipment and pulled me to the surface. In those few perilous seconds, he managed to save my life."

Tim swallowed, and paused to collect himself. No matter how many times he told the story, he couldn't escape the pain. "Then Hart said, I remember his exact words, 'Don't go stepping into any more bomb craters, knucklehead.' Two seconds later, a blast of gunfire split open his skull.

"I blacked out after that…woke up in sick bay on the ship. The medical aide told me they'd taken three bullets and some shrapnel from my arm and amputated it. So that's the story. Now may I hear my program?"

"Sure." Will rose and began firing an imaginary rifle. "Rat-a-tat-tat! Get the yellow bastards! Whatcha listenin' to?"

"I *was* listening to the news. MacArthur — Nimitz — the Allies just signed the surrender papers aboard the *U.S.S. Missouri* in Tokyo Bay."

"I thought the Japs gave up weeks ago."

"This makes it official." Tim sighed and shut off the radio. No use trying to hear anything with Will around. "Strange people, the Japanese. The diplomats all showed up wearing top hats and frock coats, as if they were going to a formal reception — or a funeral."

"I wish it *was* their funeral. Don't you?"

"No." Tim tensed in frustration. "We've had enough death and destruction."

"But the Japs *started* the war. They bombed us first."

"So they did." Much as Tim hated to admit it, part of him shared Will's hostility. He could forgive the Japanese people, he could even forgive the Japanese soldiers and sailors who'd been following orders, but never, ever, could he absolve Tojo and the military leaders who ruled the government. "Tell me again, Will. What's happening today?"

"Your sister Eevie's gettin' hitched. You know, the sexy redhead all the guys —"

"Don't be crude. I seem to recall that Yvonne is *your* sister, too. We're due in Burlingame at three?"

"Yeah. Whaddya think of the guy she's marryin'?"

"I like Marc Greenfield a lot."

"He's rich, I guess. They own that big fancy store on Union Square. But he's not our kind."

"Not our kind?"

"Yeah — Greenfield."

"You mean Jews aren't 'our kind'?"

"Some are." Will smiled. "I like Jerry Steinberg okay. He told me a funny story about this little girl who went to Fleishhacker Zoo with her mother, and she said, 'Mommy, I've seen all the elephants and monkeys. Where are the fleishhackers?' "

Will burst into laughter, but Tim's frown quickly sobered him. "Well, okay. But I heard that Hitler did the Jews a lot of good. He made anti-Semitism unpopular."

Tim's fist clenched in anger. "Who told you that garbage?"

"Betsy's husband, cousin Jeremy."

"Well, cousin Jeremy's wrong. *Dead* wrong! Hitler was a cold-blooded maniac —" He stopped mid-sentence, feeling himself about to explode. What right had Jeremy Hughes to poison the boy's mind? And why did Will listen to bigots like that? Didn't he ever think for himself?

He and Yvonne had tried their best to get along with Will and his little sister, Katie. They were Clara's children, the offspring of their father's second wife. Their father's first wife, his and Yvonne's mother Alice, had died of cancer five years prior.

Tim and Yvonne had always been close, but had little rapport with their half-siblings. Will was assertive and difficult; Katie was shy and withdrawn.

"We'll talk later." Tim rose impatiently. "Give me a hand with that boutonniere, will you?"

Limousines lined up two thick along the driveway leading to the Main House at Rosemont, the Stockton summer estate in Burlingame. In the background loomed a handsome French Colonial mansion, stately and imposing, behind a pair of white marble pillars.

Scents of wisteria lent a tropical feel to the warm September air, as guests made their way down the stone path to the Wedding Garden. Rows of chairs on the lawn faced a raised terrace lined with tall vases of anthurium and sprays of white orchids. A trellis of honeysuckle vines formed an archway.

Inside the house, Yvonne "Eevie" Stockton cast a last glance at the mirror in the master bedroom. She smoothed the bodice of her white Alençon lace wedding dress, marveling at her stepmother Clara's good taste. She'd never heard of the delicate French needlepoint fabric, but Clara had insisted on nothing less for the custom-made gown.

Patting down her auburn hair, Yvonne adjusted the veil of tulle that floated atop the diamond tiara she'd borrowed from Clara. The two women had had their clashes over the years, but Clara had been generous and helpful with their wedding plans.

The reflection pleased Yvonne. Her lovely features were subtly emphasized, thanks to the professional makeup artist Marc had ordered for her; he would be so proud.

"You look like a princess," cooed her cousin, Betsy Hughes, standing back to admire. "Still sure you want to go through with this?"

Yvonne glanced around nervously. The bridal party had already left. "Paul's *dead*, Betsy. You know how hard we tried to find him. He did promise to come back after the war and I waited. I've waited *years* for Paul. If he were alive, he'd have gotten word to me by now."

"Does Marc know you're in love with someone else?"

"He'll never know, and it doesn't matter. I'll always love Paul. But I can't bring him back to life."

A sharp knock sounded, and James Tyler Stockton, quite tall and imposing with aquiline features, appeared in the doorway — resplendent in cutaway and striped trousers. He approached the bride.

"A banquet for the eyes," he murmured, assessing his daughter with pride. He had the strongest urge to tell her how beautiful she was, but he resisted. Shows of emotion were embarrassing.

"You all right?" she asked.

He wiped his forehead. "Frankly, my sweet, I'm not too anxious to give away my prize production."

"Look at it this way, Papa. You're not losing a child. You're gaining a discount at S. Greenfield's."

"In that case," he smiled, taking her arm, "let's not keep the young man waiting."

Betsy Hughes stood by her cousin Tim in the receiving line. She felt awkward and self-conscious in her pink bouffant Matron of Honor dress, and wished she were home. Life on their ranch in Marin was simple and serene. She had come to hate society events, where everyone stood around sizing up everyone else. Her husband Jeremy, on the other hand, thrived in such situations.

Tim glanced down. "How're you doing, Bets'?"

"I'm okay. Jeremy ran off to the bar. He's good at remembering names. I never can."

"Just smile and be your sweet self."

Poor Betsy, he thought. Betsy Kettering Hughes, daughter of James' sister, Maggie Stockton Kettering, was married to a racist snob. Jeremy Hughes had quit his bank job two days before they eloped, and now called himself a "gentleman farmer" — actually, a do-nothing bum who lived off his wealthy wife. Rumors of heavy drinking, mistresses, and gambling debts were undoubtedly true. To know Jeremy Hughes was to dislike him.

The parade of guests seemed endless, until suddenly, a smile broke across Tim's face. "Look who's here! How've you been, Lou Ella?"

The young woman who stepped up to shake his hand was about five feet tall, full-breasted, and overdressed in a red suit with beaded trim. She wasn't a beauty in the classical sense, but her skin was smooth, her nose turned up prettily, her lips were full, and her eyes glowed with excitement.

"Congratulations, Tim. Your sister's a knockout! How'd you get the Rabbi and the Reverend to keep the ceremony so brief?"

"Clara warned them to stay under twenty minutes — or else!"

Lou Ella laughed. "That's Clara. I was upset to hear you'd been wounded, but I hear you're doing great. How long's it been since we've seen each other?"

"I left the *Herald* the day after Pearl Harbor, so — almost four years. By the way, I read the paper religiously and your political essays are quite, quite excellent."

"Really? Your father thinks I'm left of Mao Tse-tung."

"Dad barks a lot more than he bites — forgive cliché. Does he ever give you time to relax and enjoy life?"

"No, but I make time for myself. I'm not a bad cook." Slow down, she told herself. Don't sound too eager. "Actually, I'm got a small pot roast stewing at home and I'm making potato pancakes tomorrow. Would you — like to join me?"

"Will the potato pancakes keep till Friday?"

"You bet." She drew a card from her purse. "Here's my address. Come around seven. Very casual. Whoops! I'm holding up the line."

"Don't forget the apple sauce." He grinned and tucked the card in his pocket.

Chapter Two — 1945

By five-fifteen, the wedding reception was near full peak. Wine, whiskey, and champagne flowed. The temperature had dropped to a more comfortable 80, and a six-piece combo kept the crowd lively. The newly-weds, dressed in their traveling clothes, were having a last fox-trot.

Marc Greenfield found his wife's ear. "When can we escape?"

"Soon." Aware of the glances coming their way, Yvonne snuggled closer. They made a striking pair, she knew, and she knew Marc thought so, too. He cared a great deal about appearance — attracting people, impressing them, charming them. Merchandising was his life.

Sometimes she teased him, saying that he was only interested in her decorative value. He would deny it vigorously, answering that as much as he loved the gift wrap, he loved the contents more.

She wanted to believe him for many reasons, not the least of which was his religion. An unfortunate experience, where a good friend was blackballed by Yvonne's high school sorority because she was Jewish, had turned Yvonne into something of a crusader.

Marrying a Jewish man made a public statement, simply that Yvonne Stockton felt all human beings were equal, regardless of color, ancestry, or how they worshipped. The realization that "Mrs. Greenfield" might not be asked to join the Junior League or the Burlingame Country Club had only strengthened her decision. She wouldn't want to belong to any group that so discriminated.

Most of her friends applauded the marriage. Though the Stocktons had the old money and social position, Marc gave every indication that he would be a leader both in business and the community.

And while her friends were starting wedded life in small apartments, she and Marc were moving into a three-story house on Pacific Avenue, complete with garden and live-in housekeeper.

Yet Marc was so much more than his superficial assets. Courtly manners, maturity, wit, the ability to converse intelligently on almost any subject, reminded her of the best qualities of her father. And unlike the other men she'd dated, most of whom were in awe of her brains and beauty, Marc made her feel feminine and vulnerable. And that new role as part of a pair, rather than as a fiercely independent woman, was some-how satisfying.

"You must be dying in that wool suit," he said. "Wouldn't you like a cold drink?"

"No, thanks, Marc. I can stand it if you can."

"I can stand anything with you in my arms. Have I told you lately that you're the most exquisite woman I've ever had the pleasure to marry?"

"And the only one, I hope," she said, laughing. "You don't look too shabby yourself — for a dedicated bachelor who's just given up his freedom. Your family even seems resigned to your marrying a shiksa, or whatever they call me. And by the way, I've got the best-looking husband here, or anywhere."

Marc wasn't movie-star handsome, but he had impeccable taste and a natural elegance. Suntanned skin, horn-rimmed glasses, and slightly irregular features, framed by wavy black hair, gave his face a look of distinction. His attire was typically flawless: navy blazer; Swiss voile shirt, sheer as a handkerchief; doeskin trousers; tasseled English loafers.

Marriage to Marc, she realized, wedded her to both a man and a dynasty. The night they became engaged, he had recounted his family history.

Founded in 1876 by his grandparents who emigrated from the Netherlands, Ann and Simon Greenfield's small shop on Mission Street had started out selling Ann's lace and needlework pillows and Simon's gold leaf frames. Petite, dynamic Ann ran the business at a time when women couldn't even vote. Her hallmark was quality, the very finest, and that soon came to be recognized.

A steady procession of carriages from Nob Hill and Pacific Heights kept the couple so busy they hired helpers and expanded their inventory. In 1905, they built a Market Street store that crumbled to the ground in the next year's quake and fire.

Restaurants and shops quickly sprang from the ashes, however, and S. Greenfield soon had a nice new downtown location. Thanks to Ann's efforts, the Greenfields began to enjoy a solid place in local social circles.

Meeting "under the clock" at the St. Francis was a ritual among the female elite, followed by Monday lunch in the hotel's Mural Room — a tradition Ann rarely missed. The secret was to know "Ernest," who alone masterminded the seating according to wealth, social position, and the amount of currency that found its way into his pockets.

Ann loved to show off her gowns and jewels at the San Francisco Opera, where she held court in a private box. Together and on their own, the couple contributed to charities of all faiths, and enjoyed a reputation for civic concern and philanthropy.

Sadly, however, only a year after the quake, Simon Greenfield succumbed to cancer, leaving Ann and their two grown sons, Herbert and Lawrence, to take over the store. Herbert wanted no part of it, and went on to become a semi-successful artist. Not so Larry, who stepped in to help his mother. She found him wise, capable, and shrewd, and soon began to depend on his advice.

Ann lived to be 94; her death in 1943 freed Larry of maternal obligations and he found himself getting reacquainted with 32-year-old Marc, his only son. Marc had been working in the store since he was a teenager, and though his father hadn't spent much time with him, Marc realized that his dad had been grooming him, and gradually giving him more and more responsibility.

The new father-son closeness had its pitfalls though. Sometimes their tempers flared, but Marc was staunchly loyal and shared his father's dreams for the future.

Early in 1945, 62-year-old Larry Greenfield realized that his own store policy meant he would have to retire in three years. Wanting to leave his mark on the city he loved, he hired gifted architect Timothy Pflueger to design a handsome new store — one that would grace their newly-acquired Union Square location for years to come.

Plans were underway, in fact, when Marc told his father that he was getting married. At first Larry balked at his son choosing a gentile, but once he met the beautiful, strong-willed Yvonne, he saw the futility of objecting. The Stocktons, after all, *were* a fine old (and wealthy) San Francisco family. Things could be a lot worse.

By the time Yvonne and Marc announced their engagement in April, S. Greenfield & Co. was a business at its peak, the largest fashionable women's clothing store in the city.

While some local businessmen sought to play down their religion, the Greenfields took pride in their Jewish identity, and their continued patronage of the arts earned them the kind of social position usually reserved for WASPS — White Anglo-Saxon Protestants — and such old San Francisco names, as Crocker, Flood, Spreckels and Huntington.

Yvonne saw only one drawback to her marriage to Marc: maintaining an image. No more running downtown hatless and gloveless, no more rummaging through the Emporium's bargain racks, no more romping through Julius Kahn Park in her dad's old shirt and rolled-up jeans. From now on, Mrs. Marcus Jacob Greenfield would be expected to look and act like the wife of the prominent department store heir. What a bore!

At the same time, though, she was not about to surrender her own style — a bit flamboyant for Marc, yet too much a part of her to change.

"Some of our wedding guests seem to be settling in for the winter," Marc murmured, glancing around.

"Papa knows how to get rid of them. He turns off the booze."

"Speaking of booze, look who's coming our way."

Yvonne peered over her husband's back. Cousin Betsy's spouse, Jeremy Hughes, was weaving unsteadily toward them. "Oh, God, I think he's smashed."

"You *think?*"

"Hey, sweetie-pie." Heads swiveled as Jeremy stumbled up and pushed the newlyweds apart. His black hair was tousled, his bow tie askew. "I wanna dance with the bride."

"Another time, pal," said Marc. "We're about to leave."

"Lesh trade partners. No, lesh not. I don't have a partner." Giggling, he grabbed Yvonne by the waist.

Marc shot her a questioning look. Yvonne nodded assurance; she could handle him. "Where's your wife, Jeremy?"

"What wife?" He squeezed her tightly. "You're beau'ful, ya know?"

"Betsy's your wife, Jeremy. She loves you. You should be with her."

"Who's Beshy?"

A firm hand clamped down on Jeremy's shoulder. Marc was shorter and slighter than his adversary, but fixed him with challenging eyes. "I'd hate to have to deck you on my wedding day, old boy, so suppose you let go of my wife."

"Your wife? I thought she was my wife!" Laughing uproariously, Jeremy released her. He turned, and to everyone's relief, staggered away. An usher helped him down the steps.

"Swell family I'm getting into," teased Marc, as the dance ended.

"Don't blame us for Jeremy. He's poor Betsy's mistake. But I do feel

21

rather guilty. I introduced them."

"You told me they went together for years before they got married. Betsy must've known what he was like."

"I guess she thought he'd change." She kissed Marc on the lips. "Anyway, you were brave and fearless and came to my rescue. What a lovely way to end our wedding day."

He smiled and drew her closer. "Slight correction, Mrs. Greenfield. That's *not* how we're ending our wedding day."

Clara Stockton inserted a silver bookmark in the novel she was reading, patted cold cream on her chin, and was about to switch off her bedside lamp when the phone rang. She glanced at the clock. Who in God's name would be calling at midnight? "Yes?"

"Mrs. Stockton," said a breathless voice. "I hate to disturb you at this hour, but I just arrived in San Francisco and I'm very anxious to talk to Yvonne. Is she there?"

"Who is this? Are you a friend or a boyfriend?"

"Both, I hope."

"I'm sorry, but you're too late. Yvonne's on her honeymoon."

A stunned silence. "When — did she get married?"

"Yesterday. Do you want to leave a message?"

"Yes. Tell her I kept my word." The receiver clicked and he was gone.

"One of Yvonne's rejects?" asked James, rolling over.

"A strange one. He said something about keeping his word, then hung up without leaving his name. That girl has too many disappointed suitors. I hope she chose the right man."

"Marc's bright. Wouldn't mind having him work for me."

Clara seized the opportunity. "What's wrong with Will?"

"His age, for one thing. I don't hire teenagers as editors. Besides, I haven't given up on Tim yet."

"Well, you should. He's happy with what he's doing."

"Hogwash. Would you want a brilliant young man in the prime of life to give up the prospect of journalistic immortality for the mere sake of being happy?"

"Go to sleep, James."

He sighed and pulled up the covers. "Good-night, my love. Pleasant dreams."

Chapter 3 – 1945

After four years devoted almost exclusively to the war effort, San Francisco faced a difficult transition. Lured by the high wages of wartime industries, thousands had poured into the Bay Area — men with wives and families, seeking temporary lodging. Most fell in love with the city and decided to stay.

Unprepared for the influx, citizens faced long lines everywhere. Sidewalks were jammed with crowds, stores ran out of supplies. But as fall drifted into winter, downtown San Francisco braced for dramatic changes, knowing that R.H. Macy & Co. had bought O'Connor Moffat & Co. on Stockton Street, while Woolworth razed the Flood Building to erect a Market Street five-and-dime. S. Greenfield & Co. also had plans, to turn the old Butler Building at the corner of Geary and Stockton into a stunning marble and granite fashion haven.

At the same time, many citizens were surprised to learn that the Fairmont Hotel on Nob Hill was intending to add — horrors! — a tower thirty stories high. Mayor Roger Lapham formed a board of prominent persons to assess the situation.

James Tyler Stockton, asked to join the group, was unable to spare the time, and suggested his son Tim replace him on the committee. Tim at first declined, then at Clara's urging, accepted.

Driving to Lou Ella's apartment that Friday evening, Tim thought about the meeting he'd attended earlier in the day. The group dedicated to studying the city's current and future needs was comprised of his father's old-money cronies (cigar-smoking, whisky-loving types who'd never had to earn a living), newly-rich millionaires, the mayor's sycophants, and a few industrial leaders.

They'd spent an hour deciding that the Fairmont had a right to erect a tower, but Tim's only suggestion, on another subject — a campaign to counter the racism engendered by the war — was vetoed. Not that it wasn't important, the committee members assured him, but getting businesses back on their feet, promoting foreign trade, and attracting tourists took precedence.

The meeting had left Tim with a sense of frustration. The men had shown themselves mainly concerned with their own interests — who would contact which wealthy friend or club member for funding, who knew which politician to approach for favors, and how these actions would affect their personal and corporate bank accounts. As the chairman politely pointed out, "Sorry, Mr. Stockton, but you can't run a city on brotherly love."

Lou Ella Manning inhaled the vapors of the pot roast simmering in the Dutch oven, and nodded approval. That last pinch of rosemary had done it. Time to take the potato batter out of the refrigerator, she decided, glancing at the clock. She would fry the pancakes fresh, and serve the apple sauce at room temperature. Everything had to be precise yet seem effortless. Tim must not have the slightest inkling of the pains that had gone into this dinner.

She thought back to the first time she had seen Tim Stockton, shortly after he came to the *Herald* in the summer of 1941. Everyone knew he and his father were at odds about his working there, but rumor had it they'd made a deal: Tim would stay for a year. After that, if he wasn't happy, he could leave and go to medical school — with his father's full support and blessing.

On her way to the newsroom, Lou Ella had spotted the good-looking young man, frowning under his glasses as he stood in the corridor arguing with his father.

Their voices lowered as she passed, but later, office gossips reported that James had no patience for his son's principles. The situation had exploded when Tim refused to cover a diplomat's speech at a private club that excluded minorities.

The father-son dispute sparked debates from the press room to the copy desk. Younger employees sided with Tim; journalists had a moral obligation — not only to observe society, but to change it. Older reporters backed James; a journalist reported the facts. Period.

Lou Ella had taken a chance and approached Tim. "You were brave to stand up to your father," she said, after introducing herself. "No one around here has the guts."

Tim chuckled. "I guess our disagreement is no secret. Does everyone here know everything that goes on?"

"Only if it happens in the hallway."

"Well, it doesn't much matter. My Dad wouldn't budge. He just gave someone else the assignment. Besides, the worst he can do is fire me, and that would be admitting defeat. He's got a year to try to make me into a newspaperman."

They'd chatted for a few minutes, and to Lou Ella's surprise, all the rumors she'd heard about Tim proved correct. He wasn't high-hat or patronizing in the least. On the contrary, warmth, charm, and a good-natured modesty seemed to flow naturally.

Quick research had turned up his age. At 22, he was five years her junior — not enough to matter. He lived at home on Jackson Street with his parents, his pretty sister Yvonne, and two half-siblings. He liked Jeannette MacDonald/Nelson Eddy movies, drove a '36 Ford roadster, and had no special girlfriend.

In the months that followed, from June to Pearl Harbor, Lou Ella managed to bump into Tim in the coffee room several times a week. He learned that she had grown up in the Bronx, and was the youngest of three daughters of a high school principal and his wife.

After winning a scholarship to Columbia University, she graduated *cum laude,* got her master's in liberal arts, and came to the West Coast hoping there would be more opportunities for women in journalism. Lacking experience, she finally accepted the only job she was offered — as city-desk secretary on the *Herald,* soothing irate subscribers and distributing memos.

Her break came on the night of a stabbing in the Twin Peaks area, with no reporters around to cover it. She begged to go, scooped the town with her exclusive interviews, and became the first woman to join the editorial staff. An offbeat, creative approach to stories earned her a promotion to feature writer. Then came the war.

"Chance" meetings with Tim ended abruptly when he joined the Marines. Lou Ella lost no time calling on Clara at her American Women's Voluntary Services office and volunteering to help. Working evenings and weekends, she typed Clara's letters, wrote her speeches and press releases, organized her files, and made herself invaluable.

Clara, Tim's stepmother, was only seven years older than Lou Ella, and found her bright and amusing. The two became friends. Lou Ella was rewarded with an invitation to Yvonne's debutante party, which she attended, but was disappointed not to see Tim there. Later came an invitation to Yvonne's wedding, and this time, she knew she'd see him.

"Am I too early?" Tim handed his hostess a straw-covered bottle tied with a red ribbon. "I could smell that pot roast half way up the street."

"Mmmm — and I love Chianti. Thank you!"

Lou Ella beamed, and led the way into a small parlor, aware that he would be viewing her from the rear. Weight was a constant enemy, but she had shed twelve pounds for the Stockton/Greenfield wedding, and was aware that no unsightly bulges would spoil her curves.

A green-and-white striped couch and armchair surrounded a wooden coffee table, shaped like a bear on all fours. On it sat a pair of Raggedy Ann and Andy dolls, a framed photo of her parents and sisters, and a tray of cheese and thin-sliced French bread. Flames sizzled in the fireplace and the clanging sounds of "Chloe" bounced off the record player.

"You call that music?" asked Tim.

Her eyes twinkled. "I think Spike Jones is a genius — the way he spoofs popular songs. Oh, I know there's a place for 'Sentimental Journey,' but I'd rather listen to 'Der Fuehrer's Face' — raspberries and all."

"A hopeless romantic."

"Actually, I am — at least where Nelson Eddy's concerned."

"You like Nelson Eddy? Me, too!" Tim glanced around the room, not knowing what to make of his unconventional hostess. Plants and flowers were everywhere: ivy on the mantel, geraniums atop a cabinet. On the wall, next to a reproduction of Joe Rosenthal's picture of the flag-raising at Iwo Jima, a colored tapestry repeated the journalistic credo: "IF YOUR MOTHER SAYS SHE LOVES YOU — CHECK IT OUT!"

"What a terrific den," Tim finally said.

"I'm afraid it's too formal," she teased. "This apartment's tiny, only four rooms, but the view from the bedroom's irresistible. No seduction implied."

"Killjoy."

"Fix you a drink?"

"Whiskey, neat, if you have it."

She reappeared a moment later with a bottle and two glasses. "So, Mr. Timothy Stockton — what are you up to these days?"

He waited for her to get comfortable, then sat beside her on the couch. "Trying to furnish my new apartment. Trying to get involved in the community. Trying to decide what to do with my life."

"What happened to medical school?"

"I thought about it all the time I was in the service. Then I learned something about myself. A doctor has to be objective — but I found I couldn't detach the blood I saw from the guy who was bleeding. When I came home, after what I'd seen, I knew I couldn't stomach cutting up dead bodies. It's as simple as that."

"Are you disappointed?"

"Very. In the hospital, on the ships, I was always talking to guys. I could sit for hours listening to their problems, consoling them." He reached for his drink. "And all the time, I kept asking myself: why me? Why should I be allowed to live when my best friend and two-thirds of my men were butchered before my eyes?"

"Your best friend?"

"Yes. I was feeling homesick on the troopship, so I checked the roster and one name jumped out at me: Hart Doyle. The Doyles and the Stocktons, as you may know, were newspaper competitors and rivals from way back, when they had a shooting match over something one of them wrote."

"I heard about that."

"So I looked up Hart Doyle, and found he was the real thing — the great-great-grandson of Egan Doyle, who was shot by my great grandfather, Anthony Stockton. Hart didn't give a hoot about any of that. He told me all about growing up a liberal in a highly conservative family. I talked about my background, too. At one point, when I showed him a picture of my baby sister Katie, he even got teary."

"How sweet."

"From then on, we were inseparable. The day we attacked the Japs, he gave his life to save mine. And I found out I wasn't as tough as I thought. My only real regret, about not going to med school, is that I won't be able to heal people."

"Nonsense! There are hundreds of ways to heal people. You could become a psychologist."

"A psychologist?" he repeated, startled.

"You're a good listener. You said so yourself. You like to help people solve problems. Why not do it professionally?" Not giving him time to respond, she went on, "You could open your own practice and work with patients one to one. Of course you'd have to go back to school."

He scratched his head. "It's an intriguing idea…but let's not get too serious. Tell me about you. I know you're a brilliant reporter. How'd you move up so fast?"

"I was lucky. I was the first woman to win the Stanford Journalism Fellowship. I spent all of last year at Stanford studying postwar problems. Then I worked up my nerve. I told your father if he wanted me back at the *Herald*, he'd have to make me political editor."

"What'd he say?"

"He screamed and hollered and offered me a salary just above poverty level. I almost took an assistant professorship at the university, but he came through at the last minute."

"Lucky for him. Luckier for me." Tim smiled as she refilled their glasses. "You know, I haven't felt this relaxed in ages. You're a special lady, Lou Ella. I shouldn't say this, but you're even more beautiful than when I left."

A sudden glow flushed her cheeks. "Why shouldn't you say it?"

"Because you're a woman at the peak of youth and attractiveness, and I'm a one-armed veteran groping helplessly around —"

"Timothy Stockton, don't you dare start feeling sorry for yourself! You're one of the kindest, brightest, nicest men I've ever met. You have an extraordinary ability to put people at ease and make them feel good about themselves. And you're nutty if you don't use that."

His eyes shone with amusement. "Anything else?"

"Yes. I'll help you look into colleges to get your Ph.D. Why not give psychology a try? You've never turned your back on a challenge."

"I have to think —"

"Well, start thinking while I get dinner on the table." She picked up the empty bottle. "And you'd better be good and hungry."

The evening passed quickly for Tim, who found himself flattered and fussed over as never before. The few girls he'd dated since he'd been home were always younger than he. For the most part, they were the spoiled, giggly daughters of his parents' friends, who expected to be taken dinner-dancing at the "Frantic" — their nickname for the St. Francis

Hotel. Or else they were neurotic frizzy-haired students Yvonne had met at the Art Institute.

Lou Ella's concern for his welfare, her interest in encouraging him even to the point of being somewhat bossy, touched him — and made him feel wanted for himself.

Lou Ella was sincere in her admiration, if not altogether altruistic. The desire for power and position had burned inside her since she was a teenager. Growing up in an academic atmosphere where status meant just as much as intellect, she had known the importance of cultivating both. Behind the carefree manner, a human dynamo was waiting, watching — patient as a leopard at a watering hole.

"Your future husband is one lucky guy," said Tim, walking to the door, "but he'd better be prepared to look like a beached whale."

"Well, there's no 'lucky guy' in my life." She gave a self-deprecating shrug. "Besides, when and if I ever marry, I want to put my husband first, and make our relationship the most important thing in my life. As long as I'm working, I can't do that."

"Hey, Miss Political Editor, this is 1945. A lot of women keep their jobs after marriage. Your husband would be a first class jackass if he asked you to give up the career you've worked so hard for."

The perfect response. "You really think so?"

"I know so." He paused and took her hand, resisting a strong temptation to draw her close to him. "It's been a super evening."

"I meant what I said. I'll even be your first patient."

He twirled an imaginary mustache. "And lie on my couch?"

She laughed. "Look, some people are coming here tomorrow at five to talk about recalling the mayor. It won't happen, of course, but I have to hear them out. Why don't you come over about six? We'll eat leftovers and make some inquiries."

"Are you sure?"

She opened the door. "Of course I'm sure. Goodnight, dear Timothy."

Chapter 4 — 1945

To many San Franciscans, the marriage of post-deb Yvonne Stockton to Marc Greenfield signaled a turning point in Judeo-Christian relations. Along with the Greenfields, several European-Jewish businessmen had already achieved prominence in banking and retailing and become active in the city's cultural life.

Names such as Stern, Koshland, Fleishhacker, Haas, Hellman, Schwabacher and Dinkelspiel began to appear regularly in the pages of the *Herald*, and other newspapers as well. While the prestigious Pacific-Union Club had no Jewish names on its rosters, both the Olympic and the Bohemian Clubs welcomed Marc Greenfield as a member.

Yvonne, in turn, found herself more sought-after than ever. Her name heading a fundraiser not only stood for glamour and social position, but for youthful energy, commitment, and concern. Her one regret was that all these activities took time from her sculpting — a hobby that was gradually slipping away.

In the spring of 1947, Yvonne slowed her hectic pace long enough to produce the first Stockton grandchild, a healthy nine-pounder named Benjamin Simon Greenfield. Two days later, Tim paid a visit to Children's Hospital.

Yvonne's private room in the maternity ward was awash in flowers. Cards and telegrams lay stacked on a table.

"This place looks like a funeral parlor," teased Tim, kissing his sister's cheek and handing her a box of chocolates. She looked unusually radiant, he thought, propped against a lace pillow. The clunky string of beads around her neck was undoubtedly a gift from one of her artist friends.

Yvonne beamed. "How'd you know I was craving something sinful? What's the latest? Are you still in love?"

"I came to talk about *you*. Motherhood certainly agrees with you. Now you can produce a whole brood of little Greenfields."

"I am *not* a reproductive machine. Have you seen your new nephew?"

"No. Does he look like me?"

"Not in the least. He's adorable."

Tim grinned and perched on the side of her bed. "I won't stay long.

Where's Marc?"

"Where he always is — down at the new building. He says the store's going to have the most beautiful ladies' lounge in the country, with black and white marble floors and gold-plated faucets. I said too bad only half the population would see it. Oh, dear — you just missed my dear friend, Beth. She made me this amber necklace. Isn't it lovely?"

"No," he said, "and no, I don't want to meet your dear friend Beth. Yes, I'm in love, and yes, I happen to think Lou Ella's the greatest thing since frozen orange juice. She sends congratulations, by the way."

"Tell her thanks."

They sat in awkward silence a moment, until Tim sighed. "All right, Eevie. Speak your piece."

"It's none of my business."

"There we agree."

"Well, it's just that, sometimes, Lou Ella seems so bossy. And she *is* five years older than you. Wouldn't you like to meet a sweet young thing your own age? Or younger?"

He rolled his eyes. "Did I meddle in your love life?"

"You couldn't. You were away."

"And I wouldn't. So keep your pretty nose out of mine. All I know is I don't have to put on airs or play any games with Lou Ella. She makes me feel wanted wherever we are, whatever we do. I've never been happier."

Yvonne's face softened. "In that case, I'm glad for you both. What do Clara and Papa say?"

"Clara isn't thrilled. Dad says she's smart and pushy. They'd both like to see me marry some professional virgin from the Social Register."

"Are you thinking about marriage?"

"Not at the moment."

"Well, you'd better sleep with her pretty soon, so you know what you're getting into — pardon the pun."

"Thanks, Dr. Greenfield." Her advice was a bit late. He and Lou Ella had been sharing a bed for more than a year. "Anything else?"

"When do you get your Ph.D.?"

"Next year, with any luck."

Before she could comment, a nurse walked in carrying a tiny, screaming bundle. "Excuse me, sir," she said, pushing Tim out of the way,

31

"I think Benjamin's hungry."

"What a magnificent child! The image of his uncle."

Yvonne took the infant to her breast. The crying stopped as soon as he found what he wanted.

"I'll let my nephew dine in peace," said Tim, noting his sister's blissful absorption. He patted the baby's head and moved to the door. "Be seeing you, old chap. *Bon appetit.*"

Chapter 5 — 1948

In 1948, two years since the demolition of the older building, S. Greenfield & Co.'s flagship store on Union Square finally opened its doors. The public loved the new addition, delighting in its striking art-deco-modernism and simplicity of line. Columnist Herb Caen proclaimed it "austere, white, magnificent," but "all too visible (where) most husbands are concerned."

In other parts of the city, the mayor's committee was getting results. Three hundred national retailers and manufacturers were considering moving to the Bay Area. And to almost everyone's relief, and despite Mayor Lapham's best efforts to dump them, San Franciscans voted overwhelmingly to save their beloved and historic cable cars.

As many residents had hoped, postwar redevelopment programs were bringing a rush of new jobs and vitality. Hotels and restaurants were again prospering, thanks to the lifting of travel restrictions. And happily, Tim Stockton's persistence paid off, and San Franciscans became the first in the nation to embrace Japanese designs and products.

Shortly thereafter, a covey of rag-tag writers, musicians, poets and painters began to cluster in North Beach coffee houses, forging the heart of what would later be known as the Beat Generation.

Tim and Lou Ella's elopement in the spring of 1951 surprised no one in the Stockton clan, and came as a relief to Clara, who hadn't wanted to host a big wedding. She adored Tim; he was kind and gentle, and never stubborn like Yvonne. His sensitivity appealed to her; he always seemed to be worrying about someone else. Yvonne, on the other hand, mainly worried about herself. Clara hadn't much cared who Yvonne married; just getting her out of the house was a blessing.

In her heart, Clara would have liked Tim to marry someone of his own class who would fit in with the family. Lou Ella, unfortunately, did not. Her clothes were cheap and garish, and she had little in common with Yvonne or Marc. Will didn't relate to her on general principles, Katie was indifferent, and James accepted her with reluctance. Tim deserved better, James felt, than to marry one of his employees.

On the other hand, Lou Ella was pretty, in an ordinary sort of way, and tough and shrewd enough, Clara now realized, to have wormed into her good graces during the war. But as she often reminded James, it was Lou Ella who pulled Tim out of his postwar lethargy and steered him into a satisfying profession, even if it wasn't journalism.

Tim had finally opened his own psychology practice, catering to shell-shocked veterans. He enjoyed his work and seemed happy with his life. For that, they owed Lou Ella endless gratitude.

Tim and Lou Ella's long-awaited honeymoon in Bermuda ended abruptly when President Harry Truman fired General Douglas MacArthur from his Far East command — an action that brought the couple winging back to their Nob Hill apartment.

Lou Ella was no fan of the egocentric General whose philosophies often clashed with Truman's. But he was news. A week after he was relieved of his duties, the 71-year-old hero arrived in San Francisco on a flight from Tokyo. The *Herald's* headline proclaimed: "MACARTHUR RETURNS." Lou Ella Stockton's byline made the front page. It began:

> *"General Douglas MacArthur came home last night to*
> *San Francisco's wildest welcome. Hundreds of thousands*
> *of cheering fans gave the five-star General of the Army a*
> *tumultuous welcome, that often lapsed into a near-riot."*

The next morning, Mayor Elmer Robinson proclaimed "General Douglas MacArthur Day," and invited all citizens to attend ceremonies at City Hall. Although no press was allowed in the hotel, Lou Ella bribed a busboy and sneaked in, climbed the back stairs to the General's floor and waited for him to emerge from his suite. When he did, she quickly introduced herself and rode down with him and his party in the elevator.

"Are you bitter, sir," she asked, elbowing her way up next to him, "about being removed from your command?"

He stared straight ahead with no change of expression. If her pushiness annoyed him, he didn't show it. "The President and I had serious disagreement over prosecution of the action in Korea," he answered, in his rich, sonorous voice. "But he is Commander-In-Chief of our armed forces, and like any good soldier, I obey commands from my superior."

"Sir, there's a rumor that you may run for President. Any truth to it?"

His reply played like a recording. "Many people have urged me to do so, but it is far from my thoughts at the moment. I'm happy to be home, and looking forward to addressing the Congress in Washington."

"Do you fear for the future of America?"

"America is at the beginning of the trail, not the end. This country's greatest accomplishments and contributions to the history of man are yet to come."

"That's all, Miss." An aide shoved her aside as the elevator came to a stop. "You're not even supposed to be in here."

"I know that," snapped Lou Ella, scribbling in her notebook, "but I am."

Early in May, Clara and James gave a family dinner to honor the newlywedded Lou Ella and Tim. Marc and Yvonne Greenfield, who now had two young sons at home, attended. So did 22-year-old Will, currently working at the *Herald's* copy desk, and 12-year-old Katie. Shy and distant, she seemed to be off in a fantasy world.

James' sister, Maggie Stockton Kettering, was also there, with her daughter Betsy. Finally divorced from Jeremy Hughes, Betsy was eight months pregnant by her new husband, a rather stuffy, social-registered businessman named Foster Pickett.

By now, Clara had replaced her predecessor's gaudy dining-room furnishings with beige satin draperies and a mahogany Biedermeyer table that expanded comfortably to seat twenty-four. A soft candle glow lit the Rosenthal place settings and Steuben goblets. In the center of the table, a heart made of red roses floated in a bowl of gardenias.

"Smells great — like a senior prom." Tim grinned as he helped Lou Ella into her chair.

Yvonne took a seat at her father's left. "Papa, do you remember when I was little and you took me to Rosemont, and showed me all those gardenia plants in the old solarium? I see that room so clearly."

"What happened to it?" asked Marc.

"It's a guest room now."

"Your father wants to sell Rosemont," ventured Clara, ringing for Maxwell to start serving. "We need a family vote."

Maggie Kettering heaved her oversized bosom and stared at her brother. "Selling Rosemont? That's the first I've heard of it."

James frowned. "My wife's announcement is like Mark Twain's death — greatly premature. I couldn't possibly sell the Burlingame property without talking to you, my dear sister, since you own half of it. But it's a

35

thought that bears discussing."

"Why? Can't you afford the upkeep?" Maggie chortled at her own joke. In the last decade, both their estates had nearly doubled in value.

Yvonne wrinkled her nose. "Papa, why would you even *think* of selling Rosemont?"

"Because I'm 61 years old and much to my regret, all too mortal. When Maggie and I sail off to the Great Beyond, you kids are going to be left with a big financial headache. The gardener's bill alone would buy half of S. Greenfield's fur salon."

"I doubt that," said Marc, smiling.

"Not to mention pool maintenance, caretaker's salary, gardeners' wages, insurance, taxes, and so on."

Maggie eyed him suspiciously. "Does someone want to buy us out?"

"Since you ask, yes. A developer did approach me, and it's not a bad idea. We could get top dollar, Maggie, and leave solid cash investments to our children, instead of saddling them with a white elephant."

"But I like Rosemont," protested Will, "and Katie does, too. Tell Dad how much you like to swing in that hammock by the pool and read your stupid Oz books."

"They're not stupid." All heads turned to Katie, who sat with down-cast eyes, fidgeting with a pigtail. "And I don't care if he sells Rosemont or not."

"I don't care," singsonged Will. "Do you care about anything except your silly books?"

Katie looked to her mother for rescue. Clara obliged by rapping her glass. "Time for a toast. First of all, let me say how pleased we are to welcome Lou Ella to the family. James and I —"

"You needn't speak for me, my love."

"Oh? Would you care to speak for yourself?"

"As a matter of fact, I would." He rose to his feet, threw out his chest, and assumed his chairman-of-the-board stance. "Timothy, my boy, I've always hoped you would take your rightful place as head of the news-paper your great-grandfather founded. I haven't given up that hope and I never will. But in the meantime, I have two brief announcements.

"The first is that as of this day, May 11, 1951, our Stockton Corp-oration is ready to go on the air with KSTO. That stands for K-Stockton, of course — the television channel we've been setting up for nearly a year."

"Bravo! Congratulations!" rang out the voices. Yvonne clapped and Will hooted.

"Thank you. Fred Hawkins, my executive editor, has already left the *Herald* to run the station, and I've every confidence he'll do well by our investment."

He paused a few seconds, then quickly turned to his right. "My second announcement has to do with our guests of honor. Lou Ella, now that you're a Stockton, your rightful place is on the masthead. As a token of the family's affection, I'd like to offer you a position more suitable to your new status. I confess I never thought I'd choose a woman for the job, but it's one you've earned and richly deserve. How would you like to be the new executive editor?"

"I — I'd be thrilled, Mr. Stockton." Startled, Lou Ella beamed. She hadn't expected a promotion so soon, and her heart was thumping. Resisting the urge to ask if that meant a raise, she smiled and said, "You're most generous. Thank you, indeed."

"That's swell of you, Dad," grinned Tim.

"What's so swell about it?" Will glared at his father. "I'm a flesh-and-blood Stockton and all you do is hide me behind that friggin' copy desk! It's not fair to make *her* a bigshot and not your own son."

"Young man," snapped James, furious that his grand gesture was being questioned, "You are nowhere near as accomplished a journalist as Lou Ella in any sense of the word. You have yet to show me that you have even the most basic skills necessary to become a reporter."

"I'm a Stockton, aren't I?"

"An accident of birth does not qualify you to run a newspaper, or for that matter, even to work for it. I've told you repeatedly what I expect from you, and all I've gotten back are whines and complaints."

"You've never given me a chance. It's always been Tim, Tim, Tim. You've never given a damn about me and you fucking never will!" Throwing down his napkin in a rare gesture of defiance, Will rose and stalked out of the room.

"Come back here this minute," shouted James. "Don't you dare leave! I forbid it!" Getting no response, he clenched his fists. "You'll be sorry, young man."

"Calm down, James," said Clara, rushing to comfort her husband. "Will doesn't mean what he's saying. Remember your heart."

"We've spoiled him rotten, Clara. In my day, we worked for everything we got. Now these kids want to come in five minutes out of college and take over the business."

"If my son used that language," growled Maggie, "I'd disown him!"

Yvonne smiled across the table. "Welcome to our happy family, Lou Ella."

"Your brother's bride is rather aggressive for my taste," said Marc, driving home from the dinner, "but she got what she wanted, and Tim does seem happy. How old is she, anyway?"

"Lou Ella's thirty-seven. Hard to believe they've been together five and a half years." Yvonne began pulling pins from her head, shaking loose her coppery tresses.

"That jersey dress makes her look like a balloon. Can't you take her into the store and get her some decent clothes? She's family now. What she does reflects on all of us."

"Oh, Marc, don't you ever stop worrying about how people dress and how it affects your reputation?"

"That's my business, sweetheart." He shifted into low at the crest of a hill and began a slow descent. "I hate to bring this up, but the last time you came into the store, you weren't even wearing a hat."

"Do I get twenty lashes? Burned at the stake? You'd like me to wear nothing but little black dresses or Christian Dior suits with sailor hats. You'd like me to spend half my life shopping, and the other half schlepping my wardrobe to the dressmaker every six months to raise and lower the hems. Right?"

He sighed. "If you mean would I like you to be conscious of fashion trends, you bet I would. There's a whole new look today. It counteracts the severity of the war years, and brings back femininity."

"You sound like a press release."

"Because I'm excited, sweetheart. Fashion's being revitalized. Mainbocher's sent us some slinky cocktail dresses that would fit you perfectly. Chanel has a stunning line of tailored suits. Schiaparelli's designs are cigarette-slim, and Balenciaga's hour-glass silhouette knocks your eyes out. They'd all look sensational on you."

"I'm your wife, Marc, not a walking advertisement for S. Greenfield and Company."

38

The silence was almost audible. "Honey," he finally said, "You're an exquisite woman. You have a marvelous eye and a knack for putting yourself together. You could walk in with a potato sack tied around your waist and you'd still look better than half the models."

"That's irrelevant, Marc. I have strong feelings about the message my clothes convey. I'm not a fashion slave. I love earthy colors and natural fabrics that celebrate life — all life, not just the snooty world of haute couture."

She stopped herself. They had argued the subject a hundred times and gotten nowhere. Why was she even bothering? Marc would never understand her guilt about living a rich, spoiled life, while soldiers and civilians were getting slaughtered in Korea, babies were starving in India, and Negroes' homes were being fire-bombed in the south.

She tried for a new subject. "Did you think Papa looked strained tonight?"

Marc snickered. "If my son talked to me that way, I'd look strained. Too bad Will's allergies kept him out of the Army. They might've made a man out of him. But the one who really looked tense was poor little Katie. Why is she so uncomfortable at family dinners?"

"Katie's from another planet." Yvonne shrugged. "I can't get through to her at all. Once I asked Clara if she'd had an affair with a Martian, but she didn't think it was funny."

"The Stocktons are a strange breed." He reached across the seat. "Especially you."

She laughed and took his hand. "And your family's normal?"

"No," he said. "The Greenfields are worse."

Chapter 6 — 1953

James Stockton's fatal heart attack at the age of 63 coincided with the signing of the cease-fire that led to the end of the Korean war, an event that relegated the publisher's passing to a black-bordered box at the bottom of the front page.

Inside the first section, however, Lou Ella wrote a glowing obituary, complete with photos, quotes, and anecdotes. Mayor Elmer Robinson ordered the City Hall flag flown at half-mast, and delivered the eulogy at the crowded funeral in Grace Cathedral.

Clara sat through the ceremony determined to maintain composure. She had tried for so long to get James to heed the doctor's warnings to slow down, it was almost a relief to have the dire predictions come true. But towards the end of the service, she buried her face in her hankie and cried — not unaware that the tears were partly for herself.

The future held no illusions for Clara. Learning to cope as a widow would not be easy. At forty-six, she was young and attractive enough to remarry, but the prospect of adjusting to a new mate, plus the fear that any prospective husband might be a fortune hunter, made remarriage unlikely — at least, for the present.

Still, she was sad and lonely, walking in the park long hours in the daytime, crying herself to sleep every night. How often she thought of that other man in her past, the one who'd captured her soul. And how often she wondered what life would have been like, had she left James to marry him. Had she followed her heart, her lover might still be alive.

The next morning after the funeral, Will Stockton breezed past his father's secretary, Helen Hopkins, who tried in vain to stop him. Lou Ella was sitting at the publisher's desk.

"What're you doin' in Dad's chair?" he challenged.

Lou Ella looked up calmly. "We have a paper to get out, Will. When the boss isn't here, the second-in-command takes over."

"Who made you second-in-command?"

"Check the masthead."

"The masthead don't mean a fucking thing. He was my father and I should be in charge."

"It doesn't work that way, Will," she said, returning her attention to the file in her hands. "I'll be glad to talk with you later, but right now, I'm swamped."

"It's not your job and it's not your office. I don't want to call my mother, but I will if I have to."

"Do that, by all means." She offered him the phone. "I haven't time to argue. Now will you get out, or do I have to call security?"

"Why — damn you, bitch!" he sputtered, and slammed the door.

The terms of James' will indicated that Maggie Stockton Kettering owned 40 percent and James owned 60 percent of the Stockton Corporation. James bequeathed 20 percent to Clara, and 10 percent to each of his four children, with Katie's share in trust to Clara until she became 21.

After the reading of the document, Will made immediate claim to his father's title of publisher, demanding a showdown vote. Tim responded angrily, insisting that Will was unqualified. By naming Lou Ella executive editor, Tim contended, James had designated her as his successor. Verbal warfare broke out. Accusations flew across the room. The attorney postponed the vote for a week.

The day after hearing the will, Tim and Lou Ella called on Maggie Kettering. She assured them that she had no intention of watching her inheritance slide down the drain under Will's "leadership," and promised them her vote. Her 40 percent along with Tim's 10 percent meant 50 percent — a good start, but not enough. A 50/50 tie would favor Will, the blood heir.

Next, Tim visited his stepmother. Clara opened the front door herself, wearing a black sweater and slacks, and gave him a hug.

"How's my favorite problem solver?" she teased, as she ushered him into the parlor. Burning logs in the fireplace helped warm the room. "Come sit down. Where's Lou Ella?"

"I wanted to see you alone." He perched on the edge of a sofa.

"All right." Clara took a seat on the opposite couch. "Let's get to the point, Tim. I hate to see the family torn apart this way. Couldn't Lou Ella be flexible? She'll still be executive editor. The only difference will be that Will's publisher instead of James."

"Mother," he said, trying not to sound exasperated. "Will has no experience — nada, zilch, nothing. He's my brother and I respect that, but he doesn't know the first thing about publishing a newspaper."

"He hasn't paid his dues?"

"He hasn't even applied for membership." Tim tried to keep his voice from rising. "Don't you see? Giving Will that kind of responsibility with his history and inexperience will destroy everything that generations of Stocktons have worked all their lives to create. If Dad wanted to put Will in a position of authority, don't you think he'd have done so?"

"James didn't understand Will. He treated him like a second class citizen. It's time we gave the boy a chance."

"At what price? The 'boy' is 24 years old! Giving him 'a chance' could cost us everything — not only our reputation, but our bank accounts. Are you willing to risk that?"

"Nonsense. James has an excellent staff who would work with Will. Lou Ella isn't the only person who can do the job. And you're not exactly objective."

"You're the prejudiced one, Mother. Lou Ella's proven herself. Will's proven himself, too — with temper tantrums and drunk-driving arrests. If any stranger with Will's background came looking for a job, we'd throw him out on his ear."

"But Will's *family*." She rose and walked to the hall, signaling that the discussion was over. "I'm sorry, Tim. But I know in my heart what's right for my son — my youngest son. Nothing will change my mind. Maybe with time, you and Lou Ella can open your hearts to your brother."

Tim started to answer, then stopped himself. If he spoke his thoughts, they'd probably never talk again. With an angry nod, he turned and headed for the door.

"Tell me quick," said Lou Ella, as her husband entered the apartment. "What'd she say?"

"She said no." Tim strode to the bar. "Wanna drink?"

"I'll fix one for you. Was she unpleasant?"

"Just stubborn. Her brain's so full of soap bubbles, she actually thinks Will could do the job."

"Did you tell her about — the other?"

"No. I didn't have the heart."

Lou Ella set his vodka on the table and folded her arms. "So where do we stand?"

"We have 50 votes, Maggie's 40 and my 10. On the other side, Clara has her 20, plus Katie's 10 and Will's 10. That makes 40. Eevie's the swing vote. If she goes with us, we'll win 60 to 40. If she goes with Clara, it's a 50/50 tie, and we lose."

"Can you talk to Eevie again? She knows Will's a problem. Does she think Clara might get mad and disinherit her?"

"No, it's not that. When Clara dies, her shares go to the four of us — equally. That's in Dad's will. But Clara's crazy about Eevie's boys. Eevie even calls her 'Nonna' now. I don't know that she'll want to cause a family rift."

"Your sister's no shrinking violet."

"I've talked to her twice, Lou Ella. There's nothing more I can do!"

"Okay, okay, don't get mad." She bent down and smoothed his forehead. "What will be, will be."

Despite her accepting words, Lou Ella hadn't the slightest intention of sitting back and letting fate decide her future. The next morning, she called Yvonne and asked her to lunch. To her surprise, Yvonne agreed to meet at noon.

Lou Ella's jaw was clenched as she handed her keys to the parking attendant. Striding past the overgrown tiki idols guarding the entrance, she pushed open the carved-wood doors to Trader Vic's — San Francisco's favorite dining spot. In only two years, since "Trader" Vic Bergeron had changed the name of his Hinky Dink's eatery in Oakland to Trader Vic's, and opened a branch in the city, "Vic's" had become the town's premier power restaurant.

"Hello, Mrs. Stockton." The Maitre d' greeted her warmly. "Mrs. Greenfield's already here, at your table."

"Thanks, Bill, and say hi to the Trader." The realization that Yvonne was three minutes early gave Lou Ella hope. Maybe she was equally anxious to talk.

Like a robot set on automatic, Lou Ella headed for the Captain's Cabin, the "inner sanctum" reserved for favored localities. The lighting was soft, the air cool, the décor subdued. Commemorative plaques, nautical mementos and signal flags covered the wood-paneled walls, giving the room an intimate, clubby atmosphere.

Half the tables were occupied, including Lou Ella's booth in a back corner. Yvonne Stockton Greenfield sat sipping a Mai Tai. She smiled as her sister-in-law squeezed onto the banquette.

"Have a taste?"

"Thanks, but I've got to be sharp today. The head of the Fair Rent Committee's coming at two, then some guy who says he can prove the Rosenbergs were innocent, then a staff meeting to discuss the Key System strike...you get the idea."

"I do." Yvonne opened a cigarette case. "Smoke?"

"Thanks, I will. How's Marc? The kids?"

"Everyone's fine except me. Lou Ella, I absolutely hate these family squabbles. If I side with you and Tim, Clara and Will won't speak to me. And if I side with Clara, I lose you and Tim. How can I win?"

Lou Ella thought a few seconds before answering. "I know it's awkward for you. I'd give anything for it to be otherwise. But so much more than my job and my ego are at stake: lives, families, the city's fate, the future of the whole Stockton Corporation. You could lose a major part of your inheritance."

"How?"

"Well, for one thing, this is a critical period for the *Herald*. A few bad moves and we could go under."

"How far are we lagging?"

"Third, after the *Examiner* and *Clarion*. When the *Examiner* offered Herb Caen $500 a week to write for them, and your father refused to pay a cent over $400, we lost our biggest draw."

"Penny wise, pound foolish. Papa was good at that."

"Well, I'm determined to get Herb back and I'm also determined to pass the *Ex* in circulation. It's going to take time — maybe two years, maybe ten. But right now, the *Herald* needs a transfusion and I'm willing to give blood. Put me in the driver's seat, and I promise you a colorful, upbeat newspaper that all San Francisco — all the nation, in fact — will be talking about."

Yvonne listened intently, never taking her eyes off Lou Ella, as she heard how complicated and sensitive the job of publisher was.

When the waiter brought their salads, Lou Ella caught her breath. "I rest my case," she said, exhaling. "Shall we eat?"

"You'd make a marvelous saleswoman." Yvonne reached for her fork. "Does my big brother know we're meeting?"

"No, he feels we've pestered you enough. But I'll tell him tonight.

I never lie to him."

"How's he doing? Personally, I mean."

"He still has nightmares about Tarawa. He still loves the 49ers. But otherwise, he's absorbed in his work. The one thing he really understands is war trauma. He's helped dozens of 'hopeless' cases."

"And knowing Tim, he probably doesn't charge them."

Lou Ella laughed. "Let's say I'd hate to have to live on what he earns."

"The family really owes you a lot. He wouldn't have made it this far without you."

"That's nice of you to say." The compliment astonished Lou Ella. Her sister-in-law had never shown her much warmth. "I love Tim more than anything in this world. He's been through such hell, I hate to see him suffer now when it's so unnecessary. If only Clara weren't so blind about Will. If only we could tell her the truth about him..."

"Well, we can't."

"She'll find out someday."

"Not from us." Yvonne faced her companion with challenging eyes. "Let me play devil's advocate. What would you do if Will became publisher?"

Lou Ella speared a chunk of chicken. "I'd be out of there before you could blink. And I'd take the first decent job offer that came along — competitor or not."

Chapter 7 – 1953

The stockholders' meeting took place around Clara's dining room table on a Sunday afternoon. Three lawyers were present: two representing Clara and the Stockton Corporation, and one hired by Tim to represent him and his wife. Neither Marc nor Lou Ella, the in-laws, had been asked to attend.

Maggie Stockton Kettering chatted with Betsy, her future heir, who came to support her mother. Maxwell, the butler, passed coffee, tea, and madeleines. Will doodled on scratch paper. Tim and Yvonne sat in silence, avoiding each others' eyes.

Clara graced the head of the table, looking more like an elegant matriarch than a grief-stricken widow. Graying hair, carefully styled and sprayed, framed her lovely face. The weight she had lost since James' death had hollowed her cheeks considerably, adding to the aura of aristocracy.

Not without premeditation, she wore the white silk hostess gown Yvonne had given her for Christmas.

"Is everyone served?" she asked in a pleasant voice.

Getting a nod from Maxwell, she rose and clasped her hands. "We all know why we're here," she began, "and thank God James isn't around to see his family torn apart by pettiness and ambition."

Tim scowled. Her allusion seemed aimed at Lou Ella.

"The *Herald*, as you know, is privately owned by the Stockton Corporation. You also know how the proxies are distributed. Each percentage point equals one thousand shares, or for the sake of this tribunal, a single vote."

"It's not a tribunal, Clara," said Tim. "No one's on trial."

She stared at him in surprise. He had never called her by her first name before. "Well then, shareholders' meeting, kangaroo court. Whatever."

"Do get on," urged Maggie.

"We're here to vote on a simple question: whether the Stockton legacy continues as it always has, in the hands of a bright, capable male heir, or whether we turn the paper over to an outsider —"

Tim froze. "My wife's an outsider?"

"She's not a blood Stockton. My grandsons Ben and David Greenfield are Stocktons, and so is Betsy's son, Tyrone Pickett. But until one of

46

them grows old enough to carry on the tradition, Willard Hayes Stockton is the obvious male heir."

"In other words, you want Will to be publisher," said Yvonne, somewhat impatiently.

"Yes. Lou Ella can stay executive editor, and the family will be united again." She turned to the lawyer on her right. "Avery Andrews will now take a vote."

The attorney, stiff and formal in his pin-striped suit, scanned the faces. "Does anyone wish to speak?"

"If you mean me," said Tim, wearily. "I've nothing to add that I haven't said to my family in person — except that if Will becomes publisher, Lou Ella will not stay on. She'll resign and possibly go to work for the *Examiner*. So your plan to unite the family, Clara, would serve the opposite purpose."

"Duly noted," said Andrews. "Mrs. Stockton, would you put your proposal in the form of a motion?"

"I move that Willard Hayes Stockton be named publisher of the *San Francisco Herald*."

"I second the motion," said Will.

"What a surprise," snapped Maggie.

"If you're all agreed, we'll go around the table. Are you recording this?"

The second lawyer nodded.

"We'll start with you, Mrs. Kettering. How do you vote?"

"The only way a sane person can — to save the *Herald* from my nephew's rank incompetence. *Against* the motion."

He skipped Betsy. "Mr. Timothy Stockton?"

"Against."

"Mr. Willard Stockton?"

"In favor."

"Mrs. Greenfield?"

The room grew silent. Yvonne folded her arms and frowned. "This is insanity! Papa would never have allowed this travesty. I decline to vote."

The lawyer spoke in a monotone. "Then I must inform you, Mrs. Greenfield, that failure to vote will be recorded as against the motion."

"Oh, damn the legal crap!" She glanced across the table. "I love and adore you, Tim, but I have to agree with Clara that we can't divide the family. If Lou Ella really cares about us, she won't desert us when we need her. She'll stay on, work with Will, and they'll learn to get along. That's the only solution I can see. Therefore I most reluctantly, and under strong protest, vote…in favor."

"Whoopee!" Will jumped to his feet and tossed his papers in the air.

The lawyer banged a gavel. "Please, Mr. Stockton. The meeting's not over."

"It's over as far as I'm concerned. I'm goin' out to celebrate."

"And get drunk?" frowned Tim.

"Good and drunk. And if your sweet little wifey wants to take her dubious talents over to the fucking *Examiner,* be my guest!"

Betsy's hand reached out to restrain Tim, whose clenched fist seemed headed for its mark.

"Willard!" cried Clara, horrified. "Sit down!"

"Not on your life, Mamacita. I got a hot tamale waitin' to celebrate with me, and this little number don't like to be kept waitin'."

"*Doesn't,*" she corrected angrily. "I'm warning you, Willard."

He blew her a kiss. "Ta-de-dah!"

The door slammed and he was gone. Avery Andrews waited a few seconds for the shock to subside. Then he turned to Clara and said quietly, "I'm sorry, Mrs. Stockton, but we still need to record your vote."

Pale and shaken, Clara stared down at her hands. Tales of her son's swearing and drinking had always passed over her — unnoticed, unheeded, unwanted. But now she could no longer afford that ignorance. Too much was at stake. Too many lives were involved. Everything James had worked and struggled for could be ruined by her refusal to see what he and everyone else had seen so clearly.

Her lips trembled as she finally raised her head and spoke in a low voice. "Would anyone object to making Will assistant general manager of the television station?"

A second of startled silence as the room echoed a unanimous "No." Tim held his breath.

"Then — in the interest of my late husband and the paper he devoted his life to, I'm afraid I must vote against my own motion." She rose and pressed a hankie to her mouth. Waves of nausea told her she was going to be sick. "Excuse me," she mumbled, and dashed out the door.

Part 2

A Soldier Returns

Chapter 8 — 1955

No one knew exactly why Mayor Elmer Robinson appointed Yvonne Greenfield to the artist's seat of the San Francisco Art Commission. Some said it was because she was rich, prominent, and dabbled in sculpture.

Others thought Yvonne got the nod because she'd fought so hard for her friend Benny Bufano. Despite rumors that he was a Communist, she had succeeded in getting his 18-foot granite statue of St. Francis placed in a prominent location — the steps of the Church of St. Francis of Assisi in North Beach.

Whatever the Mayor's reasons, Yvonne was pleased to be recognized as an artist, even though she rarely lifted a chisel anymore. The decision scored a nod of approval from *Examiner* columnist Herb Caen, who generally avoided mention of his former employers, but couldn't resist noting what a work of art Yvonne Greenfield was.

Mature for her 33 years, Yvonne had definite ideas about what she wanted to accomplish — as did the Commission's president, paper tycoon and philanthropist Harold Zellerbach. Whenever they clashed on a subject, he would take her to lunch at his favorite downtown restaurant, El Prado, where they would dine and bicker until one of them gave in. She soon learned his Golden Rule: whoever won the round would be expected to return the courtesy in some form.

Watching him rule the Commission with dedication and fervor, gently twist arms, and trade favors for favors, was an education. She admired him tremendously; he cared about the city with a passion equal to hers.

Beauty shops were nothing more than shrines to narcissism, Yvonne mused, as she sat under a dryer in Mr. Dale's hair salon overlooking Union Square. The latest *Vogue* lay on her lap unopened. The clothes, jewels, and fabulous faces gracing the pages were as irrelevant as ever, and she wondered, for the thousandth time, how she could have married a man whose interests were so unlike her own.

Yet all considered, their ten years together had been reasonably happy, and had produced two magnificent children. Ben was eight already, a bright, curious boy, with his father's gift of charm. No one had any doubt that Ben's future was in sales and merchandising. Five-year-old David, on the other hand, was quiet, serious, and showed signs of becoming a scholar — perhaps a college professor, his mother thought, or a lawyer.

Watching them grow had mellowed her as a woman, and somewhat subdued her flamboyant style of dressing. Fashion was a low priority in her life, yet marriage to Marc, as she had foreseen, meant being dressed and groomed every minute of every day.

Lanvin, Patou, Jacques Fath and all the Paris designers were blossoming forth in vivid colors, and as long as Yvonne's outfit was the latest "haute" style, and came from the store, Marc was pleased. Even when she picked up the boys at school, she was expected to look and act like the wife of a prominent merchant — an expectation she found herself resenting more and more as time passed.

Not that she blamed Marc. On the surface, he was everything he had promised to be: strongly protective of his family, successful in business, active in the community. From time to time, however, there were rumors. Marc was seen leaving the Ritz in Paris with a striking brunette. Marc was seen dining in Philadelphia with a leggy blonde. Marc was spotted shopping in Rome with a famous Italian model.

The rumors, she guessed, were probably true. But she also knew the affairs were matters of the flesh, not the heart. Much as the knowledge hurt, there was little she could do to stop his philandering, so she chose to ignore it. In truth, she felt somewhat guilty, too. The image of Paul Amory, the only man she had ever loved in a truly romantic sense, was always with her. She could still recall their first meeting at the Stage Door Canteen in 1943.

She and Betsy had been going there every Sunday to act as hostesses to the troops. Awkward and self-conscious, Betsy liked to pass soft drinks and doughnuts, then stand back and watch the men fight for a dance with Yvonne. At least once a night, Yvonne would have to discourage some eager young G.I. determined to learn her phone number, or to meet her later at the Music Box bar on O'Farrell Street. "I'm very flattered," she'd say politely, "but it's against rules."

On this particular night, the large hall was jammed with men in khaki and navy uniforms. They chatted in groups, stood alone, sat at tables. Almost all puffed cigarettes, as they shared stories and laughter to cover their anxiety.

"Cut a rug, Miss?"

A sailor with rosy cheeks smiled shyly. Yvonne always seemed to get the baby-faced 18-year-olds, fresh from the farm. Not that she minded — that's why she was there — it was just hard, sometimes, making conversation. Her voice sounded like a recording. "Thanks, I'd love to. My name's Yvonne. What's yours?"

The dance seemed endless and the sailor asked for another.

"I wish I could, but we have to circulate." She started to walk away when a strong hand shot out and gripped her arm.

"Not so fast, Yvonne."

She spun around, ready to blast whoever was taking such first-name liberty. Then she stopped as if paralyzed. The soldier towering over her was the most striking-looking man she had ever seen. Lean and well-built, with smooth chestnut hair, he had a square jaw and clean-shaven skin that glistened as if he'd just spanked it with bay rum. His features were chiseled and symmetrical, yet his expression seemed somehow detached from his extraordinary good looks.

"Do we know each other?"

"No. But I know you."

"I doubt that." Her poise was starting to return. "We're mystery girls here. No last names, no phone numbers. Love us and leave us; those are the rules."

"Not my rules." Without asking, he slid his arm around her waist and began to dance. The beat was fast, and several couples were jitterbugging, but he held her close to him.

"All right, soldier. Just what *do* you know about me?"

"You're 21 years old, secretary of your senior class at Mills College, and you're planning to be a sculptress. If you want anonymity, you shouldn't be written up in your father's newspaper."

"But the article didn't say when I'd be here."

"I know." His tone was half-accusing. "I've been coming every night looking for you."

She felt a tremor of excitement. He'd seen her picture, read about her, and wanted to meet her. How different he was from the young soldiers and sailors with their awkward approaches. "Why were you looking for me?"

"Does it matter?"

"Do you always answer questions with a question?"

"Do you?"

Her laughter was spontaneous. "No. But fair is fair. You know all about me."

"What do you want to know?"

"Everything. We may never see each other after tonight so you might as well be honest."

"In that case, my name is Paul Amory and I'm a bastard."

"Literally or otherwise?"

"My mother was a photography student working part time at the Ritz Hotel in Boston. She had a brief fling with a traveling politician; when he came back in six months, she informed him she was having his baby. He gave her a generous settlement never to reveal his name. She took the money and bought a camera shop. Three months later, I was born."

"And you never knew your father?"

"She told me he was dead — until I was sixteen. Then, when he *did* die, about 8 years ago, she told me the truth."

So Paul Amory was 16 plus 8 — 24. "What did you do?"

"I went crazy with curiosity. I drove to Washington to meet my step-mother and two half-brothers, but the servants wouldn't let me in. I came home to Boston and thought about writing my story for the newspaper. My father was well-known on the east coast. But my mother objected. She didn't want everyone knowing she had an illegitimate child."

"I can't blame her. Did you have any proof?"

"Yes. My mother had to sign a document saying she'd been fully compensated by my father, and promising never to contact him or his family. But the paper didn't say anything about *my* not contacting them."

"Why didn't you show it to your half-brothers?"

"I didn't know she had it until I enlisted, and there were questions about my birth certificate —" He stopped and looked down. "Hello. You must be cousin Betsy."

"Sorry to interrupt you, Sergeant —"

"Paul."

"Nice to meet you, Paul. Mrs. de Baubigny's been watching you, Eevie, and she says you've danced with Paul long enough. She wants you to circulate."

"Unbelievable!" sputtered Yvonne. "This place is like a prison."

He released her. "What time do you finish?"

"She can't tell you that. It's against —"

"Hush, Betsy. I'm through at eleven."

"Good," he said. "I'll be waiting."

And Paul Amory *was* waiting for her that night, in the shadow of a doorway across the street. Yvonne smiled to herself, remembering the argument with Betsy and finally sending her home in a cab...remembering the thrill of holding Paul's hand as they walked to her car...then driving him down Geary Street...the long hours talking, talking, talking on the sandy beach... the way he'd looked at her.

Nor would she ever forget the next night, when he'd taken her face in his hands and said good-bye. He wouldn't kiss her, he explained. It would have made leaving her even more difficult. But then he couldn't resist and he finally did kiss her...and he made her a promise...a promise that he'd come back for her after the war. And she'd promised she would wait for him...forever.

"You're cooked, Yvonne." A wisp of a man in a pink silk shirt lifted the dryer off her head.

"Good. I get claustrophobic under that thing."

He tested a strand of hair. "You know the old line: 'You have to suffer to be beautiful.'"

"Nothing personal, Dale, but if I hadn't promised Marc I'd get my hair done every week, you'd never see me again."

He followed her to a chair and began removing curlers. "Big party tonight?"

"No. Just one of Marc's designers coming for dinner."

"Pity." He reached for a brush. "No one will see my coiffure. Say, doesn't your brother own Channel One?"

"No, Dale, Will doesn't *own* Channel One." God forbid, she thought. When Will first heard that his mother had voted against him at the proxy meeting, he was so furious, he vowed to have nothing more to do with her or the family.

After a year of pouting, however, he had gone to Clara, apologized, and asked for a job. She promptly installed him as assistant general manager at KSTO, with the understanding that Fred Hawkins was his boss, not the reverse. And so far, miraculously, Will seemed to be getting along.

"Will *works* at Channel One," she explained. "Why?"

"I wouldn't mind being interviewed about the latest hairstyles. I could bring pictures — or even live models."

"Why don't you phone Will directly? My name won't do much good as a reference, but you're free to use it."

"Thanks. I may do that."

By the time Yvonne finished at the beauty shop, the day was almost over. She stopped to pick up Marc's shirts at the French laundry, drove to the Owl Drug Store for the children's cough syrup, and finally, climbed out of the car in her garage.

Their Swiss *au pair* would be bringing the boys home from the park in a few minutes. They would scream for food, but the nanny would herd them into the tub, dress them in their robes and "jammies," feed them a cracker or two and make them wait. Under house rules, dinner was a family affair — unless, of course, there were guests.

"Brought you some goodies, Dagmar." Yvonne set her packages on the kitchen table, then peeked into the steaming pot. "Mmmm — smells yummy. What time did I say we're eating?"

"You said seven-thirty, Mrs. Greenfield. I have everything timed. I can't make it a second earlier."

"No, no, that's fine." Dagmar had a tendency to forget who worked for whom. But she was honest, and a decent cook — and Yvonne had learned to make allowances.

Upstairs, she took a quick shower and slipped into a new at-home gown Marc had brought her. Her closets bulged with more clothes than she could wear in a lifetime.

How she missed rummaging through sale tables, the way she and Betsy used to do, or browsing through the racks at Livingston's and the City of Paris! What fun it would be, she thought, to buy something — *anything* — that wasn't "the latest model" from the designers' salon of S. Greenfield.

She also realized that, as Betsy once told her, "Most women would kill to have problems like yours."

Chapter 9 — 1955

After a shower, Yvonne entered the family room, stooped to pick up a metal soldier, then switched on the television and settled on the sofa to open the day's mail. A news commentator was describing the uproar after Allen Ginsberg's reading of his poem, "Howl" at the Six Gallery in North Beach.

"Oh, no," Yvonne groaned, as the announcer led into their next feature, a special report on World War II prisoners of war. Stories about the war or anything remotely connected to it were anathema to her. Reliving that horror was not her idea of entertainment.

She rose to change the channel when a face flashed across the screen — a face that paralyzed her.

She stared at the image in shock and disbelief; then it disappeared. As she continued to gape, the host of the show came on with what seemed to be an endless report on war camps. Finally, he began to introduce his guest: former POW, recipient of the Bronze Star and Purple Heart, winner of the Sigma Delta Chi National Journalistic Fraternity Award for General Reporting, and currently, chief editorial writer for the *Boston globe*. The sound of his name made her gasp and sink to the couch.

"Suppose you tell our viewers: does time heal all wounds?"

"Time heals *some* wounds." Paul Amory spoke in measured tones. His voice was deeper than she remembered, and his appearance astounded her. Still strikingly handsome, he sat tall in his chair, garbed in a dark turtle-neck and well-worn sport coat, and looking decidedly older than his years. She knew his birthday; November 4, 1919. He would only be thirty-six. Yet his hair was streaked with gray, his brow etched with ridges. His eyes were cool and detached, as if they had seen and suffered more than they could bear. A deep scar stretched from his cheek to his neck.

"Would you explain, Mr. Amory?"

"I'll try. Most GIs hated the regimentation, the rugged training, the time spent away from homes and families. We loathed the sergeants who became bullies with the least amount of authority. We detested the thought that we were there to maim and murder an enemy we'd never seen."

"And those memories are still strong?"

"Nature has a way of burying the bad memories. Most veterans want to remember their buddies, the camaraderie, the girls they met, the excitement and stimulation of war."

"And you?"

"Mine wasn't the kind of experience you can bury."

"Suppose you start at the beginning. How were you captured?"

Paul folded his arms. His discomfort was obvious. "I don't like talking about myself — but I know I owe a debt to history."

He paused for concentration, then continued. "I volunteered for a secret mission to the Philippines in January of 1944. A submarine took me from Perth, Australia and landed me late at night on Lamon Bay — across the peninsula from Manila. My job was to coordinate Philippine and American guerilla activities against the Japanese, and make preparations for a U.S. invasion."

"Were you alone?"

"Yes. It would've been suicide to travel in a group. The guerrillas met me and took me to their headquarters. But before I could do what I was sent to do, one of the Philippine guerrillas turned informant. I was captured by the Japanese. They beat, tortured, and almost starved me, for a month."

Yvonne swallowed hard; tears slid down her cheek.

"And then?"

"They shipped me to Japan with some other American POWs to Fukuoka Camp 17 on the island of Kyushu. The camp officers forced us to work twelve hours, seven days a week in the mines. The conditions were miserable, and the camp commandant was a sadist."

"How did you live through all that? What kept you going?"

"I knew that sooner or later we'd win the war and I could go home to my girl. Unfortunately, by the time I got back to California she was on her honeymoon."

"Had you written her from prison camp?"

"We weren't allowed to send mail. A team from the International Red Cross visited us, took the names of our loved ones, and promised to notify them we were safe. So I assumed she knew where I was — but I guess she got tired of waiting."

The narrator inclined his head in a show of sympathy. "Are you now married?"

"No." Paul smiled his rare smile, and for a fleeting moment, looked

57

like the idealistic young man she remembered. "No woman would put up with me."

"How did the experience affect you?"

"You don't live through a Japanese prison camp without changing. I came home a different man. I'd used up all my patience — all my drive to save the world. Instead of entering law school as I'd planned, I took an easier route and became a journalist."

"Easier route? Your achievements contradict you."

"I'm not saying journalism's a free ride. Far from it. But for me it was the easy way. I couldn't handle going back to school — not intellectually, not emotionally, not physically."

"And the Purple Heart?"

His hand inadvertently touched his scar. "Oddly, I was hit by friendly fire, a bomb fragment from an American B-29 strike in the last days of the war."

"Forgive me, but you look older than 36."

Paul managed a hollow laugh. "There's no maid service when you're a guest of the Emperor of Japan."

Yvonne could no longer hold back the sobs. The image of him being tortured and brutalized, and all the time dreaming of coming home to her, was almost unbearable. Why hadn't the Red Cross notified her? Why hadn't he called the second he was released? If only someone had told her he was alive. If only she'd waited longer. If only, if only, if only...

"Two last questions, Mr. Amory. Do you think Hollywood movies portray prison camps realistically?"

"No."

"Do you hate the Japanese?"

"No. I can't waste my energy hating anybody, especially a whole race. But I won't do anything to help their economy."

The host thanked his guest and led into a series of commercials. Yvonne switched off the set, wiped her eyes, and tried to collect herself. What madness for Paul to feel that because he'd changed in the prison camp she would have loved him any less. How could he think she was that shallow — or fickle — or unfeeling?

Impulsively, she grabbed the phone. But by the time she reached the Boston television station, Mr. Amory had left.

The next morning, after a night of fantasies and conscience-wrestling, Yvonne made several calls to the *Boston Globe*. Paul was always "unavailable," and she didn't leave her name.

Her inclination was to catch the next plane to Boston, but Benny was getting bands on his teeth that day, and she had a calendar full of commitments. Even if she could get away, how would she explain it to Marc? Or to herself? What kind of trouble was she courting?

Yet in her own mind, she had no alternative. Paul still possessed her heart; he always had and always would. And at that moment, the cost to her marriage didn't seem to matter.

A scheme began to take shape in her mind; If she couldn't go to Boston, perhaps she could lure him to San Francisco. Claiming to be a reporter writing a feature on prize journalists, she called the *Globe* again and requested background information on Paul Amory. Then she alerted Helen Hopkins, her father's secretary now working for Lou Ella, that a batch of personal material was arriving from Boston.

Three days later, she took the elevator, to the third floor of the *Herald* Building, and hurried down the hall to the editorial offices. Carved moldings and oak paneling decorated the walls of the waiting room. The furnishings were still sparse, a hangover from her father's reign of penury.

She approached the desk. "How's my partner in crime?"

"Overworked and underpaid. Same old story." Helen Hopkins grinned up at her.

"You didn't say anything to Lou Ella, did you?"

"Not a peep. We gals have to have some secrets. Here's your packet — it's a thick one."

"And here's yours." She handed her a gift-wrapped box. "If it's not your color, you can change it."

Helen blushed. "You didn't have to do that."

"I wanted to. Is our leader in?"

"She's at a staff meeting, but she'll be back any minute."

"Thanks. I'll wait in her office."

Behind the closed door, Yvonne tore into the envelope. A stack of clippings fell out, most with Paul's byline. One was a picture of him receiving an award. A separate sheet gave his background and education. A note from the promotion director invited her to call if she needed more information.

Yvonne scanned the articles eagerly. Paul's early stories showed substance but lacked style. His recent editorials, however, delighted her. The writing was as crisp and virile as he was — each word carefully chosen, each sentence honed to glistening clarity.

A wave of excitement crept over her as she began to think her plan might work. All she wanted, she told herself, was to see him again...to be able to explain that she hadn't known he was imprisoned...that she would never have gotten married if she'd thought there was any chance he was alive.

She would ask him if he still loved her, and if he said yes...well, she couldn't let herself think any further. Somehow, they would solve the problem together.

"What a nice surprise!" Lou Ella strode into the office. Her walk was steady, her voice clear and confident. Two years of carrying the mantle of publisher had both hardened and humbled her. The job had proved more difficult than she anticipated, yet her lively, imaginative stories were slowly transforming the stolid journal into an entertaining and sometimes irreverent newspaper, with a growing readership.

Yvonne smiled innocently. "Would you believe I just stopped by to say hello?"

"Not for a minute." Lou Ella sat down in her swivel chair and returned the smile. Any resentment she'd had for her sister-in-law's vote at the shareholders' meeting had long faded. "What's on your mind?"

"I came to solve your problem — your search for the most perfect managing editor."

"I have a managing editor, though he's far from perfect."

Yvonne lay the envelope on her blotter. "I saw this journalist on television the other day. He was so bright and articulate, I phoned the *Boston Globe*, where he works. I said I was writing a story on prize-winning reporters and needed some background info."

"Why?"

"I remember all the problems Papa had finding qualified people, and this man really impressed me." So far, she had managed to be truthful. A few omitted details, perhaps, but no outright lies.

"What does he do at the *Globe*?"

"He's chief editorial writer."

"What makes you think he'd want to come here?"

"You'd offer him a better job."

"Do I look insane?" She didn't wait for an answer. "I'd have to be, to hire a man I'd never met, move him and his whole family across the continent —"

"He's single."

Lou Ella tried to hide her impatience. Yvonne's story was strange at best. There was more to her request — much more — but she hadn't the time or energy to find out what it was. "Suppose he got here and I didn't like him?"

"Won't you at least read his editorials?"

"Okay, but later."

"I get the hint." Yvonne moved to the door.

Lou Ella came around her desk. Now that her visitor was leaving, she could afford to be friendlier. "Will we see you at Clara's on Christmas Eve?"

"If I survive eight days of Hanukkah. Marc's got me taking the kids to his parents' every night to light the candles and get presents. They're really excited."

"Lucky kids. I only had one holiday."

"Will you get back to me, Lou Ella?"

"You bet," she said, reaching for the doorknob. "Drop by again."

The following Tuesday, Yvonne called Lou Ella. No, she hadn't had a minute to look at the material. Yes, she promised she would do so that very day.

"I finally spoke to Mr. Amory," she reported the next morning. "He has no desire to come west."

"You called Boston?" Yvonne felt her heart race. Lies and deception had always been foreign to her, and she was surprised that she could dissemble so easily. "What did you say?"

"Very little. He knew who I was. He reads the *Herald*, and thinks it's the finest paper in the west."

"What else?"

"I told him I liked his writing. He's got guts and fire, the way Tim used to write before he went to war."

"What did Mr. Amory say?"

"He said he had no traveling plans at the moment."

Her brain was reeling. "You offered him a job?"

"Not in so many words. But he knew I was putting out feelers. You're not a bad talent scout."

"So — he knew why you were calling?"

"Yes. Look, Yvonne, I have to run. I'll see you Saturday night."

"But maybe —"

"I'll walk you to the door."

Marc Greenfield slept soundly. Having trained himself to snooze through the cries of his children and just about everything else, Yvonne's nocturnal restlessness failed to disturb him.

By morning, she had made a decision. There was no time to think about possible consequences. As soon as Marc left for work, she phoned the *Boston Globe*. A secretary told her Mr. Amory was in a meeting. She called back, saying it was personal. Mr. Amory was still unavailable. The third time, she told the secretary: "Please tell him it's Yvonne in San Francisco."

After a short wait that seemed interminable, she heard his voice in the receiver. He sounded friendly but clearly impersonal. "Hello, Mrs. Greenfield."

"Paul — thank God! I was afraid you wouldn't talk to me. How'd you know my married name?"

"I read the *Herald*. I see your picture. You're as beautiful as ever. Are you the reason Lou Ella Stockton called me?"

She laughed, relieved not to have to pretend with him. "Well, yes. She doesn't know about us. But she was very impressed by your editorials. She wants you to come out and talk to her."

"How did she happen to read my editorials?"

"I saw you on TV and sent for them. I heard what you said, that you thought I got tired of waiting for you. I wanted to tell you it's not true. The Red Cross never notified me, or if they sent a letter, I didn't get it. I waited and waited. I thought you were dead."

After a short pause, he asked, "What difference does it make now?"

"I waited two years for you. I would've waited forever if I'd known you were alive. That's the truth, Paul. You have to believe me."

"I believe you. But you also heard me say that I came back a very different person. I'm not that same innocent, optimistic young man with dreams of reforming the world."

"So what? Did you think my love was that flimsy?"

"Don't get emotional, Yvonne. What happened years ago is over. We were two kids who fell for each other. Today, you have a husband and a family. You have children, for God's sake!"

"Don't you understand? You're the only man I ever loved — the only man I ever will love."

"I should hope that's not true. You made a wise choice. You married a man who gives you things I could never have given you."

"I didn't care about any of that! Paul, do you love me?"

"I haven't thought about it lately."

"I don't believe you."

"It doesn't matter what you believe. If things had gone our way, the ending might have been different. But they didn't."

"Words can't destroy what we had. I've never stopped loving you."

"I'm not a home-wrecker," he said firmly. "Good-bye, Mrs. Greenfield."

Chapter 10 — 1956

The mid-fifties saw the blooming of the Beat Generation, a rumpled group of poets, prophets, and pacifists better known as "beatniks" — a word coined by columnist Herb Caen.

Lou Ella Stockton, always anxious to explore ("exploit" her critics said) the unconventional, sent a reporter in disguise to three popular North Beach spots: The Co-Existence Bagel Shop, The Cellar, and the heart of the Beat movement, the all-paperback City Lights bookstore. Its owner, a tall, lanky poet named Lawrence Ferlinghetti, was facing charges for publishing Allen Ginsberg's "obscene" poem, "Howl."

While the reporter admired Ferlinghetti, he was unimpressed by the large numbers of hangers-on — mostly young people in their 20s and 30s who affected the sandals and beards of their peers, but did little more than sit around coffee houses decrying the Establishment.

The reporter's story concluded that beatniks, for the most part, were intellectual charlatans, fond of marijuana and other stimulants, impersonal sex, and hearing themselves pontificate. The story shocked, angered, and stirred controversy in local circles — exactly as Lou Ella hoped it would.

Mind-searching and identity-seeking were also taking place in other parts of town. Psychotherapy became the popular play-toy of Pacific Heights matrons, besieged businessmen, and sparring spouses. The main difference between those who spilled their souls in upper Grant Avenue coffee shops and those who did so on a psychiatric couch, was the willingness — and ability — to pay $25 an hour.

Yvonne Greenfield was among the latter. The analyst she chose was a stern Freudian who believed in letting his patients ramble on and on without comment. But he strayed long enough to set down an immediate rule: no more cuddling in bed with sons Ben and David. Young boys, he insisted, were sexual sponges who shouldn't be having erotic fantasies about their mother.

Her problem, however, had nothing to do with her sons.

"I've tried everything to keep busy," she told Dr. Mink, during a session in late April. "I'm chairman of four different Art Commission committees, I have more responsibilities than I can handle, but I still can't stop thinking about Paul. I came to you for help but all you do is sit there judging me and not talking. Why do I bother to come?"

"Maybe I did have a repressed childhood," she went on, not waiting for an answer she knew she wouldn't get. "But I've been coming to you five times a week since January, and I'm tired of lying on this couch babbling to myself. In fact, I don't think I'll come anymore. Do you mind?"

She waited a few seconds. "You won't answer? That's *dumb,* Dr. Mink. Well, I guess I'll go to Boston to see Paul. I'll ask him point-blank if he loves me, and if he does, I'll be tempted to restructure my life. Any parting advice?"

"Let's talk about your hostility," the doctor said, after a short silence. "Are you sure you're angry at *me*?"

"Just partly." Her voice softened. "I'm mad at Paul for rejecting me, I'm mad at Marc for screwing around, I'm mad at Clara because she probably threw away that Red Cross letter umpteen years ago, and I'm frustrated because you won't answer my questions." She stood up and reached for her purse.

"Yvonne," he said, "I'm not sure you're ready to stop therapy. Think it over and call me in a few days."

"I don't need to," she said firmly. "I'm not coming back."

Late that night, Yvonne tried to sound casual as she crawled into bed with Marc. "When are you going to New York, honey?"

He switched off the lamp. "Tuesday. By the way, hems are going up to 16 inches."

"You want me to have all my clothes shortened again?"

"Call alterations. They'll send someone to the house. You'll be a style-setter — the first in town with the new look."

The new look. Just what the world needed. After a pause, she casually said, "I've been thinking I might go east with you. I could use a vacation."

"Vacation! I've got three days of meetings and a week-end convention in Cleveland. I'll be running every second."

"That's okay. I'll visit museums and galleries, and who knows?" Dr. Mink had inspired her to voice her feelings. "I might even buy some clothes for myself."

He frowned. "That shrink's putting ideas in your head."

"How could he? He never talks to me. Besides, I'm not seeing him anymore."

"Really?" Marc rolled over to face her. "What happened?"

"Not a thing. He tried to relate everything to my sex life, and since I've only slept with one man, he didn't have a lot to work with."

"That reminds me of a limerick:
'The late psychoanalyst, Freud,
Was at normalcy very annoyed,
But bugger your brother,
Or knock up your mother,
And the great man would be overjoyed.'"

Yvonne chuckled. "That's my doc. I'm sure he's convinced I'm suffering postpartum penis envy or something."

"Did he suggest a cure?"

"Yes. I'm to go east with you."

Marc groaned and turned on his side. "Go to sleep, sweetheart. We'll talk tomorrow."

By morning, Marc had accepted the inevitable. Once his wife made up her mind to do something, no amount of persuasion would sway her. Despite her stubbornness, he never doubted that he truly loved her; his infidelities were just ego games and had nothing to do with their marriage. He would simply make a few calls and change his plans.

"Maybe you're right," he announced at breakfast, trying to sound enthusiastic. "It might be good for you to get away for a few days. But I won't be able to see much of you that weekend."

"That's okay. I'll keep busy." The stab of guilt she felt was quickly canceled by the notion that his weekend plans might include female companionship.

"I've been thinking," he went on, "we could both use a vacation. What would you say to two weeks at the Royal Hawaiian? No kids, no phones, just you and I sipping rum punches on the beach. I checked my calendar. I could leave May fifteenth."

His offer stunned her. How could she make plans to go away with Marc until she knew what was happening with Paul? The guilt came back tenfold as she realized that his philandering was relatively harmless, while her plans could have far deeper consequences.

Taking her silence for assent, he kissed her forehead and grabbed his briefcase. "Don't forget the hems, sweetheart. Time to show those gorgeous gams again."

The minute the garage door closed, Yvonne ran upstairs to her desk. She could think of little but Paul anymore. He seemed to be lurking in every thought...every action...almost becoming an obsession.

Lou Ella's secretary, Helen Hopkins, had managed to get Paul's home address, and Yvonne decided to write. She would tell him that she was coming to Boston, and would ring his doorbell Saturday. If he didn't want to see her, he didn't have to be home. But he would have no way to reach her and tell her not to come.

She scribbled several sentences, crossed them out, tried again, and finally wrote:

"Dear Paul,
I'm leaving for New York tomorrow, and plan to fly to Boston on
Saturday, May 5th, to take you to lunch. I'll expect to pick you up
at your home address sometime between noon and one.
Yours, as always,
Yvonne"

She sealed the letter. Her plan was as transparent as she was. She knew he would see right through any attempt at deception.

The weekend was a flurry of preparations. Late Tuesday afternoon, she and Marc landed at New York's Idlewild Airport. A long limousine delivered them to the Hampshire House, where they checked into a rose-filled suite overlooking Central Park.

For the next three days, they barely saw each other. Yvonne's friends took her gallery-hopping, to theater, museums and restaurants. Early Saturday morning, Marc left for Cleveland, and Yvonne caught the air shuttle to Boston.

She had planned carefully for the occasion: a beige silk shirt-dress, matching cashmere cardigan, high-heeled spectators. Her hair was soft and loose, and despite Marc's urging, longer than was currently chic. Light makeup, so expertly applied it seemed invisible, heightened her natural beauty.

Dr. Mink would have insisted that she probe her motives. Was she hoping to seduce Paul? Did she want a long-term relationship or a love affair? Was she really willing to sacrifice her marriage? Possibly her children? Fortunately, Dr. Mink's methods no longer mattered.

One question, however, did need answers. Surely, Marc would ask what she'd done over the weekend. Worse yet, what if he came back to surprise her and found her gone? She quickly dreamed up a story. An old school chum named Coralyn lived in Boston. She would explain that she'd called Coralyn to say hello, and on impulse, gone to see her. Simple as that. She'd gone too far with her plan to worry about it now.

Chapter 11 — 1956

Paul Amory lived in a section called the North End. "Beacon Hill it ain't," was the cabbie's comment on approaching an area of shabby-looking stores and rundown buildings.

A few blocks past the commercial strip, however, the neighborhood improved. The cab pulled up to a small red-brick duplex, one in a row of identical houses. Yvonne checked the address, paid the driver, and instinctively cautious, waited till the cab was out of sight. Then she hurried up the stairs.

Every nerve in her body tensed with anticipation as she rapped the brass knocker. What if he wasn't there? What if he *was* there? Would they embrace? Kiss? Shake hands?

The door opened, and she found herself facing the man she had met — and fancied herself in love with — thirteen years earlier. He looked as striking as she remembered, even more so in his jeans and plaid shirt — but such casual dress made her wonder if he'd gotten her letter. "Hello," was all she could blurt.

"Hello, Yvonne." His voice was cool and pleasant, betraying no sign of his own emotion. "Welcome to my palace. As you can see, a woman's touch is badly lacking."

Was that a hint? An invitation? She forced a smile and followed him into the living room. Woven matting covered the floor. Painted walls displayed awards, maps, and several colorful abstracts. His furniture was ultra-simple; Swedish modern, she guessed. Shelves overflowed with books and records, and a fat black man grinned at her from a silver frame on a piano.

"I haven't been to many bachelors' homes," she said, trying to sound casual, and somehow, to explain her nervousness. Being there made her realize how little she knew about him — his interests — his hobbies — what kind of person he had become.

"Care for a drink?"

"Thanks, not a thing." She took a seat and clasped her hands to still their shaking. "You're looking wonderful, Paul. The TV cameras don't do you justice."

"My boss says I don't look a day over sixty." He sat down opposite her. "And you haven't changed at all, except to grow more beautiful."

Before she could reply, he said, "The world's finest Italian food is only two blocks away. Can you walk in those stilts?"

She laughed. "I didn't think my awkwardness showed."

"It doesn't." They sat in silence for a long moment, then he offered her a cigarette.

"No thanks, I quit two years ago."

He lit one for himself. "What brings you to the East Coast?"

"I wanted to visit friends, and some galleries and shops. My husband's family owns a department store, as you probably know, and Marc gets livid when I'm seen in other stores. Here it doesn't matter, that is, as long as I don't, God forbid, buy retail."

He laughed. "My mother was like that. She used to say everything was negotiable, even taxes and doctor bills."

"Is your mother — ?"

"She died in '46, eight months after I came home."

"Oh, I'm sorry. Did you ever call your half-brothers?"

"Yes, and they still refused to see me. Ironically, their snub got me into journalism. I was mad enough to write about my late father and my reluctant half-brothers, and take the story to the *Globe*. They wouldn't print it, but they offered me a job."

"They must have liked your writing. Where are your brothers now?"

"One died in a small plane accident. The other, last I heard, had a drug problem. Are you hungry?"

"Starved."

"Let's go, then," he said. "You're in for a treat."

Acting had never been one of Paul Amory's talents. Today, however, he had no choice but to try. He hoped he was giving a plausible impersonation of a man in control of his emotions.

Ever since Lou Ella's call from nowhere, he'd known instinctively that Yvonne was behind it — that somehow, some way, he'd see her again. Contrary to what he'd told her, she had always been an unfinished passage in his life...a source of hurt and frustration, as well as the object of his fantasies. And he knew they were just that — fantasies.

Yet hard as he'd tried to love others, no woman had ever affected him the way Yvonne did. He doubted any woman ever would. The only reason he read the *Herald* was to see an occasional picture of her, or read what she was doing. Somehow, it made him feel close to her.

So there he was, incredibly, sitting opposite her, playing the cool, detached reporter, when all he wanted to do was smother her in his arms and never let her go. He thought back to the night they met, how they'd stayed on the beach till dawn, how he'd had to knot his fists to keep from grabbing her. Then, it was the war that stopped him. Now, it was a much greater obstacle: a husband and children.

"Paul, this is fantastic." Yvonne plunged her fork into the pasta and twirled it around her spoon. "You probably eat here all the time. Why don't you weigh 200 pounds?"

He smiled. "I like to walk. Boston's a walking town."

"So's San Francisco."

"They have a lot in common: water on three sides, populations of 700,000, more or less, and about the same number of square miles — 49, I think." Small talk was not his forte. But anything to keep the conversation moving.

"True," she said, "but San Francisco is sinful and scandalous, and full of crazy beatniks. Boston is traditional and respectable, no?"

"Not always." He refilled her wine glass and tried to sound casual. "Tell me about your life. Are you happy?"

"Reasonably."

The next question came out before he could stop it. "Is your husband good to you?"

"Yes."

Just as he feared. A wife-beater would have eased his guilt. He shut off the dangerous thoughts. "Then suppose you tell me why you're here. The real reason."

His directness relieved her; she hated being evasive. "All right. I haven't been the same since I found out you were alive. I even went to a psychiatrist to chase you out of my head, but it didn't help. I know it's crazy. I know it's destructive. But you've been in my thoughts, day and night."

Her words stirred him. They were words he'd dreamed of hearing for years. Yet now that they were being spoken, he couldn't respond the way he wanted to.

Sensing his reluctance, she went on, "I feel incomplete without you, Paul, as if we have some obligation to the love we had for each other."

"Not love — infatuation. With so little time together, we had to compress our emotions and give them a name. Can't you see that none of that matters now? I meant what I said before: your life is with your husband and children."

"I'd never leave my children. But they could learn to love you and you would love them."

"That's insanity, Yvonne. The only reason I decided to see you today is to tell you to forget any ideas you might have about our getting together. It's not going to happen."

"What if I came to you in a year or so and I was single?"

"Yvonne," he said gently, "you and I live on different planets. I couldn't possibly exist on yours, any more than you could be happy on mine."

"You didn't think so thirteen years ago."

"I was young and naive. I thought passion could solve everything."

"You mean economic problems?"

"Economic, social, ideological — our whole value structures clash. Your taxi ride from the airport probably cost what I earn in a day."

She paused a moment, then added, hesitantly, "If you moved to San Francisco, Lou Ella would pay you a good salary."

He shook his head. "San Francisco's your town, not mine. It belongs to the Stocktons and the Crockers and the Greenfields, and all the great dynasties that make it what it is. Here, at least I have my own identity. I sit on several boards, I work on charter reform for the mayor, I'm president of the Chamber of Commerce. It may not be much of an identity, but it's mine — all mine."

"Then we'll live here."

He shook his head. "Life isn't a fairy tale. Even if I did still care about you, even if I *had* loved you, love *doesn't* conquer all."

She nodded, as if in agreement. Let him play hero all he wanted. Soon they'd be alone and she would test his almighty will power. "Tell me about your work. Is it very demanding?"

Relieved to have a new subject, he answered patiently. He spoke of the rigors of his job, his hopes to tour India and Africa, and the obligation he kept putting off: writing a history of his years in a prison camp.

They stayed at the restaurant long into the afternoon, forgetting time until the sky began to darken.

"Something wonderful happens when we're together," she said softly.

"It happened those two nights on the beach, and it happened again today."

He said nothing, not wanting to acknowledge how strongly she affected him. Across the table — so near he could touch — was that same sweet, beautiful face; the eyes that melted him, the lips he wanted so desperately to kiss. All he could think of was to pay the check and escape while he was still coherent.

"I'm calling you a taxi," he said, the moment they were inside his flat. Yvonne laughed. "You that anxious to get rid of me?"

"Yes!"

"I'll call my own cab." She set her purse on a chair and slipped off her shoes. "Can't we have a cup of tea?"

"*After* you call."

"Yes sir, General." The wine had relaxed her and renewed her confidence. She gave him a mock salute and lifted the receiver, holding down the button as she dialed and pretended to order a car. Then she walked up to him in the living room. "Why are you so jittery?"

He retreated instinctively. "You know why. Now put on your shoes and stop acting like a child."

"Would it be a crime to kiss me good-bye?"

"You asked me to kiss you once before. I told you I wouldn't...I couldn't. Remember?"

"As if it were yesterday. But then you did. I remember how your lips felt. Do you remember?"

"All too well." The words slipped out.

"Oh, Paul, why can't we have this time for ourselves? Why can't we make believe it's 1943 and we're just a soldier and his girl in love?"

Slowly, deliberately, he lit a cigarette. "I knew this was lunacy. I should've left town."

"It isn't lunacy. It might be if we were going to hurt anyone, but I'm going back to my husband. He doesn't know you exist and he never will. I can't promise to forget you, but I can promise never to call or write or try to see you again, if that's what you want."

"That's exactly what I want." He tossed his cigarette in the fireplace. "In exchange for that promise — ?"

"Just give us the present."

"Impossible," he said, turning away.

"Please, Paul. I want so much to stay with you tonight. I don't have to be back in New York till tomorrow. We'll never have this chance again."

"No," he repeated, not quite as emphatically.

"Haven't we waited long enough?" She took a step towards him, sensing a desire as strong and compelling as her own. Her hands crept up his back, spread to his shoulders. She felt him respond ever-so-slightly.

Standing on tiptoe, she kissed his neck, her lips brushing gently across the nape. He stood still, not daring to move. Then she slid to his ear. "I love you," she whispered. "You want me as badly as I want you. I can feel it."

"Yvonne," he said hoarsely, "Don't do this to me."

Again, she moved her lips across the back of his neck, feeling him shudder at her touch. Suddenly, impulsively, he whirled around to face her. Their bodies met with a need so urgent, she felt dizzy. At last she was in his arms, where she so desperately wanted to be, holding him, clinging to him, almost crying with joy and relief as he pressed her head to his chest.

He tilted her chin and found her mouth, kissing her as he had dreamed of — tenderly, passionately, feeling his being melt into hers. There was no stopping now, no time to pause and think what they were doing....

Her pulse quickened as he unbuttoned her dress and let it fall. She stood immobile for a moment, then stepped out of it. He reached for her straps and slid them off her shoulders, marveling at the fullness of her breasts.

Her nipples firmed to his touch as her hips began to sway in slow rhythm. He tore off his clothes and within seconds, they were lying on the floor, naked bodies pressed together as eager hands and tongues explored each other. His urgency grew until he could no longer hold back. He entered her with a low moan and flowed into her, controlling himself till he felt her strong arousal, then thrusting them both to a plane of passion where nothing else mattered.

And when it was over, he held her tightly, regretting his weakness and making excuses to himself, all the while knowing that he had never loved another woman that way — that she returned his depth of emotion — and that they still had the whole night ahead of them.

Chapter 12 — 1956

Flying home Sunday night, with Marc dozing peacefully on the seat beside her, Yvonne struggled to master her emotions. Every second took her farther and farther from the man she adored and a challenging new life she yearned for, now even more than before. Yet she had been so anxious to give herself to Paul, she had struck a devil's bargain: a night together in exchange for a lifetime apart.

Once home and back to her routine, she tried to pretend the trip was a fantasy — a daydream that had never happened. But it had happened, and the prospect of giving up the rare love that they shared overwhelmed her with sadness. The only person she could trust to keep her secret was Betsy. But Betsy was happy now, with her second husband and their five-year-old son; she didn't need to hear her cousin's problems.

So Yvonne found a new psychiatrist, a young woman whose unorthodox approach had been written up in the *Herald*. Unlike Dr. Mink, Charlotte Newman M.D., Ph.D., M.P.H., considered herself eclectic, and did not believe in the silent treatment.

Her office was a pleasant, sunlit room on the second floor of a Sacramento Street medical building. The decor was homey, with flowered upholstery and children's paintings on the walls. Doctor and patient sat facing each other, chatting as if they were friends. After hearing about Paul for the better part of the hour, Dr. Newman asked Yvonne what she wanted to do.

"I want to be with him," she shrugged. "Right now, I want to give up everything to go back to Boston and marry him."

"Marriage is more than good sex."

"I loved him long before we made love. The fact that he was a great lover is a wonderful bonus, but our feelings go much deeper."

"Do you enjoy sex with your husband?"

"I can take it or leave it. We've been married eleven years. Marc is kind and predictable, but I know he has affairs, and that colors our relationship."

"Did Paul satisfy you?"

"Yes." Blood rushed to Yvonne's cheeks. "I hate to think how many women he's practiced with."

"How do you feel about that?"

"Irrationally jealous. I can't let myself think about it." A self-conscious tilt of the head. "I've wanted men to kiss me, hug me, even to touch my breasts, but I've never wanted a man inside me — possessing me — the way I wanted Paul."

Dr. Newman smiled. "How are you otherwise?"

"So-so. Marc wants to take me to Hawaii for two weeks but I can't face it. I feel terribly guilty and yet —"

"Don't even think about making a decision now. You need time to develop perspective — to look at your beautiful family and realize how miserable you'd be if you ruined their lives. Paul must be a very ethical man, and smart enough to see that you couldn't possibly live in each others' worlds."

"Why couldn't we? I love him enough to give up everything except my children. But he made me make that awful bargain. I can't even send him a postcard."

"He's wise, Yvonne. Far wiser than you. Suppose he'd been a playboy with no conscience?"

"But that's the point. His integrity — his values — that's just what attracted me in the first place. Sometimes I want to drive to the bridge and jump off."

The doctor stiffened. "Suicide is quite often an act of hostility. You'd destroy the lives of everyone you love, especially your sons. You do show signs of depression. You may not get well in a week or a month, but you will get well, I promise you. I'll be here to help as long as you want me."

Yvonne liked Dr. Newman, continued to see her three days a week, and made a sincere effort to move on with her life. One evening, when Marc was working late, she attended a gathering in the City Lights bookstore in North Beach.

Convinced that "Howl" was a mystical sonnet rather than scatology, and certain that Paul would be on the side of a free press, she joined a group of writers and artists who supported publisher Ferlinghetti through a long obscenity trial that he eventually won.

Harold Zellerbach was no fan of the literary counter-culture, and had tried several times to interest Yvonne in his projects, but not until he mentioned the summer concerts led by Boston Pops' conductor Arthur Fiedler, did he get a positive response. Anything that had to do with

Boston attracted her, although working with the flirtatious Maestro turned out to be a bit of a challenge.

Taking charge of the concerts held in San Francisco's Civic Auditorium left her little time for brooding, but the healing process was as long and tedious as Dr. Newman had warned. Sometimes she felt angry at Paul for making the decision for both of them. It was her life, her marriage, her children. What right did he have to dictate her behavior? But the question was moot; he had already done so.

She had been home from the east several months when a call came from Betsy. Her mother, Maggie Stockton Kettering, had suffered a stroke, lapsed into a coma, and died in the ambulance. Yvonne felt an immediate sense of loss. Close as she was to Betsy, she hadn't seen much of Aunt Maggie, except at family gatherings. But she'd been fond of her.

"I'll be right over," she told Betsy.

"No, Eevie, I'm okay." Betsy blew her nose. "Mom's had hypertension for ages. The doctor warned us she could have a stroke at any time. Why don't you go see Clara? She's taking it pretty hard."

Clara upset by Maggie's death? Not likely, thought Yvonne. The sisters-in-law had been friends at first, then angry rivals during the fight for control of the *Herald*. In recent years, they had learned to tolerate each other for the sake of appearances.

"Good idea," said Yvonne, not wanting to argue. "I'll pay her a call, then I'll be here if you need me."

After phoning the news to Marc at the store, she called her stepmother. To her surprise, Clara sounded shaken, and said yes, she'd be grateful for a visit.

Minutes later, Maxwell answered the door and escorted Yvonne to the upstairs den. Clara sat warming a brandy snifter as she gazed out the bay window. "Come in, come in," She ordered.

Yvonne took a chair, marveling, as she always did, at Clara's composure. "My condolences about Maggie."

"Same to you." Clara tried to sound nonchalant. "How's Marc? The boys? Care for a cognac?"

"No, thanks. Everyone's fine." Something was wrong. Clara never drank in the daytime — nor was it like her to be evasive. "You and Aunt

Maggie weren't very close."

"No. We disliked each other intensely."

"Then why are you so upset?"

Clara was pensive for a moment, and finally, blotted a tear on her cheek. "It's not Maggie," she said softly. "It's your brother, Will. We had words, and poor Katie heard everything."

Yvonne and her stepmother had always avoided revealing their feelings to each other, but Clara had set the tone. "I've never asked you this, but what's wrong with Katie? She doesn't relate to any of us. I'm her sister, yet I can barely talk to her."

Clara shook her head. "Katie spends half her life buried in books and the other half watching that television set I made the mistake of buying. I want her to come out at the Cotillion next year, but she's so painfully shy."

"Can't you send her to a therapist?"

"She won't go. But the real problem is Will. I'm afraid — well — I'm afraid he'll never get married." She looked to Yvonne for a shocked reaction. There was none.

Yvonne sighed. "What you're about to tell me, Nonna, is old news. Tim and I have known for a long time."

Clara gasped. "You knew Will was a — ?"

"We knew he had no interest in women. But it was Will's secret, and not ours to tell you."

"Oh, dear Lord!" Clara's hand shot to her head. "Thank God James isn't here!"

Yvonne touched her arm in a rare gesture of affection. "Being gay is no tragedy, Nonna. Now Will can stop pretending. That may be why he's been so hostile to the family all these years."

"He's angry at me?"

"At all of us. He had instincts he didn't understand at first. When he did understand them, he was ashamed, and frightened that someone might find out, especially his father. So he made up stories about girlfriends and sexual conquests. But when resentment built up and he drank too much, his rage would come out."

"How do you know all that?"

Yvonne managed a smile. "I spent hours discussing Will with my shrink. She met him at my last cocktail party. He brought a young man he said was a business associate. When they left, she said there was no question they were lovers."

Clara drained her snifter and sat up. "Oh, dear Lord! Who else knows about this?"

"The point is, Nonna, it doesn't matter. Half the artists I know are gay, as they call themselves, and they're wonderful, creative people. Will was born to be different; he didn't ask to be. And if *we* don't love and support him, who will?"

Thoughtful for a few seconds, Clara tried to absorb it all. "I was sure you'd be as shocked as I was. Instead, you make me see what a silly old fool I am. I'm afraid I reacted badly."

"Then call Will." Yvonne pushed the phone toward her. "Tell him you love him and that you're happy he doesn't have to pretend any more."

"But I'm not happy. Will was my last hope for a grandson to carry on the Stockton name."

"My sons and Betsy's will carry on, with or without the Stockton name." Yvonne lifted the receiver and dialed. "Here, Nonna," she said firmly. "Talk to your son."

Will was at home scrambling eggs when the phone rang. He decided not to answer, thinking it might be another angry family member. But on the tenth ring, he grabbed the receiver. "Yeah?"

"It's your mother, Will. Don't hang up — please! I'm sorry if I hurt you."

Will moved the frying pan off the burner. "You're not pissed?"

"If God created you to be different, then that's the way it is." Not knowing what to say to the startled silence on the other end, she set down the receiver.

Yvonne grabbed it. "Will, it's me, Eevie. Your mom was just calling to say you don't have to pretend any more. We all love you and we want you to live your life whatever way you want. Are you there?"

"Yeah…"

Hearing the emotion in his voice, she quickly said, "Well, you'd better get out your dark suit. If you wear that horse blanket sport coat to Aunt Maggie's funeral, she'll come down from heaven and punch you in the teeth."

And she clicked off.

Chapter 13 — 1956

Maggie Kettering had left instructions for cremation and a private ceremony. After the service in a small church, Lou Ella Stockton, Will Stockton, and Marc Greenfield returned to their offices. Betsy and Foster Pickett left with their son Tyrone, and Clara and Katie Stockton drove home with Maxwell. Tim Stockton had picked up his sister.

"I'm worried about you, Eevie," he said, when they were alone in the car. "You don't look well."

"I'm fine." Yvonne glanced sideways. "It's great the way that you've learned to master your prosthesis. You can drive, type, do most anything."

"Quit changing the subject. When was the last time you went to a doctor?"

"You don't give up, do you?"

"I know you too well, Eevie. What's going on?"

She exhaled a long sigh. "All right, if you must drag it out of me, Marc and I are fighting about clothes again."

"Something else is bothering you. When you came home from New York, you had a strange expression and I thought you were just tired. But that hangdog look is still there."

"I know." She turned to him impulsively. "Do you remember Paul Amory?"

"The guy you were so nuts about during the war?"

"Yes. I thought he was dead, but he isn't. He lives in Boston. I saw him when I went east."

"You *saw* him?"

Too emotional to stop, she blurted out everything — from the first glimpse on television to their passionate reunion. "I'm thinking of leaving Marc," she declared, almost in tears, "but Paul won't even talk to me."

Tim stopped the car in front of her house, turned off the motor and faced her. "Let me tell you a quick story. I came home from Tarawa a pretty screwed-up jerk. All I could think of was my own misfortune. I forgot about the guys still living that horror in the Pacific, and the guys who came home on crutches and wheelchairs, and the guys who never came home. I had a single thought: *My* life was over. I wanted to die."

"Seriously?"

"Yes. The only thing that kept me sane was that you were getting married and I was damned if I'd ruin your wedding."

"I didn't realize —"

"I was a good actor. Then I saw Lou Ella at your reception. In a matter of days, everything changed. She showed me what a jerk I was to heap all this self-pity on myself when I had so much to be grateful for — and so many people I could help. Suddenly, I had a reason to live."

"Our situations are different."

"Not very. Here's Yvonne Greenfield, one of the most beautiful, glamorous women in the world, with a husband who adores her, fantastic kids, youth, health, brains, more money than she can spend — and she's moping around, crying to her shrink because she's got the hots for an old flame in Boston."

"I love him."

"Wake up, Eevie. Love is more than happy hormones. You've seen this guy three times in your life — three times in 13 years. Do you know his middle name? Do you know his medical history? Do you know what kind of women he's been sleeping with? Do you know anything about him, except that he's good-looking and great in the sack?"

"I know he has wonderful integrity."

"Oh, swell." He rapped the steering wheel with his metal claw. "Fly off to Boston. Ruin the lives of Marc and your children and all who love you. Is that what you want?"

"Marc's been — unfaithful," she said, her voice cracking.

He reached out and drew her close. "I'm sorry, sweetheart. I know you're hurting. But you haven't thought this through. No matter what Marc's done, he adores you. Forget Paul. He doesn't want you. He doesn't love you. Where's your damn pride?"

She lay her head on his shoulder, tears rolling down her cheeks. "I miss him so much, Tim. I'm going out of my mind."

"You've got a massive infatuation. That's all it is. He's not crying for you, or he wouldn't have let you go. And if he's that sexy, he's probably got a whole stable of girlfriends."

"Probably." She wiped her eyes.

"Forget him, Eevie. He's got his own life and his own world. Go home and hug your kids."

Toward the end of the year, Yvonne began to feel familiar changes in her body. A test confirmed her suspicions; she was six weeks pregnant — the result of the short trip she and Marc had taken to Hawaii.

At first, the news distressed her. Having Marc's baby would add another link to the marital chain that bound them. Still clinging to the hope of a life with Paul, unrealistic as it was, she felt reluctant to take on the burden of a third child.

Against Dr. Newman's advice, she decided to phone Paul. Marc was the father; there was no question about that. And yet, if there was any chance that Paul might relent and give their relationship a chance, she would surrender her unborn baby. Surely he would understand that this new development negated their agreement.

Repeated excuses from Paul's secretary, however, made her realize he wasn't going to take her calls — or her letters, which came back unopened.

Dr. Newman tried to help her accept Paul's rejection and approach her pregnancy with a positive attitude. Marc was thrilled to learn of his pending fatherhood. He did his best to convince Yvonne that the baby was a gift from God — a gift, he prayed, that would lift her out of her strange depression.

Marc's wish was soon granted. Despite everyone's hopes for a girl, the birth of an eight-pound boy on May 3, 1957 was a joyous occasion. Yvonne lay in bed two mornings later, watching the infant sleep in her arms. She had forgotten the miracle of childbirth. The beauty and perfection of his tiny face warmed her spirits.

In previous births, she'd been anxious to get back in shape and return to her activities as soon as possible. But this time, her main thought was to be a mother. The realization that she could have lost everything, including her precious sons and exquisite new baby, made her feel ashamed. Guilt clouded her happiness, and she promised herself that once she got home, her three children would get as much of her time, love and attention as they deserved.

Glancing down at her infant, she tucked in his blanket. He bore no resemblance to his father, or for that matter, to anyone. Several silky red hairs were his only distinguishing feature.

A smile of contentment crossed her face. "Samuel Isaac Greenfield," she whispered. "With that name, you'll never get into the P-U Club."

Chapter 14 – 1956

The Garden Court of the Palace Hotel looked its glittery best for the Society-with-a-capital-S event of the year: San Francisco's Debutante Cotillion Ball.

Austrian crystal chandeliers sparkled under the dome-shaped ceiling, amid stately marble columns and leafy trees. It was the ideal setting for the men in their custom-made tails, some with red sashes proclaiming them members of the Floor Committee, and their table companions, the relatives and friends of the young honorees.

A crowd of nearly 2,000 had gathered to witness the annual rite of passage of 27 hand-picked debutantes — among them, a very frightened Katherine Marie Stockton.

Clara sat tall in her chair, nervously puffing a cigarette, surrounded by her two sons. Will whispered in her ear. "Katie'll be fine, Nonna. Don't worry."

"But I *do* worry. Poor Katie's only doing this to please me." Clara turned to Will with silent affection. Had Yvonne not intervened, she might never have understood Will's difference. Now she felt she was just beginning to know her son. And the relief of not having to pretend anymore had gentled him considerably.

"Try to relax," he said, pushing over a champagne glass.

"I'm a fool," she groaned. "I never should have forced Katie do this, but I thought it would give her confidence. Ever since James died, she's become almost a recluse."

"How can she be a recluse? She gets good grades. She's been accepted at Mills College."

"She says the girls snub her. I —"

Clara's words were interrupted by the fanfare announcing the traditional 10 PM presentation. The orchestra segued into "A Pretty Girl Is Like A Melody." One by one, the "buds" in their white ball gowns and elbow-length gloves, clutching fresh bouquets, stepped through a portal on the stage. They smiled as their names were announced, curtsied to the parents and committee members, and were officially introduced to San Francisco Society.

Nineteenth in the procession, Katie appeared pale and lifeless. Mousy brown hair framed a small, pinched face. Her eyes were downcast, her step hesitant. The flowers trembled in her hands. Unlike the smiling, confident girls who preceded her, Katie seemed petrified.

The highlight of the presentation came when the girls' escorts, resplendent in their tails and white carnations, raised their batons to form a crossed-swords arch. The debs passed beneath it. Katie managed to get through the ritual, and when the fathers claimed the girls for the customary first dance of the evening, she fell into Will's arms with a shudder of relief.

"Oh, Will," she said, "I'm suffocating! How can I get out of here?"

"Relax, sweetie-pie. You can't go till you dance with your escort."

"My dumb escort doesn't want to dance with me any more than I want to dance with him. He's just here, because he happens to be Betsy's snooty neighbor."

They danced in silence for several minutes, until Will felt a tap on the shoulder.

"May I?" Tim smiled as he cut in and circled Katie's waist. The right sleeve of his topcoat, folded at the elbow, hung limply at his side. On special occasions, the prosthesis came off. "You look pale, honey," he murmured in her ear. "Are you all right?"

"No! I hate all this fuss and pretense and phony stuff."

"No one claims the Cotillion is anything but a longtime tradition. It's something young girls do to please their parents — and sometimes themselves."

"It was okay for Yvonne. She's beautiful and charming. But I'm ugly and everyone hates me."

"Katie, Katie," he said soothingly, "you're not ugly and no one hates you. Tonight will be over all too fast, and years later, you'll be proud to show your picture to your grandchildren."

"I'm *never* getting married. Oh, Tim, it's so hot in here. I feel like I'm choking. Can't we sit down?"

"Sure we can, honey." He took her arm, walked her to the table and sat her next to her mother.

"She's having a mild panic attack," he whispered to Clara. "I think we should take her home."

"Yes, of course. It was a big mistake." Clara passed her daughter a cup of coffee. "Take a few sips of this, darling. We can leave whenever you want."

Katie took the coffee, stared blankly for a minute, murmured, "Thanks, Mom" — then tilted the cup and poured it down the front of her two-thousand-dollar white silk ball gown.

Part 3

The Love Generation

Chapter 15 — 1960

In the early sixties, San Francisco was a city of growth — but progress was slow. In one of her weekly editorials, Lou Ella Stockton pointed out that the only signs of "redevelopment" to date were the wrecking balls on giant cranes crashing into homes and deserted buildings.

It wasn't long, however, before tall, glassy apartments began to appear on Nob Hill and various residential sections. Soaring office towers sprouted in the Financial District. New hotels and department stores sprang up around Union Square.

At the same time, Anti-Vietnam War marches and free speech demonstrations were gaining momentum. Frustration bubbled to the surface everywhere — not only on college campuses, but in homes and meeting places, in North Beach cafes, and particularly, among a growing group of young people who frequented a section of Haight Street, near Ashbury. Their goal, they would soon proclaim to the world, was to spread peace and love.

The Bar Mitzvah of Benjamin Simon Greenfield in early March of 1960 was crowned by evening festivities at the Fairmont. Benjamin's grandmother, Clara Stockton, had left the hotel earlier, but his parents, Marc and Yvonne, stayed to party — making fools of themselves, Katie Stockton thought, watching them do some awkward new dance called "the Twist."

She lasted as long as she could bear the noise and cigarette smoke, then excused herself, claiming an early morning class. Tim walked her to her car and made sure she locked the doors.

Driving home to Jackson Street, Katie's mind drifted back to the last big party she'd attended with Tim — the calamitous Cotillion. Even now, three years later, the thought of having to parade on stage in front of all those people made her shudder. Spilling coffee down her gown hadn't been the best idea, but she had panicked. Thank God Clara had wrapped her in a coat and whisked her out of there.

The next day, Clara had dragged her, crying and protesting, to a psychiatrist — the same kind, patient doctor Katie was still seeing. He had told her that her problems were not unique and that he could help her, which he had. After several weeks, in fact, she became so attached to him, she couldn't bear to go off to college.

At first, Clara was determined Katie would go to Mills, as both Yvonne and her cousin Betsy had done. Then the psychiatrist intervened. He convinced Clara that Katie was highly susceptible to anxiety attacks, and that being alone in strange surroundings could trigger repeated episodes. Sufficiently scared, Clara agreed to keep Katie living at home while she attended the San Francisco College for Women, a small Catholic university.

To everyone's relief, Katie seemed to be adjusting, even making friends with Lily Chow, the only Chinese girl in the school. The two "misfits," as they saw themselves, found comfort in each others' company. Clara was pleased; at last, her daughter had a friend.

Thinking about Lily made Katie smile as she drove home along Jackson Street. Their standing movie date on Sunday was the high point of the week. Parking by the curb, she hurried up the brick pathway to the house. Not even a porch light gleamed in the darkness, a holdover, she assumed, from her father's frugal regime. Being out at night was scary. She glanced behind her several times to make sure no one was following. Once inside, she locked and double-bolted the door.

Flipping the light switch, she saw that everything was in its place; the polished parquet floor, the Fortuny-covered walls with their priceless Corot paintings. Beaming down on the foyer was the eighteenth-century crystal chandelier that her mother had been so thrilled to find in a Paris antique shop.

Upstairs, Katie tiptoed to her room. She changed into her nightgown and crawled into bed, too tired even to read. Thoughts of the party floated through her head; how beautiful her half-sister was, and how much everyone admired her. She loved Yvonne as one loves a distant goddess, accepting their physical differences and 17-year age gap as hopeless barriers to intimacy.

The chasm wasn't Yvonne's fault, Katie realized. It was her own. She didn't want a one-sided relationship, and what could she offer a woman like that? God was unfair to have given Yvonne so much and dealt her so little. But whoever said God was fair?

Jealousy, however, was not part of Katie's nature. A sophisticated man like Marc Greenfield would never be attracted to someone like her, and that was fine, because she wouldn't know how to talk to a man like that.

Several boys had asked her out over the years, but only, she was sure, because her family was rich. What would it be like, she wondered, to have a man who didn't know she was rich and truly cared for her?

Dozing between consciousness and slumber, she was jolted awake by a sudden, loud noise. Frightened, she switched on her lamp, walked cautiously down the hall to Clara's room, and opened the door.

What she saw made her freeze in horror. Her mother was standing over the body of a man. Blood streamed from a hole in his chest, spilling onto the carpet. Pale and shaking, Clara dropped her gun to the floor, then plucked an envelope from the dead man's fingers.

Katie gasped and covered her mouth, unable to speak.

"I — didn't mean to kill him," Clara stammered. "He — was a burglar. He threatened me. Are you all right?"

Katie nodded mechanically, still speechless. Her mother took a few seconds to collect herself, then called an ambulance, her lawyer, and the police. She folded the envelope and tucked it in the pocket of her robe.

"W — what's that?" Katie finally asked.

"I'll explain later. Please don't mention it to anyone."

"All right." Katie sank onto the bed. "What happened? Who is he?"

"I don't know him — he broke in. He must've come through a window in the back. Oh, God!" Clara exhaled deeply and began to pace. "I was just going to bed when he confronted me and demanded my jewels. I went to the drawer and gave him my diamond necklace. He demanded more money, threatened me. Then I saw your father's pistol.

"I grabbed the gun, told him I was calling the police. That's when he lunged at me. I was sure he was going to kill me —"

Tears clouded Katie's eyes. "But — If *he* got in, *anyone* could get in. We're not safe here!"

"Katie darling, please calm yourself." Clara sat down and put a shaking arm around her daughter's shoulder. "I've lived in this house for thirty-three years. Your father and *his* ancestors lived here before that, and this is the first time there's been any sort of problem. Tomorrow, I'll have bars put on all the windows."

"What about tonight?" Katie asked, sobbing.

"You can sleep in here with me. Now stop worrying. Where are those pills the doctor gave you?"

"In my room. But I'm scared to go in there."

"No one's going to hurt you, darling." She helped Katie to her feet. "We'll go in together."

The ambulance came first and pronounced the victim dead. Within minutes, Clara's attorney and the police arrived. Avery Andrews was a tall, striking-looking man with wavy white hair combed back from a high, aristocratic brow. His face was narrow, his nose straight, his mouth un-smiling. It was a stern, determined face, lacking warmth and compassion.

He stood by Clara's side as various strangers swarmed the bedroom, taking photographs, measurements, and lab samples. Homicide inspector Chet McGuire listened to Clara's story and asked questions. "We could not find any tools on your burglar, Mrs. Stockton, only the diamond necklace you say you gave him. Did you see any tools?"

"No, I — don't remember…"

"He wasn't a pro; no gloves, no tools, no bag to carry his loot. And why would he leave fingerprints everywhere? Why would he show his face? If he was going to burglarize you, why wouldn't he wait till you went out? It doesn't add up."

"What are you saying?" demanded Andrews.

"I'm saying that it's strange, that's all." McGuire tried not to be disrespectful. He knew who Clara Stockton was. He also knew her story had more holes than a fishnet. But she had connections, and she'd been shrewd enough to call in a high-powered lawyer. "You're sure you've never seen this man before?"

"Yes, positive."

He glanced at the dead man's wallet. "Ever heard the name Albert Hogan?"

"No."

He moved toward the bed. "You say it was a noise that woke you, Miss Stockton?"

Katie sat shivering on the edge, wrapped in a blanket. Her frightened eyes darted around the room.

"Miss Stockton?"

"Can't you see the girl's in shock?" Andrews looked to Clara. "Shouldn't we call her doctor?"

"Perhaps we should — although I gave her a sedative." Clara cradled Katie in her arms.

The lawyer turned to the officer. "Have you no feelings? No sensitivity?"

"All in good time, Mr. Andrews. This is a crime scene. I must insist that nothing be touched in here until our investigation is completed. That may take several days. With all due respect, Mrs. Stockton must have another bedroom in this mansion."

Andrews started to protest, but Clara stayed his arm. "It's all right, Avery. Katie and I can use a guest room. May — we go now, Inspector?"

McGuire's eyebrow lifted imperceptibly. "Yes, of course. Goodnight, Mrs. Stockton."

Chapter 16 — 1960

Katie awoke the next morning with a dry mouth, an aching head, and a confused mind. The barbiturate had knocked her out for eight hours, but hadn't dulled the horror of the previous night.

The sight of her mother sleeping peacefully in the next bed made her feel sick. Only hours ago, her mother had shot and killed a man — a vital, breathing human being who was loved — maybe had a wife and children. Now he was lost to them forever, just as her beloved father, James Stockton, would never come back to her.

Gradually, memories of the scene began to return. Even in her shocked state, she had thought it odd that her mother would call a lawyer. If the shooting was self-defense, why did she need Avery? And why was the policeman asking so many questions, as if he didn't believe her? What was in that envelope she'd been told not to mention?

Blankets slid to the floor as she climbed out of bed and reached for her robe — then just as abruptly, dropped it. Where did she think she was going on a Sunday morning?

With a sigh, she stumbled into the bathroom, slipped off her night-gown and stepped into the shower, turning the control to high. The steaming water almost scalded her, soaking her skin till it was red and stinging. Still, she felt dirty. Was she trying to wash away the taint of lies? Every instinct told her that what happened was wrong. Yet her mother was a good, kind person, hardly a cold-blooded murderer.

The body lying in a puddle of blood had been neatly dressed in khakis and a white shirt. Maybe the man had been desperate to buy food for his family or medicine for his wife. Even if he did rob rich people and scare them half to death, he hadn't deserved to die.

She turned off the water and grabbed a towel. Lily would be calling soon, wanting to go to a movie. What would she say? "Sorry, Lil. My mom killed a man last night and I'm too upset."

Angry, groggy, a jumble of conflicting emotions, she sat down at her desk and scribbled on a pad. "Dear Mom, I'm going for a walk. Please tell Lily I'm sorry about the movie and I'll explain Monday. Don't worry, I'm fine. Love, Katie."

She threw on a pair of pedal pushers and a sweater, and tied back her hair in a ponytail. Tucking a wallet in her pocket, she left by the front door. For no particular reason, she headed east on Jackson Street to Fillmore, then down a series of steep hills toward the bay, walking briskly until she arrived at the newly-built Safeway.

The sprawling supermarket covered a full square block of the Marina district opposite Yacht Harbor. Adjacent to the lineup of boats was the stretch of lawn known as the Marina Green. Usually, she stopped to watch the children fly kites and play on the grass. Today, she passed without noticing them.

By the time she entered the store, she was dazed and confused, and trying to remember why she had come. After several minutes of wandering up and down aisles, she suddenly began to weave. Feeling herself about to faint, she reached for a shelf to hold on to, when a strong hand grabbed her elbow.

"I've got you," said a voice. "You won't fall."

Startled, she found herself staring at a young man in a tattered shirt and dungarees. He was tall and lean, with half his face hidden under a flowing black beard. A thick crop of hair, parted in the middle, spilled over his shoulders. Around his neck hung several strings of colored beads.

His eyes shone with concern. "You all right?"

"Kind of w-woozy."

"Let's get some air. Breathe deeply." He held her arm as they walked to the door. "I freaked out myself once, on the steps of City Hall. The government was witch-hunting for commies. A bunch of us came over from Berkeley to protest. The fuzz started beating up on us, and I lost my cool and slugged one. They busted me for two weeks."

Punching a policeman didn't seem to have much relationship to feeling faint at Safeway, but at least he was trying to comfort her, and that was kind of him. She stood on the curb of the parking lot, taking long breaths of the invigorating air. Finally, she released his arm. "Thank you. I — I think I'm okay."

"Was all that just a stunt to meet me?"

Blood rushed to her cheeks. "No, I — took a Seconal last night —"

"What's a classy chick like you doing taking phennies?" He grinned at her. "I'm Jason Morris."

With effort, she smiled back. The rules against talking to strangers could be waived for once.

"Hi, Jason." Still, she was wary. Her father had warned her that the

Stockton name meant big money to people, even people she liked and trusted. But that would hardly apply to a young man who had no idea who she was. "I'm Katie Stockton."

"Hi, Katie Stockton. Care to stroll by the water?"

"Well, you — your shopping —"

"I wasn't shopping, I was gathering energy. You see, the modern supermarket is a sensual smorgasbord. Vibrations from natural products recharge the human battery, that is, except for the symbols of capitalist cruelty. Have you ever thought how many cows are murdered to make your hamburger? How many innocent fish go into your tuna surprise?"

"Are you a vegetarian?"

"I'm a humanitarian. I never eat anything that had a face."

A trace of a smile crossed her lips. "What a lovely, sensitive thing for you to do."

"I try to put myself in the animals' place. Take a jar of pickled pigs' feet. How do you think Mrs. Pig feels about that? Would you want your babies' feet pickled in oil?"

Her eyes twinkled for a fraction of a second. This shaggy-haired hippie with the odd sense of humor was bringing her back to life. She had even managed to forget about last night for a few blessed minutes. "You're weird."

"And you're wonderful." He turned to her in the crosswalk. "What sort of things do you believe in?"

"How can I answer that? I don't even know you."

"That's easy. I'm a nice Jewish boy from Los Angeles. My grandfather's name was Moscowitz before he changed it to Morris, and my parents sent me to Hebrew School as soon as I could talk. Fortunately, it didn't take. I can sit cross-legged in Golden Gate Park and get off on the Koran a lot faster than I can recite some meaningless ritual. Do you believe all that religious junk?"

"I believe in God. I've never —"

"It's pure BS. Religious leaders don't want us to think for ourselves, they just want us to repeat what they tell us: God is merciful, God is omniscient, God is omnipotent. God forbid we might ask a question or two. Like how come this great merciful God lets people kill and torture each other?"

"It does seem odd."

"Now we're grooving! Hey, let's sit on the lawn and tune into each other's auras." The touch of his hand on her arm startled her and made her recoil.

He stared in surprise. "Something I said? Onion breath?"

"I'm sorry. I'm especially nervous today. It's — I can't talk about it." She turned away. "I'd better go home."

"Wait! Don't go away mad. I can show you some breathing stuff that'll help."

"Thanks, but I —"

"You don't really want to leave. You know you want to stay with me."

She hesitated. The morning was crisp and clear. The Golden Gate Bridge glistened in the sunlight, and the blue-green water of the bay seemed calm and reassuring. Going home meant having to face her mother, maybe her lawyer and the police, having to relive the trauma so fresh in her mind.

With a shy smile, she dropped to the grass and clasped her hands around her knees.

Jason lay on his back beside her, arms folded under his head, his gaze fixed on the water. After several minutes, he broke the silence. "It's not healthy to keep things bottled up, Katie."

He was right. She wanted desperately to confide in someone, and who better than a stranger who knew nothing about her, and whom she would probably never see again. "You won't tell anyone?"

"Who would I tell? No one gives a flying fart about anyone else's problems. They've got too many of their own."

His language embarrassed her, but if she mentioned it, he'd think her square. "Well, a burglar broke into our house last night and my mother — my mother shot him."

"Dead?"

"Dead."

"Wow." Jason pulled himself to a sitting position. "That's heavy stuff. Where was your father?"

"He's dead. I'm a half-orphan." She had never described herself that way before. The word sounded hollow and frightening, as if she'd been deserted by everyone she loved.

"Did you call the fuzz?"

"Mom did. It was awful. They acted like she did something wrong.

She was only defending herself."

Jason's voice was sympathetic. "You've had a rough time, kiddo. I had no idea you were dealing with shit like that." Gently, he asked, "Would you like to come see my pad, Katie? No hanky-pank, I'll just play you some sweet music, read you a few of my favorite passages and try to help you through a rough day."

"Oh, I couldn't impose. Don't you have plans for today?"

He nodded sideways. "A friend and I were going over to San Quentin to protest the gas chamber — they're gonna kill Caryl Chessman — but they're gonna murder him anyway, so we might as well save our energy. And with all that bad karma, there's still good karma, because I met you. You shouldn't be alone at a time like this."

His concern seemed genuine. "Where do you live?"

"In the Haight."

"Isn't it kind of scary there?"

"We've got a few creeps hanging around, but most of 'em are cool. And where else could I rent four rooms for 75 bucks a month?"

"That's amazing." She didn't volunteer that her father's trust fund paid her a weekly allowance of $300. "How do you get there?"

He held up his thumb. "High mileage, low maintenance, and it doesn't foul the air."

The thought of hitchhiking panicked her, yet instinct told her not to suggest going home for her car. A Presidio Heights mansion and a new Mercedes would be hard to explain to a man who paid $75 a month rent.

"I'd like to see your pad," she said, after a long moment. "But if I pay the fare, could we please take the bus?"

Chapter 17 — 1960

Jason Morris lived in the most dilapidated building Katie had ever seen. The gray stucco exterior was grimy and graffiti-ridden. Leaflets and newspapers were piled in a dusty corner of the lobby. Even the elevator was out of order.

By the time they climbed eight flights of stairs, they were panting. "I used to — leave the door open," he gasped, searching for a key. "I'd have two, three guys crashing here every night, until they ripped me off."

"How awful! What did they steal?"

"A lot of stuff that didn't matter. I mean, I was pissed as hell when they took my stereo. But now I'm cool. I don't get hung up on material things anymore."

"Then why lock the door?"

He pushed it open. "Because I don't want to come home and find some junkie freakin' out in my bed."

A thick, sweet smell enveloped her as they entered a large room. Bright-colored posters glared from the walls. Books, magazines, and soiled ashtrays littered the bare wooden floor. A couch with visible springs, a coffee table with a cracked glass top, a portable heater, and a king-size bed with a single blanket were the only furnishings.

"Buckingham Palace it ain't," he said, shoving aside a curtain to let in light, "but then, I'm no queen, either. That's like a joke. Ever read Kahlil Gibran?"

"Yes. I loved *The Prophet*."

"Hey, far out. Maybe we can read it together." He traced a zigzag in the window dust. "Look, Katie. I know this place is a freakin' mess, but I wasn't expecting company. Don't get turned off."

"I'm not turned off." She was, in fact, fascinated. Her sheltered life had never permitted friendship with anyone too poor to buy bed sheets.

"Ready for the grand tour?" A tiny kitchen had a sink full of dishes and a grimy card table. "This is the banquet hall."

"Do you cook?"

"Only on Thursdays — chef's night out." He led her into an even smaller room. "That's the shower that doesn't work, and that's the john where I pee. Are you hungry?"

"Not very."

"When did you last eat?"

"Ummm…yesterday."

"I thought so. You dig lentil soup?"

"Sure. Ever cut up hot dogs in it?"

"Are you crazy? Do you know what's in those things?"

"No." She followed him back to the kitchen.

"If I tell you, it'll blow your mind." He took a jar from the refrigerator, emptied it into a pot, and turned on a hot plate. "Chandra, my neighbor across the hall, makes me a batch of soup every week. She uses all organic ingredients, no meat, no preservatives."

Katie nodded politely. The fact that she was even thinking of eating that gray-brown gruel made her realize how hungry she was.

"I'll tell you a story about hot dogs," he went on. "When I was in high school, I had this buddy, Lee — a practical joker. One night, we got his parents' car for a double date, and he took along this hot dog. Lee and this chick were in the back seat making out, but when she wasn't looking, he put the hot dog in his pants and put her hand on it. She pulled away, the hot dog came with her, and she let out a scream you could hear for six blocks."

Katie didn't know whether to be shocked or amused. "Was she angry?"

"At first." He stirred the soup, tasted it, and resumed stirring. "Then she laughed hysterically."

Lunch was looking less appetizing by the minute.

"I'm so middle class you could puke," he went on. "My old man's a postman. He spends the better part of his life dodging dog shit. My mom's hooked on soap operas, my sister's sweet sixteen and all screwed up, and I was a pre-law student on a scholarship, till I dropped out of Berkeley in January."

"Why'd you drop out?"

"I got sick of it. I still had a year of college, at least four of law school. After all that, maybe I'd pass the bar, maybe I wouldn't. And for what? So I could drive a Cadillac and buy my wife a mink coat? Screw that. All I really wanted was to get laid and get stoned."

The statement pained Katie. She couldn't offer him either pleasure.

"What's your bag?" he asked.

"I'm a junior at S.F. College for Women."

"Studying — ?"

"French and English lit. I suppose I'll be a teacher someday."

"You and your old lady live alone?"

No need to mention Kai and Maxwell. "Yes, but I'm thinking about getting a place of my own — an apartment with a guard at the door so burglars can't break in."

"You're talking mucho dinero. Big bread."

"My father left me a little money — enough for rent."

"Lucky you. Do you have a car, too?"

"Yes. At home."

"Far out! Maybe we can drive to Muir Woods one day. Hey, hey, whaddya doin'?"

"I might as well wash the dishes while we're standing here." She pushed up her sleeves and turned on the faucet. "Where's the soap?"

"If you insist, it's under the sink." He handed her a sponge and winked. "Go easy on the water."

Clara Stockton patted her hair nervously. She would have liked to be almost anywhere but where she was. "Are you sure we shouldn't give the poor woman time to recover?"

"I'm your lawyer. Trust me." Avery Andrews helped Clara out of the Cadillac as they parked in an alley off Valencia Street.

"I don't think $500 a month is enough. We should pay her at least a thousand."

"It's more than enough, Clara, and I'm going to ask you for the last time. Are you sure you want to do this?"

She exhaled audibly. Her heart was racing, and the lack of sleep had sapped her energy. The reality of the incident was taking its toll. "Yes, I'm positive. Just because the shooting was self-defense doesn't make it any less tragic for his family."

"Very well. As long as you insist on taking this ill-advised step, we have to act now. If any new evidence should surface, it could look as if you're paying her off."

"What new evidence?"

"Have you told me everything?"

"Yes, of course," she said, in a tone that closed the subject. No one must ever know the truth. Too many lives would be shattered. Guilt was a burden she would have to bear alone.

South of Market Street was foreign country to Clara. Except for a childhood visit to Mission Dolores, and the fact that everyone said the weather was great, all she knew about the Mission District was that the early Spanish settlement of churches, cemeteries, and beer gardens had evolved into an area of low-rent housing and tawdry shops. Most of the residents were Mexican or Latin American.

Two young girls, playing hopscotch on the sidewalk, stopped to gawk at the well-dressed couple in the big car. Their stares heightened Clara's discomfort, as she and Avery climbed three steps to a rundown brown shingled house.

A woman finally answered the door — mid-thirtyish, with dangling earrings, scarlet lips and straight black hair. An orange sweater and velvet pants hugged her short, stocky frame.

"Come in," she said, in a heavy accent. "I am Rocio Hogan."

"Avery Andrews. Nice to meet you. And this is Clara Stockton. Our deepest condolences. We're very sorry for your loss."

The widow glanced briefly at the woman who shot her husband, said nothing, and led her visitors into a small, cluttered living room. Unmatched furniture surrounded a wooden table strewn with ceramic knickknacks and a gold-plated crucifix. On the wall, painted on black velvet, a fierce-eyed leopard crouched, ready to pounce. The odor of spices and garlic mingled with the smell of dime store perfume.

"May we sit down?" Clara asked. Her knees were trembling.

Rocio Hogan glared at her. "My husband no burglar. He no steal nothing!"

"I'm — so terribly sorry."

"Please, Mrs. Hogan." Avery stepped between the women. "May we take a seat and talk calmly?"

"I no wanna talk calmly. I got three kids in school. I got mortgage on this house. I got bills, bills, bills, and no money nowhere. What I do?" Tears poured down her cheek, leaving thin trails of mascara.

Avery's look warned Clara not to speak. "We came to help with your problems, Mrs. Hogan. Did you make a list for me?"

"I don't need no list. Here!" She reached up, snatched a pile of papers from a shelf, and plunked them in front of him. "This is list. All bills!"

He took a handful and glanced at them. "Looks like you owe a good deal of money. Your husband was unemployed. How did he expect to pay these?"

"He say no worry," she sobbed. "He say he get big money."

"Did he say where he was getting this big money?"

"No. He say we be rich and he buy me nice clothes, nice earrings."

"My client feels very strongly for your loss, Mrs. Hogan. But your husband committed a felony — a serious crime that would have sent him to prison. Mrs. Stockton wants to help you and your children."

The widow dried her eyes and looked up. "How much help?"

"She's willing to pay all these bills, the costs of a funeral, and give you a monthly pension —"

"How much?"

"Three hundred dollars. All you have to do is sign a few papers, promising that neither you nor anyone in your family will ever make claims against my client or her family."

"I better see lawyer."

"Go ahead. Hire a lawyer. If you take it to court, you'll lose your case, and you won't get a cent. You'll be stuck with all your old bills plus a new set of legal bills. If that's what you want, we're wasting our time here." He started to get up.

"Wait!" Rocio Hogan pursed her lips. She appeared to be thinking. "I got three kids. They eat, eat, eat. I got big house. No money."

"I suppose we could stretch it to $325."

"*Cinco*. Five hundred."

Avery rose to his feet. "I can see we're not getting anywhere."

"Wait!" she ordered again. "How high you go?"

"We made you a generous offer. You have several thousand dollars worth of bills here, which we're willing to pay, plus another five hundred for the funeral, *plus* you'd be getting $325 a month for the rest of your life." He looked across the room at his client. "Would you be willing to go to $350?"

Clara nodded. She would give the poor woman whatever she wanted. She hated Avery's game but she paid him to know what he was doing.

Avery shrugged. "All right, Mrs. Hogan. Three hundred and fifty dollars — that's $4200 a year and a great deal more, I'm sure, than your husband ever earned as a dock laborer."

"He earn good when he work. You make it $500 and I sign papers right now."

"No, I'm sorry. That's out of the question. We were trying to do something nice for you."

"It's okay, Avery." The tactics — the taunting — were suddenly more than Clara could stand. What Al Hogan had done was wrong. What she had done was worse. Much worse. "Give her the $500. No, make it $1,000."

The lawyer shot her a black look. "That's $12,000 a *year!*"

"Is okay. You give me papers. I sign."

Barely restraining his anger, Avery filled in the number and handed the widow a neatly typed document. "Are you sure you know what you're signing?"

"Not to ask for no more money."

"Yes, but I want you to read this carefully."

She scanned the sheet, took the pen from his hand and scribbled her name on the four copies he put in front of her. Then she asked, "When I get my money?"

"As soon as I get back to the office, I'll put a check in the mail to you." He forced a smile. "Congratulations, Mrs. Hogan. You're quite a business woman."

She winked smugly and tapped her head. "Rocio Hogan no fool."

Chapter 18 – 1960

Katie Stockton stretched out on the couch. Jason, sitting cross-legged on the floor, fingered his wooden recorder. She had survived the broth with no ill effects, cleaned the kitchen while he meditated, then listened in rapt attention as he read aloud from *The Prophet*.

"That was Bach," he said, setting down the instrument. "Sweet and harmonious, the way life should be. The way life could be."

"If what?"

"If everyone were cool. If people didn't get uptight about making bread and trying to screw each other." He fixed her intently. "Want to turn on?"

The question was one she'd been dreading. "I don't think so. I'm scared of drugs."

"You should be. Some are real downers. But you can't get hooked on pot. Hell, that phennie you took last night is a hundred times worse."

"I hate pills."

"Wait'll you try *pakalolo*. It's the Cadillac of cannabis. This cat I know gets it straight from Hawaii. I've been saving some for a special occasion."

"Don't waste it on me."

"Why not? You're special. It's like sex. You start with the best. That way you're not disappointed."

He disappeared and came back almost immediately with a portable radio playing classical music. He joined her on the couch, emptied a small packet of grass onto a thin paper, rolled it, and lit it. "Now watch what I do."

His eyes closed as he inhaled, held his breath for five seconds, then blew it out in a slow stream. "Relax and breathe deeply," he said, passing her the cigarette. "Keep the smoke in your lungs as long as you can."

Frightened but curious, she followed instructions. "I don't feel anything."

"You will. The pure stuff goes right into the bloodstream."

After three more puffs, she sat up stiffly. "It couldn't be working already, could it?"

"You groovin'?"

"Yeah…I feel…kind of floaty." Suddenly she grabbed his arm. "I'm scared, Jason. I think I'm losing control..."

"Easy, honey. Cool it. I'm right here. I won't let anything happen to you. Just relax, let the good thoughts flow...let yourself drift...oh, man, that's beautiful..."

They passed the joint back and forth several times. "How d'ya feel now?"

"Groovy," she said, smiling. A sense of elation swept over her as she felt herself soar. The thought of last night flashed through her brain and vanished.

He put his arm around her. "This is what life's all about, Katie — feeling high, feeling good, feeling love. There's only one thing better."

"What's that?"

"Making love when you're high. All your senses are turned on. It's like nothing you ever felt..."

"Yeah..." The suggestion would have been unthinkable five minutes earlier. She lay her head on his shoulder. "Tomorrow — maybe I'll try."

Difficult as it was for him, Jason kept his promise not to touch Katie. He felt attracted to her and he didn't know why. She wasn't pretty in the usual sense, and she wasn't the least bit sexy. But she had a tight, firm little body, and he was certain she was a virgin. What a challenge it'd be to make her first time so enjoyable that she'd remember it for the rest of her life.

Strange, he thought, that a 20-year-old college student could be so naive...

Late that afternoon, when the marijuana wore off, Katie walked into the kitchen. Jason was warming more soup.

"I'd better go," she said. "May I use your phone to call a cab?"

"I don't have one, but Chandra does. I'll take you over there, if you're sure you want to leave."

His comment astounded her. "I've taken up hours of your time. How can I ever thank you for getting me through today?"

"By letting me get you through tonight. Not what you're thinking. I'll sleep on the cot. I just don't dig your spending another night in that house of horrors."

"I don't dig it, either." Impulsively, she reached up and touched his cheek. "You're such a kind, generous person, Jason. I've never known anyone like you."

He took her hand and pressed a key into it. "Then go home, Katiebird. Get your pajamas and your toothbrush, and come back to me."

"I'll come back," she promised. "But not tonight."

Chapter 19 – 1960

The sky was already dark by the time the cab pulled up to the stately mansion on Jackson Street. Katie straightened her clothes, loosened her pony tail, and prepared to tell her story. She had never lied to her mother, and she was not about to start.

Untypically, the front porch light was on. The minute she opened the door, Clara came running down the stairs. Katie had never seen her look worse: hair tossed back in a bun, face pale and drawn, eyes red and swollen.

"Oh, Katie darling, thank God you're all right!" Clara hugged her tightly, almost hurting her. "We've been worried to death."

"I'm sorry, Mom. Didn't you get my note?"

"That was eight hours ago. Where have you been?"

"Walking. Sitting. Reading with a friend."

"What friend? Lily said she hadn't talked to you."

"Just a friend I met. Oh, Mother, what's the difference? I'm home. Were the police here?"

"Of course they were." Clara's tone was half motherly concern, half-frustration. "Oh, Katie, you can't just run out the door when things go wrong. This was the worst day of my life. I needed you with me, and I didn't need the added worry of trying to find you, or of trying to explain to that nosy Inspector McGuire, that I didn't know where my daughter was. How could you be so thoughtless?"

"Thoughtless?" The accusation startled Katie. "I — I didn't shoot a man last night. You did."

"A man who broke into our house. Would you have wanted me to let him rob us and rape us and whatever else he was going to do?"

Her words stirred up all the old fears, and for a moment, she hated her mother for preying on that weakness. Jason had made her feel good about herself; comfortable, relaxed, even secure. He had scared away the demons, and now her mother was calling them back.

"W — what was in that envelope?"

Clara's eyes flashed in alarm. "You didn't tell anyone?"

"No, I kept my promise. What was it?"

"Nothing important. I'll explain when all this is over." Her relief seemed tangible. "Right now, I promised to call the inspector as soon as you came in. Avery's upstairs, thank God. He's been my rock of support through all this madness. Have you eaten?"

"I'm not hungry."

"Well, Kai's off, but Maxwell made some sandwiches." Her face softened. "Please, Katie dear, you really had us worried. The next time you have a problem, come talk to me. But don't go running off. I love you and I'll always be here for you."

Carefully lifting the skirt of her hostess gown, Clara ascended the stairs. Katie stood watching — hurt, perplexed, trying hard to be patient with a mother she wanted to understand but probably never would.

Worse yet, Katie reflected, it seemed as if her mother had never tried to understand her, never attempted to see the world through the eyes of a daughter so opposite from herself. How could Clara possibly know what it was like not to be pretty and witty and charming?

With heavy step, Katie climbed to her room and began to take off her clothes. She knew she should be grateful to be back in her clean, comfortable surroundings, but she couldn't stop thinking about Jason. What an extraordinary afternoon they'd spent! How she'd hated to leave him all alone in that dingy apartment with nothing to eat but a bowl of muddy lentil soup.

A knock made her grab a robe and hurry to the door. Avery Andrews stood scowling at her. "It's about time you got home, Katherine. Where have you been?"

"With a friend."

"What friend?"

"Someone you don't know."

"Someone of good character, I hope. But that's not why I'm here. Your mother talked to the police. They're coming tomorrow at ten to question you."

"Question *me*? About what?"

His brow wrinkled in consternation. "A burglar was shot dead in your home. You were the only one here with your mother. They have to know if you saw or heard anything unusual."

"I didn't. I was sleeping."

"You'll have to make a statement. Tomorrow at ten."

"Phooey," she muttered to herself. "Why couldn't she have shot him in the arm? Or the leg? Why'd she have to kill him?"

Avery's eyes flashed as he called on his courtroom control. "Have you no sympathy for what your mother's been through, Katherine? What would you do if you woke up in the night with a stranger standing over your bed? You'd grab a gun if you had it, wouldn't you? And since we're on the subject, don't you think you might've stayed around to support her at this difficult time?"

"I'm sorry." Katie started to tremble. "I — I guess I was thoughtless. But last night was terrible for me, too. I'll never forget seeing that poor man lying in his own blood. I was upset this morning and I had to get away."

The lawyer shook his head. "Why your mother puts up with your nonsense is something I'll never understand."

What nonsense? she wanted to ask, but he was already striding down the hall. Tears flooded Katie's eyes at this latest, unexpected rebuke. What had she done that was so awful? And what right had he to scold her that way? He wasn't her father. He wasn't even her stepfather, though she suspected he'd like to be.

Feeling more rejected and resentful by the minute, she stepped into the shower and scrubbed herself clean. All she could think of were Jason's words: "Go home, Katiebird. Get your pajamas and your toothbrush, and come back to me." By the time she finished showering, her decision was made.

Dressing quietly, she once again reached for her notepad, and wrote: "Dear Mom, I'm obviously a burden to you and Avery, so I'm going to spend the night at my friend's apartment. Please don't worry. I'll be home for the 10 o'clock meeting tomorrow. Love, Katie."

She checked down the hallway; all was clear. Quickly and quietly, she taped the note to her door, stuffed several pillow cases full of sheets and blankets, and tiptoed down the stairs.

Jason's building didn't look quite so depressing at night, Katie decided, as she stood outside his door, wondering whether to knock or use the key. She chose the former.

He answered, wrapped in a towel. "I had a hunch you'd be back," he said, grinning. "Caught me in the tub. Hey, what's all that?"

"Sheets, blankets, dinner."

"Set 'em down. Make yourself at home." A few minutes later, he emerged from the bathroom wearing a clean T-shirt and jeans. "Did you say dinner?"

"I stopped at the Deli and got us two hero sandwiches — all cheese and pickles, no meat."

"Even yours?"

"Sure. What you said makes sense. From now on, I'm going to be a vegetarian, too."

"I really dig that, Katie. Most chicks wouldn't care." He sat down beside her on the couch. "But hey, I don't have the bread to pay you back."

"It's okay. I'm grateful to be here. My mother and her lawyer boyfriend treat me like a five-year-old."

"I'd offer you some liquid tranquilizer, but I'm out of booze."

She laughed, opened the box and handed him a sandwich. "You're really broke, aren't you. Do you ever work?"

"You mean like, how do I pay the rent?" He chomped into the bread. "*Man,* that's good! I'm the unofficial janitor here. I do odd jobs for the owner so I haven't had to put out any cash yet. Chandra feeds me in return for painting and fixing up her pad. And when I really hit bottom, I sell a little dope."

"That's terrible! You could go to prison."

"I could also starve." He peered into the box on her lap. "Is that a mirage or do I see some joy juice?"

"Can't have hero sandwiches without wine. Got a corkscrew?"

"Does a tennis player have balls?"

They demolished everything; pot only increased the appetite, he explained. After dinner, he hugged her and kissed her cheek. They lay on his bed for a long time talking and listening to music. She had made up the cot for herself, but instead, dozed off in his arms and slept soundly until morning.

Chapter 20 – 1960

Hoping to avoid a confrontation, Katie tried to enter the house quietly. No sooner had she opened the door, however, than she heard Clara's voice, "In here!"

She found her mother sitting in the living room, her face tense with worry. "Where were you all night?"

"I was with a friend. A male friend. But nothing happened."

"You spent the night with a man and nothing happened?"

"That's right. I'm still a virgin." Katie slipped off her coat and dropped to the couch.

"Who is this man? What do you know about him?"

"That he's kind and decent. His name's Jason Morris."

"Where does he live?"

"On Haight Street."

"Oh, dear God! How did you meet him?"

"At the Marina Safeway. He caught me as I was about to faint."

Clara bit her lower lip, determined to keep control. "Does this — man know your name and where you live?"

"He knows my name. He never asked my address."

"He can find out easily enough. We'll have to hire a night guard."

"Because of Jason?"

"Oh, Katie dear, you can't trust these people." Clara tried hard not to sound hysterical, but how could her daughter be so incredibly naive as to pick up a stranger and spend the night with him? She believed that Katie thought nothing happened. Katie had never lied to her. But what else would a man want with her?

"Jason doesn't want material things, Mother. He was a pre-law student at Berkeley..."

The doorbell broke into her sentence. Avery Andrews appeared, followed by Inspector McGuire who interrogated Katie for over an hour. He told her that Albert Hogan was an unemployed dock worker who left a wife and three children. Had she ever seen or heard of him prior to the shooting? All her answers were negative.

Finally, both men left and Katie faced her mother, puzzled. "Why was the Inspector asking all those questions?"

"It's their nature to be suspicious, particularly if someone has wealth or connections. And I think the Inspector was unhappy with the press."

"What press?"

"The *Herald* story made me sound like a heroine. The other papers played it down." Clara sighed. "Katie, darling, it's a closed chapter now. Let's put it behind us."

"You haven't told me what was in the envelope."

"It was a letter someone wrote to the burglar a long time ago. If I'd showed it to the police, they'd have asked a million more questions. It's not important."

"It is to me. It might help me understand why you shot Mr. Hogan."

"I told you why. Now please get dressed. I'll drive you to school."

Clara's dictatorial attitude seemed to bring all Katie's fears to the surface. Her new-found independence — the wonderful freedom she felt with Jason — was being snatched away. Deep resentment began to rise.

"I'm not going to school." The words sprang out before Katie could stop them. She had never openly defied her mother before. "I'm going back to Jason. If you'd like to see what kind of person he is, I could bring him home for dinner."

"Have you lost your senses?" Clara's voice trembled. "Do you really want to bring some stranger you picked up at a store into our house?"

"He's not a stranger, he's my friend."

"Let's not argue, Katie. I don't want you to see him again."

"I'm sorry, Mom. For once in my life, I don't care what you want."

"Can't you see he's got you brainwashed? He could — make you a drug addict — sell you into white slavery! Anything! Now please go upstairs and get dressed!"

"And if I don't?"

"If you dare to spend another night with that man, Katie Stockton —" The words stuck in Clara's throat; she didn't want to hear what she was about to say. "I've worried about you for almost 21 years. I've loved you with all my heart, protected you, done everything I could for you. Now I don't know you any more. If you go to that man, if you *sleep* with him again and expect to bring his germs and diseases into this house, you're very much mistaken. You won't be welcome."

Katie froze. She had expected harsh words, anger, reproach. She had not expected to be banished from her home. Too stunned to cry, she turned and fled the room.

Smoking grass was a lifesaver; it soothed and relaxed Katie's shattered nerves. Even the knowledge that Jason had traded her mother's Porthault sheets for two joints didn't matter. She was back on his couch and they were high together — wonderfully, gloriously high.

Later in the day, they went shopping at the neighborhood market, bought shirts and overalls at the Army surplus store, and picked up a table and chairs at a thrift shop. After putting away the vegetables and rearranging the apartment, they shared a second joint.

Katie's worries dimmed for a few hours, but that evening, she was forced to face the realization that she had no home to go to. A new set of fears set in. What if Jason grew tired of her? What if he threw her out, too? Maybe she had been too quick to leave Jackson Street. Maybe she should have been more understanding of what her mother was worried about and the torments she was suffering.

Sensing her mood, Jason put his arm around her. "Don't be sad, Katiebird," he whispered. "I agonized for days, after I dropped out of school. But it was the right decision for me and yours is the right decision for you."

"How do you know?"

"Because I know. I'll bet anything you've spent your life trying to please your mother. Repeat after me. `I'm my own person now. I'm beautiful and I'm free.'"

Katie felt herself glow. No one had ever called her beautiful before. She reached up and touched his hand. "You're right, Jason. Now — at last — I can have a life for myself."

The next two days went up in smoke. Jason traded Katie's twenty dollar bill for a fourth of a kilo of grass. Unused to such abundance, they indulged freely. On the third day, however, she awoke with a headache.

"Your body's telling you to lay off for awhile," he said. "I'll run to the store and get you some aspirin. Uh — I'll need some money."

She handed him another twenty. "That's the last of my cash. We'll have to get to the bank today."

Alone in the apartment for the first time, Katie moved through the rooms in silent fear. Every noise...every shadow...seemed to hold threats of disaster. The throbbing in her head grew worse. With it came nausea and vomiting. In a moment of despair, she thought of her mother. Surely Clara would forgive her, come get her and take care of her. All she had to do was phone. But the sound of a key in the lock changed her plans.

"Here's the aspirin," said Jason, handing her a bottle. "You look white as a snowman. Are you okay?"

"I think I'm dying."

"Better lie down. I'll get you some water."

Two hours later, Katie awoke from a heavy sleep. The headache was gone and she was famished. Jason insisted she stay in bed while he made her orange juice and scrambled eggs.

"By the way," he said, as she was cleaning her plate, "I spent the rest of your twenty bucks. I got something I think you'll like."

Visions of Blum's chocolates and sugar doughnuts flashed to mind. "How thoughtful of you. What is it?"

"Ever read about lysergic acid?"

"The stuff they use to unclog toilets?"

"No, no, this is a new hallucinogen. Not even on the street yet. Some researchers in Canada have been running experiments and found that it alters consciousness — opens doors to your inner self. Aldous Huxley said it made him one with the universe."

"Is it really an acid?"

"Not the kind that burns you. I got a buddy, Wally, whose cousin works at the Stanford Research Institute. They're studying the drug — they call it LSD — and guess what I talked him out of?" He opened his palm to reveal two small blue pills. "Genuine Sandoz pharmaceuticals — pure as gold."

"Isn't it dangerous?"

"Nah, they give it to volunteers every day. But the thing is, we can't do it together. One person takes a trip to inner space, and the other acts as kind of a tour guide, keeping him linked to reality." He extended his hand. "Ladies first? Or shall I?"

Anxious to prove she trusted him, she popped one into her mouth and washed it down with the last of the juice.

"I'll be damned," he muttered, with a touch of apprehension.

"I'm off to see the wizard," she hummed cheerfully. "How long before I crawl into my brain?"

"I don't know, Katiebird. We'll just have to wait and see."

Forty minutes later, Katie lay stretched out on the bed, alert and nervous. Jason was sprawled beside her, his hands clasped on his chest. Strains of Scheherezade filled the room. The air was thick with expectation.

Suddenly, she spoke. "Wow. I see them."

"What?"

"Belly dancers. Eunuchs in jeweled vests. The palace. It's gorgeous!"

He sat up excitedly. "What else do you see?"

"A king in a velvet robe trimmed with ermine. Beautiful maidens in flowing harem pants." She inhaled happily. "But Jason, I know I took a pill and I'm hallucinating. I can switch the pictures on and off, like a movie screen."

"Far out." He turned to face her, propping himself on his elbow. "Those are all benign visions. What *don't* you like? What are you afraid of?"

As he spoke, she stared at a group of fingerprints on the near wall. Gradually, they grew bigger...rounder...blacker, sprouted legs and began to crawl. An army of giant tarantulas was marching toward her! With a shudder of loathing, she blinked twice and they disappeared.

"What do you see?" he asked.

"Spiders. But I knew they weren't real and I made them go away."

"Amazing," he said. "What else?"

"I don't feel at one with the universe — at least, not yet." She closed her eyes, appeared to concentrate for several seconds, then slowly opened them. Her voice sounded miles away as she murmured, "Poor Daddy. He wanted another Yvonne, but he got me instead..."

One by one, memories began to pour forth, each recalling another. Katie's whole childhood spilled out in a rambling monologue that seemed to have no end. Her reminiscences were tinged with the realization that she felt like an outsider in her own world...constantly frustrated by her inability to relate to people, even her own half-sister.

Jason was fascinated. The world of nannies and butlers, luxury cruises to Europe, and a summer estate in Burlingame was not the world he knew. Katie's preoccupation with her father surprised him at first, then became clear. Aware that he favored his older, more attractive daughter,

James Stockton apparently made a conscious effort to understand and be close to Katie. When he died, he left a gap in her life that no one else could fill.

The drug lasted well into evening, giving Jason the freedom to ask questions he wouldn't have dared ask earlier — and allowing Katie to answer honestly. Both seemed touched by their new intimacy. In the darkness, Jason held her tightly.

"We're one with each other now," he whispered. "Have you ever experienced anything so beautiful?"

"No — never."

"Dearest Katie, I want so much to be close to you in every way. Do you think — I want you so badly — would you be willing to try making love?"

"I — guess so," she said reluctantly. "If it's important to you."

"Oh, my darling." Jason fell on her greedily, his hands opening her bathrobe and exploring her slim young body. In his eagerness, he was not as gentle as he'd planned. Despite her whimpers of pain, he lost control. A few quick thrusts and the act was over — to his frustration and her great relief.

Guilt was inappropriate, he told himself. If she hadn't held out on him so long, he'd have had more staying power. "Are you okay, honey? Did it hurt a lot?"

"Not as bad as I expected." But neither had it been the least bit enjoyable. The invasion of her private parts, the grunting, animalistic urgency, the sticky semen dripping down her leg — all disgusted her.

"You'll like it better when you get used to it."

Don't hold your breath, she thought. But at least they'd conquered another big hurdle.

The next morning, Katie awoke naked, snuggled against Jason's chest. Her memory was hazy. She had taken a small blue pill and they'd made love...once, maybe twice. Yes, he had entered her a second time during the night, been less rushed and more thoughtful. It hadn't hurt as much. That was all she remembered.

The apartment was strangely quiet as she lay there, listening to his breathing, wondering what had happened to her calm, orderly life. In less than a week, her mother had killed a man, and she had dropped out of college and moved in with a stranger. She had lost not only her virginity, but her best friend, Lily, who for some reason, hadn't bothered to return her phone calls. Well, so be it. They had nothing in common anymore, anyway.

At the moment, Katie's sole concern was making a new life for herself and sorting through her values. Maybe Jason was right; all that mattered was getting laid and getting stoned — or at least, getting stoned. The other activity she could easily forego.

Chapter 22 — 1960

Meeting Katie had been a stroke of luck for Jason Morris. Much as he professed to scorn capitalism, having enough money to buy good dope and good food was a welcome luxury after months of scraping to stay alive.

He had never known anyone with Katie's generosity, probably because no one he knew could afford to be generous. Money was not what originally drew him to her, but it was, he had to admit, a welcome bonus.

He found her kind and sensitive — almost too sensitive. The hurt of her mother's "rejection," seemed to pervade everything she did, whether they watched Ed Sullivan on their new TV set, or made love. Only when she was high would she consent to have intercourse, and that disturbed him. He was used to randy chicks who grabbed his crotch and wanted sex as much as he did. Good sex was mutual sex, and he missed it.

By the summer of 1961, their life had settled into routine. For the first time, Katie was aware of what was happening in the world — as well as in her personal world. John F. Kennedy had become the 35th U.S. president, and Jason felt he was a good man, but the Vietnam War was accelerating.

In the meantime, she'd hired a lawyer named Philpott who contacted Avery Andrews and made sure she got her weekly checks from her trust fund, but he was *not* to give her address to anyone.

Both Clara and Tim, however, wrote letters and passed them on to Avery Andrews who sent them to Philpott. Clara's note was brief but loving: her daughter could come home any time she wanted; Katie didn't bother to answer.

Tim's note brought tears. He was worried and wanted to see her. She wrote back with no return address: she loved him, she was fine, and for the moment, she needed to be left alone.

One afternoon in July, she returned from a doctor's appointment with the news she'd suspected. "It's official," she told Jason, as she set down her purse. "I'm two months pregnant."

"You can still get rid of it."

"You won't eat anything that had a face, yet you're willing to have me kill our unborn baby?"

"Well, hell, that's your decision. But how'll you climb eight flights of stairs? How'll we take care of a baby?"

"I talked to the landlord this morning. He's willing to rent us the whole first floor, all three units, and let us make one big apartment. I'll pay for everything. Please say yes, Jason. I really want this baby."

"I dunno." Jason dug into his pockets. His voice was shaky. "If we do it, what name would you give him?" He stopped suddenly. "You're not thinking about marriage?"

"No, don't worry. But I did tell the doctor I'm Mrs. Morris. And if you didn't mind, I'd want to give the baby your name."

He breathed a loud sigh. "I guess I can live with that, but I gotta be honest, Katie. I can't promise I'll be around permanently. And I sure as hell can't support the kid. That lawyer of yours need to draw up a paper saying I won't ever have to pay child support. And right now I gotta go. There's a peace rally in Golden Gate Park."

"Oh, thank you, thank you," she cried, hugging him. "I'll have Philpott make sure you won't be financially responsible. You won't be sorry."

On February 15, 1962, a seven-pound girl came into the world. Katie called her Melanie Stockton Morris, despite Jason's preference for such names as "Star" and "Cosmic Edition."

Much to his surprise, he found his daughter irresistible. She was blue-eyed and blond — like her maternal grandmother, Katie said, with delicate features and soft, pink skin. Her sweet smile melted all his apprehensions.

Jason even gave up his aversion to "servants," and let Katie hire a runaway teenager named Christi to help. By the end of the year, Christi was feeding Melanie solid foods and watching her crawl happily across the floor.

Some months later, Katie happened to spot a picture in the *Herald*. She showed Jason her half-sister, Yvonne, standing with Mayor George Christopher and some other dignitaries. Jason couldn't help admiring the woman's energy, which, he said, "leaped off the page."

His approbation spurred Katie to get involved; she promptly joined a group of activists protesting cruelty to animals.

By 1963, Jason had shaved his beard and cut bangs in honor of his new idol, Mick Jagger. Katie's generosity now allowed him to fly off to Washington to become one of 200,000 marchers in a Civil Rights demonstration. That November, Kennedy's death saddened Katie, but had little effect on her life.

More and more, she found satisfaction staging demonstrations outside medical labs and picketing fur stores. Once, riding in an elevator behind a lady in a leopard coat, she took a pocket knife from her purse and slashed the garment down the back — an impulse that cost her four hours in jail, a huge fine, the cost of a replacement coat, and serious lawyers' fees.

In quieter moments, she was content to stay home with Melanie, still incredulous that God could have given her such a beautiful baby daughter.

By the mid-sixties, Katie was growing increasingly restless in their apartment. Urged by such "celebrities" as Harvard Professor Timothy Leary to "Tune in, turn on, drop out," more than 70,000 frustrated young people had flocked to the Haight-Ashbury district, crowding houses, doorways, parks and streets.

Reporters happened to discover the "flower children," and suddenly they were everywhere. Pictures appeared on the covers of *TIME* and *Newsweek*. Gray Line began bringing busloads of tourists to the "Haight," to view these colorful peace-lovers called "hippies." And the word "psychedelic" entered the American vocabulary, never to leave.

The hippie men wore long hair, beads, tie-dyed shirts and surplus army jackets reflecting their contempt for war — and in some cases, bathing. The women, decked in Elizabethan frocks and flowing dresses, sported buttons that read, "I'm What's Happening" and "Ban the Bra!"

Both sexes "raised their consciousness" with "harmless" marijuana and acid, and passed around bubble pipes of peace.

What seemed a gentle, idealistic movement on the surface, however, had an ugly side. Increasing drug abuse, squalor, poverty, mental illness, sexual promiscuity and venereal diseases were only a few of the problems that began to afflict the flower children.

Chapter 23 — 1965

One afternoon in April, Jason strolled into the kitchen and grabbed a beer. Katie set down a cake pan. She had planned to clean up before talking to him, but he was around so rarely. "Jason, could we talk for five seconds?"

"Sure. You've got four left. Where's Melanie?"

"Christi took her to a friend's house. That's what I want to talk about. The streets are so full of pushers and junkies and weirdos these days, it's not safe for a child anymore. This is no place to raise a three-year-old."

"Fine. Shall we get a penthouse on Nob Hill?"

"Jason, I'm serious. You know I got some money from Daddy's trust fund when I was 21. We could buy a small house in the Richmond district or the Sunset."

"Shit, Katie, we've been all through this. I've become a parasite — or worse, a damn hypocrite, sponging off a rich chick. At least I can tell myself I haven't sold out completely as long as I live here, with people who think and act like I do."

You could get a job, she thought, as she had many times before. "My only concern is for Melanie."

"The answer is no, we're not moving. Now if you'll excuse me, I'm about to brave the pushers, rapists, and perverts and take a stroll down Haight street."

He slammed the front door, leaving Katie crushed. She had summoned all her courage to speak out, and he hadn't even listened. What could she do? She couldn't complain about grass; she still smoked it herself, although she was gradually switching to alcohol. Gin and orange juice had similar numbing effects, and at least they were legal.

What frightened her most was all the new hallucinogens: mushrooms and peyote and sugar cubes soaked in LSD. Everyone was raving about them and calling them "mind expanders." Some of the longest nights of her life had been nursing Jason back from bad acid trips.

With a sigh of weariness, she walked down the hall to her bedroom, grabbed the latest "Animal Lovers" newsletter, and curled up on a chair. No sooner had she settled than the buzzer sounded.

"Darn," she muttered. Living there was a danger — she was too accessible to the crazies. A man's face appeared through the window in the door. Katie looked twice, gasped, and flung it open. "Tim!"

He greeted her with happy laughter and an outstretched arm. "My baby sister's all grown up. God, I've missed you, Katie. I couldn't stay away any longer."

She hugged him tightly and fought back tears. "I never thought I'd be so glad to see anyone. You look wonderful! I thought I was family-proof. How'd you find me?"

"A friend of a friend works at your bank. May I come in?"

"Of course you can come in!" Katie led him into the living room. "How's Lou Ella? How's Will? How's Mom?"

"Lou Ella's got her hands full, but she's coping. Will's a different person since he came out of the closet. He's got a lover and they're happy as newlyweds. He's even doing great at the TV station."

"That's wonderful. How's Yvonne and her kids?"

"Growing like beanstalks — the kids, not Yvonne."

Her voice dropped. "And Mom?"

"In the hospital, Katie. She had a mastectomy. That's why I came. I thought you'd want to know."

"Oh, dear. Is she all right?"

"We think so. The cancer hadn't spread."

"Is Avery Andrews still chasing her?"

"No. He caught her for awhile, but she wasn't interested in wedlock so he married another wealthy client and Mom said good riddance. She's at St. Francis Hospital, if you want to call."

"Yes, of course I will. I hope she'll let me visit her. I really miss the family. Philpott said you were thinking of selling Rosemont. I told him to give you my proxy."

"We just sold it, Katie. You'll be getting a chunk of money soon. I hope you're investing wisely." He grinned. "You were such a shy little girl, and now —"

"Now I'm a shy old lady of 26. Oh, Tim, we have so much catching up to do. Would you like some tea? Coffee? Let's have a drink."

"Not a thing, thanks. Is your young man around?"

"No, Jason's out. And so's your niece."

"My what? Are you married?"

"No. Jason's not the marrying type. But he *is* Melanie's father."

A frown crossed his face. "Katie, it's not fair to your daughter to grow up a bastard. For her sake, you should tell everyone you're married, or at least, that you *were* married when you had Melanie. Promise me you will?"

"Well, sure, I guess so. If you think it's important."

"I do. How old is my niece?"

"Three. Wait'll you meet her, Tim. Melanie's the sweetest, prettiest little girl you've ever seen, but she won't be home for hours. Can you stay awhile?"

"Thanks, but Lou Ella's expecting me." He glanced around the room. Cheap cotton draperies, a pair of throw rugs, a couch and a wooden bench were the main furnishings. Toys, dolls, and building blocks were scattered everywhere. He shook his head in frustration. "What the hell's going on, Katie? Why are you living like this?"

She shrugged. "Jason doesn't want his friends to think we have money. I've been trying to get him to move into a house across town for Melanie's sake, but he won't. He says his roots are here."

"Do you love him?"

She thought a minute before answering. "Yes. He's my best friend, and he's good to Melanie. But we're not lovers anymore. He has a harem of 'chicks' he sees and I couldn't care less. Sex was a bore."

Tim controlled his reaction. "Does he work?"

"Not at a job. But he's very handy around the apartment."

"I don't understand you. You're young, you're bright, you've got money, you've got every advantage in the world and you live like a beggar. Christ, Katie, I stepped over a roach the size of my thumb in the hallway. Don't you think Melanie deserves better?"

"You didn't kill it, did you?"

"The roach? No, the big fellow's still there. What about it, Katie? Doesn't Melanie deserve better?"

"Yes. But I can't leave Jason."

"The hell you can't!" Tim's eyes flashed with anger. "You've no right to deprive her of a decent education and a chance to grow up with girls from good families, instead of these loonies and junkies. Think *hard* about what you're doing to your daughter, Katie."

Katie did think about it. After Tim left, she thought of little else for the next week. She watched Melanie blossom and start to talk in sen-

123

tences and begin to observe the world around her. Soon she'd be asking questions, and picking up Jason's foul language.

Tim's visit had also awakened strong feelings for her mother. Katie had promised to call the hospital and did so, but whoever answered said Mrs. Stockton was sleeping, and took Katie's name and number. The fact that Clara didn't call back was a blow to Katie, and strengthened her resolve never to contact her mother again.

One morning, she knew what she had to do. When Jason walked in the bedroom after a long night out, she tried to talk to him.

"I don't have time to rap," he said, unbuttoning his shirt. "I'm being picked up in twenty minutes."

"Which 'chick' is this?"

"Trudy. The cute little redhead from the surplus store."

"How old is she — 14 or 15?"

"Hey, I thought we understood each other. You're my old lady. She's a chick. What's the big deal?"

"The big deal —" Katie forced herself to speak, "is that I can't live here any longer. I've decided to move."

Jason set down his clean shirt, dumbstruck. "I saw this coming. Ever since your brother showed up and filled your brain with horseshit."

"I wanted to move long before Tim came. I don't want to move to get away from you. I need you, and so does Melanie. But she deserves a better life."

His face was grim as he resumed dressing. "I can't hack this neurotic Karma. If you want to split, split."

"Okay, then, we will." His calm reaction stunned and hurt her. She hadn't expected him to give up his child and his meal ticket so easily, but she'd planned what to do if he did. "I'll leave you a check for seven thousand dollars."

"Oh, Christ, Katie." He shook his head. "If I had any balls at all, I'd tell you to keep your damn money. But I sold my soul ages ago. I've been wanting to open an Indian restaurant with Chandra, and that'll put us in business."

"Great. I hope it works out for you." They faced each other awkwardly. "Well — I guess that's it. I'll be gone when you come back, but I'll let you know where we'll be. You'll come see Melanie, won't you? She'll miss you terribly."

"Sure I'll come see her. I'll come see you, too — if your butler won't throw me out."

His banter didn't fool her. She sensed he was hurting almost as much as she was. "I love you, Jason. I'll never forget what you've done for me. You've given me the strength to be able to take a step like this."

He held out his arms and they embraced. "I love you, too, Katiebird. Remember the night we read Ecclesiastes? 'A time to weep, and a time to laugh.' There's a time to every purpose under the heaven. I guess this is our time to be apart."

"It doesn't have to be," she wanted to say, but all she could do was nod sadly and turn away.

Part 4

Melanie

Chapter 24 — 1967

The summer months saw increased fighting in Vietnam along with the growing spread of civil rights and peace protests. Nowhere were the antiwar voices more spirited than in San Francisco, where a mass migration to the Haight-Ashbury was reaching its peak.

Yet for many of these idealistic "flower children," the Haight had become a nightmare. More and more, it seemed their main goal was to share a "higher consciousness" induced by drugs.

The scary part, Katie thought, as she trimmed a rose bush in her new garden, was that she might still be living there, protecting the cockroaches, if Tim hadn't come by and given her the push she needed. A week later, she had hugged Jason good-bye, packed up Melanie and Christi and moved to the Fairmont Hotel.

The search for a home had been easier and faster than expected. Although she had planned on a modest residence, one look at the handsome brick mansion on upper Broadway with its sweeping bay view and lovely Thomas Church garden, and she was sold. She could hardly wait to see Jason's face when he visited. He might even beg her to take him back.

Much to her disappointment, Jason only visited once that first year — to introduce his new wife, Trudy. His marriage pained Katie deeply. He had seemed so averse to commitment. For Melanie's sake, however, she pretended to be pleased.

In only six months, Jason had lost Katie's $7,000 going-away gift in his natural foods restaurant. He'd worked in a health food store for a few months, then gotten a job as "research assistant" in a new magazine called *Rolling Stone*.

"We only sold 5,000 copies of the first issue," he had told Katie, "but I know it's going to take off. All I need is a loan of $2,000 to invest." After extracting a promise that he would come to see Melanie more often, Katie wrote him a check.

The prospect of reuniting with her family was one Katie dreaded, not having seen anyone except Tim for the last seven years. But Tim had begged her to attend the wedding of her nephew, Ben Greenfield. When Yvonne sent a note saying how much they all missed her, and that they were looking forward to meeting Melanie, she relented. Melanie did have a right to know her family.

The wedding of Ben Greenfield and his fashion model bride took place at Temple Emanu El on Arguello Boulevard, followed by a reception at the Mark Hopkins Hotel on Nob Hill. After all the toasts and wedding cake, Marc Greenfield took his wife's arm.

"Do you think it'll last?" he whispered.

"Why not?" Yvonne clicked open a compact and checked her makeup. "Twenty-two years ago they said we'd never last."

"Only 22 years? It seems like forever."

"Rat!"

"I meant that nicely." A waiter came by with a tray, and Marc handed his wife a glass of champagne.

"Well, okay. You're a lovable rat, even if you do pick on Sam."

"A ten-year-old boy should have responsibilities. You don't do a child any favors by spoiling him." He dropped his voice. "Who's that girl over there? She looks familiar."

"Oh, my God. It's Katie!" Grabbing his arm, she hurried across the room to where Katie stood, clutching five-year-old Melanie's hand. Yvonne embraced her half-sister warmly.

"Katie Stockton Morris, you can't avoid us any longer. And why have you been hiding this exquisite child!" She bent down to Melanie. "Hi, sweetheart. I'm Yvonne, your aunt."

"What's an aunt?"

"I'm your mother's sister. And this is my husband, your Uncle Marc."

Marc patted her head and kissed Katie's cheek. She hadn't changed much, he thought; a little older, a little heavier, still the same social misfit. Whoever sold her that Pucci print should be executed at dawn. "Welcome back to the fold. We've missed you."

"Thanks." Katie smiled shyly and sipped her champagne. Marc and Yvonne were still such chic, beautiful people. They always made her feel tacky. "I'm sorry I've been out of touch. I knew you'd disapprove of my life style and — Jason."

"That's my Daddy," piped Melanie.

"Are you divorced?" asked Yvonne.

"We've been apart for two years. But we're good friends."

"What about you, young lady?" Marc directed his question to

Melanie, amazed that Katie and her hippie friend could have produced such an adorable child. "Are we going to see more of you from now on?"

"I don't know. Do you have a little girl I can play with?"

"Sorry, honey. All I have is three boys. But I run a big store downtown and if your mother will bring you into our toy department, I'll let you pick out any toy you want."

"*Any* toy?"

"That's right."

"And take it home?"

"For keeps. Would you like that?"

She looked up. "Say yes, Mommy!"

"Yes," said Katie, laughing. "Marc, you're spoiling her."

"She's a winner, Katie. I'll bet she's photogenic, too. I'd love to use her in one of our Christmas ads."

"Thanks, but we keep a low profile. We're three helpless females — including our housekeeper Christi — living alone. I worry about kidnappers."

Yvonne nodded approval. "You can't be too protective these days." Her eyes shone with curiosity. "Does Jason live nearby?"

"Daddy lives in the Haight-Ashby," said Melanie.

"Ashbury," corrected Katie, changing the subject. "Now catch me up on your children. What's the groom been doing?"

"Ben's going back to Dartmouth to get his MBA in marketing," said Marc. "Then he's coming to work at the store. David's a pre-med student at Brandeis. He wants to be a surgeon, God knows why. And Sam over there — our ten-year-old baby —"

"Isn't he gorgeous?" Yvonne beamed at her youngest son. "He's on a mystery-book kick right now. Wants to be another Conan Doyle. By the way, Katie, the kids were thrilled with that exquisite silver tray you sent."

"I'm glad." She glanced across the room where Clara, her mother, was standing with her brother Will, talking with guests. "Hope you won't mind if Melanie and I just slip away. And please stop by the house one day. You, too, Marc. I'd like to show you my garden."

Yvonne ignored her outstretched palm and gave her a solid hug. "We'd love to come by, Katie — very soon."

Chapter 25 — 1971

The early 1970s saw San Francisco reeling from the Haight-Ashbury disaster. What *TIME* magazine had hailed as "the vibrant epicenter of America's hippie movement" was over, and according to the *San Francisco Herald,* there was little evidence that the flower children had benefited society.

Gone were such landmarks as the Psychedelic Shop, the Diggers Free Store, Happening House, and the Hip Job Co-op. City Health inspectors shut down the last of the unsanitary communes, merchants moved their stores to better parts of town, police arrested drug dealers by the dozens. Homes and buildings were left to deteriorate.

What remained lacked any resemblance to the days when Katie first lived there, sharing Jason's hopes for a world of peace and love. Sadly, the Haight-Ashbury had become a shrine to dreams and visions gone sour.

The day before Christmas, Katie Stockton Morris sat at her breakfast table, reading stories about her old district with conflicting emotions. While she fervently thanked God she was out of there, she couldn't help feeling sad for Jason, who was still determined to change the world.

"More coffee, Mrs. Morris?"

Katie smiled. After all they had been through, Christi was now insisting on formality. She claimed it suited her elevated status as "personal maid" to the mistress of the house.

"No, thanks — just my usual."

A clatter of footsteps made Katie look to the door, and in stormed nine-year-old Melanie, her hands planted firmly on her hips.

"Mom! We have to talk."

"Calm down, dear. We can talk over breakfast."

"I won't calm down! Carolyne called and told me to look at yesterday's *Herald.*" She slapped the sheet on the table and pointed, "Who's that?"

The paper gave Katie a start. A three-column photo of her mother, Clara, silver-haired and regal at 64, stared from the page. The caption read: "Mrs. James Tyler Stockton was honored at a luncheon. A proclamation from Mayor Joseph Alioto acknowledged her 30 years of service as trustee of the Brett Stockton Memorial Museum."

Katie had dreaded this moment, but she was prepared. "That's your grandmother."

"You said she was dead."

"I know I did, Mel. I couldn't tell you the truth until you were old enough to understand."

"Understand *what*?"

"It's a long story. Sit down."

Still pouting, Melanie folded her arms and perched on a chair. "Well?"

"Many years ago, before you were born, your grandmother Clara woke up one night and found a burglar in her room. He tried to attack her, so she grabbed a gun Grandpa James had given her, and shot him."

"Did he die?"

"Yes. I was terribly upset, as you can imagine, and the next morning, I went for a long walk. That's when I met your father."

"At the M'rina Safeway."

"Yes. I knew he was a good, kind person. I wanted to see him again and Grandma Clara wouldn't let me."

"Why not?"

"She thought he was a bad man. She said if I left the house to see him, I wasn't her daughter anymore and I couldn't come back."

Melanie gasped. "Why was she so mean?"

"She thought she was protecting me, but I went to see your father, anyway, and you know the rest."

"You got married and lived happily ever after till you got divorced."

"Something like that." Katie winked a thank you as Christi set down her morning screwdriver.

"Did you ever try to make up with Grandma Clara?"

"I called her once, when she was in the hospital. I left my name and number. She never called back."

"Oh, Mommy, I hate her!" Melanie jumped up and threw her arms around her mother. "I'll never speak to her either. Never!"

"I don't want you to hate her. She's not a bad person. She just doesn't seem to want us in her life."

"Like Daddy doesn't want me?"

Katie felt a stab. "What do you mean?"

"He loves his new wife better'n me."

131

"Nonsense, honey. He's busy working on the magazine. Trudy told me she hardly ever sees him these days. What time are they picking you up for dinner?"

"Six o'clock." Melanie squirmed out of her mother's arms. "I gotta go call Carolyne."

Jason and Trudy arrived at 6:30, apologizing for being late. Melanie hugged her father and curled up on his lap.

Katie marveled at the changes in Jason. His cropped hair was combed and neat, taking years off his appearance. Gone, too, was the hippie talk and the sickly-sweet odor that used to permeate his clothes. The familiar dungarees and sandals were replaced, incredibly, by a camel's hair sports jacket, turtleneck, and slacks.

Even Trudy had clipped her reddish-brown locks, added a touch of lipstick to her pretty face, and exchanged her granny gown for a pink wool suit with gold buttons.

"Life obviously agrees with you two," said Katie, from behind her bar. "Scotch, Jason?"

"White wine, please. Say, was that a butler who answered your phone yesterday?"

"No, that was Bill, Christi's new husband. She was going to leave us and move in with him. I suggested he move in with her instead, and work for us."

"He's real nice, Daddy," said Melanie. "He fixed my swing."

Katie served her guests, mixed herself a drink, and sat down. "You said you had something to tell us?"

"Yeah, I'm quitting the magazine. It's gotten too big — too commercial. The good news is that when I sell my shares, I'll have enough to buy into a film production company."

"Isn't that super?" Trudy's eyes gleamed with excitement. "Jason's going to star me in his first movie!"

"What kind of movie?"

"A love story with a message," said Jason. "A powerful visual protest against censorship."

"Can I be in it?" asked Melanie.

"*May* I, and no, you can't." Katie felt her heart sink. "Honey, run down to the cellar and bring up some white wine, please."

"You're tryin' to get rid of me."

"That's right. I want to talk to your father alone for a minute."

Growling, Melanie slid off her father's lap and disappeared. Katie stared at Jason. "Now it's pornography?"

"We don't consider lovemaking pornography."

"Oh, my God!"

"Hold on, Katiebird. Don't judge me until you see it."

"You won't expose Melanie to anything like that, will you?" Katie's immediate thought was to protect her daughter from this latest, horrifying menace.

"For Chris' sake! We're taking her out for a veggieburger. We'll bring her back in an hour, virginity intact."

"Please, Katie," begged Trudy. "Don't close your mind. Wait until the picture's finished. It won't be the least bit offensive."

"You're going to be proud as hell of me," said Jason. "Just you wait and see."

The sun was setting slowly in a sky streaked with orange. Silent shadows began to steal into the bedroom where Melanie Morris lay sprawled on her bed. Absorbed in a book, she failed to hear her mother's tap at the door.

Katie entered and switched on the light. "How many times have I told you not to read in the dark?"

"Sorry." Melanie's gaze shifted. Games, records, and books were strewn across the covers. "Thanks for the party, Mom."

"Thirteen's a big birthday."

"I wish it were sixteen." Melanie closed the book and eyed her mother with affection. Hard to believe she was going on thirty-six. She didn't look or act that old, though her hair had wisps of silver and her waistline was expanding. "Wasn't it nice of Daddy to stop by? Imagine those awful people kicking him out of the movie business! You were wonderful to get him a job with your contractor and help him buy a house. You should see how nice they fixed up my room."

"Nicely."

"Mom, do you think you'll ever marry again?"

Katie raised an eyebrow. "What brought that up?"

"Just wondering. My friend's mom got remarried and Carolyne's new brother picked her up today. He's eighteen and positively dreamy."

"So now you'd like a dreamy new brother?"

"I wouldn't mind. How come you won't get married?"

"I didn't say that. How much birthday cake did you eat?"

"You always change the subject." Melanie tilted her head. "Do you think you and your mother will ever make up?"

Katie's reaction was surprisingly calm. "I doubt it."

"If I called Grandma Clara some day, d'ya think she'd see me?"

"No, and don't waste your time worrying about it." Katie headed for the door. "Are you coming down to dinner?"

"After all that cake, I'd barf on the tablecloth."

"A simple 'no' will do. Take off your party dress, then, and put on your pajamas."

Sleep was late in coming that night. Melanie tried to deal with all that was happening in her life. Starting high school in the fall might be fun if she were going to a public school like Lowell, but her mother had insisted she go to Hamlin's, of all things, a private school with no boys.

Melanie had shot up to being one of the tallest girls in her class. Her eighth grade teacher had said she showed leadership skills, and had talked to her about becoming a lawyer, but Melanie had her own plans for the future — plans she hadn't even told her friends. They'd think she was crazy to want to be a movie star.

Acting seemed easy when you watched other people do it, but Melanie knew better. You had to train your voice, walk a special way, hold your head high, and learn all sorts of skills and tricks. Maybe Mom would treat her to acting lessons that summer.

Strange, she reflected, that such a nice person as her mother had no husband. Strange, too, that she couldn't forgive her own mother after all these years. What was Grandma Clara's side of the story? There she was, living only five minutes away, and Melanie couldn't even call her on the phone.

Or could she? The more she thought about it, the more she realized nothing was stopping her. They couldn't put you in jail for going to see your own grandmother, could they?

She knew the house on Jackson Street almost as well as she knew her own. She had walked and roller-skated past there more times than she could count.

On a cool, crisp Sunday in June, Melanie called down to the garden. "See you later, Mom. I'm going for a walk." Taking a last look in the mirror, she straightened the skirt of her velvet dress, took the ribbon out of her hair, put it back, took it off, and put it back again. Finally, she buckled her Mary Janes and quietly left the house.

Minutes later, she was glancing up at her grandmother Clara's great Tudor mansion with its tall protective hedge — wishing she hadn't come, but determined to follow through. Only last month, trying to sell Girl Scout cookies, she'd rung every doorbell on the block but that one. Maybe by the next cookie sale, it wouldn't look so forbidding.

She pushed the button gingerly. Seconds later, Kai, wearing a white uniform, appeared. "Yes?"

"I'd like to see Mrs. Stockton, please. I'm her granddaughter."

"Is she expecting you?"

"No, it's a surprise."

"Well, come in and wait here."

"Thank you." Melanie watched nervously as the petite Asian woman climbed the impressive spiral staircase. The house was full of antiques and old paintings, like a movie set. She almost expected Scarlett O'Hara to come sweeping down the stairs.

Kai returned quickly. "I'm afraid there's some mistake. Mrs. Stockton doesn't have a granddaughter."

The words inflamed Melanie. "She does, too!" Dashing past the maid, she bolted up the stairs and poked her head in three doors until she came to a bedroom. An elderly lady sat at a desk.

"What's going on here?" she asked.

"I am too your granddaughter!"

Before Clara could answer, Kai appeared in the doorway. "I'm so sorry, Mrs. Stockton. She flew up here — I couldn't stop her."

"That's all right, Kai. I'll handle this." Clara eyed the intruder. "Whoever you are, young lady, please go home."

"I'm going, Grandma Clara." Melanie folded her arms. "But first I have something to say. Maybe you and my mom don't get along. That's your business. But I'm an innocent child, so I think it's really dumb of you to hate me."

"How could I hate you? I don't even know you."

"Well, I don't know you either. But at least I was nice enough to come visit. That's more'n you ever did for me. And now that I've seen you and I know how you act towards innocent children, I'm going home!"

She turned and started for the doorway when a voice commanded: "Wait!"

Melanie froze, wondering if her hostess was about to call the police.

Clara peered over her glasses. "Come here, please."

Too frightened to speak, Melanie turned and approached cautiously.

"You're prettier than your mother. And you've got the gall of your father." She peered closely. "What's your name?"

"Melanie Stockton Morris."

"How old are you?"

"Thirteen."

"Has anyone ever told you that you look like me?"

"No. Do I?"

"I'll show you a picture." Clara rose, tightened the sash of her silk robe and strode to her closet. She pulled a scrapbook from a shelf, then walked over to a loveseat. "Come sit down."

Melanie obeyed meekly. The voice wasn't sounding quite so angry.

Clara flipped pages until she came to a faded photo of a young girl. "Ah, there we are. That was taken at the opening of the Steinhart Aquarium in Golden Gate Park. The hair's longer and I wasn't quite as tall as you, but otherwise..."

Melanie gasped. "Wow!"

"Startling, isn't it." Clara shut the scrapbook and set it aside. "So I suppose you are my granddaughter after all. No one else could look that much like me." Her voice softened. "Now what's this all about, Melanie? Who sent you here and why did you come?"

"No one, honest. My mother doesn't even know I came. I wanted to hear your side of the story."

"What story?"

"Why you and Mom — Katie — don't speak."

"That's a question you'll have to ask your mother. I love her and I miss her terribly. Now, have you satisfied your curiosity?"

"Not really."

"Well, that's too bad, because you have to go home."

"May I come again?"

"I don't know why you want to see a crabby old lady."

"Because I want to love you. You're my grandmother."

A catch in the throat made Clara pause. She waited a few seconds, then spoke. "Yes, I suppose I am. All right, you can come again. Next Sunday, if you like. But not this early. Come about noon and we'll have a sandwich."

"I'd like that, Grandma."

Clara turned her head, walked to her bathroom and shut the door, just in time to hide her tears. How in the world, she wondered, could shy Katie and her hippie lover have produced such a charming little girl? Where did she get her passion and her fire? Of course she knew exactly where — as the buried images began tumbling through her brain.

Returning to the armchair at her desk, Clara capped the ballpoint pen and set aside a pile of papers. It was no use trying to work. Too many memories were flooding her head — one in particular.

Many, many years ago, on a night she remembered vividly, she and James had just finished dinner when the doorbell rang. He opened the door to find two strange men facing him. They were neat, clean-shaven, and looked to be in their twenties.

"Mr. James Tyler Stockton?" One man had stepped forward. "My name is Hart Dixon, my friend is Al Hogan. We represent a group of citizens concerned about our country's isolationist policies. Could you spare five minutes?"

James's inclination had been to slam the door. But he resisted. If he ever decided to run for mayor, he'd need groups like that behind him. "I don't usually see callers at home, but you're here, so you might as well come in. This is my wife, Clara Stockton."

"Pleased to meet you, Mrs. Stockton." Hart Dixon extended a hand; she shook it cautiously.

The men followed James into the living room, a formal parlor with dramatic 30-foot ceilings, oak paneling, and to Clara's long-time frustration, purple-fringed sofas.

"Make yourselves comfortable, gentlemen. Care for a drink?"

"No, thanks." Hart Dixon had remained standing while his companion sat. "If you don't mind, sir, I'll get right to the point, You must be aware that the threat of fascism grows more menacing every second. President Roosevelt said as much on his visit here in July."

James poured himself a cognac. "I'm also aware that the 1935 Neutrality Act was designed to keep us from meddling with warring nations."

"With all due respect, Mr. Stockton, your readers deserve to be informed. They need to know what's happening right now, and what they can do to protect themselves. If I may explain..."

James had listened intently to Hart Dixon's rhetoric. It was a speech the publisher could have predicted, and yet, the young man's delivery was riveting. He had a gift for eloquence. Nothing about him — not his talk, his manners, his dress, nor his handsome, sensitive features — stamped him as a working man.

When the monologue ended, James faced him. "Who are you, Mr. Dixon? Where are you from?"

"I'm a native San Franciscan, sir, and a graduate of Harvard. Does what I'm saying make sense to you?"

"It makes sense, because you're educated and well-spoken. That doesn't mean I'll act on it."

"Will you at least think about it? The message must get out."

Hart Dixon's words nearly triggered James' usual response: "If you've got a message," he'd growl to his reporters, "call Western Union." Instead, he said quietly, "You have my promise. And I want you to go back to your group and tell them that you had a private audience with James Stockton. I'm always —" He frowned at the sound of footsteps. "What is it, Kai?"

"Mr. Powell's on the phone. Shall I say you're busy?"

"No, no, I'll talk. My guests were just leaving. Goodnight, gentlemen, my wife will show you out."

As James disappeared down the hall, Hart Dixon stepped forward and spoke softly. "I've heard of your grace and beauty, Mrs. Stockton. May I say — without offending you — that the reports don't do you justice?"

Clara beamed at the good-looking stranger. A tingle of excitement made her blush. "Compliments never offend me if they're sincere."

"I don't have time to be insincere."

"Then thank you. I'm flattered."

His look was bold and presumptuous. "We'll meet again, Mrs. Stockton. I feel it in my blood."

Chapter 28 — 1975

And so it had begun, a totally unexpected romantic affair. No one was more surprised than Clara, who'd never dreamed she could be unfaithful. But Hart had called and called on various pretexts, and finally, just to tell him once and for all to stop bothering her, she'd agreed to take a walk with him. The walks had become longer, the talks more intimate, and soon, almost before she knew it, he'd awakened feelings and emotions she had never experienced.

His real name, he'd told her, was Hart Doyle — son of Fitz Doyle, a rival publisher, and one James hated. But that was the least of Clara's concerns. Some weeks later, when James got attacked for an editorial he'd written, and landed in Stanford Lane Hospital, Clara — in a weak moment — agreed to visit Hart in his home. What happened there was all too predictable.

A continuing life of deceit, however, was impossible for Clara, and she knew from the beginning that her place was, and always would be, with James. Her heart breaking, she broke off the affair, only to discover that she'd gotten pregnant while James was hospitalized.

In the meantime, James had gone back to the office and immersed himself in work. When Clara realized her situation, there seemed only one course of action: she put on James' favorite perfume and her sexiest silk negligee and seduced him. Learning she was pregnant some months later, James never gave the slightest thought to the possibility that the baby might not be his.

Hart Doyle had no knowledge of this development. Aching and badly depressed, he'd respected Clara's position and agreed not to call or try to see her. No one knew her guilty secret, and no one ever would. She would guard it with her life.

Katherine "Katie" Marie Stockton had come into the world without fuss or fanfare. But as she grew, she seemed very different from her siblings. And now, seeing Katie's daughter Melanie with all the guts and determination Katie lacked, Clara had little doubt that Melanie had inherited those fiery genes from her grandfather, Katie's *real* father, Hart Doyle.

What kind of God, Clara wondered, would play a trick like that, endowing this delightful child with the charm and aggressiveness of her old lover, and making her almost an exact replica of her shameful grandmother? Could she dare to hope that one day Melanie might bring Katie back to her? Nothing in the world would thrill her more.

Melanie thought about changing her clothes before reporting her adventure to her mother, then decided that would be dishonest.

Katie looked up to see her daughter coming down the steps to the garden. "What are you doing in your party dress?"

"I went to see Grandma Clara."

Katie set down her shears, more puzzled than angry. "Why?"

"I just wanted to. You never said I couldn't."

"I thought you'd know better." She sighed. "Well, I'm sorry you had to be hurt. I could've told you she wouldn't see you."

"She wouldn't, so I ran up to her bedroom. She was mad at first."

Katie stared in disbelief. "You went up to her bedroom? Uninvited?"

"I had to. She told the maid she didn't have a granddaughter."

"Oh, my God! Then what?"

"Then she calmed down and showed me a picture of herself. She said I look just like she looked at my age. I brought up your name and she said she loves you and misses you terribly."

"Oh, Mel, I wish you'd asked me before you dashed off."

"Don't worry, Mom. She was nice to me. She even said I could come back and see her next Sunday."

"I wish you wouldn't. I don't want her saying things to hurt you."

Melanie frowned. "She can't hurt me, and if she ever says one word against you, I'll punch her in the mouth."

"Oh, dear God." Katie pulled off her gloves and slapped them in her basket. "This is all too much for me. I'm going in to lie down."

Chapter 29 - 1975

Despite Katie's disapproval, Melanie returned to Jackson Street the following Sunday. This time, her Uncle Will answered the door. She had met him once at Tim and Lou Ella's house, and hadn't paid him much attention. Yet she remembered his strange appearance: bright yellow hair that looked bleached, a thick, well-trimmed mustache, a dark suntan. Under a white jacket, he wore a pale pink shirt, open at the collar.

"Come on in, Melanie. Remember me?"

"'Course I do, Uncle Will. What're you doing here?"

"Visiting my mother. She's expecting you in the breakfast room, right through that door."

"Aren't you staying?"

"No, Sundays are quiet at the television station. I can get some work done."

"May I come see the station sometime?"

"Yes, certainly. Just call Rick, my secretary."

"You have a man secretary?"

"Why not?"

"It just seems funny. Could I bring my best friend Carolyne?"

"Sure, talk to Rick. Sorry, I've gotta run now."

Melanie stood in the doorway, watching him hurry to his Mercedes and greet a young man sitting in the front seat. It occurred to her, then, and she wondered why it hadn't struck her sooner, that Uncle Will was what they called homosexual.

Her mother had always avoided talking about sex in any detail, but Uncle Tim had explained that some men liked to make love to men. Some women fell in love with women, too, and they all called themselves gay. Uncle Tim said that what people did in private was no one's business.

Melanie found her grandmother Clara sitting in a spacious breakfast room. Sunlight streamed through the window, reflecting off the polished silver and gleaming crystal. A pair of French doors opened onto a garden — not the blooming rose bushes and lush confusion of her mother's back yard, but a delicate arrangement of rocks, bonsais, and cherry blossom trees surrounding a pond. An arched bridge completed the peaceful setting.

"Hi, Grandma." Melanie thought about kissing her, then decided against it. "I saw Uncle Will on the way out."

"You've met, have you? Do you know my other children?"

"Sure. I've been lotsa times to Aunt Yvonne's house. Uncle Marc's real nice, but Uncle Tim's my favorite. He's the one who got us back with the family."

"You and your mother?"

"Yeah. But sometimes I see Uncle Tim alone. He's more like a father than an uncle."

"Everybody loves Tim." Clara's bell summoned the maid. "We're ready to eat, please."

Melanie twisted herself into a chair. "What was Grandpa James like?"

"Your grandfather was strong — a great asset to the community, and a brilliant businessman. His leadership saved the *Herald*."

"From what?"

"From mediocrity. From becoming ordinary."

"What about Uncle Tim? What was he like growing up?"

"Tim was always a delight: sweet-natured, lively, curious, caring about everyone but himself."

"And Aunt Yvonne?"

"She was a terror. Melanie, you're not fooling me for one second. I know where you're heading, and I don't see any benefit to discussing your mother. If Katie wants to see me, now or any time, I would open my heart to her and love her as if nothing ever happened."

"Honest, Grandma? Will you tell her that?"

"Yes, if she calls. I've always wanted us to be close. She's the one who's kept us apart. And since I *am* your Grandma, you might as well call me Nonna, as my other grandchildren do."

"Thanks...Nonna." The name rolled off her tongue and gave her a secret thrill. At last, she officially had a grandmother. And the possibility that she could bring Nonna and her mother back together again was almost too wonderful to contemplate.

They chatted through lunch; Melanie did most of the talking, describing Jason and Trudy, sharing her fears of starting Hamlin's, even confiding her ambition to be an actress. Finally, she kissed her grandmother good-bye and ran all the way home.

Melanie could hardly contain her excitement. She skipped up the stairs and found her mother resting in bed.

"I have great news!" she cried, plopping down beside her, "Grandma Clara wants to see you!"

Katie turned her head and sighed impatiently. "What about?"

"Because she loves you. You're her *daughter*!"

"If I'm her beloved daughter, why did she kick me out of the house? Why didn't she return my call in the hospital? I'm not about to go crawling back on my knees."

"But Mom, I know she forgives you. She wants to see you."

"Forgives me for what?"

Instantly, Melanie knew she had chosen the wrong word. Grandma Clara was the one who wanted to make up all these years and her mother was the obstacle.

"When she's ready to apologize, she can call me," Katie said irritably. "I wish you wouldn't keep seeing her."

"But she's my *grandma*." The only way to handle this, Melanie decided, was to be patient. One day, with or without their help, she would bring these two stubborn women together.

Chapter 30 — 1979

Determined not to become the kind of domineering mother Clara was, Katie did not interfere with her daughter's visits to Jackson Street. Despite an initial feeling of betrayal, she came to realize that Melanie was as strong-willed as the rest of the Stockton women, and there was little she could do to prevent the growing relationship.

Begrudgingly, she had to acknowledge that Melanie was deriving some benefits. Leafing through Clara's scrapbooks and hearing tales about her colorful ancestors, Melanie had begun to develop a sense of pride in her family. Try as she might, however, Katie couldn't help resenting their closeness, and thus, had urged Melanie to apply to a college in the east.

Melanie hadn't objected. She had no steady boyfriend, and had long ago decided that any love relationship would have to be secondary to her career — one that had started in her freshman year at Hamlin's, and continued until Graduation Day.

Four years of school plays and four summers of drama workshops at the Linda Garry Acting School had given 17-year-old Melanie a feel for the stage and a healthy taste for applause. Her best performance, she thought, was as Class Valedictorian. The standing ovation thrilled her; could an Oscar be far off?

A few nights after graduation, Jason and Trudy joined Katie and Melanie in the Broadway house for dinner. Midway through the meal, Melanie said, "Mom, Dad, there's something I'd like to discuss with you."

Jason set down his fork. "You'd better not be pregnant."

"If I am, it's Immaculate Conception." Melanie had carefully timed her approach. By now, her parents would have had enough food and wine to be reasonably mellow. "Mom, I really appreciate your wanting to send me to Wellesley, but I've been giving it a lot of thought and I don't think it's in my best interest to go to college. I could be using those four years to gain stage experience."

"What are you saying?" asked Katie, stunned.

"Linda, my drama coach, thinks I'm ready to join the American Conservatory Theater. They have a junior workshop that does real plays, and she wants me to read for the director."

"That's more important than your education?"

Melanie looked to Jason with pleading eyes. "Dad?"

"I have to agree with your mother, Mel."

"But I'd be wasting all that time. They're looking for pretty *young* faces. I'll look older four years from now. And think of the experience and the exposure. A talent scout might discover me and whisk me off to Hollywood."

"It doesn't happen that way," said Katie.

"How would you know? You've never had to make a living." She glared at her mother, resentment flaring to the surface. "You didn't like it when your mother tried to run your life and now you're trying to run mine!"

"Mel, how can you say that?"

"Can't you and Dad give me some credit for being able to make my own decisions?" Melanie strove to sound calm. "I know what I want, and I *don't* want to go to Wellesley!"

An icy silence followed. Melanie hated being so assertive, but look where being meek had gotten her mother — nowhere.

"We'll finish this discussion in private," said Katie quietly. "Let's enjoy the rest of our dinner."

The scene replayed itself as soon as Jason and Trudy left. Katie refused to discuss any change of plans, and Melanie stomped off in anger. Early the next morning, she tiptoed down the hall and scratched lightly on a half-open door. "Are you awake?"

"I've been up for hours. Come in."

The sight of an empty vodka bottle on her mother's night stand filled her with guilt. "I'm sorry, Mom," she said, tears running down her cheek. "I shouldn't have said what I did. Forgive me?"

Katie's arms encircled her. "There's nothing to forgive. You're all I have, and I don't want to lose you."

"You'll never lose me." Melanie sniffed and reached for a tissue. "But I've been thinking some more. I'm really hopeless around the house. I can't cook or do anything, not even fry an egg. Maybe I should get an apartment and try to support myself."

The suggestion startled Katie. "Where would you live? How would you pay your rent?"

"I'd get a job. My drama coach might hire me as her assistant."

"Don't be naive. The second she hears you need money, she'll want nothing more to do with you."

"I suppose you're right. But you've always been so reasonable about things, and we've always been able to talk. Why are you pushing me to go to Wellesley?"

Katie sat silent a long minute, struggling for an answer. Overriding her intellect was the fear, almost a panic, that she could alienate Melanie by being too strict. One rift in the family was enough. "Would you consider going to a college around here? You were accepted to Stanford and they have an excellent Theater Arts Department."

Melanie thought a long minute. Then she grinned. "Well, okay, Mom, I'll go to Stanford if you insist. But I'll need a new red convertible to get there."

Chapter 31 - 1979

The following Sunday, Tim and Lou Ella came to Jackson Street for tea. Clara looked forward to the visit. She had come to like Lou Ella over the years, grateful that she'd kept the *Herald* running fairly smoothly, and even more grateful that she made Tim happy.

The formality of Clara's Louis Quinze decor was softened by the yellow floral pattern of the couch and draperies. Fresh-cut roses filled the air with fragrance. Atop a travertine mantel, Clara's imposing portrait dominated the scene.

Tim and Lou Ella relaxed on the sofa. The passage of years showed on Lou Ella's once-pretty face, now a roadmap of wrinkles. To the dismay of her brother in-law, Marc, she had never learned, or taken the time to learn, how to dress. Worse yet, she didn't seem to care. Her main concern was the newspaper. And no one, not even her enemies, could deny its initial success.

In 1953, as soon as she'd been named publisher, she had hired an assortment of columnists, assigning them every subject from marital advice, offered by a male hairdresser who called himself "The Love Queen," to a woman sports writer with a fondness for players' rumps and a memory for sports trivia that infuriated her male colleagues.

The paper's earthy tone rated a sneer from *Newsweek* magazine, unhappy with the accent on "sex and sensationalism." Scoffed a critic: "The *Herald* is like a circus barker shouting, 'Hurry, hurry! The girls are about to strip!'"

Such criticism, however, only fed the controversy that was making the *Herald* the fastest growing daily in the country. Not content simply to watch her columnists become celebrities, Lou Ella launched her famous tongue-in-cheek crusades. Among a dozen that appeared in the late '50s, the most noteworthy were the campaign to place billboards on the Golden Gate Bridge, the movement to clothe naked cats and dogs, and the suggestion to change Coit Tower from a phallic symbol to a pyramid.

In the early '60s, Lou Ella had scored a coup by luring back Herb Caen. His first column had a memorable item: he reported seeing frizzy-haired Phyllis Diller's clever comedy act, and that afterward, she'd whispered in his ear, "If you give me a good review — I won't sleep with you."

Herb brought forty thousand readers, zooming the *Herald* to first place in Northern California circulation. And despite lawsuits, union problems, financial crises and changing demographics, the *Herald* continued to maintain its lead.

No longer the staunch Republican town of years past, San Francisco was steadily shifting to the left, and Lou Ella was happy to sway with the current. The *Herald* soon became the first major U.S. newspaper to protest American involvement in Vietnam.

The appearance of "adult" movie ads upset Clara, who felt they had no place in a respectable newspaper, but she was voted down. The revenue was sure and steady, and as Lou Ella explained to the family stockholders, the theater owners would only take their business to the competition.

By the late-seventies, however, circulation had begun to lag. A mild heart attack slowed Lou Ella for a few weeks, but not for long.

"I'll be 65 next month," Lou Ella announced as she stirred her tea. "That's mandatory retirement age. My doctor wants me to quit."

"You've done a fine job," said Clara. "You deserve a rest."

"But who'll replace me? I keep hoping someone in the family — maybe Sam Greenfield or Tyrone Pickett — will come along and take over."

Clara shook her head. "Not likely. Tyrone's working at his father's investment company and Sam's down at the store."

Balding, and slightly paunchy from life in a therapist's chair, Tim sat listening while his wife and Clara chatted. He wore an eye patch, the result of recent cataract surgery, and finally asked, "What *will* you do when you retire, sweetheart?"

Lou Ella laughed. "Tim thinks I'll go crazy staying home."

"I don't care if *you* go crazy, I'm afraid you'll drive *me* crazy."

Clara smiled. Tim had given his life to his work and was still practicing.

The doorbell sounded just as Tim and Lou Ella rose to leave. Marc and Yvonne entered, followed a second later, by a breathless Melanie.

Yvonne pecked Tim's cheek. "What's your hurry, big brother? Something I said?"

Tim grinned. "Too many Stocktons in one room make me nervous." He turned to Melanie. "How's my favorite niece?"

"I'm your *only* niece, Uncle Tim. What happened to your eye?"

He raised his metal claw menacingly. "MGM signed me to play Captain Hook."

"Great! Can I get free tickets?" Melanie hugged him and strolled into the living room. "We all came at the same time, Nonna. Should I come back later?"

"You're family, aren't you? Sit down and try to behave yourself."

Marc and Yvonne settled on the settee; Melanie perched on a chair. A penchant for fresh flowers and ugly antiques, she observed wryly, were about the only tastes her mother and grandmother shared.

"What are you up to this summer?" Yvonne asked Melanie.

"Not much." She loved to stare at her beautiful aunt. Three years short of sixty, Yvonne had traded the striking good looks of her youth for an aura of grace and serenity. Soft gray hair complemented a still-lovely face, radiant with warmth and smile lines. Marc, in contrast, looked pale and drawn, a result of recent colon cancer surgery.

"To be honest," said Melanie, "I'm going batty waiting to hear from my drama coach. She promised to set up a reading at ACT, and I haven't heard a word."

"Melanie's got the Stockton stubborn streak," said Clara. "One phone call to Bill Ball or Cyril Magnin, and she'd be on her way."

"I want to make it on my *own*, Nonna. I just get bored waiting."

Clara reached for the teapot. "Boredom is the wasteland of a vacant mind. Did Mark Twain say that? If he didn't, he should have."

Yvonne nibbled a cookie. "Maybe Marc could put you to work, Melanie. Darling, didn't you tell me one of your best models just quit?"

"Yes, but she was 28 and a pro."

Yvonne shrugged. "You don't have to be Einstein to show off a dress."

"She's much too —" He stopped suddenly, appraising Melanie with a critical eye. "What size are you?"

"Four or six. But I stagger like a drunk in high heels."

He continued to regard her, scratching his chin. "It might just be a possibility. You're seventeen — and we *are* trying to attract a younger clientele."

"What would I do?"

Marc shrugged. "What they all do. You'd be on your feet for seven hours showing clothes to customers."

"Would you pay me?"

"The regular starting salary. About four dollars an hour."

"Wow! When do I start?"

"Stop talking nonsense," Clara scolded. "Melanie could be improving her mind. Why should she waste her summer being a salesgirl?"

"It'd be a wonderful experience for her." Yvonne's voice was strong and calm. She and Clara had been disagreeing for half a century; arguments were no novelty. "She'll learn how to apply makeup, how to walk, how to wear clothes, how to charm an audience. If she wants to be an actress, she couldn't get better training."

Melanie tried to contain her excitement. "But what if Linda, my drama coach, calls?"

"Tell her you've made other plans." Marc peered into a small black date book. "Do you have a Social Security number?"

"No."

"Get one first thing in the morning and be in my office by eleven."

"That's ridiculous," said Clara. "I'll give her an allowance. She doesn't need to stand on her feet all day selling clothes."

"But Nonna, I *want* to."

"What will your mother say?"

The question startled Melanie. Her grandmother must really be agitated to bring up Katie. She rose and kissed her cheek. "I'm going home to find out. And if she objects, I'll just pack up all my rock'n roll records and my hamster cage, and move in here with you."

That evening, Yvonne called Lou Ella. The sisters-in-law made no pretense of being close, but respected each other and shared a tendency to be direct.

"Clara mentioned that you're looking for a replacement for yourself at the paper," said Yvonne.

"Yes — ?"

"What about Paul Amory, the *Boston Globe* editor who went to *The New York Times*? You talked to him back in 1956, remember?"

Lou Ella did remember. She had thought at the time there was something strange about Yvonne's eagerness to recruit Amory; now she was sure of it. "How could I forget? He's won almost every award, including two Pulitzers. And he's got one of the most coveted plums in journalism:

a weekly column on the Op-Ed page of the *Times*. Why would he be interested in a small metropolitan daily?"

"All he can say is no."

Lou Ella didn't need Yvonne's help but she couldn't afford to alienate her. "Okay, I'll have Helen give him a call him next week."

"Thanks, Lou Ella. Let me know what happens."

Yvonne berated herself as she replaced the receiver. A 57-year-old grandmother shouldn't be having romantic fantasies. But her heart was beating like a teenager's.

Chapter 32 — 1979

The handsome white marble building known as S. Greenfield & Company had been a local landmark for more than forty years. To discriminating shoppers world-over, the S. Greenfield label meant the highest quality you could buy.

Over the years, Marc Greenfield had become something of a local celebrity, quick-witted and quotable. Once he told Herb Caen, "When my dad hired Tim Pflueger to build this store, he told him to make it pigeon proof, so it has no ledges. But the other kind of pigeons — the tourists who buy ten French designer gowns at a glance — will always be welcome!"

The remark delighted Marc's iconoclastic wife Yvonne, but several French designers vowed to boycott the store. They never did, of course. Why let pride get in the way of business?

Melanie Stockton Morris waited nervously in Marc's outer office, admiring the attractive, impeccably-groomed employees, certain she looked tacky by comparison. After trying on half a dozen outfits from her closet, she had settled for a white cashmere turtleneck, a dark green blazer and a plaid skirt. Katie had told her the skirt was too short, but it showed off what Melanie considered her best feature: her long, shapely legs.

Marc's stunning secretary, Vicky Anne, did little to ease her visitor's anxiety. A vision of chic, with slicked-down blonde hair tied back with a velvet ribbon, and a black wool sheath molded to her slim frame, she seemed too perfect to be real. "You may go in now, Melanie."

"Thanks."

Her uncle's office was stark and modern. A large Diebenkorn abstract served as backdrop to a pair of white leather chairs. Facing them was a clear Lucite desk with steel trim. A striking portrait of Yvonne shared wall space with a window overlooking the grassy plaza and pigeon sanctuary known as Union Square.

Marc came around the desk to greet his niece. "Sorry to keep you waiting, sugar. All set?"

"I'm scared to death."

"About what? If you're no good, I'll fire you. C'mon, I'll take you down to meet Darci."

The gown salon was divided into two sections; one featured European designers, the other, American. A double rack of garments tempted bargain hunters with final reductions.

A few feet from the elevator, a young Eurasian woman stood quietly arranging a suit on a mannequin. She stepped back and studied the outfit from several angles. Then she retied the bow at the neckline.

"It's not the blouse, Darci, it's the jacket. Try turning up the collar."

"Good idea." She smiled and spun around. Coal black hair, geometrically cut, contrasted with pale ivory skin. Almond-shaped eyes, a chiseled nose and full lips formed a breathtaking face. A gold-belted body suit showed off her figure.

"Darci Lin, meet Melanie Morris, and vice versa.

"Hi, Darci. Boy, you're skinny, too. Doesn't anyone eat around here?"

Darci regarded her up and down, as if she were a statue. "Good bones."

"Remember, Darci. No special favors for my niece. Treat her like everyone else. If she can't hack it, out she goes."

"Thanks for the vote of confidence, Uncle Marc."

"You're in good hands, sugar. Catch you later." He blew a kiss and disappeared into the elevator.

Melanie stared after him. Where was he going? How could he desert her like that?

"Don't be nervous." Darci took her arm. "Let's go into my office. We need to fill out some forms before I send you up to the beauty shop."

"Beauty shop?"

"Your uncle thinks you can do couture. That means the long hair has to go."

"But it's one of my best features."

"Leave your appearance to us. What you need to work on is poise — confidence — a saucy manner that says, 'I'm young and beautiful. Screw the world.'" She opened the door to a small office and pointed to a chair. "Sit, please."

Melanie tried not to act shocked. "My Mom didn't want me to work here, but I told her I was going to, anyway."

"Why did she object?"

"She thinks I'm parading my body or something. But that's silly. I've had four years of training to be an actress."

"Then showing clothes should be a breeze." Darci gave her a clipboard. "Fill this out."

Melanie complied, and gave it back. "Do I *have* to get my hair cut?"

"Trust me, you'll be pleased. Then we'll do makeup and wardrobe."

"I must really be a disaster."

"Let's say you're a challenge. Now get your pretty ass up to the sixth floor."

Later that day, Melanie hardly recognized herself as she tottered around the fitting room on 2½ -inch heels. Darci had fluffed up her new, short bob, given her a quick lesson in makeup, and dressed her in a $2,200 suit.

"Fabulous," she said, admiring her handiwork. "How do you feel about yourself?"

"I'm young and beautiful and screw the world, right?" Melanie giggled. "Don't I wish I felt that way."

"You will. Stand tall. Remember to make yourself as attractive as possible so women will want to buy whatever you're showing."

"You won't just turn me loose out there, will you?"

"Didn't you tell me you trained to face audiences?"

"Acting's different. The dialogue's all written. You don't have to think of things to say."

"I'll tell you what to say: `Isn't this Bill Blass suit *divine*? It comes in ivory, charcoal, and emerald, custom-made to your measurements in six weeks. I think the ivory would be absolutely smashing with your coloring.'"

"Then what? Do I fall to the ground and kiss their feet?"

A hint of a smile curled Darci's lip. "Only if they buy. Now change into your smock and we'll have a bite in the employee's lounge."

The two young women sat at a table, finishing their chicken salads. Most of the lunch crowd had departed, leaving the cafeteria almost empty.

"Why do you keep looking around?" asked Melanie. "Are you expecting someone?"

"No." Darci opened her purse and took out a cigarette. "Never smoke. It's a rotten habit."

"Darci, I've told you everything about me — all my family secrets. Now it's your turn. It's impolite to ask your age, isn't it?"

"Yes. But I was born in New York 26 years ago."

"Why'd you come to San Francisco?"

"I was married to a man who wanted to move here. He promptly fell in love with his secretary. It's so ridiculously cliché. He divorced me, married her, divorced her, and now I hear he's married again. Wouldn't you think, with that track record, a woman would know better?"

Melanie shrugged. "But you're so beautiful. Why would anyone leave you? You must have millions of men chasing you."

"There's only one I want and he's not interested."

"Really? Let's snag him before he gets away. C'mon! I'll help! Let's go after him."

Darci laughed. "This isn't a hog-roping contest." She squashed her cigarette in the ashtray. "Anyway, I've got to do some client-humoring. We have this rich old lady who orders all her clothes by phone. A few months ago, she gave me a half hour of instructions about style, colors and size, and I sent a car full of clothes to her home. They all came back the next day — with no explanation."

"How rude!"

"Well, I happened to see this woman at the theater a few nights later, and I realized she was ordering the size she *used* to wear, not the size she was. So we assembled another batch of clothing, sizes 14 and 16. We removed the tags, replaced them with tags that said sizes 8 and 10, and guess what!"

"She kept everything."

"Gold star. Now, Miss Sassy, are you ready to face the world?"

"No. I want to hear all about your mystery man."

"Nice try, sweetie. But it's time to make a few bucks for the Greenfields."

The first week on the job was rougher than Melanie expected. Having to be dressed, groomed, and wear high heels all day was a chore. By the time she came home to soak her feet, she was exhausted. At one point, she prayed that her drama coach would call and give her an excuse to quit.

But Linda didn't call, and Melanie wouldn't allow herself to give up. Marc and Yvonne had put themselves out to arrange the job, and poor Darci had spent hours trying to make her into a model. She couldn't let them all down.

Besides, it was an education. Little by little, she was tuning in to the retail scene, not particularly liking what she saw, but fascinated by the intrigues, the petty jealousies, the straights who mocked the gays and vice versa, and all the backstage manipulations.

The life of a department store model, she realized, was anything but glamorous and exciting. Most of the customers she saw were snooty dowagers with social-registered names, or spoiled young women who had either married or inherited wealth, and thought nothing of paying several thousand dollars for a dress. They all seemed to feel that spending that kind of money entitled them to special treatment. Good thing they couldn't hear what the sales people said behind their backs.

On the first day of Melanie's second week, Darci was fitting her into a suit, when a male voice boomed, "Ladies, are you decent?"

Before they could answer, Ben Greenfield strode into the dressing room. Built like his grandfather James Tyler Stockton — tall, broad-shouldered, husky as a halfback — his presence was commanding but not intimidating. On the contrary. Darci had told her that the employees thought him a big teddy bear.

"Sorry to bust in on you, but I've been meaning to see my little cousin for a week. How're you doin', Mel? You look sensational."

She giggled. "I feel like a ten-year-old dressed up in her mother's clothes."

Darci plucked a pin from her lips and fastened a silk rose to the lapel. "Don't worry about your 'little cousin,' Ben. She's a survivor."

"I'll bet she is."

"Everyone's been really great to me." Melanie's eyes sparkled. "Except

Darci. She's a slave driver."

"You don't look too mistreated. Well, I can see you ladies are busy. If you need anything, let me know."

"Thanks for stopping by, Ben," said Melanie. "That's really nice of you."

As soon as the door closed, Darci unpinned the rose. "This suit's all wrong on you. Slip on the blue Valentino."

Melanie unbuttoned her jacket. "Wasn't that cute of Ben to come by? I like him better'n his brother. David's a brain surgeon. He's too serious."

"Blue's your color. Definitely."

"Then there's my youngest cousin. I haven't seen him in ages. Do you know Sam?"

"Yes." The answer was clipped and decisive, and seemed to close the subject. "You're swimming in this skirt. Lift the jacket and I'll see if I can pin it."

"Do you ever see him around the store?"

"Who?"

"Sam." Melanie stared at her. "Why are you acting so funny?"

"I'm *working!* Hold still."

"Did you have a run-in with Sam?"

"No."

"Ouch! You don't have to stab me. Did you and Sam go out?"

"None of your business."

"Aha! Methinks we struck gold."

"Melanie, you can be so damned infuriating! Yes, if you must know. We went out."

"And?"

"And nothing."

"You're lying."

Darci slammed down her pincushion. "All right, I'm lying. Sam and I went out for eight months — until just a few weeks ago. We had wonderful times together. Then I had to screw it up by falling in love with him."

Shock froze Melanie's face. Could it possibly be? That raunchy kid with the bushy beard and pony tail? "We *are* talking about Sam Greenfield, aren't we?"

"Do you have a problem with that?"

"No, it's just — well, I haven't seen him since he came to the house ages ago. I was about 12 and I guess he was 17, and a real smarty pants. Then he went off to Wharton."

"Don't you see him at Christmas? Family gatherings?"

"I told you my mom and Nonna, my grandma, don't speak. Nonna has the family on holidays but we don't go. We celebrate with my Dad and Trudy. Sounds like a soap opera, doesn't it. I guess I think of Sam Greenfield as more my generation than yours."

A smile melted Darci's face. "For your edification, Ms. Morris, I am not yet senile. I'm four years older than Sam and it didn't make a whit of difference."

"Then what went wrong?"

"If you must know, I couldn't go on being casual, watching all the beautiful models throw themselves at him. He said he loved me but he wasn't ready to make a commitment."

"Oh, no." A light clicked in Melanie's brain. "Sam Greenfield is your mystery man?" Not waiting for an answer, she ordered, "You *can't* just give up. If you really love him, you have to fight for him."

"The voice of experience."

"I'll go see him. I'll talk to him."

"If you repeat one word of what you just wormed out of me, I will personally mash your skull into sawdust. Capeesh?"

"I can take a subtle hint. But I still don't know why you're mooning over Sam Greenfield. Yuk!"

It didn't take long for Melanie to seek out her youngest cousin. Unlike Ben, who at least had the courtesy to say hello, Sam apparently couldn't be bothered. But in fairness, she hadn't made any effort to see him, either.

Her motive was part curiosity, and part wanting him to see her all dressed up. Besides, he *was* her cousin, and they should acknowledge each other.

Soon after the store opened the next morning, she took the elevator up to Marc's office and poked her head in the door. "Hi, Vicky."

The secretary glanced up coldly. "Yes?"

"I'm looking for Sam's office. Could you please direct me?"

"He's not there. I just saw him walking down the hall."

"Thanks." She turned quickly and rounded the corner. A long-legged figure strode ahead of her. "Sam?"

The man stopped and looked over his shoulder. "Is that you, Melanie?"

"I wasn't sure you'd recognize me." She grinned and walked up to him. "You sure look different."

"And you're all grown up."

She shifted her weight awkwardly, not knowing what to say. Gone was the straggly pony tail, the beard, the arrogant manner. This was a Sam she had never known; clean-shaven, immaculately dressed with a rose in his lapel, strikingly handsome with dark wavy hair and liquid brown eyes. She suddenly felt sad for Darci. Who wouldn't hate to lose such a dreamy-looking guy.

"How's it going?" he asked.

"Uh, it's only my second week. But it's fun, and Darci's teaching me a lot about clothes and makeup and stuff." The bait was out; she awaited his reaction.

"You're lucky. She's a special lady."

"She likes you, too."

A rush of color flooded his face. "Wish I could stay to chat, but I'm late for a meeting."

"Oh, that's okay. I just wanted to say hi."

"Glad you did. Let's have a family pow-wow one of these days." He turned a corner and disappeared.

Melanie stood rooted, letting the shock register. What an incredible-looking couple he and Darci must have made. A wave of empathy swept over her, along with feelings of resentment. Why had Sam been so cruel? With him at her side, Darci had had everything a woman could want. Now all she had were regrets.

Part 5

The *Herald* Angel

In the third floor executive offices of the *San Francisco Herald,* Helen Hopkins pressed a buzzer on the intercom. "I called *The New York Times* again, Lou Ella. I've left two messages with Paul Amory's secretary."

"Keep trying. It's important."

A day later, at last, the call came back. Lou Ella recognized the warm, resonant voice. "You won't remember me, Mr. Amory. We haven't talked in 23 years. But I've followed your career at every turn. I'm a great fan of your column."

"I remember you very well," he said. "How can I help you?"

"I'm calling to ask whether you and your wife would be interested in taking a trip to California, as our guests."

"For what purpose?"

"I have to retire for health reasons. The *Herald* badly needs a fresh infusion of ideas and vitality — a new publisher, to be exact. We're interviewing a few select people and I'm hoping you'll be among them."

"Save your money, Mrs. Stockton. Number one, I have no wife. And number two, I'm quite content where I am."

"Is there anything I can say or do to make you at least think about it?"

He chuckled. "I'm flattered, but no."

"Have you ever been to San Francisco?"

"Briefly. During World War II."

Something clicked in Lou Ella's brain. Suddenly, the facts began to make sense. Yvonne must have known Paul Amory. She was a dynamic beauty in those days and they probably had a romance. "You met my sister-in-law Yvonne during the war, didn't you?"

"Yes. How is she?"

Lou Ella saw her advantage. "Going through hell right now. Her husband's seriously ill with colon cancer, so she has no time for the paper's problems. If you could just take one day off and come, say, Thursday night, you could sit in on our editorial meeting Friday, and be home by Saturday. We're in a bad way, Mr. Amory. Might you reconsider?"

"I'll call you back."

"Ladies and gentlemen, the Captain has turned on the seat belt sign.

We'll be landing at San Francisco International Airport at approximately 4:45 P.M. Pacific Standard Time."

Paul Amory checked his watch. Twenty minutes to go. The sky was bright with sunshine as the plane cleared the clouds and began its slow descent. Paul could hardly believe he was returning to San Francisco for the first time in 36 years. He thought back to himself as a young soldier — brash, idealistic, determined to remake the world.

Somehow, he felt he had failed that young man. As assistant to Abe Ross, executive editor of the world's most influential newspaper, Paul was at the top of his profession — but although he could express his opinions in his weekly column, he couldn't do much about them. Ross was both king and dictator at the *Times,* and had little patience with ideas that weren't his own.

Rows of miniature houses appeared in Paul's window as the plane continued to descend. His thoughts turned back to Yvonne. How he had agonized over the decision, weighing the pros, the cons, wondering what she'd be like, wanting almost desperately to see her, struggling to understand his own motives.

Was he being heroic, coming to the rescue of Yvonne's failing newspaper, or was he being selfish and secretly hoping that her husband...no, no, he couldn't allow himself to think that. And even if it happened, he and Yvonne were different people in different worlds.

He forced himself back to the present. Would he see her that evening? How would he react? Why was he still clinging to romantic memories that should have died decades ago? And why had he dropped everything to fly 3000 miles to help save a failing city newspaper?

The reason was simple: she needed him.

Chapter 35 - 1979

A neatly-lettered placard with his name greeted Paul as he stepped off the ramp into the San Francisco Airport. He approached the sign holder. "I'm Paul Amory."

"Hello, sir, I'm Mr. Stockton's driver."

An older man stepped forward. "And I'm Tim Stockton, Lou Ella's husband. Welcome to our fair city."

Paul smiled, noted the amputation, and shook his host's hand. "World War II?"

"Battle of Tarawa. Yvonne mentioned you were a guest of Emperor Hirohito."

"Yes. The food was wretched and the maid service worse."

Both men laughed as Tim led the way to a white Cadillac parked in the press zone. Tim found himself responding positively to the journalist's easy manner, not to mention his distinguished appearance: six-foot-four inches, topped by thick white hair and handsome features. As a younger man in uniform, he must have been impressive. "Lou Ella and I are very grateful to you for coming out."

"I hope I can be of help. Any news about your brother-in-law?"

"Marc's in bad shape, I'm sorry to say. But Yvonne's going to try to get away for dinner. I hope you're free."

"I have no plans."

"Good." Tim joined Paul in the back seat, delighted to meet the man he had heard about for so many years. He was fascinated to hear Paul's war experiences, and by the time they reached the Fairmont Hotel, they were swapping stories like old war buddies.

To everyone's dismay, however, Marc was having a bad night, and Yvonne wasn't able to leave him, so Tim and Lou Ella took Paul to dinner at Trader Vic's. The next morning, Lou Ella introduced Paul at the *Herald's* editorial meeting, the daily ritual of exchanging ideas and sorting out which news reports deserved headlines.

Paul spent the rest of the day scanning recent issues, touring the offices and printing plant, interviewing editors and reporters, and charming all who were anxious to meet him.

Tim and Lou Ella's Russian Hill penthouse was imposing in its panoramic view of the city, but the owners had no desire for a showplace. Their living room was furnished simply, with overstuffed chairs and sofas, shelves of knick-knacks, classical records, and pre-Columbian sculptures they'd bought in South America. A stack of art books and a faded arrangement of artificial flowers decorated a coffee table.

That evening, Tim puffed his pipe as he sat with Paul Amory, exchanging views on why President Carter's approval rating had dropped so low. Lou Ella excused herself to answer the door, and returned a moment later, followed by Yvonne — flushed and breathless. "Sorry to be late."

Paul stood up quickly. He hadn't been prepared to see her, at least not so suddenly. He'd have planned what to say, rehearsed how to act, done a run-through or two, but she caught him off guard. He was almost afraid to look at her, but he had no choice. He hoped his voice wouldn't betray his emotion. "Hello, Yvonne."

She shook his hand and smiled, no longer feeling the need to pretend anything to Lou Ella. "You're wonderful to come help us with the paper. We're in a terrible bind."

He felt himself blush. The sound of her voice recalled thousands of moments he'd relived in the prison camp. And now there she was standing before him, slimmer and more fragile than he remembered, but just as breathtakingly beautiful. "How's your husband?"

"He was sleeping when I left. Our youngest son, Sam, is with him." Yvonne sat down, and a maid handed her a glass of wine. Paul noticed her hand was trembling.

Lou Ella turned to Paul. If she'd sensed any tension in the air, she wasn't letting on. "Won't you end our suspense and tell us what you found out today?"

Relieved to be able to talk business, he took a small notebook from his pocket, glanced at it, then closed it. "I'm going to speak frankly. Please remember, it's just one man's opinion. If I had to put my first impression into one sentence, I'd say The *Herald* is like Oscar Levant's definition of Hollywood: strip away the tinsel and you find the real tinsel underneath. It's mostly fluff with very little substance."

"We're not *The New York Times*," retorted Lou Ella, defensive.

"He knows that," said Yvonne. "Let him talk."

Unfazed, Paul continued. "To start with, you have too many features and second-rate columnists, and too few investigative reporters. You need to clear away the dead wood and overhaul the newsroom."

Tim's face lit up. "I've been saying that for years!"

"First priority should be to reshape and expand your coverage. Add a World News section. Open a Washington bureau. Consider putting out zoned editions to compete with suburban dailies. Above all, don't give in to machine journalism. Your reporters shouldn't spend the bulk of their time editing U.P. and A.P. copy. They should be writing their own stories."

Lou Ella frowned. "You're talking major expenditures."

"Whatever you invest will come back to you, particularly money you spend to hire top talent."

"We're trying to hire you," said Yvonne, with a hint of a smile.

"I'm flattered, but you don't want me. I'd have to have total authority, and no employee has that. Remember A.J. Liebling's line? 'Freedom of the press belongs to those who own one.' In your case, though, the owners may have to share some authority. Whoever takes over Lou Ella's job at the *Herald* will have to tackle tough subjects. Arouse passion and controversy. And he or she has to know that the owners support him every step of the way."

"We certainly *would* support him," said Lou Ella.

"At the same time, have your staff institute long range planning. The real news isn't just what's happening today. It's what's going to happen tomorrow and all the tomorrows to come. You have a great advantage. You live in a fabulous city where things change rapidly, people feel strongly about issues, people speak their mind. What will San Francisco be like in five years? Will the cable cars survive? The Presidio? Do you need a suicide barrier on the Golden Gate Bridge? Will rents continue to rise?"

Lou Ella heard a pause and jumped in. "I know you're trying to give us a broad impression, but what we really need are specifics. Could you put some ideas in writing?"

"I'll type up my notes as soon as I get back to New York."

"But right now," Lou Ella persisted, "what do you see as our biggest problem?"

Paul exhaled visibly and took a few seconds to think. Then he spoke hesitantly. "I'd have to guess it's television. The tube is stealing your headlines, your readers and your advertising dollars. The only way you can compete is by offering a new depth of investigative journalism — supplying information your readers can't get from the hastily-prepared news broadcasts."

Discussion turned to more worldly subjects at dinner. After the meal, Paul pleaded exhaustion, thanked his hosts and asked to be excused to call a cab for the airport. Yvonne insisted on driving him, and they left the penthouse together.

No sooner had the door closed than Lou Ella turned to her husband. "When did they have their affair?"

"Affair?" Tim asked innocently.

Lou Ella burst into laughter. "You Stocktons can never lie with a straight face. Actually, I can't blame her. That's one gorgeous man!"

Tim grinned. "I rather fancy him myself — aesthetically speaking, that is."

"Are you going to tell me?"

Her expression told him there was no escape. "All right. They met at the Stage Door Canteen, fell in love — or at least infatuation — and he shipped out. They promised to reunite after the war. Eevie waited for him. He wrote that he was going off on a dangerous mission and that was the last she heard from him. Some time later, she learned he was missing in action, and assumed he was dead."

"Enter Marc?"

"Yes, she got married. Then, years later, she found out Paul had been interned in a Japanese prison camp. He thought that the Red Cross had informed Eevie of his imprisonment, but the message never reached her. She thinks Clara saw the Red Cross logo, figured it was a request for money and tossed it out. But the moment Ecvie heard Paul was alive, she flew to Boston, saw him, and came home. That's all I know."

"Is that when they had the affair?"

"You'll have to ask Eevie."

"I don't need to. Did you see the way they looked at each other? They're probably heading for a motel as we speak."

"With Marc in the hospital? Please, dear, give my sister a little credit."

"I give her lots of credit." Lou Ella's eyes flashed with mischief. "If I know your sister, we haven't seen the last of Paul Amory."

A heavy mist cooled the night air, floating over the Bay and enveloping Alcatraz. Pale lights on the Oakland Bridge flickered through the haze. A man, in overcoat and slippers, pattered down the Russian Hill incline, walking his bichon frise. In the distance, a foghorn sounded.

"That brings back wonderful memories," said Paul, as he helped

Yvonne into the car.

Stay calm, she told herself, as he came around to sit beside her. Don't blow it. "I sometimes wish we were those two innocent kids on the beach. Wouldn't it be nice to go back and start our lives over?"

"Regrets are useless," he said gently.

She drove down Hyde Street toward the entrance to the freeway.

"I like your brother," he offered, a minute later. "Does he know about us?"

"Yes."

"He's very much like you: sensitive, intelligent, direct."

"Were you ever married, Paul?"

He laughed. "Not that I know of."

"Why not?"

"If I couldn't have the woman I wanted, I didn't want anyone."

"You could've had me."

"No, you belonged to another. And I'm genuinely sorry about your husband. What's the prognosis?"

"It tears me apart to see him suffer. The doctor says he could go in a month — or a year."

"That's why I came. I knew you were in trouble."

She controlled an impulse to reach for his hand. "I appreciate it more than you know. Is there any way I can persuade you to become our new publisher?"

"No. My life and work are at the *Times*."

"Are you happy there?"

"My boss can be a tyrant. But otherwise, yes."

"You could be 'boss' here. The family holds all the shares and they don't want to lose their biggest investment. Anything you did would be fine with us."

"Thank you." He hesitated a moment. "I didn't want to upset everyone at dinner, but the *Herald*'s problems are considerable."

"I know." She glanced at the clock. Every second was precious. "Tell me about your exciting life. I wanted to write you every time I read you'd won another award, but I knew you'd return my letters."

He smiled. "I had to be strong for both of us. My life has pretty much been all work, no play. I'd rather hear about you and your family."

Conversation flowed easily, as it had the few times they'd been together in the past. When they arrived at the United Airlines entrance, she said, "Please think about our offer. You can name your conditions."

He climbed out with his bag and came around to her side. "The years have been kind to you, Yvonne. You're even lovelier than before."

"Will I see you again?"

"I'm only five hours away if you need me."

I need you now, she wanted to say. I need you to hold me and to help me be strong for Marc and my children. I need you *desperately*. Please don't go away. But all she could murmur was, "Have a safe trip."

Paul's recommendations, impressively thorough, arrived a week later. Carrying them out would require a strong, experienced leader. Lou Ella's letter requesting a bill came back from Paul marked, "No charge; my pleasure." She mailed it to Yvonne, with a note saying, "He's as gracious as he is brilliant."

The next eight months passed slowly for Lou Ella. People had begun to hear reports about a new deadly form of cancer that attacked gay men. The *Herald* always toned down reports that might seem unfavorable to gays, thus earning a reputation as a "fag-rag" — a name Lou Ella didn't mind. She had welcomed articles describing homosexuality as a genetic quality, predetermined by genes. Who would *choose* a lifestyle that made him or her subject to continuous prejudice?

At the same time, she continued her quest for a publisher. The more journalists she interviewed, the more frustrated she became. Paul had spoiled her. No one had his qualifications, or even came close. The stress of a possible strike, the continuing drop in circulation, loss of advertising, and the defection of her executive editor to the *Examiner* — finally landed her in the Intensive Care Unit at St. Francis Hospital.

Tim called Yvonne from the emergency room. Lou Ella survived the coronary, but wouldn't be able to go back to work for months, if at all.

"Oh, Tim darling, I'm so sorry," said Yvonne. "I'll be right over."

"No, you stay home with Marc. How's he doing?"

"He's very weak. He wants me with him every second. What'll we do about the paper? Who's going to run it?"

"You'd better call your friend Paul Amory and get him out here on the double. Otherwise…there won't be a paper to run."

Chapter 37 — 1980

On Monday, April 7, a full-page notice appeared in the *Herald*. Paul had edited the copy several times, anxious to get across his message without embarrassing Lou Ella or her staff. The final version read:

To Our Readers:

Starting today, you will see a series of changes in the Herald. Some will please you, some may not. I hope to hear from you in both cases.

Let me introduce myself. I'm Paul Amory, senior editor at The New York Times. *As many of you know, publisher Lou Ella Stockton is presently recovering from illness. At her request, I've taken a year's leave to serve here as acting editor and publisher of the Herald.*

My goal will be to provide everything you want in a newspaper. We will be enlarging our talented staff with fine journalists recruited from all over the country.

We believe a newspaper must accept responsibility for everything appearing on its pages. Freedom of the press is not freedom to print slanted, morally questionable, or misleading information. To this end, we have made several changes in advertising policy, including the elimination of adult movie listings.

With your help, the San Francisco *Herald will strive to set the highest standards in the nation and continue to be a dominant voice for journalistic integrity.*

Sincerely,

Paul Amory

That same edition, *Herald* columnist Herb Caen wrote: "My new boss, Paul Amory, winner of two Pulitzers and 17 other journalism awards, is quite a prize himself — straight, unmarried, a talented jazz pianist, and a ringer for Gregory Peck. But save your dimes, gals. He says he's 'permanently unavailable,' whatever that means..."

To no one's surprise, Paul's takeover sparked a tidal wave of controversy. Liberals alleged First Amendment violations; the ACLU threatened a class action suit, claiming discrimination against adult movie theater owners; the Newspaper Guild challenged the hiring of out-of-towners, and protested the choice of a non-staff member as temporary publisher.

Perhaps the loudest shouts came from several hundred loyal *Herald* readers, vowing to cancel subscriptions if their favorite feature or columnist wasn't reinstated. Few of the readers, however, carried out their threats.

Eight weeks into the job, Paul received a call from Yvonne. She'd been caring for Marc around the clock, and he hadn't talked to her since he was back. "How's your husband?" was his first question.

"He weighs less than 100 pounds," she answered sadly. "I can't get him to eat."

"Shouldn't he be in the hospital?"

"There's nothing they can do, and he's happier at home."

"I'm so sorry. I hear Lou Ella's improving."

"She's starting to get around, thanks to you. Your coming out in our time of need made all the difference. I can never thank you enough."

"Is that why you're calling?"

"Only partly. Lou Ella came to our family meeting yesterday. I thought you'd want a report."

"By all means."

"Will, my half-brother, wants to reinstate the adult movie ads. He got Katie and Lou Ella — Tim gives her his proxy — to go along because of all the revenue we're losing. But Clara, my cousin Betsy who's very concerned about pornography, and I outvoted him."

"You're the majority shareholders, aren't you? I'm grateful."

"Will wanted to put a lid on your expenditures, too, but we rejected him."

"Will isn't too fond of me?"

"He's afraid you're not going to give gays a voice the way Lou Ella did."

"We don't cater to any group. We report the news. And you can tell Will that we have a reporter spending full time researching this new 'gay cancer' everyone's whispering about."

"Is it that serious?"

"Yes. Tell Will we strongly support the gay community, but we can't ignore a major threat to the community." He lowered his tone. "You shouldn't have to worry about the paper at a time like this."

"I don't worry with you in charge — although Lou Ella thinks you're going to have union troubles."

"We've had them since the day I arrived." His voice grew gentle. "Be strong, Yvonne. Your husband needs you to keep up his spirits. And don't forget, I'm only a phone call away."

Two days later, Tim called Paul with the news of Marc's death. At Marc's request there would be no funeral. Family and close friends were invited to drop by the house that evening. Paul did so, but Yvonne was surrounded. He kissed her cheek, expressed regrets, and left.

Chapter 38 – 1980

The following Friday, Doug Custer, the paper's chief labor negotiator, entered Paul's office. He sank into a chair and threw up his arms. "We've been talking for eight months now. We've settled with all the unions but one. The pressmen won't budge."

Paul put down the mock-up page he was studying. "How does it stand?"

"Still the manning issues. They insist on having one person for each machine. It's crazy. The new machines are triply efficient. One person can easily monitor two or three, but they say it's a safety matter. If we stretch them too thin, they'll start getting careless and lose fingers."

"Bottom line?"

"These guys want to go out. If we give in, it'll cost half a million a year. If we don't, the strike could cost twice that much or more, depending how many advertisers go elsewhere."

Paul pondered a minute. Then he asked, "What about wages?"

"That's the last step. If we can settle this, we'll go to the table to talk pay increases."

"Have they given us a deadline?"

"Not yet. But this guy Oakley who heads the union is one tough bastard. He's itching to hit the picket lines."

"Thanks for the report. You're doing great," said Paul. "Let's talk Monday."

The sky was dark as Paul left the *Herald* Building around seven that evening. He crossed the street to the deli, picked up a pastrami on rye, and headed for the garage. For some reason, he wasn't as tired as usual, and the idea of spending another weekend alone depressed him.

What he missed, he realized, was companionship. He had been so busy since coming to the *Herald*, he hadn't had time to make friends, and he'd instructed his secretary Helen to turn down all invitations. There wasn't anyone in town, except possibly Tim, he felt he knew well enough to call and invite for a beer.

Nor was there any woman in his life, other than the shadowy presence of Yvonne. She was free now, a charming, beautiful widow. But she would be mourning for months, and he respected her grief. The idea that she might once again be "available" was an idea he refused to deal with. She couldn't be expected to move to New York, and at 61, he was too old for a bicoastal romance.

Dreaming about her over the years, however, hadn't kept him from a series of relationships with attractive women, all of whom had left when he refused to make a commitment. How fortunate, he thought, unwrapping the sandwich as he walked, that his libido was not the raging fire it used to be.

He climbed into his car, finished eating, and noticed a neon sign in the distance. "O'Leary's" was the local newspaper hangout he'd heard about. Publishers didn't usually mingle with their employees, but at the moment, he didn't care.

Curious to see the place, he locked the car and strolled down the street. The bar he entered was dark and noisy. Groups of men huddled at tables and clustered along the counter. Waitresses in white shirts and black slacks scurried around with trays of glasses. In the background, a Beatles' tune flowed from an antique juke box. Beside it, a baby grand stood empty, reminding him of how much he missed the piano in his New York apartment.

Paul perched on a stool and warmed his drink several minutes. Then he motioned to the bartender. "Anyone play the Steinway?"

"Yeah, a guy comes in at nine."

"Mind if I try?"

"You any good?"

"If you like Fats Waller." Paul slid a ten dollar bill under his glass, crossed the room, and took a seat at the piano bench.

A burly black man was about to drop a quarter in the juke box. "Hey, you gonna play?"

Paul nodded and hit the keys, softly at first. His left hand walked the bass with a steady beat. Then his right hand chimed in the melody.

The onlooker listened with rapt attention. "Hey, man, where you learn stride piano?"

"Just picked it up. Recognize this?" Suddenly, Paul came alive. His fingers skipped across the keyboard, rolling out chords and arpeggios in fast, upbeat rhythm. Without dropping a note, he loosened his tie, opened his collar, and began to warble: "Every honey bee, filled with jealousy, when they see you out with me..."

Several men came over to crowd around the piano. A couple pushed aside a table to jitterbug. Paul sat spellbound, lost in his music. His hands ran wild over the ivories, suddenly transforming the gloomy O'Leary's into a lively tavern.

"Hey, Fats!" yelled a customer. "How 'bout 'Your Feet's Too Big'?"

"Well, all right then!" Paul grinned, his head bobbing and weaving. His fingers ripped across the keys as he boomed out the lyrics.

"St. Louis Blues," called another.

"Yes, yes," he cried. "Beedle, daddle, deedle, daddle, yaddle, deedle, do. Whoopee!" He launched into "Ain't Misbehavin'," followed by "Lulu's Back in Town," and worked up to a foot-stamping frenzy with "The Joint Is Jumpin'."

The crowd went crazy. Hoots and whistles filled the air. Paul threw back his head and laughed aloud for the first time in months. He forgot who he was. He forgot where he was. He forgot everything but the knowledge that he could play Thomas "Fats" Waller till his soul cried out.

When the regular pianist arrived at nine, Paul stood up and bowed to his wildly applauding audience. Politely refusing drink offers, he made his way to the exit. As he stopped to wipe his brow under the light at the door, he heard a startled voice exclaim, "Holy shit! Do you know who that *was*?"

Monday morning, Paul called back his labor expert, Doug Custer. He told him he wanted to see Oakley, the "tough bastard" who was holding up the union settlement. Custer protested. Publishers didn't get involved at that level. More important, Paul had no idea of the subtleties of the negotiating process.

Paul insisted. Custer stalked off. Twenty minutes later, a man in overalls appeared in the executive office.

"Come in, Mr. Oakley." Paul walked up and shook hands. His visitor looked to be in his late thirties, with a bright, fresh face and determined eyes. He reminded Paul of himself at that age. "Please have a seat."

"Thank you, sir."

"Let's get right to basics. I don't think your people in the pressroom want a strike any more than we do. Correct?"

"No one wants a newspaper strike, Mr. Em'ry, except possibly the radio and TV stations. But we'll do whatever we have to."

"Call me Paul. Are you willing to compromise?"

"I'm not willing to risk the safety of my workers."

"Nor am I. The safety of every man and woman on these premises is my personal responsibility. But we both know this is a question of jobs. Suppose we keep everything status quo: one person, one machine."

"What are you saying?"

"I'm saying that we'll give you what you want. In return, I would only ask, that when the people manning these machines retire, we have the option of replacing or not replacing them."

"No dice. We'd have no guarantee that you wouldn't eliminate the jobs entirely."

"Let's be realistic. In a few years, our presses will be obsolete. The new ones won't need monitors. You won't be able to make a case for them. This way, at least you'll be protecting the current jobs of your people."

Oakley took time to think. "Well, maybe. I'll have to see it in writing. Then I'll submit it to the members."

"Understood. Do we have a verbal agreement?"

"I guess so." A smile crept across Oakley's face. "That is, if you answer one question: Where'd you learn to play hot jazz?"

Paul felt himself redden. "Were you there Friday night?"

"Hanging all over the piano. I'd never heard of Fats Waller, but I went out and bought two of his records the next day. That guy could really cut it. And you ain't too bad."

"Thanks. To answer your question, I taught myself."

"No kidding." Oakley opened the door and grinned over his shoulder. "D'ya ever play parties?"

News of the agreement spread quickly through the paper. Doug Custer was annoyed that Paul had conceded so much, and begged him not to interfere in future negotiations. Both sides still had to agree on issues involving fringe benefits, pay increases, and length of contract. Labor wanted a two-year deal before renegotiating; management offered three. After two months of futile efforts, the unions delivered an ultimatum. If they didn't have a contract by midnight of the following Friday, they would hit the streets.

At this final, tense stage of talks, the summit meeting moved downtown to the Sir Francis Drake Hotel. Both union leaders and management took blocks of rooms. When their intense, often bitter debates lasted into the night, they would grab a few hours sleep, then be back at the bargaining table before dawn.

Talks, however, continued to stall. The deadline loomed imminent, so Paul decided to intervene. For three days and the better part of three nights, he sat with the union leaders, arguing, cajoling, controlling his temper and refusing to stoop to name-calling. He stood firm where he thought he should, conceded where he thought it fair, and toward the end, even when he thought it unfair. Eventually, he was able to hammer out a package acceptable to both sides.

He immediately called Yvonne and asked her approval. She phoned Betsy, who'd inherited her mother's 40 percent of the stock, and agreed to go along with whatever Yvonne wanted. Still, that was only 50 percent of the stock, and wanting to be sure, Yvonne phoned Tim. He was willing, and when Lou Ella balked at the expenditure, Tim took back his proxy so he could support Paul and his sister. With 60 percent of the directors' votes assured, and only a few hours until midnight, Paul averted what would have been a calamitous strike. It was, Tim said later, a bloody miracle.

Chapter 39 — 1980

The settlement did much to ease tensions at the *Herald*. Despite the cost, Paul felt confident he had acted in everyone's best interest. Word got around that the *Herald's* transformation was showing promise. Their newly-opened Washington bureau was sending back first-hand inside reports. Local and national stories were being fully investigated and documented. Longtime "fluff" features, the *Herald's* mainstay for more than two decades, gave way to witty satirists, acid-voiced critics, and the finest syndicated columnists.

Readers' comments, at first mostly negative, now grew increasingly positive. Thanks to special editions designed for the suburbs, circulation rose slightly, while local sales remained stable, an improvement from their downward trend.

Toward the end of the year, Paul began to think about going home. His 12-month leave would end March 1, 1981, and his employer, so said a friend at the *Times,* was getting impatient. Much as Paul hated to leave the *Herald* in less capable hands while the Stocktons searched for a replacement, it was either that or lose his job.

By mid-February, the *Herald's* circulation had begun to rise, despite the jabs of several newspapers who dismissed the disease reports as gay-bashing. All rumors about the "gay disease" became sadly true, however, when the Center for Disease Control reported cases of a rare pneumonia and skin cancer among gay men.

On a more positive note was the fact that in less than a year, Paul had managed to transform a struggling daily into a widely-read newspaper that was gaining respect among its peers. When Yvonne read the figures, she called Paul to offer congratulations.

"Thanks," he said. "I think we're finally on track. How're you doing?"

"Trying to get my life in order. Marc was such a pack-rat. My son Sam's been helping me go through his files."

Paul was silent a moment. Then he said. "I'll be leaving in two weeks."

"I know. I wish there was some way to say thank you."

"You just did."

"The offer of a permanent position still holds."

"I'd like very much to stay. But I have obligations."

"Will I see you before you go?"

"I think it's best if we don't."

"But why? Marc's been gone almost ten months. Is there any reason we can't be friends?"

"I'm being selfish," he said softly. "I don't want to have to say good-bye to you again."

At Paul's request, no fanfare or parties accompanied his departure, nor would he allow anyone to drive him to the airport. Tim and Lou Ella, effusive in their gratitude, had presented him with a Patek-Philippe watch. Many of his staff, including those who had originally opposed him, made a point to shake his hand. His farewells were quick and clean, his emotions restrained. Once on the plane, he tried to look forward to getting home, but all he could think about was what — and whom — he had left behind.

The porter at the airport broke the handle of his suitcase, the cab driver overcharged, and a notice under the door of his apartment announced a major rise in rent. Welcome back to the Big Apple...worms and all.

His return to work was hailed by a few colleagues, but otherwise unnoticed. Once at his desk, he slid easily into his old routine. Yet nothing was the same as before. The *Herald* was always on his mind. Who was handling the daily decisions? The disputes? The crises? Would all his efforts be wiped away by his successor? If the paper went under, what would it do to Yvonne?

One day, shortly before Easter, a telegram arrived from Tim. "About to sign long-term contract with new publisher," it read. "Hate to take second-best."

"Damn!" Paul slammed down the wire. His thoughts went first to Yvonne, then to the newspaper. The *Herald* was *his* baby — *his* protégé. How he dreaded picking it up one day and seeing it reduced to its former standards. He'd been thinking a lot about it recently, knowing the family had to hire a new publisher. And now the reality jarred him. This was his last chance to see a year's effort and a lifetime of journalistic experience fulfill their promise. Impulsively, not even knowing what he was going to say, he grabbed the phone.

A maid answered, then went to get Tim.

"Hello, Paul," he said cheerily. "You got my wire?"

"Yes. How're you doing? How's Lou Ella?"

"Everyone's fine, except Eevie. She hasn't been the same since you left. She can't seem to understand why you're there and she's here." He paused a few seconds before asking, "You do love my sister, don't you?"

"I've always loved her." The words escaped before Paul could stop them.

"You were happy at the *Herald*, weren't you?"

"Yes, very."

"This chap who wants your job — he's tough and hard. Not like you, Paul. You never became cynical. You didn't say much, but you knew exactly what was going on, and you cared about the people you worked with."

"I still care."

"Then why in God's name aren't you here? Eevie wants you, Lou Ella wants you, the whole goddamn staff wants you, and I want you, too."

Paul took a moment to consider. The *Times* was a big grinding machine that would thrive with or without one columnist. He had gone as far as he could in his position. By contrast, the situation was almost entirely dependent on him at the *Herald*. Somewhere along the way, San Francisco and the *Herald* had become his home; New York was the foreign country. "Does Yvonne know you sent the wire?"

"No. I didn't want to raise her hopes."

"Don't say a word to her. Just give me two weeks to get things in order."

Tim could hardly contain himself. "Does that mean what I think?"

"Tear up the new guy's contract," Paul answered, with a lift in his voice. "And tell him to keep the hell out of my office."

A flood of lights blazed outside the Greenfield house as Tim's white Cadillac approached.

Paul peered through the window. "Looks like she's expecting the Pope. I thought this was a surprise."

"Relax, old boy," said Tim. "I told her I was bringing over the new publisher. She thinks it's the other guy. Well, get out!"

"Aren't you coming in with me?"

"No. The reunion belongs to the two of you."

Paul clasped Tim's hand, then climbed out of the car. Walking to the house, he tried to still his fears. On the plane, he'd tortured himself thinking about all that could go wrong. Despite Tim's assurance that there was no other man, and that Yvonne's feelings for him hadn't changed, he felt worried and nervous. What if she didn't share his depth of feeling? What if she still loved Marc? What if her children didn't like him? What if…?

"Help me, God," he murmured as he pressed the bell.

A moment later, Yvonne opened the door. Paul held his breath. He had never seen her look lovelier. Blue silk hostess pajamas outlined her gentle silhouette. The faintest touch of makeup illumined her features.

"P — Paul?" she stammered, stunned.

"Either that or a damn good imitation." He grinned. "Are you going to ask me in or do I stand here shifting my weight like a nervous suitor?"

The word "suitor" seemed to affect her. "Yes, yes, come in, of course. Is Tim — ?"

"He's waiting in the car. He wanted me to surprise you alone."

"But what? How?"

"How I got here is immaterial. What I'm doing here depends on you. How do you feel about older men?"

His question made her relax into a smile, still not daring to believe her senses. "Tim said he was bringing over the new publisher. Does that mean —? Oh, Paul, tell me I'm not having some crazy dream."

"We're both dreaming, sweetheart — a dream that's about to come true. We've wasted too much time apart. I know I'm not being coy or smooth. I just know what's in my heart, what's always been in my heart. Whatever years we have left, I want to spend them with you."

Yvonne began to cry, softly. "I never dared to believe this could happen," she whispered. "I wouldn't even let myself pray for it. I was sure my life was over, and now — now it's about to begin again. Oh, Paul, I couldn't bear to lose you a third time. Are you really back for good?"

"For good. For bad. Forever, if you want me."

"I want you desperately, but only if you promise never to leave me again."

He opened his arms wide and gently enfolded her. "I promise, my darling. I promise with all my heart and soul. This time, I'm here to stay."

Chapter 40 — 1983

San Franciscans were in an upbeat mood. 1982 had seen the 49ers beat the Cincinnati Bengals to win the Super Bowl. The locals fervently hoped this achievement would help dilute their kook-city image.

The town was brimming with growth and promise. Despite the politics and red tape delaying the Yerba Buena Gardens, a major redevelopment project, the $125 million George Moscone Convention Center finally opened. Paul Amory, publisher of the *San Francisco Herald*, hailed the occasion as the start of a new era.

Plans for low-cost housing flourished. Some projects materialized, some went to redevelopment heaven. Real estate prices soared, as residents, particularly gays, converted the Victorian houses of the Castro and Noe Valley into picturesque "painted ladies."

Taxi drivers were among the few who profited while the city's 110-year-old cable car system underwent renovation. It took two years and $64 million, but was hailed as one of Mayor Dianne Feinstein's finest achievements. In her own words: "We have risen from the ashes before. We will do it again."

The sound of a bell startled Melanie Morris. She jumped from her chair and pressed a buzzer to open the door to her Nob Hill apartment building. Then she dashed to her closet and changed her sweatshirt for a sweater. She reached the hall just as the elevator stopped.

A short, dapper man of indeterminate age emerged. He was neatly dressed in suit, bow-tie and vest, carried an ivory-tipped cane, and walked with a limp. Dark glasses and a bristly mustache failed to hide an accusing glare. "You forgot about me, didn't you."

Melanie pecked his forehead. "Not for a second, Damon. I was just going through my pictures, trying to decide whether to send a head shot or a composite with my resumé."

"Oh, Lordy. Choose your best head shot and send one — *only* one. That's the advice I gave Michael Douglas when he was a college student. And he hasn't done too poorly."

"All thanks to your advice."

"Trust me, ducky. I've been in this racket for 25 years."

More like 40, she thought, with amusement. Damon DuBray was

a braggart, a poseur, and like many in the theater, a compulsive name-dropper. His "good friends" generally turned out to be people he'd seen on a stage somewhere, or spotted across a room. Nevertheless, under all the bluster was a man who knew theater better than any coach Melanie had ever had, and whose friendship she had come to treasure.

They had met in 1980, three years prior, when Damon, a visiting professor, led a workshop in group improvisation. Melanie had not been a top student, but after a term of his private tutoring, she had begun to show promise.

"You look marvelous, buttercup," he said approvingly. "I take it you survived graduation?"

"Barely. But I got my degree, so Mom's happy." She took his arm and led him into her study, a large room cluttered with movie memorabilia. Atop the mantel, a cut-out of Scarlett O'Hara flanked a plaster Oscar. Beside it stood a marble bust of Alfred Hitchcock. Framed posters shared wall space with shelves of film star biographies, plays, and textbooks, on every theatrical subject from Auditions to Ziegfeld.

She pulled a stool up to his chair. "Did you see the papers this morning? David Niven died."

"Poor chap. As charming in person as he was on the screen. We used to double-date on the Riviera." He took a gold watch from his vest. "Now let me get this correct. You're reading for the Golden Gate Repertory Players?"

"Yes, and I'm dying to play Antigone. I don't have a single leading role on my resumé. My agent will want that."

Damon took off his sunglasses. "You have an agent?"

"Not yet, but I will. I have a trust fund from my grandmother."

"I seem to be missing something." He pulled a handkerchief from his pocket, shook it open, and wiped his lenses. "Do you plan to go to the agent store, pluck someone off the shelf, and pay the cashier?"

"No, but I plan to write on my resumé that I have independent means. I'm willing to work absolutely free until I make a name for myself."

"And some top agent's supposed to leap at the chance to make fifteen percent of nothing?"

"Well — just in the beginning."

Damon leaned forward and took her hands. "Dear pussycat, how

184

naive can you be? You must know that hundreds of college drama departments spew out thousands of drama majors every year. So do charm schools, modeling schools, acting schools, beauty pageants, talent contests, and the like. These would-be Gables and Garbos are every bit as willing to work their derrieres off — not to mention other parts of the anatomy — in exchange for experience."

"I'm different. I'm going to be a star."

"Do tell." His sigh was audible. "Well, pass me that script, Miss Hepburn. But just remember, if the casting director sees Antigone as a big-boned woman with black hair, you could give the finest reading in the world and not be chosen."

"Why do I get the feeling you're preparing me?"

"Because now that I've said that, I can also say that I think you've as good a chance as anyone. Shall we begin? Remember, this is the last time you'll ever see your lover, Haemon. Take a minute to think how you feel about that. Close your eyes. Focus. Concentrate..."

Long after Damon's departure, Melanie lay in bed, the lines from Antigone running through her head like the pesky lyrics of an advertising jingle. Tempted as she was to feel sorry for herself for having chosen such a daunting profession, she also realized her blessings. Very few struggling actresses lived in a two-bedroom penthouse, or had a mother who supported them both emotionally and financially.

Ever since she started Stanford, Katie had been solidly behind her, letting her live her life and make her own mistakes. Unlike Melanie's friend Carolyne, who'd left college early to get married and was already divorced, Melanie hadn't had any serious romances. She'd gone steady several times and lost her virginity, one moonlit night, to a fellow actor. Marriage, however, had never tempted her.

In February, when Melanie turned twenty-one, Katie had made her a gift of her 10,000 shares in the Stockton Corporation. Melanie was thrilled to be a full-fledged board member, to have a seat at meetings, and ten percent of a say in all matters pertaining to the *Herald*, including the television station and the company's real estate holdings.

She particularly enjoyed seeing her family in action. Paul and Yvonne, the lovebirds, always attended together, but he did the voting, as if the shares were his. Betsy, now increasingly concerned with "morality" issues, usually voted with Yvonne. Tim rarely came, letting Lou Ella vote his proxy. Clara and Will usually voted as a team. The interplay was fascinating — a challenging new world — and Melanie was as happy to take on the responsibility as Katie was to shed it.

Not that Katie and Melanie didn't have scenes. They had screamed themselves hoarse when Melanie decided to move out of the house after graduation. But the battles were over, they were close again, and Melanie often wished there was some gift she could give her mother that money couldn't buy.

The answer came to her in a dream that night. She saw herself standing at an altar in a long, black gown, holding her hands over Katie and Nonna and saying, "I now pronounce you mother and daughter. You may kiss and make up."

By morning, however, the dream was a haze. And all that mattered, for the moment, was getting the role she longed for.

The call came for Melanie the day after the reading. "It's Shane from Golden Gate Repertory. Frightfully sorry you didn't get the lead, darlin'. I'm afraid we need a strong, willful woman who can stand up to Creon, not a wispy blonde with a soft voice."

"Oh, damn!"

"Hold on, there's good news, too. We think you'd be smashing as Ismene, who's weak and gutless. Does that interest you?"

"Yes, I'll do it. Who's understudying Antigone?"

"That role's not for you, sweets. Be here at noon tomorrow."

The Greek tragedy ran for six weeks, from November third through to December fifteenth, barely filling a 200-seat theater in the Mission District. "Downtown Arts" called the production "compelling," and wrote: "Among the supporting players, Roselyne Rafelle was excellent as the nurse, Andy Opperman made a convincing lover, Melanie Morris was effective as the sister, Ismene."

And then it was over. Weeks of rehearsals, and nothing to add to her resume but an afterthought in a local throwaway.

Damon, her drama coach, had shown up on preview night, and suggested she ask Paul Amory to send the *Herald's* drama critic, but Melanie had declined. She liked her new uncle too much to beg a favor.

Her mom, Katie, had attended the opening with Christi and Bill, and her dad, Jason, and Trudy, had shown up the next evening, despite Melanie's plea not to blink or they'd miss her. All agreed she should have been Antigone.

Chapter 41 – 1983

The night the play closed, the cast gave themselves a party in the wings. Melanie, changed into street clothes, chatted with the director till a handsome young man walked over. His head tilted as he rubbed his hair with a towel. "Did I get all the gray out? Do I look youthful again?"

"You look positively fetal." She smiled. "You were a brilliant Creon, Alex. I'm going to miss watching you strut about the stage."

"You won't have to miss me. I'm not going anywhere, except to my brother's house."

"Well, I'm going home. And I hate good-byes, so let's —"

"Have you eaten?"

His question startled her. Alex Brandon had become a good friend during the run of the play. Watching him boast and bluster as the tyrant king, listening to his beautifully-articulated soliloquies, she developed great respect for him as an actor, as well as a secret attraction. The gold wedding band on his hand, however, marked the boundaries of their friendship.

"Is that an invitation?"

"I'd be honored if you'd share a pizza with me. I'd offer you one of your own, but I've only got seven bucks."

She laughed. "Where's Madeline?"

"Maddy, I expect, is either at the flat, packing up the last of my belongings, or else depositing them at my brother's front door. She filed divorce papers Friday."

"Oh, Alex, I'm so sorry." The revelation didn't surprise her. Madeline had seemed sullen and hostile the one time they'd met.

He dropped his towel on a chair. "My wife wanted two things I couldn't give her right now: a steady paycheck and a baby. But look, Mel. I don't need a shoulder to cry on. I'd just like to be with you, if you're not too tired."

"I'm not." A minute ago, she had felt exhausted. "Is your heart set on pizza or could I tempt you with a Swiss on sourdough? I'd love to show you my apartment."

He smiled and took her arm. "How'd you know I'm a cheese-nut?"

Long past midnight, Alex leaned back on the couch with his arm around Melanie. Beside them on the coffee table, a silver bucket held an upside-down champagne bottle.

"I can't remember when I've had a nicer evening," she murmured, snuggling up to him, "even if I am a bit tipsy."

"We both needed to relax tonight. May I tell you something I'll regret in the morning?"

"It is morning, so you might as well tell me."

He inhaled, as if drawing in courage. "I've had a crush on you since the day we met. It had nothing to do with the breakup of my marriage."

"How could it? You never even flirted with me."

"Maddy didn't think so, but that's another story. I keep remembering the scene where Antigone says to Haemon: 'Ismene is pink and golden — like a fruit,' because you *are* pink and golden, like a delicate peach."

"A pickled peach at the moment."

"You're wonderful. I never imagined you'd so much as look my way, much less spend an evening with me." He raised her chin and kissed her lightly. "You wouldn't believe the fantasies I've had about you."

"I've had a few, too."

"Tell me."

"Oh, girl fantasies are different from boy fantasies. I dream about romance. One time we met at this masquerade ball in Italy. We wore masks, but we felt this enormous attraction."

"Do tell. Go on."

"An orchestra was playing — we danced till daybreak. Then we parted, knowing we'd meet again without our masks, and recognize each other immediately."

"I like my fantasies better."

"I'll bet you do." She laughed. "Do you think you'll ever go back to your wife?"

"Not while I'm drawing breath." He cupped her face in his hands and kissed her again, this time with intensity. "Dear Melanie," he whispered, "Let's go get comfortable."

Several weeks into her affair with Alex, Melanie became aware of character traits she hadn't seen before. Despite a myriad of talents she envied, Alex lacked the most essential one — ambition.

"Don't you want to be a famous movie star?" she once asked him. "Don't you want to earn zillions of dollars endorsing zit creams and dandruff shampoo?"

"You remind me of my mother," he said. "Dad was a schoolteacher, and she was always after him to ask for a raise. One day, she was bitching to a friend, and the friend said, 'Does your husband make you happy?' My mother said, 'Yes,' and the friend said, 'Then he's the most successful man in the world.'"

The message communicated, and Melanie said no more. All she knew, sadly, was that their relationship had no future.

The lease on her apartment was due to expire in six months. By then, she would be ready to move to Hollywood. She felt sure she would land a screen test, with or without Damon's help. His offer to write friends on her behalf, made her wonder if his "friends" would even know his name.

One evening in February, as she and Alex sat reading and half-watching television, an announcer spoke of *"nucular"* weapons.

"*Nuclear*, idiot!" screamed Alex. "Why do these assholes have to crucify our language?"

"You have such perfect diction," she said casually. "Why don't you try to get into radio or TV journalism?"

"Any moron can read a TelePrompTer."

"But only morons say 'nucular'. Let's send your resumé to the local stations. The worst they can do is ignore you."

"I'm an actor, not a news reporter."

"You're also broke."

"How kind of you to point that out. Tell you what, Ms. Pushy. If you're so anxious for me to get into radio or TV, *you* send the goddamn resumés." He buried his head in the latest issue of Theater Arts.

"Okay, I will. And guess what — I'm going to be your agent."

Six weeks passed without a single reply. Reluctantly, Alex agreed to let Melanie drive him around to the radio stations. The scene replayed itself everywhere. A receptionist shunted them to the personnel office where he filled out a form.

She even phoned KSTO, the family-owned TV station. Without dropping names, she talked her way into an interview. A harried little man in shirt sleeves saw them for two minutes, then dismissed them. The executive at Channel 3 was even more brusque. By the time they got back to her apartment, they were tired and discouraged.

"We'll try some out-of-town stations next," she said. "Everyone says that's where you get experience. I'm sorry we wasted the day."

Melanie's head was buried in a script for an audition the next morning when the phone rang.

"Ms. Morris?" said a voice. "This is Joe Mariano at Channel 3. You were in my office yesterday."

"Oh, yes, Mr. Mariano. Alex isn't here right now —"

"I'm not calling Alex, I'm calling you. Didn't you say you two were in a play together — that you've had acting experience?"

"Yes."

"Well, I'd like to talk to you. Can you come by this afternoon? Say, two o'clock?"

"Just me?"

"That's right. Bring your resumé."

Melanie hung up the phone in a daze, not daring to think of the possibilities. She ran to the bathroom, slapped cold cream on her face and set her hair in rollers. Then she went into the kitchen and began to make spaghetti sauce. Anything to keep busy. Anything to keep from thinking about what she'd tell Alex. Anything to keep her heart from pounding itself right out of her body.

Chapter 42 – 1983

Thanks to Damon's insistence on punctuality, Melanie arrived five minutes early for the appointment. A security guard checked her I.D. and admitted her to the ultra-modern building that housed KSAF-TV, one of the three top local stations. The stark decor seemed much less intimidating than the previous day.

Joe Mariano was on the phone when she found him in his cubicle. He waved, motioned her to a chair, growled, "Then get the damn thing fixed!" and slammed the receiver.

"Equipment trouble," he muttered, leaning forward. His short, wiry body seemed coiled to spring. "Let's not waste time, Melanie. Tell me about yourself."

"Glad to." She blessed Damon for having schooled her in the art of being interviewed. Mariano's request was the standard opener and she was prepared, neither hesitating nor stammering as she gave a summary of her credits.

He was thoughtful a moment before asking, "Are you interested in working here? That is, if you qualify, and a barrel of other ifs."

"Oh, yes!" Exposure was what she needed. Name recognition is power, Damon always told his students, and a temporary television job would look well on her resume. "Maybe I should tell you, my uncle just became general manager of Channel 1. I hope that's no problem."

"Your uncle is Will Stockton?" Mariano folded his arms. "Why haven't you gone to him for a job?"

"This was your idea, Mr. Mariano. I've never thought of a career in television. I'm an actress."

"Suppose we hired you, and he decided he wanted you to work for him. What would you do?"

"That would depend on what he offered and what kind of contract you and I had."

The girl was no fool. "All right, you've been straight with me. I'll be straight with you. I like your looks. Our cameras fall in love with pretty blondes. If you photograph as well as I think you will, and speak as well as you seem to, we can use you. Our weekend weather girl is going on maternity leave. But I'd need some assurance that if we train you and promote you, you'll stick with us for the term of your contract."

"I doubt Uncle Will would steal me away. But I'll call and talk to him before I sign anything."

"Fair enough. Have you time to do a quick camera audition? They're set up for you in Studio D, down the hall."

"I didn't bring any makeup."

"They'll take care of you." He extended a hand. "Good luck, Melanie. I hope it works out."

Several weeks later, in the outer Broadway mansion where she had lived for almost twenty years, Katie Stockton Morris stood at her bedroom window, admiring the masses of blooming roses. What good fortune to have had the services of Tommy Church, said to be the best landscape architect in California, shortly before he died. "Morrrrning," sing-songed a voice.

Katie tightened the sash of her robe. "Come in."

The door opened, and her loyal housekeeper Christi entered, wearing street clothes. "Coffee, croissants, and your usual Sunday special," she announced, setting down a tray.

"Thanks. What are you and Bill up to today?"

"We're playing carpenter, Mrs. Morris. Bill's going to build shelves for my mother's room."

"How nice of him." Katie's thoughts drifted back to the frightened teenager she had hired to help with her baby. Christi had just run away from a mother she hated — the same mother who now came to visit her twice a month. "Don't work too hard, Christi. See you tomorrow."

Katie sat down to her breakfast. She liked Sundays, the only day she had the house to herself, and could patter about in her robe and slippers, or throw on a pair of old jeans and work in the garden. She started to pour her coffee, when a figure appeared in the doorway.

"Hi, Mom!" Breathless with excitement, Melanie entered the room, planted a kiss on her mother's forehead, and pulled up a chair.

"What a nice surprise!"

"I came to tell you my good news. I'm going to be on television."

Katie looked confused. "On Will's station?"

"No, Mom, Channel 3 hired me last week. It's only on weekends, but if they like me, it could lead to other things." She told about the interview and studio test, and subsequent offer of a 13-week contract. "Aren't you glad that no talent agent has whisked me off to be a movie star?"

"I'm relieved. I kept thinking of all those lunatics in Hollywood. What about Alex?"

"Oh, that's over. He accused me of flirting with the news director behind his back, which I wasn't. Anyway, I hear he's moved in with some sweet young thing barely out of puberty."

"Are you upset?"

She giggled. "Distraught. By the way, I called Uncle Will before I signed the contract. I told his secretary I might go to work for Channel 3. He called back and wished me luck — couldn't have been nicer."

Katie's face softened as she smiled at her daughter. Thanks to some miracle, Melanie had not only inherited Clara's beauty, but her spunk and spirit as well. "When do you start?"

"Saturday, May fifth." She picked a croissant off the tray and began to nibble. "I saw Dad yesterday. Did you know that his father, Grandpa Morris, died?"

"Yes, the head of the Nursing Home called me. I've been paying his bills for years."

"Wow, that was generous of you." Melanie digested the information, then sank back in her chair. "Mom, I'm scared stiff about this TV job. What if I make a major ass of myself?"

"You won't, dear. You'll do fine."

"Damon's going to help me. He's got a friend with a video camera so I can see how I'll look on the screen." She reached for a glass of orange juice.

"Uh, don't drink that. It's got my vitamins in it."

Melanie sighed. "Vodka for breakfast?"

Katie emptied the glass in a few quick gulps. "I have to go work in the garden. Good luck, dear, and let me know when to watch you."

Part 6

Sam

"Beams of moonlight streamed through the window as the bride-to-be lay sleeping..."

A rap at the door broke Sam Greenfield's concentration. "Damn!" he muttered. Every time he tried to sneak in a few minutes of writing, someone interrupted. Saving the work on his computer, he quickly replaced it with a spreadsheet. "Come in."

A young woman with short reddish-brown hair, flawless features, and a trim figure encased in pants, entered his office and handed him a card. "Pat Stark from the *Herald*. Hope I'm not too early."

Sam rose and offered his hand. Darned if she wasn't the image of his heroine — not as feminine, perhaps, with that austere hairdo and man-tailored slacks, but every bit as good-looking. "Hello, Pat Stark from the *Herald*. You're a very pretty lady. Do you believe in love at first sight?"

"Hmmm. That's a no-win question. If I say yes, I'm a flirt. If I say no, I'm an iceberg."

He grinned and motioned to a chair. "Seriously, aren't you awfully attractive to be a reporter?"

"Where is it written that female reporters have to be dogs?"

"It's sort of unwritten." He sat down. "Care for coffee? Juice? Me?"

"No, thanks. As a matter of fact, I'm getting married in three weeks." A hint of a smile crossed her lips. What a gorgeous-looking hunk he was. And what a tease! "You're quite a contrast to your brother. Ben's serious."

"Yup, I'm the family joke. Benny and Dave got the brains."

"Ben says you got the looks."

"That and ten cents will get you a dime."

"Why do you keep putting yourself down?"

"Because I'm a misfit." Sam shrugged. She was a reporter and he knew to be cautious, but she wasn't taking any notes. "Benny's 41, only ten years older than I. He took over when Dad left us, and he's done brilliantly. Dave's a neurosurgeon in Marin. They both have kids, dogs, and wives who drive station wagons. They've found their niches. And I'm still circling the earth, trying to find a place to land."

"What are you looking for?"

"I wish I knew. Um — this is all off the record, right?"

Pat Stark took a tape recorder from her purse and set it on his desk.

"Now we are *on* the record." She wasted no time with fillers. "Your mother's a Stockton. She's Protestant and your father's Jewish. And what are you?"

Sam chuckled. "Ever met a gentile named Samuel Isaac Greenfield?"

"Does your mother care?"

He wondered why his questioner never smiled; maybe she had bad teeth. "My mother wanted us to be able to choose our religion when we grew old enough. Dad didn't. He sent us to Sunday School when we were five, so we grew up Jewish. Say, what does this have to do with your story? What's it about again?"

"Family-run corporations. Is this your office?"

"More or less." He glanced around at the custom-built furniture, the file case camouflaged in an antique cabinet, the handsome Cynthia Schuman acrylic on the wall. His own elegant setting on the seventh floor of S. Greenfield & Co. made him feel uncomfortable.

She followed his eyes. "What do you do for the corporation?"

"I've had a dozen different jobs since I came here ten years ago. Right now, I'm head of security."

"Do you feel that a family-run corporation has closer ties to all of its employees?"

Sam pondered. He disliked giving interviews, but he answered her questions with good-natured patience. Finally, to his relief, she returned the tape machine to her purse and stood up. "Ben said something about your wanting to be a mystery writer. Are you any good?"

"I don't know. I've never shown my writing to anyone."

"Would you like an unbiased opinion?"

"Thanks, no. I'm — wait a minute." He stared at her with sudden interest. "Why shouldn't I show you my book? All you can do is tell me it's hopeless and I already know that."

He opened a drawer and extracted a thick folder. Hand it over quickly, he told himself, while he still had the nerve. "You'll be honest with me?"

"Brutally. You have other copies?"

"Yes, one."

Nodding, she packed the papers in her briefcase and shook his hand. "Nice meeting you, Sam. Would you be available for pictures next week?"

"Sorry." He smiled as he reached for the door. "I don't do photos."

Chapter 44 – 1988

Back at his desk, Sam smacked his forehead. What had he done? How could he have been so stupid as to let a pretty woman charm him into parting with his manuscript? Ever since he'd first started writing, as a teenager, he'd been afraid to show his work to anyone, afraid the verdict would be so discouraging he'd never write again.

Yet the impulse to get a professional opinion hadn't been altogether spontaneous. For months he'd been nagging himself to make a decision about his life. Should he continue working at a job that didn't suit him, in a store that didn't need him, in a profession that didn't interest him?

Or should he escape while he was still reasonably young? But escape to what? Everyone was talking software and "high tech," and he could work reasonably well on a computer, but it wasn't a field that interested him.

And how would his brother Benny feel, Sam wondered, if he left the family business. Probably relieved. Sam had proved beyond question that he hadn't the slightest aptitude for figures, sales, marketing, or any aspect of merchandising. Worse yet, he didn't give a damn about fashion. Could any intelligent person really care that long skirts were replacing miniskirts or that Calvin Klein was heralding the return of loose, flowing trousers?

Sometimes he could hardly believe the meetings he had to attend. That morning, in fact, representatives of the Color Marketing Group had announced — no, dictated was a better word — that black would continue to be *the* shade for 1989, and that all their promotions indeed would feature black furniture, kitchens, cars, pets, even noodles darkened with squid ink. And they were serious!

Swell, he thought. The AIDS epidemic was spreading throughout the city, teenagers were bringing loaded guns to school, drug dealers were taking over the Haight, honest out-of-work citizens were sleeping in doorways — and *he* was sitting around discussing black noodles.

Six weeks after the interview with Sam, Pat Stark finally called. She had been busy getting married. She said nothing about the book, but made a lunch date, forcing Sam to wait yet another week for a verdict.

He arrived at Osteria, a small Italian restaurant near the *Herald*. Pat was seated at a table, looking stylish in a black turtle-neck cashmere and slacks. He was beginning to hate black.

"Marriage agrees with you." He took the chair opposite her. "That's the first time I've seen you smile. I was sure you had fangs."

"Some people say I do."

"Maybe I'll agree when I read your article. How's it going?"

"It runs Sunday, and you're in it."

He waited a moment, then asked, "Has anyone offered you a drink?"

"I wanted to wait and drink with you."

"Do we have something to celebrate?"

"I'll tell you more in a minute." She gave her drink order and talked about her brief honeymoon until the waiter returned with the wine.

Sam raised his glass. "To your health, and to mine — which is failing rapidly. Haven't you kept me dangling long enough?"

She spooned a speck of cork from her wine, then touched his glass. "I was hoping to loosen you up with a drink or two. I want you to be as receptive as possible."

"I'm practically a sponge."

"Well, okay. First the bad news." Her face relaxed slightly as she said, "You're not a novelist, Sam. Your characters are stereotypes and your plot drags. You tend to overanalyze, which gets in the way of your action. Your dialogue moves the story, but frankly, you're not great at casual banter."

"Aside from that, Mrs. Lincoln..."

"No, no, there's good news, too. Your descriptions are clear and vivid. Your eye for detail is incredibly keen. Your sentences are short and meaty. Your curiosity and skepticism come through. Do you know what I'm describing?"

"Yes. A poor schnook who's been deluding himself for years."

"No, I'm talking about a style of writing you do very well. You write like a journalist."

Sam swallowed hard.

"Maybe it's the Stockton genes. Whatever it is, you're wasting your time trying to write novels. You belong in the news media."

"I do?" He scratched his neck nervously. "Mom would have a stroke. She's seen too much of newspaper shenanigans. But then, who knows? She's 66, and still gets a hoot out of wielding publishing power."

The waiter came by and rattled off the day's specials.

"All I'm saying," Pat went on, as soon as they'd ordered, "is that you *are* a misfit in that store. You're an ugly duckling and you'll stay an ugly duckling until you swim with the swans."

"Who are the swans?"

"Take your pick: *TIME, Newsweek, The Wall Street Journal* — but you'll have to cut your teeth at the *Herald*. Take advantage of your heritage, but don't go in cold or you'll be resented. Educate yourself first. Subscribe to trade journals like *Editors and Publishers Weekly*. Bone up on the newest technological advances in printing. Find out what's happening with First Amendment issues."

Sam began searching his pockets. "I should be taking notes."

"Just listen. Go home and practice writing articles on your word processor. Send them to me to edit if you want. News writing is just literature in a hurry — not an original line, but true. When you get a feel for it, talk to your stepfather. But be willing to start at the bottom."

"Paul's a great guy. My mom's never been happier." Excitement was stirring within him. "But I'd better see her alone first. She may have mixed feelings. Thanks, Pat. Whatever happens, I'm truly grateful for your guidance."

Chapter 45 – 1988

A strong wind chilled the air. Sam shivered in the lightweight linen suit Benny had custom-made for him, and prayed his Beau Brummel days would soon be over.

Shoving his hands deep in his pockets, he hurried up the steps to the family home on Pacific Avenue. Strange, he thought, that his mother still lived in the same house she and his dad bought when they were married. The beautiful, free-spirited Yvonne and the seemingly conventional Marc had had a good marriage, even with their age difference.

His father, Marc, had been a traditionalist whose family expected him to marry someone in the faith, a nice Jewish girl who'd be thrilled to wear designer labels, attend services at the temple, and join her mother-in-law volunteering at Mt. Zion Hospital. Instead, his dad had fallen for a gorgeous *shiksa*.

The only time Sam had ever seen his parents clash seriously, besides arguing about her clothes, was over him. He was 9 or 10, when Marc caught him sneaking a bottle of gin from the pantry. He could still see himself crouching behind his mother's skirt, while his father waved a cutting board and shouted that her precious baby would never grow to be a man without a good paddling. His mother screamed back that Marc was a barbarian, and chased him out of the kitchen.

Then she held her trembling son in her arms, dried his tears, and told him if she ever caught him stealing liquor again, she'd whack the dickens out of him herself.

The memory made him smile. He missed his father, but he liked Paul Amory. At first, he hadn't been sure. His mother had announced her decision to marry him without warning. She and Paul hadn't even dated, much less lived together.

But they were adults, and Uncle Tim said they'd known each other since World War II. Paul had moved his books, records, and all his various awards and trophies into her house, and to everyone's surprise, they seemed to get along splendidly. His mother, in fact, had blossomed like a cherry tree.

The sound of the front door closing gave Yvonne a rush of excitement. Sam seldom came to see her in the daytime, and that, she reminded herself, was as it should be. Much as she would have liked a closer relationship with her youngest son — with all her sons, for that matter — they were adults now, and as busy with their own lives as she was with hers.

When Sam had phoned to ask if he could see her alone, she was sure the subject was romance. He hadn't been seriously involved with anyone since that pretty Eurasian model, years ago.

His new interest, she conjectured, was either pregnant, married, or not Jewish. The first two conditions might pose problems, but the third had no import. Regardless of what his father used to say, all that really mattered was the girl's character and her ability to fit in with the family.

Approaching footsteps made Yvonne set down her pen and take off her glasses. Next to her desk, in the spacious bedroom she now shared with Paul, a wall showed off family portraits and photos. Out of respect to Paul, there was only one of Marc, part of a group picture. Across the room, overstuffed chairs and a small balcony looked down on the pink rhododendron bushes of the British Consulate.

"How's the world's most glamorous grandmother?" Sam kissed her and pulled up a chair. "And how's my handsome step-dad?"

"Fantastic. Paul's the dearest man who ever lived — besides your father, of course."

"I told him he'd better be good to you or I'd see him in the alley."

Yvonne smiled adoringly. She couldn't look at her "baby" without beaming. Why she favored him over the others, and felt so much closer to him, she would never know. "I take it you're in love, too."

"Me? Good Lord, no!"

His answer both surprised and relieved her, perhaps because she knew she would never think any girl good enough. "Are you in trouble? Do you need money?"

"No, again." He laughed and patted her hand. "Relax, Mom. I'm here about business. I'll get right to the point. You know I've never been happy working at the store. Forgive cliché, but I'm a fish out of water. I've always had this dream that someday I'd write mystery novels."

"You should be ready for a Pulitzer by now."

"Not quite. But I showed a few chapters to this reporter, Pat Stark, from the *Herald*. She said the novel was hopeless, but that I write like a newspaper man. She thinks I should go into journalism."

Yvonne's eyes flashed with interest. "Really? What a wonderful idea!"

"Mom — you mean it?"

"Of course I mean it. Newspapers are as much a part of your heritage as the retail business. Paul's been looking for an administrative assistant. He'll be thrilled to have you."

Sam's face fell. "No, no, if I wanted that kind of work, I'd stay at the store." He leaned forward on his chair. "I want to write, Mom. I want to work on challenging stories that take digging and probing."

"Have you ever done anything like that?"

"For the last four weeks, I've been reading everything I could on the subject. I've been writing articles every spare minute, and Pat's been criticizing them."

"Is this Pat — a close friend?"

"A married friend."

"Good. Then she can be objective."

"She says I need experience, and that I wouldn't stand a chance in a zillion of getting it, if I weren't who I am."

"The point is, you *are* who you are." Yvonne reached for the phone. "I'll call Paul."

"No, wait." He stayed her hand. "I can talk to Paul. I can talk to Benny. The only one I worried about was you. I was afraid you'd seen so much of newspaper politics, you wouldn't want me involved. But — you're sure it's okay?"

"It's a lovely idea. Haven't I always supported you? Your father used to say I spoiled you wicked."

"He was right." Sam grinned and leaned back in his chair, relieved and cautiously excited. "Thanks, Mom. So now that that's settled, what's that box of papers? You still going through Dad's stuff?"

She nodded. "I thought I was done, but I just found this notebook. Your father was writing a family history for the store's centennial in 1990."

"Benny might want to see that. He's planning a big hootenanny."

Yvonne looked thoughtful. "Say, what about you finishing this history? It'd give you a chance to do some of that digging and probing, and be a wonderful tribute to your father's memory."

Sam shook his head. "But — well, sure, I'll take it home and look it over."

"Do try, darling. Oh, and you are going to talk to Nonna, aren't you?

It wouldn't hurt to have her approval."

"I'm way ahead of you, Mom. I'm stopping by Jackson Street this evening."

Chapter 46 — 1988

Bundled in a long white robe with a fox collar, Clara Hayes Stockton waited in her sitting room, savoring the prospect of Sam's visit. She hadn't seen her favorite grandson in months, and was delighted to hear he was coming by. At the same time, she wondered if he was in trouble. Young people had a way of suddenly materializing when they needed you.

The bell rang shortly before eight. Maxwell the butler, bald and slightly bent over after 37 years with the family, greeted Sam warmly. "She's in her parlor."

"Thanks, pal." Sam bounded up the stairs, strode into the room, pecked his grandmother on the cheek and grinned. "Hi, Nonna. You're looking well for an Eskimo."

"I suppose you're cold," she growled. "Do you want a blanket?"

"No, thanks. I dressed for the occasion." He made a show of tightening his wool scarf, then grabbed a footstool. "May I sit at your feet?"

"Better take a chair, so I can look at you. You've grown since I last saw you."

"It hasn't been *that* long." No mistaking the reproach in her voice. "This is June. It was only March. Ben picked out some shoes for you and I delivered them. Remember?"

"I don't remember what I had for breakfast." Her tone was starting to soften. She just missed him and wished he'd call more often. "What's on your mind? Are you in trouble?"

"No," he laughed. "But I thought you'd want to know I'm thinking of leaving the store."

"Are you unhappy there?"

"It's just not something that I want to do for the rest of my life. I'm thinking of — well, trying my hand at journalism. A reporter friend said I might have some talent in that direction."

"Have you talked to Paul?"

"No, I wanted to talk to you first. I — was hoping you wouldn't have any objections."

"Don't be silly," she scolded. "You're half-Stockton, aren't you? It's in your blood. Why shouldn't you be a journalist?"

Sam's eyes widened. He held his breath. "You serious?"

"I certainly am. I've always hoped that you or Betsy's son, Tyrone

Pickett, would join the *Herald's* staff. But just between us, that Tyrone's a snooty brat. I can't stand him."

"I can't, either." A wave of relief swept over him. "I'm so glad, Nonna. I was afraid you might think we have enough journalists in the family. I know I have to see Paul, but I'm not sure what to say to him. How did Grandpa James get started? — or did he just inherit a newspaper?"

"You don't know your family history?" She hesitated a moment, then asked, "Are you pressed for time?"

"No." He smiled and moved to a more comfortable seat on the couch facing her. "Not at all."

Clara settled into her armchair, her thoughts drifting back to the late '20s, and the day she met James Tyler Stockton. He was guest-lecturing at Stanford, where she was a sophomore. His talk on the responsibilities of a free press was strong and moving, and so was he. When at last the assembly adjourned, she made a point to tell him how much he inspired her, and how she hoped to become a poet.

The young woman's adulation and beauty apparently inspired him as well. He invited her for a tour of the *Herald* the next day, then took her to lunch in the Garden Court of the Palace Hotel.

Five months later, while cruising the bay on a friend's yacht, James told her that her flaxen hair glowed in the sunlight and her smile melted his heart. Ever since he'd lost his precious Alice some 15 years prior, life had been an emotional wasteland. Would she do him the kind honor of becoming his wife?

The proposal flattered and thrilled her. They spent long hours trading memories of childhood. His had been privileged, overseen by parents who worshipped money, the Social Register, and God — in that order. Hers had been equally pampered and protected, but with a focus on philanthropy and the arts.

By the time she married the imposing and highly eligible James Stockton, she never doubted that she could run his house, rear Tim and Yvonne, the children of his first wife, Alice, and still have time to pursue interests of her own. How naive she was!

"Yes, Sam, Grandpa James did 'just inherit' the *Herald*, but there's a history there. The Stocktons go all the way back to the Gold Rush in

1849. Your grandfather was always quick to point out that we were no relation to Commander Robert F. Stockton, the early California military governor, who gave his name to Stockton Street.

"It was 1865, as I recall, when Grandpa James's grandfather, Anthony Stockton, and Anthony's brother Brett, started the *San Francisco Herald* as a neighborhood news sheet."

Sam was fascinated. "I sort of remember that."

"But as the years passed, and circulation continued to rise, Anthony and Brett began to develop an exaggerated sense of their own power. I think it was in the late '80s when the *Clarion,* a rival newspaper, denounced the brothers as 'monsters of greed and depravity,' or something like that. All I know is that hotheaded Anthony Stockton took a Colt revolver to *Clarion* publisher Pat Doyle's office, and shot the man dead."

"Wow!"

"A well-bribed jury voted for acquittal, but as Anthony was leaving the courthouse, the murdered man's son, Egan Doyle, sprayed Anthony with bullets."

"Fatally?"

"Yes. But Egan managed to avoid prison. In those days, I guess you could bribe anyone. The Stocktons and the Doyles hated each other from then on, and Grandpa James inherited the hostility, but it died with his generation. I know Tim credits Egan's grandson, Hart Doyle, with saving his life. Then minutes later, Hart was killed by Japanese gunfire."

"How horrible! How did they meet?"

"On a troopship. I knew Hart Doyle," she added, trying to sound casual. "He was a kind, gentle man — wouldn't have hurt a fly."

"That's war, Nonna, and wars are obscene. But back to history. What happened to the *Herald* after Egan shot Anthony?"

"Well, Brett Stockton turned the *Herald* over to his son, George, who was succeeded by *his* son James — that's Grandpa James, who'd started as a copy boy when he was 10 or 11."

Sam nodded appreciatively. "I'm too old to be a copy boy, but I'm willing to start at the low rung of the ladder. I wouldn't even want anybody to know Paul's my stepfather. But I'm very proud of Grandpa and my heritage."

Clara smiled, enjoying her memories. "I wouldn't tell this to another soul, but your grandfather was a bit of a fraud. None of the arts he supported so visibly held the slightest interest for him. Museums bored him, he didn't know a flute from a fiddle, he slept through opera, and he thought ballet was for sissies. But he was brilliant — and a good man."

"Sam," she said, suddenly growing serious. "Paul can't go on forever. See him, talk to him, don't be afraid to tell him your dreams. It would please me *enormously* if you were to carry on the family tradition. There's really no one else."

"I love you, Nonna." Sam held back tears as he walked over and embraced her. "Thanks for the encouragement. You won't be sorry — I promise."

Chapter 47 — 1988

Sam had always felt more like a Greenfield than a Stockton. As prominent as his maternal heritage was, it was his father's philosophy, his father's religion, and his father's profession that dominated his upbringing. So close and family-oriented were the Greenfields, in fact, that Sam had never sought a relationship with the Stocktons. Except for his grandmother Clara, the rest were virtual strangers.

Life was odd, he thought, as he stood outside the *Herald* Building, a tall, square, sheath of a structure topped by a 40-foot clock tower. His ancestors had founded the paper, his Aunt Lou Ella had published it for almost three decades, now his stepfather Paul Amory ran it — and he had never been inside the door.

Heeding the security guard's instructions, he got off the elevator at three, followed the hall to the executive offices and approached the receptionist. "Uh, hello. Sorry to disturb you."

Helen Hopkins glanced up from her video display terminal. "Hello, Sam. Have a seat. Paul will be right with you."

"Thanks." He regarded the woman with curiosity. "Pardon me, have we met?"

"Not officially. I'm Helen. I've worked for your family for 41 years, first for your grandfather, then Lou Ella, now Paul. I remember when you were born — 1957, wasn't it?"

"Wow. What a memory."

"I took the call from your father at the hospital. Lou Ella had bet on a girl. She lost a bundle on you, and she took it out on me."

Sam chuckled. "Sorry about that."

"It's too bad you never knew your grandfather."

"Was he as ferocious as they say?"

"At times. But James Tyler Stockton was the finest newspaperman I've ever known. He had a gut instinct for what sold papers. Nothing could stop him. Once, when the presses broke down, he took off his coat and crawled inside to thread the paper through the rollers with his own hands."

Sam smiled. "How funny that you and I have never met. You're practically part of the family."

"Thanks. I like to think so."

"Well, I hope we won't be strangers any more." He parked himself on the wooden bench, opened a magazine and closed it. Why was he feeling so nervous? He had every reason to be confident. His mother and grandmother were firmly behind his move. But Paul still ran the paper.

Strange, he mused, how rarely he saw his Stockton relatives. They used to share holidays when he was a child, but the Greenfield clan grew too big, with grandchildren of all ages. And the Stocktons — Clara, Tim, Lou Ella, and Will — seemed to prefer quieter celebrations now. Sam wondered if Katie and Melanie ever joined them, then he remembered that Clara and her daughter Katie didn't speak.

What a screwed-up family! He loved Nonna, but couldn't understand her rift with Katie. Tim seemed a nice guy, Lou Ella was wrapped up in the newspaper, Will and Katie were distant. Benny once told Sam that the Stocktons had never forgiven Yvonne for marrying a Jew. Maybe so. Katie took up with a Jewish guy, too, Jason something, and look where it got her.

To Sam's relief, the door opened after a short wait. Paul emerged, smiling and affable. "Come in, Sam. Sit down. Tell me, to what do I owe this pleasure?"

"I'd like to say it's purely social, but it isn't. I have a request."

"I'm happy to help if I can."

The office, Sam noticed, as he followed Paul inside, was just as pretentious as he'd heard, with its ornate moldings and high-backed red velvet chairs. Gold-framed etchings of early San Francisco lined the walls; heavy silk draperies framed the windows. He could see Grandpa James in that pompous setting, but not Paul. His stepfather belonged in a sparse, utilitarian office, as devoid of frills as he was.

Sam chided himself for noticing Paul's wrinkled suit, but he couldn't help it. Working at S. Greenfield had taught him all the wrong values.

Paul sat down behind his desk. "What's on your mind?"

Sam perched on the edge of his chair. "Okay — I met one of your reporters, Pat Stark, who was kind enough to read something I'd written and thought I had possibilities as a journalist. I came to ask if you might find an opening for me on the paper."

"You're leaving the store?"

"I hope to, but I haven't told Benny. I've never been happy there."

The implications of Sam's request impressed Paul. If Sam proved to have potential, a few years as a reporter, another five as assistant to the publisher, and one day, he might be able to fulfill the family tradition and take over. "Does your mother know you're seeing me?"

"Yes, and Nonna, too, but I made them promise not to put any pressure on you. The decision is all yours. If you decide to hire me, I'll give you 1000 percent of myself, and I'm willing to start anywhere. I'll even take out the garbage. If you don't want to hire me, you don't need to explain. I'll just crawl away quietly."

Ignoring his attempt at humor, Paul spoke without hesitation. "Of course I'll hire you, Sam. And I'm delighted that you want to work here. But let's get something straight. I won't treat you like everyone else. I'll be tougher, much tougher, on you. If you've got what it takes, I'll be very pleased. If not, we're still friends. Okay?"

"That's great! When do I start?"

"There's a temporary opening in the Modern Living section. Come in Monday. I'll tell Ruthe Garchik. She'll be your editor."

"Isn't that fashion and society?"

"You expect me to put a novice in the newsroom?"

"Uh, no, that's fine."

"Remember, no special privileges. You'll earn minimum wages and benefits, and you'll be expected to join the Newspaper Guild. If there's a strike, they're sure to stick you out front with a picket sign and run your face on the evening news. How would your mother feel about that?"

Sam rose. "Knowing her, she'd probably love it." He grinned. "I'd better go before you change your mind."

Paul walked him to the door and patted his shoulder. "Good luck, Sam. And welcome aboard."

The Modern Living section of the *Herald* was a large office area that housed a horseshoe-shaped table for illustrators, layout people, and copy editors. Surrounding it were a half-dozen reporters' desks. Several looked as if they'd been struck by a hurricane. Papers, books, dirty ashtrays and stained coffee mugs were strewn at random. Neatness, apparently, was not a priority.

Atop a green file cabinet sat stacks of Bay Area dailies from previous weeks. Beside them, a wall of cubicles bulged with Monday morning mail. Sam had gotten there early, and was studying *The Associated Press Stylebook* when his editor arrived.

Ruthe Garchik, a surprisingly soft-voiced woman in her mid-fifties, assigned him a desk and asked a reporter to make sure he knew how to use the video display terminal. Sam had hoped his presence would go largely unnoticed, but by the end of the day, every employee there knew who he was. It was somewhat disappointing to hear from Pat Stark that he'd been tagged "His Gucciness." Only time (and a more casual wardrobe) would prove to his co-workers that he wasn't a spy for management.

The next morning, Ruthe stopped at his desk. "You have a background in fashion, Sam. What about covering the Leukemia Society luncheon at the St. Francis today? You could do a piece from the male point of view. Does a man look at the models' figures or the clothes? That sort of thing."

Sam's response was immediate. "I'll do it if you want me to, but I'd better warn you that I've suffered through too many of the damn things. I don't react to the models at all. All I see is my watch and how soon I can escape."

"Hmm —." She tapped her lip with a pencil. "What *does* interest you?"

"Sports, crime, mysteries, people, the world, politics — any chance you could send me to the Democratic convention next month?"

"None. That's not our bailiwick." She spoke over her shoulder as she hurried to answer her phone. "I need three fresh ideas, Sam, and I do mean fresh. Research them. Polish them. Write a one-page query for each. Then we'll talk."

The *Herald's* city room, often a madhouse of frenzied reporters clicking away at their computers, was virtually deserted. Sam liked to come in on Saturday mornings. Working without interruption, he'd been able to finish three good story proposals for Ruthe and leave them on her desk.

Another advantage was access to the morgue. Reference books, files, and microfiche went unguarded for several hours, and he could read and rummage through the shelves at leisure.

On this particular day, he decided to research his family. If enough material was available, he might be able to finish the history his mother wanted without spending too many hours. The Greenfield file, all on microfiche, was divided and labelled: "Benjamin/David/Sam; Isaac; Marcus; Simon; S. Greenfield & Co.; Yvonne/see Stockton."

Turning the knob on the viewer, he moved the film across the screen till he found his own name. The clippings were few: a birth announcement, a mention of his Bar Mitzvah, a reference to the Pat Stark interview of 2/10/88. Everything he would need, including his parents' and grandparents' obituaries, and all his father's awards and accomplishments, were there.

The Stockton file was slightly larger, starting alphabetically with Alice. There were lengthy clips on Anthony and Brett; Clara's wedding — and a headline that instantly drew his eye: "SOCIETY MATRON KILLS BURGLAR."

As far back as Sam could remember, he had heard stories about Nonna shooting an intruder. Nothing specific was ever said, but he had sensed there was more to the incident than attempted robbery. Scanning the front page of the *Herald*, he read that an alleged burglar, Al Hogan, had broken in late at night, terrorized the prominent widow, and then demanded her jewelry.

> *"Fearful that the perpetrator might harm Katherine, her 20-year-old daughter sleeping down the hall, the victim surrendered a diamond necklace. When the alleged burglar attempted to attack the victim, she picked up her late husband's revolver and shot him in the chest. He was pronounced dead at 12:48 A.M."*

The case was "under investigation," according to authorities, yet that was the only clipping. No follow-ups, no police reports, not even the usual recap of the intruder's history. Sam made a note of the date, and brushed through the rest of the Stockton file: Edith, George, James, Katherine's birth announcement, Lou Ella, Margaret/see Kettering, Betsy/see Pickett, Timothy, Yvonne/see Greenfield, Willard.

"Digging for skeletons?"

Sam looked up to see a man in a stained mackintosh and crumpled rain hat peering over his shoulder.

"Caught in the act. Hi, I'm Sam Greenfield."

"Mike Dill, better known as Kosher. So you're the heir apparent."

"Not too apparent, I hope. How long have you been around?"

"Oh hell, kid." He swept off his hat and stuffed it in his pocket. "I was a copy boy 30 years ago. You shoulda seen the morgue in those days — skinny old broad right out of Central Casting stood at the counter barking orders."

"To whom?"

"Everyone. She was keeper of the treasure — boxes of old clippings stacked one on top of each other, right up to the ceiling. Reporters would send us to retrieve some ancient story, and we'd have to scrounge for hours. Those were the bad old days. Nice meeting you, kid. I gotta run."

Sam swung around on his chair. "Say, Kosher, do you have any idea how I could get some *Examiner* clips?"

"Yeah, sure. I got a friend. What do you need?"

"The week starting March 13, 1960."

"Could you narrow it down?"

"Sunday to Thursday. News sections."

He scribbled the date on a pad. "I'll need a double sawbuck to cover costs."

Sam laughed and took out a twenty.

"And don't go blabbing. You didn't get anything from me."

"Hell, no." Sam swiveled back to his machine. "We've never met."

Early Monday morning, an envelope was waiting on Sam's desk. Inside, he found four unlabeled sheets of film. Knowing the librarians wouldn't show up until 9:00, he crossed the city room to the morgue and slipped the microfiche into the viewer. Kosher had come through.

The *Examiner* report of the shooting incident was short and factual.

The last paragraph indicated that, "Several questions remain unanswered and will require further investigation." A follow-up four days later, however, reported that the case had been closed due to "lack of evidence."

Lack of evidence of what? What could be clearer than shooting an intruder in self-defense?

Back at his desk, Sam looked up Dill in the *Herald's* inside phone directory. No answer on his extension, so he left a message, then checked his own slot for mail. Nothing.

For the first time in his adult life, he realized, he actually enjoyed the work he was doing. Even the open competitiveness of his colleagues was a welcome change, so different from the petty jealousies and the back-stabbers at S. Greenfield & Company.

Thanks to reading, studying, and writing sample stories late into the night, he was learning fast. Ruthe had run his first feature, Dennis Day's obituary, with only a few changes, but he had to completely rewrite his first article, a half-humorous look at how women choose their political candidates. The fourth draft had passed inspection, however, and he'd rejoiced to see his work in print. Especially his byline.

Later that day, Sam was en route to Mike Dill's desk when he saw him in the hall. "Say, aren't you the guy they call Kosher?"

"And you're His Gucciness, Lord of the loafers. Welcome to our Disneyland, kid. And good-bye."

"Nice to meet you, too," Sam called as the reporter strode away.

A few minutes later, he phoned him and spoke softly. "You didn't have to run off. I just wanted to thank you for the film."

"That's why you called?"

"No, actually, I need another favor. How can I get some police files?"

"You say Dukakis won the nomination yesterday? Gee, How'd I miss that?"

"C'mon, Kosher. No one's listening."

"No kidding. Sonny Bono's his running mate?"

"I need a contact."

"Thanks for the tip, kid. Call me any time."

A click sounded in Sam's ear. Swearing under his breath, he phoned a longtime family friend, a judge, who explained that he was sorry, but couldn't help, either.

Sam's mind was churning, and he wasn't sure why. What was he hoping to prove? What did it matter why his grandmother shot a burglar 28 years ago? Did she really do the shooting or was she covering up for someone? Could Aunt Katie have shot him? Was keeping that terrible secret the reason Katie was so strange?

At the same time, he was trying to make as little work for himself as possible. Yet his curiosity — all his mystery-loving detective instincts — were piqued.

The next evening, thanks to a personal plea enhanced by a fifty dollar bill, Mike Dill was able to provide printouts of the police file. Sitting on his bed, propped against a backrest, Sam read the typed report carefully, surprised to learn that the late Avery Andrews had been on the scene right after the police arrived. According to the document:

> "Clara Stockton reported that, 'The burglar lunged at me and I was afraid he was going to kill me, so I pulled the trigger.' Mrs. Stockton stated she was pretending to get cash from her dresser drawer and got the gun instead. Hogan carried no tools, and wore no gloves or mask. He was a known political activist, but had no record for burglary or violence.
>
> "Mrs. Stockton's story has major discrepancies. At first, it appeared her daughter might have done the actual shooting, but Clara Stockton's fingerprints were the only ones on the gun. Mrs. Stockton claimed she didn't know how the man got in the house, but there was no sign of a break-in. After interviewing the maid and butler, it was clear neither could have let the alleged burglar in. A thorough investigation is recommended."

The initial summary, signed by Officer Chester McGuire, was dated March 12, 1960. Ten pages of lab reports and notes followed, including an interview with Katie, and a letter from Avery Andrews detailing the terms of Mrs. Stockton's agreement to provide for Hogan's family.

The investigation was abruptly halted on March 15, 1960. Either the police decided there was no reason to continue, or Clara used her connections. It occurred to Sam that the key to the killing was Katie, who might have stored away memories she hadn't told the police. But his reclusive aunt was not likely to share secrets with a nephew she hardly knew.

He wondered if her daughter, his cousin Melanie, might intercede. He hadn't seen Melanie since he'd bumped into her at the store nine or ten years ago. She was pretty, he remembered, but hopeless in those sophisticated couture gowns. Last he'd heard she was doing weather reports for Channel 3. He'd give her a call one of these days, but not at the moment. The job took all his time, and some of his co-workers were a bit too eager to see him fail.

Part 7

Cousins

Chapter 49 — 1989

Melanie Morris studied her hair in the monitor. The floor manager had just given the one-minute signal to airtime for the six o'clock news, and she was nervous. Her co-anchor, Ronn Ackerman, was in Sacramento interviewing Lieutenant Governor Leo McCarthy about the attempt to get seven local counties declared disaster areas. Tuesday's horrifying earthquake, 7.1 on the Richter Scale, was the worst to hit the Bay Area since 1906.

Channel 3's reporters were all over San Francisco covering the damage, and Ronn had warned her she might have to carry the show alone. As Susie Bigelow, her executive producer, made clear, she would have to double her concentration in order to pick up last minute cues.

Melanie glanced at the intro copy she would be reading on the TelePrompTer, and wondered how long the Loma Prieta earthquake, named for a mountain peak near its epicenter, would dominate the news.

Several months earlier, KSAF had adopted a structured format: each broadcast would have to include one crime story, one sex-related feature, one animal tale, and a bulletin that affected viewers' pocketbooks. Despite the station's unchanged ratings, management insisted it was too soon to evaluate the success of the new format.

Such rigid guidelines, however, violated every journalistic standard Melanie had learned in the night courses she'd taken at City College. The textbook stated explicitly that you didn't mold news to fit a format, and you didn't titillate viewers, you enlightened them. But she was dealing with reality, not ideals, and unfortunately, she hadn't the clout to protest.

"Here we go. Fifteen seconds."

Melanie's lovely face was replaced on the monitor by a station promo. The TelePrompTer sat just above the camera, positioned so it would appear that she was looking into the viewers' eyes.

For an instant, her mind flashed on the hundreds of hours she had spent mastering the electronic marvel that unrolled her script line by line. What a struggle she'd had, learning to read the copy without moving her eyes or her head, as if she were watching a Ping-Pong game. She had even trained herself to memorize the next story lead-in, so she could have time for some friendly byplay with Ronn.

The floor manager raised five fingers, then four, in a silent countdown. Melanie's adrenaline began to flow, as it always did just before air-time. "Heightened awareness" she called it. A gaffe on videotape could be remedied, but a live blunder was forever. The red light blinked. Melanie began.

"Good evening, everyone. I'm Melanie Morris, and this is Channel 3's Eye On The World, six o'clock edition. Ronn Ackerman is on assignment. He'll be back tomorrow. Tonight's special reports include the continuing aftermath of the quake: three dead as a broken gas main fire sweeps the Marina; protesters storm police lines in Santa Cruz; and vice-president Dan Quayle tours the ruins and leaves without seeing Mayor Agnos — an action His Honor calls 'a cheap publicity stunt.' These and other stories, coming up."

Melanie's dazzling smile brightened the screen as the camera's light winked out and the first of four 30-second commercials appeared. Susie Bigelow flipped the speaker switch in the glass-paneled control booth. "Do we have wire copy yet?"

Melanie nodded, waving a bulletin handed her a moment earlier.

Helicopter footage of the fire in the Marina District led the news, with a human interest story about the fireboat Phoenix, due to be "retired," yet when the water mains broke, the fireboat's portable hydrant was able to pump water from the bay and subdue the flames.

Three minutes of video followed. A one-minute feed from the network announced that Chevron and General Motors had pledged major donations to San Francisco quake relief. Before the animal story, Melanie teased her viewers with promos for upcoming programs, then finally, she wrapped it up. "That's it for Eye On The World, six o'clock edition. Thanks for watching. We'll be back at eleven."

KSAF segued into the network news, and Melanie detached her lapel mike. She headed for the door, almost bumping into Susie. The short, stocky brunette, her nest of curls framing a perpetually wrinkled brow, stood in sharp contrast to the long-limbed anchor.

"We're previewing footage on the emotional effects of the quake," said Susie. "Studio B."

"Now?"

"In ten minutes."

"Okay." The brief exchange satisfied Melanie that the show had gone reasonably well. Compliments were nonexistent; management didn't want anyone to get cocky and demand more money.

She slowed her step as she passed through the newsroom, where the latest events were gathered, sifted, and nurtured. Activity slackened for the night shift, but never stopped. The chemical smell of print and toner, the buzzing phones, the clattering Teletypes and fax machines, the wall monitors and giant schoolroom clocks representing time zones around the world...all formed the heart of the news operation.

Back in the crowded office she shared with her co-anchor, she slipped off her shoes, settled comfortably in her chair, and leafed through a stack of messages. Among them was a speaking request from the California Club, a dinner invitation from a Park Commissioner she'd interviewed, a reminder of the press opening of (yet another) Union Square boutique, and a brief note, to call...Sam Greenfield? What on earth could her long-unseen cousin want?

A machine answered his phone. She started to leave a message. A click sounded. "I'm here, Melanie. Just trying to avoid a certain party."

"Is she that bad?"

"Worse." Sam laughed. "You and I have got to stop meeting every ten years. People will talk."

"I won't tell if you won't. I was flabbergasted when Nonna told me you were leaving the store to work at the *Herald*. What happened?"

"I didn't belong at the store. I was extra baggage. How've you been? Still doing the weather?"

"I'm a news anchor now. Don't you ever watch TV?"

"Only midnight movies, and not many of those lately. How'd you get from weather to news?"

"Hard work. Lucky timing." The cliché answer rang hollow in her ears. Her cousin deserved better. But did he really want to hear about the long hours she'd spent with her coach Damon, watching herself on camera and trying to perfect every gesture, every nuance, every inflection of her voice?

Those first years flashed through her mind: learning how to read the weather charts and deliver her lines in a professional manner; learning how to hold the pointer gracefully; learning how to go right on when she made a mistake, and never to stammer or giggle.

Competition in the "glamour media" was far too keen for management to care about anyone's feelings. So far, she'd been lucky. Viewers had responded to her good looks and easy delivery. The voice that had been so wrong for Antigone was an asset for television; it was soft and clear and filled with a distinctive cadence.

Melanie's first break had come when the news director agreed to let her do a weekly consumer review, on condition that she write and research it herself. The three-minute feature was popular, but it took another two years before she was assigned to cover local events.

Friendship with a Diocese priest gained her an exclusive interview with Pope John Paul II on his historic visit to San Francisco. The network picked up the footage and ran it during sweeps week. Results were positive. When an opening at Channel 3 appeared some months later, she was asked to fill in as a weekend anchor.

Eventually, Melanie earned a regular spot on the evening news, but no one ever told her she did well, or that she had the job "permanently." As far as she knew, she was still on probation.

"What about you, Sam?" she asked. "What happened when the quake shut down the paper?"

"Instant chaos. No printing facility, no computers, no wire service. Actually, that's why I'm calling. I'm doing a piece on how the media dealt with the earthquake. Were you at the station when it struck?"

"Was I ever!" A little publicity never hurt, and the station loved it. "It was like a scene from a disaster movie. I was standing at the assignment desk, checking the story board with one eye and watching the pitchers warm up in Candlestick Park with the other. It was 5:04 P.M., just before the game. Then all of a sudden, the whole building began to rumble."

"What'd you do?"

"I ignored the first few seconds. When it got worse, I grabbed Susie — Susie Bigelow, my producer — and dashed for the doorway. One of the monitors came crashing down, filling the room with black smoke. Then the power went off and the phones went dead."

"Were you scared?"

"Petrified! When the shaking finally stopped, we all came out of our corners. I said, '6.5,' Susie said, '8.' Everyone began guessing what it was on the Richter. That broke the tension. We were dark another ten minutes before the emergency generators kicked in."

"Then what?"

"Well, within half an hour, people started bringing in amateur video footage, including that incredible tape of the Bay Bridge collapsing. Ronn — my co-anchor Ronn Ackerman — and I stayed on the air till ten P.M. telling about relief efforts. Everyone was wonderful. In the words of Dan Quayle, 'It was heart-*rendering*.'"

Sam chuckled. "You're very articulate, Melanie. Still planning to be an actress?"

"Good Lord, no. I finally got my drama coach to admit my acting talent was limited, at best."

"Ever think of going to the network?"

"Sometimes...but I love San Francisco too much to live anywhere else. And I could never leave my mother."

"How *is* the mysterious Katie?"

"She's okay; not so mysterious, just shy, and I guess you'd say introverted. Nonna keeps me up to date on the Greenfields, so I know your family's well. I hear the store's having a centennial next year."

"Say, I'm glad you mentioned that. There's something I want to ask you. Could I entice you for a quick sandwich one of these days?"

Social lunches were time-wasters, but a cousin, especially one she hadn't seen in a decade, rated an exception. "Well, I do eat now and then."

"Just as I suspected. Wednesday, Balboa Cafe at noon?"

"How will I recognize you?"

"Wear high heels and wobble," he said. "I'll recognize you."

Chapter 50 — 1989

The popular Fillmore Street restaurant was a long, narrow room with a polished wood bar taking half its space. Two young men, attractive in their V-neck cashmeres and designer jeans, sat on stools, sipping Bloody Marys. In the rear, six tables were set with crisp white cloths, vases of fresh flowers, and napkins folded into pyramids.

Sam sat by a window gazing out at Greenwich Street, marveling that two first cousins — both single, both working in the media, both living in the same city — could be virtual strangers.

No one in his family knew much about Melanie, but Katie was the real enigma. Every time Yvonne had invited her and Melanie to dinner, Katie had an excuse; she was ill, she was expecting Jason and Trudy, she was going to Carmel for a few days. Eventually, Yvonne stopped calling.

The sound of footsteps made Sam look up and gasp. An incredibly beautiful woman was walking towards him. Her stride was quick and confident, her bearing tall and regal. A beige sweater draped across her shoulders was loosely knotted over a tailored blouse and camel's hair skirt. She wore no jewelry except small gold earrings and a watch. Large blue eyes twinkled cheerfully. "Mr. Greenfield, I presume?"

Sam jumped to his feet, aware of the wonderful aroma of lemon shampoo. Melanie looked as fresh and clean as her fragrance, and seemed unconscious of the effect she produced. "Whatever happened to that cute little teenager all dressed up in fancy clothes?"

"She grew up — and so did you."

"Have I changed much?"

"Radically." She sized him at a glance; longish hair, tweed sportcoat, white shirt opened at the collar with a dangling necktie, khaki slacks. The same good-looking features and cocker spaniel eyes, only now, they sparkled with mischief. Gone was the custom-tailored suit, the manicured nails, the boutonniere. "You don't look like a prig any more."

He laughed. "You did say *prig*, didn't you? What are you drinking?"

"Nothing, thanks. I have to get back to work. Could we just have lunch?"

He signaled the waitress who took their orders. Then Sam cocked his head. "Tell me, Melanie. When you knew me at the store, was I rude and arrogant?"

"No, you were pleasant. But I was mad at you for breaking up with Darci. She was a fabulous lady. I tried to call her after I left the store, but she was gone. Do you know where she went?"

"She eloped with some rich guy in the liquor business and moved east. But you're right. She was a fabulous lady. What about you? Engaged, involved, in love with anyone?"

"Only my job. I couldn't handle a relationship right now."

"I know what you mean." Admiration filled his voice. "You seem so, well, together. Knowing your background, I expected — how shall I put it — a full-blown neurotic?"

She smiled. "I grew up being melodramatic. Everything was a crisis. I was sure I was going to be a great actress. I've tried to shed that phony theatrical veneer, but maybe I'm still playing a role: the calm, cool woman you think you're having lunch with."

"My insincerity alarm hasn't gone off yet."

"That's reassuring." She laughed happily. He was more entertaining than she expected. "What about you? Are you content at the newspaper?"

"At the moment I'm ecstatic. Paul needed extra quake coverage, so he switched me to the newsroom. Finally, I'm a full-fledged reporter. They even put '*Herald* Staff Writer' under my byline."

"That's terrific. What's Paul like as a boss?"

"I love the guy. But he cracks a mean whip, and my butt's first in line."

Melanie laughed. "It's always that way, isn't it. Family connections are greatly overrated. Mom gave me her company stock when I was 21, so I see Paul at board meetings. I think he's dreamy. And the way he and your mother look at each other, you could die! I love Uncle Tim, too, but he watches me like a vulture every night and faxes me all my mistakes."

"At least he cares. When we spoke on the phone, you said your mother was okay. Is she really?"

"She's a worry. She had her 50th birthday last week, and I begged her to have a party, but she said she had no friends. I can't get her out of the house. And off the record, every time I visit, she's — well, inebriated."

"What about professional help?"

"She won't go. She doesn't think she has a problem."

"Does she live alone?"

"She has a wonderful couple, Christi and Bill, but they're leaving at the end of this year."

"And Nonna? Mother and daughter still don't speak?"

"No, sadly. Two stubborn women cutting off their noses. My fondest dream is to get them back together. I just don't know how to make it happen."

"Who's the most reachable?"

"Nonna."

"Then talk to her. Tell her your Mom's in trouble and see if she'll make the first overture."

"She says she already did. She wrote Mom years ago that she loved her and she could always come home. Mom didn't even answer her."

The waitress set down sandwiches and Melanie checked her watch. "Sorry, Sam. I didn't mean to unload on you. Didn't you say you had something to ask me?"

He broke open a roll and buttered it. Their meeting was going so well. He hoped his question wouldn't change the mood. "*My* mom wants me to write a family history for the store's centennial, so I've been digging into the archives. I came across the famous shooting incident back in 1960. Do you know anything about Nonna killing a burglar?"

A warning bell sounded in Melanie's head. "What does that have to do with the Greenfields? Your mom, Yvonne, was Nonna's step-daughter. You and Nonna have no blood relationship."

"As far as I'm concerned, Nonna's my grandmother and I'm devoted to her. She married my grandfather, she raised my mother, and she's always treated me like her grandson."

Impatience edged Melanie's voice. "If you care about her, why do you want to stir up bad memories?"

"I wouldn't hurt her for the world. But aren't you curious? Haven't you ever wondered how such a dear lady could actually kill a man?"

"No! I put that to rest a long time ago, and you should, too." Her voice was rising.

He chewed his lower lip a few seconds, then nodded. "You're right. I won't include it. But a part of me still wants to know what happened. Your mother may hold the key. Would you be willing to ask her what she remembers?"

"Why should I?"

"Look, Melanie, the record's there for all to see. If our children come to us in twenty years and ask if their great-grandmother was a killer, I want to be able to answer them with facts, not evasion."

Thoughts raced through Melanie's brain. She had a reason of her own for wanting answers. If she could find out exactly what happened that night, she might be in a better position to heal the rift with Clara.

"Tell you what," she said, after a pause. "I'm stopping by Mom's house tomorrow. I'll mention it casually and see what happens."

A wave of appreciation swept over him. "Will you call me Friday?"

"Yes. But don't get your hopes up."

Driving down to the *Herald* half an hour later, Sam could not get his mind to function. After spending days gathering earthquake data, he was ready to write his big story. But all he could think about was the amazing woman he had just left.

The attraction was strong and sudden. Under that striking exterior, he sensed a sweetness and a vulnerability that probably mesmerized every man she met. The fact that they shared a grandfather, James Tyler Stockton, was irrelevant.

Or was it? Was it incestuous, he wondered, to have such feelings? The only drawback to cousin relationships was the possibility of having defective children. But who needed children? He stopped himself mid-thought. How had he let himself get carried away so fast? Had he lost his reason completely?

"Tell me this isn't happening," he muttered, half-aloud. "Tell me I'm having a dream."

But it wasn't a dream. Melanie Morris, his scrawny, sassy, baby-faced cousin had come back into his life in a startling new way. And he hadn't the slightest idea what he was going to do about it.

"And we're clear!" yelled the floor manager.

Melanie unsnapped the microphone hidden under her collar. "Damn aftershocks," she murmured. "Just when people think it's safe to move home, everything starts rattling again."

Her producer nodded agreement. "What's worse are those damn merchants gouging everyone, charging 10 bucks for a bottle of water. I need you for a promo later."

"I'll be back in an hour. I'm just going to see my mother."

"Well, drive carefully. It's pouring out."

Melanie always stopped to chat with the cameramen. Two minutes of effort was a bargain price for their friendship and loyalty. An anchor was only as good as her team. She'd never forget the night the Tele-PrompTer operator misinterpreted a remark she'd made as a racial slur. The machine had mysteriously sped ahead, leaving her to stutter and stammer her way through the broadcast.

The night wind was chilly and the streets slippery. Hard to believe the earthquake had only struck nine days ago, she thought, as she headed uptown to Broadway. Broken windows were evident everywhere, and buildings were still roped off with yellow bands, but on the whole, the town was mending.

Parking her car in the driveway, Melanie opened her umbrella and hurried to the front door. The thought of questioning her mother made her anxious, and for an instant, she regretted having given in to Sam. But she would be honest and simply explain his request.

She found Katie sitting in her robe and slippers playing solitaire in the den. Years of garden sunshine had etched her face with spidery wrinkles. Strains of Schubert accompanied the crackling logs in the fireplace.

Melanie sat down by her mother. "Who's winning?"

Katie continued shuffling the cards. "I am. You looked very pretty tonight, but you're too skinny."

"I've weighed 118 pounds for the last ten years, Mom. And Uncle Tim only found one mistake. He faxed me that it's pronounced 'me-heil' Gorbachev, not 'mik-ale.' What a character!"

A black nine found its way to a red ten.

"Sam Greenfield took me to lunch yesterday," Melanie ventured.

"That's nice."

"He's quite a hunk," she went on, almost surprised to hear herself say it. "He's writing a family history for the store's centennial. He came across an article about the shooting incident in 1960."

Katie shrugged. "That has nothing to do with the Greenfields."

"I know — but he's curious. Would it bother you to talk about it?"

"I've told you everything I know." An edge crept into her voice. "The only one who knows more is Clara, and I'm sure she won't discuss it."

"Did you believe her story?"

"I don't know." Katie set down her cards. "There *was* something that puzzled me — an envelope. She took it from the dead man's hand. She made me promise not to say a word to anybody. That was so long ago."

"What was in it?"

"She wouldn't tell me." A nervous shudder. "I don't know why you're bringing up such unpleasant matters."

"Sorry, Mom." Melanie reached across the table for her hand. It was cold and trembling. "I guess my greatest dream is that you and Nonna will make up some day."

"What for? She doesn't want me in her life."

"But she does. Suppose, just suppose, she were to call you. Would you see her?"

"I don't know." Katie picked up her glass and headed for the door. "I'm tired and I'm going to bed."

Sam sat at his desk in the newsroom, his fingers on the keyboard, the phone at his side. Sleep had eluded him most of the night. After watching Melanie anchor the early news, he'd taped her doing the late news, and played it back several times. Never had he seen anyone so graceful, so feminine and appealing. His fantasies were wild and disturbingly carnal.

The call finally came as he was biting into an apple. "Sam?"

He spit the pieces into his hand. "Yup, I'm here, Melanie. Caught you on the news last night."

"Uh-oh. Another critic in the family."

"Not me. I thought you were fantastic. Kind of a younger, prettier, sexier Diane Sawyer."

"Really?"

"No. Watching you is agony, but someone has to do it. Did you talk to your mother?"

"I tried. The subject was too touchy."

"Oh, God, I'm sorry. Did she say anything at all?"

No reason to mention the envelope. "Only that it's a waste of time trying to find out what happened. Please drop it, Sam. You'll just cause more grief."

"Why? It's strictly for my own enlightenment."

"San Francisco's such a small town. What if Herb Caen gets wind of what you're doing?"

"He's not interested in old news. Now stop worrying that beautiful head and tell me if you like opera."

"Yes, but —"

"I have my mother's box seats for *Aida* tonight. Will you go with me?"

"You mean like a date?"

"Does it have to have a name?"

"Well, yes — no. I mean, for God's sakes, Sam, we can't go out."

"Where is it written?"

"It's incest."

"It's nothing of the sort. We're not even full-blooded cousins. And I happen to know you don't do the eleven o'clock news on Friday nights. So I'll pick you up at seven-thirty. Black tie."

"Save your breath. I'm not going."

"Why not?"

"Sam, I'm *not* going out with you and that's final."

"What if I promise not to probe anymore? What if I promise to drop my investigation, stifle my curiosity, and never mention the shooting again — if you'll go to the opera with me."

"That's blackmail."

"No, it's extortion. Seven-thirty?"

She sighed into the phone. "Seven-thirty."

This is lunacy, Melanie thought, as she zipped the back of her floor-length Adolfo. She'd only worn the black beaded gown once before, to an awards dinner, and everyone said she looked smashing. So here she was, fussing with her dress, her purse, her jewelry — things she normally didn't care about, and all to impress a man she shouldn't be seeing in the first place.

On the other hand, why shouldn't she? Sam was right that they weren't "full-blooded" cousins. Their mothers, Katie and Yvonne, were only half-sisters. And besides, they were just going to the opera, not flying off for the weekend.

Yet even as she tried to talk herself out of being excited, her nerves were tingling. Ever since the day she'd chased him down the hall at the department store, she had thought Sam Greenfield was one of the most charming, adorable men she had ever met. But never, even in her boldest fantasies, had she dared to hope he might be interested in her as a woman.

The clock said 7:30, and she realized she hadn't told him where she lived. Her fears were allayed two minutes later, when the doorbell rang. On the way to answer, she reminded herself that nothing could come of this date. No matter how weak the family connection, her parents, his parents, and the world in general, saw them as cousins. And cousins didn't get romantically involved.

Front row seats, one box to the left of center, afforded the best view of stage and orchestra Melanie had ever seen. The performance was impressive; she adored the pageantry and thrilled to the Triumphal March. At intermission, she and Sam strolled across the marble lobby, greeting friends and acquaintances, aware of the admiring stares. She said it was his cowlick; he said it was her wobble.

Later, as they left the Opera House, he took her arm. "Do you keep a diary?"

"No." She glanced up. "Why?"

"Because we're about to have our first fight and someone should record it for posterity."

"Oh, dear. I'm having such a nice time. What are we going to fight about?"

"Your introducing me as your cousin. Would you please stop?"

"You *are* my cousin."

"People get the wrong idea." He unlocked the car door and helped her inside. "They think we're platonic."

"We are."

"I'm not." He came around, took the driver's seat and pretended to leer. "In Shakespeare's immortal words, 'Your place or mine?'"

"I don't even clink glasses on the first date."

"You're pretty square. What kind of a family do you come from?"

"A nutty one." They both laughed.

"At least we don't have to go through all that 'Where were you born?' jazz. It's strange. Every woman I've ever liked has been older, brunette, and gentile. What's a nice half-Jewish blonde doing in my life?"

"I'm not in your life."

"You are, too." He started the motor. "What kind of food do you like — French? Italian?"

"If you don't mind, I'd like to go home."

"Good idea. You'll need your sleep because I'm picking you up at nine tomorrow. We'll drive to Marin and have a picnic on top of Mt. Tamalpais."

"I can't see you tomorrow. I'm busy."

"Then we'll have dinner. I'll take you to my favorite Mexican place."

"I'm busy."

"You won't see me again?"

She sighed. "It's not personal. It's biological."

"I'm not asking you to have my child, I'm asking you for a cheese enchilada. There's a difference."

"We can't pretend we're just two unrelated people. We're —"

"Not the C-word!"

They drove in silence till they reached her flat. "I know you don't want to hear this," he said, turning her key in the lock, "but I can't remember when I've enjoyed an evening so much."

She blew him a kiss and stepped inside. "Thanks, Sam. Give my love to the family."

Even with a rather long list of chores, the hours seemed to drag on Saturday. Melanie couldn't help thinking that she could be enjoying the sunshine — and Sam — on Mt. Tamalpais. The evening was worse; it took all her effort to be pleasant to her date. Was she doomed, she wondered, to compare Sam Greenfield to every man she went out with?

Shortly before noon on Sunday, two dozen roses arrived. The card said, "Let's adopt." Puzzled for a second, she quickly understood Sam's reference to the progeny of cousins, and felt a warm glow. Then she tore it up.

Visiting Nonna that afternoon, she made no mention of Sam. But she did confide worry for her mother, and worked up the nerve to ask, "Would you ever consider calling your daughter?"

"I wish I could." The subject pained Clara. "But she has no feelings for me. When I had my mastectomy, Tim told me he visited her in the Haight-Ashbury, and that she promised she'd call me. I waited and waited. Every time the phone rang, I prayed it was Katie. It never was, and I was devastated."

"But she *did* call you! She told me so. And *she* was devastated because you didn't call her back."

Clara's brows shot up. "When did she tell you that?"

"Ages ago. When I first asked why you two hadn't made up."

Tears welled in Clara's eyes. "I wish I'd known. I never got any sort of message."

"Probably some nurse got busy and forgot to tell you. But it's not too late. I saw Mom a few days ago, and asked if she'd see you if you called. She didn't say no."

"Really?"

"Honestly! Oh, Nonna, please say you'll come with me to visit her. The alcohol problem is getting worse, and together, maybe we can convince her to get help."

"Of course I'll go, darling." Clara hugged her granddaughter. "If she'll let me back into her life, I'll be the happiest old fossil alive."

As Melanie was leaving the Jackson Street house, a man who looked familiar was approaching. A young boy was with him.

"Dave Greenfield," smiled the man, offering his hand. "It's been a long time, Melanie. This is my son, Peter. He'll be eight next week."

"Dave! Oh golly, forgive me." She blushed in embarrassment. He was thin and sandy-haired, and stamped with that weary expression common to overworked doctors. He bore little resemblance to his brother, Sam.

"Peter, this is your long lost cousin Melanie Morris. Remember the pretty lady I showed you on television?"

The boy nodded shyly.

"Hi, Peter, and happy birthday next week." Melanie shook her head in wonderment. "I don't think I've seen you since your wedding, Dave."

"That was fourteen years ago."

"You haven't changed much."

He covered a yawn. "'Scuse me. I'm getting too old for all-night surgeries. But how do you tell the mother of a nine-year-old gunshot victim that you need your sleep?"

"Your life must be wonderfully rewarding."

"What about yours? I try to catch you on the late news. Say, maybe you'll come have dinner with us one night. I'll get that crazy kid brother of mine to bring you over."

"Thanks, Dave. I'd like that. Bye, bye, Peter. Say hi to your Mom."

She hurried down the stairs, hoping Dave wouldn't realize she'd forgotten his wife's name. What would happen, she wondered, if he did call Sam and invite them over. Would it encourage Sam if she accepted? Would it be asking for problems? Or would it be a wonderful, memorable evening?

She already knew the answer.

Chapter 52 — 1989

The daily roses that arrived at Channel 3 became the talk of the station. Melanie refused to reveal the source, which stirred even more curiosity. One colleague even went so far as to call the florist, but with no luck.

After a week, Melanie dashed off a note: "Dear Sam, The flowers are beautiful but please stop. The boxes go right to the patients at St. Francis Hospital. Your devoted *cousin*, Melanie."

Sam's gifts continued, however: books, perfume, and a small box from Tiffany, which went back to the store, unopened. For whatever reason, the invitation to Dave's dinner never materialized.

On a Sunday afternoon in mid-November, Melanie drove to the house on Jackson Street. Her grandmother, remarkably alert at 82, had called Katie as promised, and talked to her briefly. Reluctant at first, Katie finally agreed to the meeting, and invited Clara to come to her house. This was the day Melanie was to bring mother and daughter together.

"You ready, Nonna?" Melanie called, stepping inside the front door.

A voice came from the living room. "I've been ready for half an hour."

Leaning slightly on a gold-tipped cane, Clara approached her grand-daughter and nervously asked, "How do I look?"

Melanie pretended to appraise her. "Hair's in place, a touch of pow-der and lipstick, navy blue coat and shoes. I pronounce you perfection!"

"She probably won't notice."

A definite possibility, thought Melanie, praying that her mother would be sober.

Minutes later, parking in front of Katie's house, Melanie decided not to use her key. She rang the bell. An eternal wait, or so it seemed until the door opened. To Melanie's relief, Katie had taken the trouble to put on a dress and clean herself up. Strong perfume masked the usual smell of liquor.

The sight of Katie sent tears streaming down Clara's face. Impul-sively she opened her arms and enfolded her daughter. Katie let herself be embraced, holding back at first, then hugging Clara in return, and letting go with her own tears.

Melanie gave a silent prayer. She had dreamed of this moment all her life. "You're looking great, Mom," she told Katie, as the women separated. A short period of awkwardness, then Melanie added. "Let's go sit in the living room."

Clara dabbed at her eyes. She was back in control. "Your home is lovely, Katie dear. Are those roses from your garden?"

The question was welcome. "Yes, I try to spend every afternoon with my flowers. I guess I get my love of flowers from you."

"You have a knack for arranging them." Clara forced a smile. Katie was pale, bloated, and looked malnourished. "Do you have a gardener or do you do it all yourself?"

This was safe territory. Katie went into a detailed explanation of the different types of roses, what grew well and what didn't. She served her guests tea and cookies, pouring with a shaky hand. Her relief was tangible when Melanie said, "I think we've stayed long enough. Perhaps we could come again, Mom?"

Before Katie could answer, Clara rose. "Will you come to dinner sometime, Katie?"

"I'd like to," she said, still reluctant to call Clara 'Mother.' "I'm glad we — got together."

"So am I." Clara sensed some of the same old shyness. She had to draw on all her will power to keep from hugging Katie again.

On the short drive home, Clara expressed concern. Melanie reassured her that they had taken the crucial first step to bring Katie back into the family. Little by little, with love and caring, they hoped they would get her to seek treatment.

The following Friday, Christi phoned to say that Katie hadn't left her room or eaten solid food in 48 hours. Melanie called the family internist, Dr. Saitowitz, and they met at Katie's bedside. He wanted to put her in the hospital. Katie refused to go. She promised to eat her dinner, and gave her word that she would show up first thing Monday morning at the detox clinic.

The situation weighed on Melanie's mind that Sunday night. Her mother was due to enter the alcohol rehab unit in the morning, and she might need some bolstering. She decided to walk the full ten blocks to

236

Katie's house.

The last rays of sunshine poked through the clouds and cold wind rattled the trees, typical weather for November. Melanie tightened her muffler, turned up her collar, and quickened her pace.

As she rounded the corner to Broadway Street, a silver Porsche pulled up to the curb. Sam Greenfield rolled down the window and tipped his '49ers cap. "Need a lift, ma'am?"

"Oh, no," she groaned. "What are you doing here?"

"Just passing by." He drove beside her as she walked. "Freezing those beautiful buns off?"

"Go away, Sam."

"Can we talk after you see your mother?"

May we talk, she thought, Katie's eternal corrections echoing in her ear. "No. I have to work tonight."

"I'll wait for you."

"I might be hours."

"Then I can drive you back to your car."

The realization that he had been following her from Jackson Street annoyed her. "Please go away, Sam. I can't deal with you now."

Not waiting for a response, she strode up to Katie's front door, turned the key and entered. The hall was dark and strangely quiet. Christi and Bill were off for the day.

"Mom?" she called. "Anyone home?"

Concern fast turned to alarm. Dropping her purse on a bench, she raced up the stairs. The bedrooms were empty. So was the sitting room. She peered through the window; no one in the garden. Where could her mother be? She never went walking. She never saw friends. She hadn't driven a car for years.

"Mom!" she shouted, her voice becoming frantic, "where are you?"

A faint whirring sound at the bottom of the stairs made her step cautiously into the living room. She quickly discovered a played-out record spinning on its turntable. Fear swept over her as she scanned the room — then stood paralyzed. Her mother's crumpled figure lay on the floor by the piano.

With a gasp, Melanie fell to her knees and felt for a pulse. Thank God! It was beating faintly. Then she noticed, with horror, that the back of her mother's head was sticky with blood. Panicked, she jumped up and dashed out the door. The Porsche was just pulling away.

"Sam!" she screamed, waving her arms, "Help!"

Brakes screeched. Sam was out of the car in seconds. "What is it?"

"Katie's hurt!"

He followed her inside. "Is she breathing?"

"Barely."

"Don't move her," he said. "I'll call 911, you call her doctor."

The ambulance arrived within minutes. Melanie rode inside with her mother, Sam followed in his car. Dr. Saitowitz, luckily, had been at the hospital, and was waiting at the California Pacific Medical Center emergency room. He disappeared down the hall with the stretcher.

An hour later, he came back, his face grim. "We have to operate, Melanie. We're trying to reach a neurosurgeon."

"Try my brother," said Sam.

"Pardon?"

"I'm Sam Greenfield, Melanie's cousin. My brother's Dave Greenfield, a neurosurgeon in Marin, and one of the best."

"What are you waiting for?" said the doctor. "Call him!"

Shortly before midnight, Sam and Melanie sat in anxious silence, sole occupants of the surgical waiting room. Much as he wanted to comfort and reassure her, he was sensitive to her needs. When she felt like talking, she would let him know.

As if reading his mind, she closed her magazine and returned it to the rack. "How long has Mom been in surgery?"

"About four hours."

"Please go home, Sam. You must be exhausted."

"I'm not leaving you."

"I can't begin to thank you — especially after I was so rude."

"You had every right to be. I was trying to be cute and you were dealing with a major problem." How beautiful she looked when she was sad.

"Mom was supposed to go into a rehab clinic tomorrow. I guess this was her last hurrah. She —"

Suddenly a door opened, and Dave Greenfield appeared, his face an impenetrable mask. He shook his hair out of a green surgical cap as he walked.

"She made it," he said, drawing up a chair. "I can't tell you much except that she's breathing. Her heartbeat's steady but I don't know when or if she'll regain consciousness."

Melanie's mouth dropped. "You mean — ever?"

"Katie has a condition called alcoholic-nutritional cerebellar disintegration, Melanie. Too much booze, too little food. Sometime this afternoon, she went on a drinking spree. She may have blacked out and wakened with lower-extremity dysmetria, which means she couldn't control her legs. Couldn't walk."

"Oh, God."

Sam took Melanie's hand.

"She probably tried to get up. Her knees buckled and she fell, striking her head against a hard object. The ambulance report said she was found at the foot of a piano bench."

"What's the prognosis?"

"Not good, Melanie. She's in a coma, so she's not suffering. It's too soon to say any more."

The bleak picture sent Melanie sobbing into Sam's arms. He held her close to him, patting her head and telling her not to worry. He was there for her; he would always be there for her.

"Sam?" Dave asked, looking on quietly. "Is there something you haven't told me?"

Sam had almost forgotten his brother was standing there. "Yeah, Dave," he replied as he stroked Melanie's hair. "I'm in love with my cousin."

Dave Greenfield knew it was not the time to be curious. Whatever relationship Sam had with Melanie was his own business. If anything of consequence was in the works, and he suspected it was, Sam would tell him soon enough.

But he couldn't help wondering how long they had been seeing each other, and how they handled the fact of their mutual ancestry. He guessed that Yvonne, their mother, would be less than thrilled to hear that her son was romancing her niece. But Melanie was so bright, beautiful, and kind. Who wouldn't fall in love with her?

After showering and changing his clothes, Dave found Sam and Melanie in the waiting room.

"You kids go home," he said. "Katie's in Intensive Care. I doubt she'll wake up tonight."

Sam put his arm around Melanie. "Will someone call us if she does?"

Dave hesitated a moment. "Uh, sure — will you both be at Melanie's?"

"Sam won't be there."

"Sam *will* be there. Dave, not a word to the family about us, okay?" He scribbled on a card. "Here's the phone number."

Too weak to argue, Melanie let Sam drive her home. He escorted her inside, insisting that if anything happened, he wanted to be able to take her to the hospital. She nodded weakly, pointed to the guest room, then collapsed in a heap on her bed.

Sam took a week of his vacation time to be with Melanie as she kept vigil by Katie's bedside. He brought soup and sandwiches from the cafeteria, and spelled her when she wanted a breath of fresh air.

At night, when the private nurse came on duty, he drove Melanie home and slept in the next room. Seeing her grace and dignity under such pressure gave him yet another reason, as if he needed one, to love her.

On Wednesday, Dave explained that Katie had contracted a form of pneumonia caused by the Serratia bacteria, an organism common to hospitals. He moved her back into Intensive Care.

At Melanie's request, Sam went to see Clara. She was shattered to hear about Katie, then encouraged Sam to get to know his cousin. "You've been a bachelor long enough," she scolded. "Melanie can introduce you to some nice girls."

Later that afternoon, Katie's blood pressure plummeted. A nurse alerted the Code Blue team, but all attempts at revival failed. At 5:18 P.M., Katherine Marie Stockton Morris was pronounced dead.

Only various Stocktons and Greenfields, plus Christi and Bill, and Jason and Trudy Morris, attended Katie's private service at the funeral parlor. Will escorted Clara, weeping quietly under her black veil. Melanie and Sam sat next to her.

The eulogy was brief and flowery, and the service ended. Clara grabbed her cane and walked over to thank the minister. Will turned to Melanie. "My condolences. I missed seeing you on the news this week."

She sniffed and wiped her eyes. "Do you check the competition?"

"Always. You're good."

"Thanks," she said, rising.

"Before you run off, Mel, how'd you like to switch channels?"

"I don't think this is the time —"

"It isn't, but my offer's genuine. I'll pay more than you're getting."

"Will, this is your sister's *funeral*!" She grabbed Sam's arm and pulled him away. "Stop me before I kill."

The rain poured steadily, muffling the sounds of rush hour traffic. Sam drove to Melanie's flat with a load of groceries. He had insisted on cooking dinner — anything to spend time with her — and she had been grateful not to be alone.

She greeted him at the door in jeans and a pink T-shirt, looking exactly, he thought, like the star of a teenage soap opera. With a nod of appreciation, she took one of the bags and headed for the kitchen.

"Did you get a nap?" he asked.

"No. I spent the day just letting myself grieve." She pulled out a package of four filet mignons. "Who's going to eat all this?"

"We are. Now scoot! Out of my kitchen. Cocktails at six, dinner at seven. Don't dress."

"Can't I help?"

He pointed to the door. "Out!"

Melanie hadn't only spent the day mourning, she had taken time to assess her relationship with Sam. During the ordeal, he had shown a depth of compassion she never would have suspected.

Her original reluctance had not only been because of their family connection, but also because she had seen him as a spoiled mama's boy, attracted to the one woman he couldn't have: his cousin. Now she began to wonder if her judgment had been too harsh. And if so, how great an obstacle was their blood bondage?

The more she knew this surprising young man, the less it seemed to matter.

Chapter 53 – 1989

Katie Morris's will left a handsome legacy to her housekeepers, Christi and Bill, generous gifts to Pets Unlimited and the San Francisco SPCA, plus bequests to several Marin garden clubs, rehab centers, and Alcoholics Anonymous branches, even though she never joined any of them. The bulk of her estate went to Melanie. And the family lawyer suggested she might want to live in her mother's Broadway Street house, but she declined. Too big. Too many memories.

In the meantime, Sam had become a most attentive suitor, shopping for groceries and cooking dinner, or arranging to have it delivered every night. One evening, two weeks after the funeral, the phone rang as they were finishing their meal.

"Hi, Vincent," he heard her say. "Yes, it was sudden. She was only fifty." A pause, and then, "No, thanks, I'm really not seeing anyone yet." Another pause. "Yes, let's talk in January. Have a good holiday."

She walked back to the table to find Sam glowering. "Who was that?"

Startled, she stared at him. "Nobody, really. A guy I dated a few times."

"Why did you tell him you weren't seeing anyone? Who the hell am I?"

"Sam, what is this nonsense? Since when do you own me?"

"I don't own you. I don't *want* to own you. But I thought I meant something to you."

"Of course you mean something to me. You've been wonderful these past weeks but now you're acting like a child. If you want to throw a tantrum over a phone call, do it somewhere else."

"Come on, Mel, am I supposed to sit around and wait while you go out with other guys?"

"No one's asking you to sit around and wait."

He tried to keep the edge from his voice. "All I want to know is if you intend to date a lot of other guys. If you do, I'm outa here."

"Is that an ultimatum?"

"Why do you have to put a name on everything?"

"It's a fair question. I don't like to be manipulated."

"And I don't like a woman who can't be straight with me."

"Then maybe you'd better leave." She threw down her napkin and headed for the bedroom, slamming the door behind her.

Sam was frustrated by their quarrel but far from defeated. Thinking back the next morning, he knew he'd been wrong. He'd acted like a whiny, spoiled, jealous child, expecting Melanie to share his commitment to their relationship. He thought he'd been so patient, never trying to get romantic, never making sex an issue. But his control had finally snapped when he heard her say she wasn't seeing anyone; if they'd been sleeping together, it never would have happened.

Anger, he realized, wasn't going to help. Obviously, Melanie needed time — time to recover from her mother's death, time to sort out her emotions, maybe even time to date old boyfriends. He wasn't afraid of the competition; he just wanted to understand the situation.

Without the joy of her presence, however, the holidays dragged. Hanukkah with his nieces, nephews and screaming grandnephews only intensified his loneliness. He answered Dave's questions with a sad shrug. Yes, he loved Melanie. Yes, they had a fight. Yes, he would see her again. No, he didn't know when. Pride and principle kept him from succumbing to the urge to call her.

He only hoped she was suffering, too.

The spat with Sam had left Melanie hurt and confused. Well-meaning friends, knowing she had lost her mother, tried to buoy her spirits over the holidays, inviting her to parties and informal get-togethers. Yvonne and Clara both asked her to family gatherings, but she had made excuses, not wanting to face Sam. Not wanting to be alone, either, she had taken her father and Trudy to Trader Vic's for Christmas dinner.

On New Year's Eve, her old friend Carolyne fixed her up with a stockbroker from Boston — a tedious evening that made her vow never to accept another blind date. At the same time, Sam's behavior distressed and puzzled her. Couldn't he even call to wish her happy new year?

Sure, they had bickered. She had been arrogant and insensitive, and she regretted it. But he had been wrong, too. If he cared for her as much as he claimed, would a few angry words, two weeks after she buried her mother, be enough to cause a permanent rift? If he was that unforgiving, who needed him?

Yet she couldn't deny the void in her life. She missed him terribly —

his concern, his adoration, even his crazy, offbeat humor. She missed the electricity of just being near him, knowing how much he wanted her, but also knowing that he respected her, and her need to let out her grief.

So many times she picked up the phone, then set it down. Calling him would be a sign of weakness. Not that she wanted to date other men; she hadn't the least desire to do so. But that would have to be her decision, not his.

The new year had barely begun when Sam arrived at the paper one morning and found a message to see Paul. What now, he wondered, as he hurried to the office.

Helen ushered him in without the usual wait. Paul was standing with his back to the door, poring through a file cabinet. He dropped some papers in the waste basket and limped to his chair.

"Good Lord!" Sam exclaimed, "What's wrong?"

"Old war injury kicking up. One of my knee joints never healed right. I need an operation PDQ or I'll be permanently lame."

"Oh, God, I'm sorry." He wasn't sure whether to be a stepson or an employee. "Please, tell me what I can do for you."

"What you can do for me, Sam, is publish this newspaper. You've only been here a year and a half, but your mother, grandmother, Tim, Lou Ella and Betsy all seem to think you can take over in an emergency. So do I."

Sam sucked in his breath. "Take over? You're asking me to take your job?"

"You can do it. I was planning to break you in gradually, but it looks like you'll have to learn on the job. Helen knows the ropes. The staff's at your disposal. And I'm only a phone call away any time of day or night."

"But what about your executive editor? How will he feel having to answer to a 33-year-old?"

"I've talked to Brady, and he fully understands. He'll support you all the way. You're a Stockton, whether you bear the name or not. You're the logical heir to the throne, such as it is."

Sam gulped, his brain reeling. "You're planning to come back, aren't you?"

"Let's see how it goes. Frankly, I wouldn't mind taking a long ocean voyage with your mother. We've never had a honeymoon. And I've pretty well accomplished what I set out to do. The *Herald*'s a first rate paper now. It's going to be up to you to keep it that way."

Speechless, Sam could only nod.

"I suggest you clear out your desk and be back here at ten. I'll be gone by then. Brady will take you into the editorial meeting and explain the situation to the others. I'm giving him a memo to read, saying that anything less than full cooperation will not be tolerated."

The magnitude of the challenge both flattered and panicked Sam. But his immediate goal was to relieve Paul of worry. "I'm sure I can handle it," he said, with a confidence he didn't feel. "Just take care of that knee and get well. You can count on me. I won't let you down."

Paul's tense expression melted into a smile. Then he reached out to embrace him. "Thanks, kid," he said softly. "You're a good man."

Chapter 54 – 1989

The weeks that followed were far more difficult for Sam than he could have imagined. Paul's knee operation was successful, but Sam found himself having to call for advice several times a day. How should he handle an editorial writer whose views had become too conservative? Should he approve moving a columnist to the back of "Modern Living" against her wishes? What about the advertiser who wanted his money back because the ad was on the wrong page? Who would replace the bureau chief who left to join *TIME*?

Brady, the executive editor, was a help, of sorts, and Helen Hopkins, who'd been there more than 40 years, was great with names and places, but the more Sam worked at the job, with its never-ending challenges, the more he began to appreciate Paul and Lou Ella, and their many years of dedication.

In the beginning, both must have faced much the same problems: the scorn of most of the old-time reporters, the "let-him-make-his-own-mistakes" attitude of some editors, the arrogant critics and columnists who disregarded memos and couldn't be bothered returning calls.

Paul's advice was always the same: "Get tough. Once they sniff weakness, you're done." And after a fair amount of bruising, Sam finally did get tough. He fought the union for the right to fire the drama critic, a fixture from the sixties, who refused Sam's request to review a charity production. He replaced an editor who ignored his memo to include weekly interviews in the business section, and he suspended a rookie reporter for being two hours late to work and smelling of booze. Word began to spread that the kid from Gucci was no pushover. Gradually and begrudgingly, attitudes began to change.

Sam began to change, too. Lack of a personal life and the sudden pressures heaped upon him turned him into a workaholic. Time lost its meaning. He had but one purpose and one goal. He would spend as many hours as necessary to prove to himself, his family, and his staff…that he could do every bit as well as his predecessors.

In rare leisure moments, his thoughts turned to Melanie. That first day they'd talked on the phone, she'd said she couldn't handle a relationship, and he had understood. But later, thinking it over, he had asked himself how any job could be so demanding that you didn't need someone to curl up with at night. Now he knew the answer. By the time he crawled into bed at night, all he could do was hit the pillow and pass out.

One morning in March of 1990, Helen Hopkins rapped on the door and entered Sam's office. "Got a minute?"

"Sure." He looked up with resignation. "What have I done now?"

"Nothing, Sam. This is personal. I'm worried about your health. You've been working too hard."

"And you've been talking to my mother again. May I remind you, Miss Hopkins, that I'm a grown man? I drive a car, I drink in bars, I vote for president, and I only pee in my pants when I'm nervous."

"You'd joke your way out of a death sentence. It's not normal to cut yourself off from people."

"Meaning what?"

"Meaning you should have a good time — go out with friends — girls..."

"Ah, now we're getting to it. What if I told you I'm madly in love with a magnificent woman, but we can't be together right now. Would that make you feel better?"

Her face lit up. "Is it true?"

"Maybe. Would you close the door on your way out?"

Invitations to civic, charity, business, and private functions began to pour into Sam's office. He knew he would have to start accepting some of them. Public relations went with the job. His first inclination was to phone Melanie and ask her to accompany him. Hadn't he waited long enough? But she was still working nights. And even if she weren't, how could he treat her as a casual date?

The prospects of resuming their relationship at that point were bleak. He was behind his desk at six A.M. almost every day, and got home just as she was going on the air. Most of the time he couldn't bring himself to watch her. He was no martyr. She hadn't given him strong reason to believe she cared for him, but he felt certain she knew the demands of his new position, and that he still felt the same about her.

On the night of June fifth, hearing on his car radio that gubernatorial candidate Dianne Feinstein had won the Democratic primary, he decided to stop by her celebration at the Fairmont Hotel. He wasn't being altruistic; a pipeline to the Governor's office would more than repay his effort. Besides that, Dianne was one of the few politicians he liked and respected.

The large hall was airless and noisy, and jammed with celebrants. Yuppies in blazers, button-down businessmen, elegant blacks, and social types in Chanel mingled with tough-looking union leaders, well-groomed career women, elegantly-dressed gays, pony tailed professors, and working people of all descriptions. The only common denominator seemed to be their happy faces.

The room was charged with positive energy.

"Mr. Greenfield?" He turned to face a pretty young woman in red. "I'm Barbara, with the campaign staff. I know Dianne will be thrilled to see you. Could we entice you to join her on the platform?"

"No, thanks. I'm just here as a friend."

"It would mean a lot to have you up there."

One of the drawbacks of his new position, Sam realized, was that people saw him as a publisher, not a person. Much as he was beginning to enjoy the prestige, he had to keep reminding himself that he represented a newspaper. Standing with Dianne before the TV cameras would be a virtual endorsement by the *Herald* — one he wasn't yet free to make. "I came to wish her well. That's all."

"We're expecting her in twenty minutes. Would you care to wait in the private lounge with Mrs. Shultz and some of the other supporters?"

"No, thanks, I haven't time. Please give her my best." He started to head for the exit, when a glance across the room made him pause. Was he seeing right? He stared hard and long, and cursed the man who blocked his view. He had to find out.

Wending his way through the mob, he managed to stop a few feet away. Indeed, it was she. And as if the intensity of his emotion somehow communicated, Melanie spun around. For a second, the sight of him seemed to catch her off guard. Then she excused herself to her cameramen and walked up to him.

"Haven't seen you for a while, Sam." Her voice rang with that lovely lilt he knew so well. Her face was impassive, her manner impersonal. "How've you been?"

"Busy. Lonely. Aren't you gracing the screen tonight?"

"Yes, I'm going back in a few minutes."

He nodded awkwardly. So much to say and his thoughts kept bumping into each other. "Do you need a lift?"

"No, thanks. I have my car."

Help me, God, he prayed. Give me words. "Melanie, I don't know where to begin. There's so much I want to explain to you."

"You don't owe me any explanation. Congratulations on your new job. How's it going?"

Her tone was more than impersonal. She might have been talking to a lamp-post.

"The job's a killer. Ever watched a hamster spin round and round on one of those wheels?" His tone softened. "You look wonderful."

"Thanks. I've got to be running. Nice to see you."

"Wait, Melanie. Could we get together later?"

"What for?" She turned and vanished into the crowd.

Sam stood rooted, reeling from the impact. In her quiet way, she had rejected him firmly, and he deserved it. All he'd had to do was phone — but how do you phone the woman you love and say, "I'm too busy to see you for the next six months."?

Later that night, he lay tossing in bed, determined to get through to her and win her back. Plots and schemes rolled around his brain, but he hated playing games, and she was far too sharp to be manipulated.

The clock said one minute to midnight. She should be home by now. Her phone rang six times before a machine answered.

"Congratulations, Ms. Morris," he said excitedly, "you're the lucky winner of the Take-A-Schmuck-To-Lunch contest. First prize is the honor of lunching with the biggest schmuck of all, Sam Greenfield. You'll meet at noon tomorrow, St. Francis Yacht Club. Failure to appear could cost a penalty: *two* lunches with Sam Greenfield."

The minute he hung up, he regretted his glibness. He'd made light of his error instead of apologizing.

"Stupid ass," he growled, and rolled back on his pillow.

Helen's note on the desk read, "Your cousin regrets she can't meet you for lunch," and started the day all wrong for Sam. It got worse. A dispute in the mailers' union was threatening to escalate, and he wasn't sure how to handle it. Paul's advice guided him, however, and five days later, his negotiators settled.

Averting the strike gave Sam a strong sense of relief, as if a block of steel had been lifted from his shoulders. All he could think about was sharing his joy with Melanie.

Knowing she usually went to the station around four P.M., he tried to reach her at home. No one answered, and he didn't want to leave another message. Instead, he decided to express himself in writing.

Fishing around his desk for a sheet of stationery, he happened to notice a letter. The board of directors of Walk-In House, a homeless shelter in the Tenderloin district, wanted him to join their panel of judges. All he had to do was attend a meeting to choose the best of a series of wall murals.

An idea flashed. Melanie had often spoken of her concern for the homeless. He remembered the night they'd passed a panhandler shivering on the street. "I know all the reasons why I shouldn't give him money," she'd said, delving into her purse, "but he's suffering. That's all that should matter."

Impulsively, Sam called Walk-In House.

"Lois Duffy? Sam Greenfield at the *Herald*. I'll be happy to join your panel of judges. May I suggest another possibility?"

The woman sounded thrilled. "By all means!"

"Melanie Morris at channel 3. She's very concerned with the homeless problem. But she told me recently how busy she is, so maybe it's best not to say I recommended her."

"Of course, Mr. Greenfield. Is there any one else?"

"No." There never had been and there never would be anyone else. "Thanks, Mrs. Duffy."

Chapter 55 – 1990

The judging session was four weeks away, but Sam couldn't wait. Before going to bed that night, he wrote Melanie a long letter, telling her how much he regretted their parting, and explaining his actions — or lack of same. Pouring out his feelings on paper was cathartic.

He wrote her again the next night, and the following night, until it became a bedtime ritual. And the more he opened his heart to her, the more he discovered the depth of his feelings.

The alarm went off early Saturday morning. At first Melanie couldn't remember why she was supposed to get up, then she recalled; she was due to judge a mural contest in the Tenderloin.

The previous night, and almost every night for the last few weeks, she had been having late supper with Vincent Rule, a good-looking, gray-haired, high-powered attorney who worked for her TV station. He was suave, older, charming and courtly. After months of missing Sam and fantasizing their bodies in every imaginable form of embrace, dating a man whose appeal was more intellectual than physical was something of a relief.

For his part, however, Vincent had made clear that his intentions were anything but "honorable"; when she felt ready to take their relationship to the next step, he would be more than willing.

Yet, just as she'd been wondering if she could have a future with such a man, Sam had bounced back into her life — warm, adorable, irrepressible as ever, with the added allure of his new position. Her strong reaction to seeing him at the Fairmont told her he was still very much in her system.

Then came the letters. At first logical and explanatory, they had become increasingly tender, loving, erotic. What was a woman to do? Follow her heart and opt for a turbulent, passionate man who was crazy in love with her, and whose family — (which happened to be her own) — was certain to disapprove? Or should she pursue a relationship with a man who seemed to offer maturity, peace of mind and stability?

Grabbing a robe, she hurried into the kitchen, squeezed a pair of oranges, and gulped down the fresh juice. Careful not to select anything expensive-looking, she slipped into a tweed pantsuit. A quick comb-out, a touch of makeup, and because she knew better than to venture alone into the Tenderloin district, she called a cab.

Walk-In House was a run-down three-story building, formerly a hotel, that had been converted into a neighborhood center. Its location was one of the seediest blocks of Ellis Street, surrounded by a Laundromat, a grocery, several bars and a pawn shop.

Sam parked in the Ellis-O'Farrell Garage, assumed his meanest scowl to scare off any would-be muggers and strode up the street. The main hall of Walk-In House was a sparsely furnished room, but large enough to hold several long wooden tables and folding chairs. In one corner, a group of homeless people gathered around an ancient television set. Others read magazines, played cards, chatted, or stared at the well-worn linoleum floor.

"Are you Mr. Kettner or Mr. Greenfield?" A heavy-set woman with over-rouged cheeks came bustling over. Three teenage boys hovered in her shadow, looking nervous.

"Sam Greenfield." He smiled and offered his hand. Her grip was like an iron vise. "Mrs. Duffy, I presume?"

"Kee-rect!" She returned his smile. "I'm afraid our turnout's rather disappointing. Eight boys worked on the project but only three showed up. I shouldn't have insisted they wear white shirts."

"Are Mr. Kettner and I the only judges?"

"No, that television lady's coming."

As if to underscore her words, a clatter of heels sounded. Sam turned to see Melanie approaching. "Speak of the angel," he muttered under his breath.

"Hello, Sam." She masked her surprise with professional cool. "You must be Mrs. Duffy. I'm Melanie Morris from Channel 3. Am I late?"

"No, we're still waiting for Mr. Kettner. He does art reviews for the *Nob Hill Gazette*."

"What is it we're judging?" Sam tried to hide his impatience. Now that Melanie had arrived, he could hardly wait to leave with her.

"Wall murals." The woman gestured to a series of eight tall panels depicting phases of the civil rights movement. "We try to encourage young people to beautify property rather than deface it."

"May I make a suggestion?" Sam drew out a checkbook. "From what

252

I see, all the murals look excellent. Suppose we make each of the eight boys a winner, and each prize a hundred dollars. I'll write a check for $800."

"Are you serious?"

"Would you agree, Melanie? As a fellow judge, does that sound fair?"

"On one condition," she said. "Make the check for 1200 dollars instead of 800. Then those poor people in the corner can have a decent television set."

"The better to see you with, my dear." Sam chuckled, scribbled the check, and handed it to Mrs. Duffy. "That should take care of everything. You won't be needing us anymore."

"How wonderfully generous!" She beamed. "But...how can I thank you? I'd love to give you a tour of the center. Won't you at least stay for coffee?"

"Perhaps another time. Do you have a car, Melanie?"

"Uh — no, I took a cab."

"Then I'll give you a lift. My best to all the winners, Mrs. Duffy."

"The boys and I thank you with all my heart, Mr. Greenfield." She slipped the check into her bosom. "Now what on earth will I tell Mr. Kettner?"

"You didn't have to go to all that trouble." Melanie climbed into the car, as Sam held the door.

"If I'd known it was going to cost me 1200 bucks, I wouldn't have." He grinned and slipped into the driver's seat. "Suppose I'd called you, would you have seen me?"

"I don't know. I've — read all your letters. I'd have to be made of stone not to be affected."

"I meant every word." He started the motor. "Hungry?"

"No, thanks. I'd better go home."

He drove in silence several minutes, sensing her anxiety. It pleased him to know the letters had helped his cause. But he mustn't press too hard. "Is anything wrong, Melanie?"

"I've been dating someone, an older man." Seeing the hurt on his face, she added, "only dating."

"That's a relief. Don't say it. I know it's none of my business. And it couldn't possibly interest you to know that I haven't looked at another woman since we parted."

"We didn't part. We had a dumb spat and you should've phoned me instead of acting like a jackass."

Her rebuke stung. He guided the Porsche up Pacific Avenue and pulled into a space at the curb. "There's a reason for this parking spot," he said, climbing out of the car. "God wants you to invite me in."

She laughed, grateful to break the tension. "God doesn't know you as well as I do. But come in, anyway."

He followed her through the door into the front hall. She excused herself to hang up her jacket. Her apartment looked just as he remembered it — neat, clean, somewhat more crowded now, with some of her mother's furniture. Fresh red roses on a table in the living room gave him a twinge.

"How 'bout my cooking breakfast?" he called, wandering into the kitchen. "I make a great cheese omelet."

"I'm out of cheese," she called back.

"Plain omelet?"

"I'm out of eggs."

"What *have* you got?"

She appeared in the doorway, trim and lovely in her tailored blouse and slacks. "Half a frozen pizza and two cans of V-8 juice."

"You gourmets are all alike." He sniffed the air. "Why do you wear that perfume when you know how it affects me?"

"I didn't know I was going to see you, remember?"

"I remember. I haven't slept for a week hoping you might be there." He walked over and took her hands. "I know I goofed, sweetheart, and I'm sorry. I've tried to tell you that a hundred different ways. Can't you forgive me?"

"I forgave you months ago."

"You did?" His face brightened. Could she mean what he hoped she meant? "Then let's put all that nonsense behind us. I ran across the most amazing facts last night. Did you know that Albert Einstein married his cousin? He wasn't exactly a dummy. Neither was FDR when he married his cousin Eleanor. And look at Charles Darwin, an expert on survival of the fittest. He and his first cousin were so happy together, they produced ten kids."

The talk of marriage gave her pause. "Sam, does everything have to be all or nothing?"

They were in sensitive territory. The wise answer would be, "No, it doesn't, honey. Take as long as you want." But they had wasted too much time already.

"I don't want to alienate you and lose you again," he said, choosing his words with care, "but neither do I want to hide my feelings. I don't see love as a halfway emotion. I've never felt this way about anybody and I don't want to go on pretending. I want all of you and I want you for as long as I live. I want us to spend the rest of our lives together and I can't settle for anything less. Is that wrong?"

At first, she said nothing. Her instinct was to back away from commitment, as she had always done. But this time, she knew she could lose him forever.

"I — want you, too." She spoke softly, her words warming him like a beam of sunlight.

"Do you mean that?"

"Try me."

He didn't need a second invitation. Leaning down, he brushed her lips — tentatively — tenderly.

"I have a confession," she murmured, pulling away slightly. "You aren't the only one who fantasizes. You've made love to me a hundred times in my dreams."

"That's not fair, having all that fun without me."

Even as he spoke, he knew that the time for jokes was over. Months of yearning caught up with him and he folded her in his arms, kissing her deeply and passionately.

She responded with a tremor of anticipation, closing her eyes to his touch, shutting out their families, their backgrounds, all the reasons for not doing what she was about to do. The feel of his lips gliding across her cheek, behind her ear, sliding down her neck... almost made her faint. His excitement was contagious. He pulled her close to him.

"I love you so, my darling," he whispered.

A delightful tingling woke Melanie's naked body as she stirred in Sam's arms. She wondered how long they'd been dozing. Their protracted lovemaking had been both exhilarating and exhausting, leaving no doubt in Melanie's mind that she had made the right decision. Not only was

Sam the kind of man she'd always dreamed of, he was an ardent, tender lover. Going to bed with Vincent would have been like sleeping with a robot.

Her gentle movements caused him to tighten his arms around her. "You're not going anywhere," he murmured drowsily. "I've waited too long to get you in the sack."

"I have to pee."

"Well, okay, just this once."

"I also have to call Vincent — unless you think I should keep my date for tonight."

"With that rose-wielding sexagenarian?"

"He's not a sexagenarian — he's Episcopalian." She rolled her eyes. "Oh, brother. Now you've got *me* making dumb jokes."

"What will you tell him?"

"The truth. He knows about you." She extricated herself from his arms and kissed the tip of his nose. "I'll be back."

Sam lay in bed with his hands folded under his head, his annoyance growing by the second. Jealousy had shafted him with Melanie once before, and he was determined not to let it happen again. But what the hell was she saying to the guy for a quarter of an hour?

When she crawled back into bed a few minutes later, his anger melted at the sight of her red eyes. "What's wrong, sweetheart? What'd that bum say to you?"

"He didn't take it well. He said unkind things about you."

"Like what?"

"That he'd made inquiries. He said the paper's in trouble and you need money to save it. My money. He said that was the only reason you want me."

"And you believed him?"

"Every word." She kissed his lips.

"Wheeee-ew!" He exhaled loudly. "Then why were you crying?"

"Because I saw what a vicious bastard he is and how stupid I've been to let silly pride keep us apart. Oh, Sam," she said, curling up to him, "I love you so much. Hold me tight and promise never, ever to let me go."

"I promise," he whispered, smoothing her hair. "By the way, sweetheart, do you think you *could* swing a small loan?"

Chapter 56 — 1990

Five weeks after their reunion, Sam and Melanie bought a three-story house on Cherry Street in Presidio Heights. The outside was unadorned white stucco with black shutters. The interior was clean and sunlit, and offered enough room so that two people, accustomed to spacious quarters of their own, would not feel crowded.

The decision to buy a house, however, compelled them to do what they couldn't put off doing any longer: tell their families. The first Sunday in September, Melanie called her father, asking if she could drop by with a friend. Trudy was out of town visiting relatives. Jason would be home all day. Thanks to Melanie's largesse, he and Trudy enjoyed a comfortable three-story home on Lake St., in the Richmond district.

Jason answered the door wearing Levis, a T-shirt, backless slippers, and a two-day stubble. The stench of beer and cigar smoke permeated the front hall. "Meant to get cleaned up," he said, kissing Melanie's cheek, "but I couldn't tear myself from the ball game."

"I'm Sam Greenfield, Mr. Morris. Nice to meet you."

They shook hands. "Greenfield? As in Katie's sister?"

"Yes, Yvonne Stockton Greenfield had the misfortune to give birth to me."

"Katie had so much family." Jason scratched his head. "I never could keep 'em straight. Care for a drink? Coffee? Beer?"

"No, thanks, Mr. Morris. We just had lunch."

Jason led the way into a cozy living room dominated by a velvet-covered armchair facing a large TV set. He turned down the sound and motioned to a couch. "Come in, come in. Sit down. Mind if I smoke? I can't do it when my wife's home."

"Daddy, the place stinks. Trudy'll be furious."

"I'll open some windows." He lit his stogie and took several short puffs. After a few minutes of small talk, he asked, "Is this a social call or do you kids have something to tell me?"

"Your daughter and I came to tell you that we love each other," said Sam. "We've been living together and we just bought a house."

He peered at them, puzzled. "Aren't you related?"

"We're half-cousins. A genetics professor at Stanford who did a study on first cousin marriages, told us very few have defective babies. And in our case, the odds are minuscule."

"Which comes first, marriage or parenthood?"

"I'm not pregnant, Daddy."

Sam laughed. "I'd marry her yesterday. She's the one who's stalling."

"I want a big wedding," said Melanie. "Or maybe a small wedding and a big reception — bridal gown with a long train, ring bearers, wedding cake, the works. Might as well do it right. You only get married once — or twice."

"Funny," said Sam.

Jason chuckled. "I like this young man. What do your parents think?"

"We haven't told them yet," Sam answered. "Mom wouldn't like any woman I brought home, and Nonna — well, she could be a problem."

"Do you work in the family store?"

"No, I'm the publisher of the *Herald*."

"Is that so? Well, you're both old enough to know what you're doing, so all that's left is to give you my blessing." His voice cracked as he struggled to finish the sentence. "Shoot, I didn't expect to get slobbery. I guess a father's entitled to cry at his daughter's cohabitation."

Melanie laughed and hugged him. "I promise we'll make it legal. A year from October. Will you tell Trudy? Right now, Sam and I have to call on my Aunt Yvonne and tell her she's about to become my mother-in-law. Yikes!"

Jason walked them to the door and smiled. "Good luck, kids. Let me know if you need a Rabbi."

"Your Dad's a character." Sam took Melanie's hand as he drove up Steiner Street. "I like him. No fuss, no pretensions. I feel as if I've known him forever."

"He liked you, too. He thinks you're a nice Jewish boy."

"Don't remind him I'm only half. God, I dread facing my mother."

"You really think she'll object?"

"We'll soon know." He squeezed her hand. "Whatever happens, you won't go back to Vincent, will you?"

"Only if you tell your mother we're living together. That sounds so yucky."

"Shall I say we're engaged?"

"Where's my ring?"

"Good idea. We'll stop at Woolworth's."

A maid ushered Sam and Melanie into the living room, a grandly over-furnished setting that Melanie knew reflected Yvonne's artistic tastes, not Marc's quiet elegance. Flowered chintz sofas flanked an antique marble fireplace. Above it hung a rare Joshua Reynolds portrait of an English Duchess. Every other available wall space was devoted to contemporary art: a Calder mobile, a series of De Kooning charcoals, and a Picasso gouache the San Francisco Museum of Modern Art had been trying to lure away for years.

Paul sat at the piano, picking out the theme from *Laura*. He stopped as soon as his guests arrived, and walked over to greet them.

"Well, well, family time," he smiled. "You're a handsome pair."

"And you're not even limping." The men embraced, and Paul kissed Melanie. Sam stood back to appraise his stepfather. "You're looking great!"

"I'm feeling great, especially since I heard about the *Herald's* jump in circulation. We're mighty proud of you, Sam."

"It's all due to your guidance. Say, we didn't mean to interrupt your playing. How 'bout some Fats?"

"Maybe later. Right now, I'd like to enjoy your visit."

"Me, too." Yvonne suddenly appeared in the doorway. "What a wonderful surprise, Sam darling. And Melanie, too! You just said you were coming by with a friend."

"She is a friend."

Yvonne kissed them both and joined them on the couch. "How's my favorite anchor person? I tell all my friends to watch my beautiful niece. I'm your greatest fan."

"No, I am," said Sam.

The hint slipped past Yvonne. "You were in mourning last year," she continued, "but I hope you'll be with us this year for the holidays. There's nothing to stop us from being a family again."

"I'd like that." Melanie tried to keep a straight face as Sam elbowed her ribs.

"What brings you two media mavens together?" asked Paul. "Something big in the works?"

Sam nodded. "You might call it a merger — of sorts. Melanie and I joined forces some months ago to work on the family history. By the way, I've finished it, Mother — hope it works for you."

He handed her a folder. "How wonderful! Thanks, darling. Ben will be thrilled, too."

"Anyway, Melanie and I found out that we liked being together. That is, on a personal level."

Yvonne's eyes widened. "You're good friends?"

"More than that, Mom." He reached for Melanie's hand. "We're in love. We plan to get married a year from October. I hope you and Paul will give us your blessing."

"But she's your cousin!" exclaimed Yvonne.

"That hasn't escaped our notice. Actually, she's my half-cousin," he corrected, then explained their research into possible genetic problems.

Paul was the first to speak. "Well, congratulations! If I had a cousin like Melanie, I'd fall in love with her, too."

Yvonne took her cue from Paul. She knew her son too well to think that any amount of logic would change his mind. "Of course you have our blessing," she said, without enthusiasm. "I think you're wise to wait a year and make sure you're right for each other."

"We could wait *ten* years," said Sam. "Nothing's going to change and nothing's going to stop us."

"It's still a bit of a shock." Yvonne's tone had turned cool. "Have you told Nonna yet?"

"No," said Melanie. "We told my father and he was pleased. Nonna's our last stop."

"She's going to be apoplectic, with all her family pride and puritan values. You'll break her heart."

"I doubt she's that fragile." Clutching Melanie's hand, Sam looked directly at his mother. "We don't need problems, Mom."

"Oh, darling, I told you I support you." Yvonne's eyes became moist. "All I've ever wanted is your happiness. You, too, Melanie dear. I just have to get used to you as a couple, that's all."

Sam smoothed her cheek. "Think of the bargain. You'll only have to buy one wedding gift instead of two."

Sam and Melanie stood nervously outside the house on Jackson Street, waiting to be admitted.

"What do you think she'll do? Disown us?" asked Melanie, answering her own question. "I wouldn't care about the money, but I'd hate to hurt her."

"I'd hate to lose the money." Seeing her expression, he added, "Only teasing, my love. Will you break the news or should I?"

Before she could answer, Clara's loyal Kai, in a starched black uniform and white lace apron, opened the door. "Why, good evening, Miss Melanie. I wasn't expecting you, Mr. Sam. Mrs. Stockton's in the garden."

"Thanks, Kai. We know the way."

They found Clara sitting on an iron bench beneath a cherry blossom tree, sipping tea. She glanced up in surprise. "Well, well, what have we here?"

Sam grinned. "It's your lucky day, Nonna. Two grandkids for the price of one." They sat on the bench on either side of her.

Clara set down her cup and faced them suspiciously. "What are you doing here together? Is some sort of family plot in the making?"

"Not exactly." Sam ran a nervous finger around his collar. "We hope you won't be upset."

"Oh, get to the point. You didn't come to see my flowers."

"We love each other, Nonna. We plan to get married. We love you, too, very much, but nothing you say or do will change how we feel about each other."

Clara stared a long moment, letting the news and its ramifications sink in. Finally, a lone tear trickled down her cheek. Her voice was soft and emotional. "Why would I want to cause unhappiness to two people I love so dearly? That's the best news I've had in years."

Melanie gasped, incredulous. "Oh, Nonna — do you mean it?"

"Of course I mean it." She wiped her eyes with a lace hankie. "How long has this been going on?"

"A few months — on and off." Sam couldn't believe her reaction. "You aren't worried we'll have deformed babies?"

"I don't give a rodent's rear about old wives' tales. The important thing is that you two exquisite children found each other and you make each other happy. Are you planning a formal engagement?"

"No," said Sam. "Mom put on a good show, but she wasn't thrilled."

"She ought to get down on her knees and thank God you fell in love with this beautiful woman. Have you set a date?"

"Sometime next October.

"Good," she declared. "Because I'm going to give you the most spectacular wedding this city's ever seen."

Later that night, Sam and Melanie crawled into bed.

"Shouldn't we tell your brothers?" she asked, snuggling up to him.

"I'm having lunch with Ben tomorrow, and I'll call Dave in the morning."

"Do you think they'll approve?"

"They've been after me to settle down for so long, they'd approve of a gorilla."

"How flattering."

"You're better looking — to me, that is. I can't speak for the gorilla."

"Sam," she whispered, nuzzling his neck. "All the years you've been single, you've must've thought about the kind of woman you wanted to marry. What was she like?"

"Oh, dark-haired, short, on the buxom side. No brains, no independent spirit, so she wouldn't challenge me and would just adore me and wait on me day and night. What about your ideal man?"

"Well, I always hoped he'd be an orphan, so I wouldn't have in-laws, and someone not used to having nice clothes so I could spoil him a little. And he'd be plain looking, not one of these pretty boy types the girls are always chasing."

"Nothing worse than a boy toy." He turned his head to her. "I thought of something else. My ideal woman would hate to make love."

"Why?"

"Well, if she *liked* it, I'd never get anything done. I'd have to spend every second catering to her needs."

"Noble creature."

"Let's see if you qualify." He took her chin in his hands and kissed her for a long time. "Did you hate that?"

"Passionately." Her arms reached up and closed around his neck. "But just to be sure — let's try again."

Chapter 57 – 1991

The following January, San Francisco was still struggling to recover from the 1989 Loma Prieta earthquake. Fissures had developed on the slopes of Telegraph Hill, a water main had failed near Civic Center, creating a large hole in the street, and long delays in repairing freeways infuriated Mayor Art Agnos, who publicly blasted the postponements as "Ridiculous!"

Despite continuing problems, certain residents of Presidio Heights remained more or less oblivious to the challenge of rebuilding the city. Clara Hayes Stockton, for one, had her own challenges to confront. Giving in to Sam's pleas to "low-key" the wedding ceremony, the 84-year-old matriarch, her mind sharp as ever, took great joy in planning as spectacular a reception for her grandchildren as she'd promised.

They'd given her a date: Saturday October 19th. The immediate family-only wedding would take place at the house on Jackson Street at five-thirty P.M. Limousines would then carry the guests to the Fairmont Hotel, where friends and relatives would await them.

Almost a year of preparation culminated in a frantic month of showers and pre-wedding parties, and what seemed to Melanie to be endless hours of fittings at S. Greenfield & Company.

Sam's big brother Ben, not one to miss an opportunity, had insisted on dressing the bride. The gown he commissioned was custom-designed in Italy by Valentino, who'd just celebrated 30 years in business, and was happy to do a favor (for which he was well-reimbursed) for his good friend at San Francisco's most prestigious department store.

"We'll do something like what we did for Jackie Kennedy when she married Onassis," Valentino's top man had told Ben. "Jackie wanted a short dress, and of course, it wasn't her first wedding. For your sister-in-law, who's obviously a virgin (giggle), we'll go full length white with a train. I see a high-neck Chantilly lace encrusted with delicate seed pearls and tiny pink rosebuds…"

And so the precious gown had arrived, made to measure, but needing infinite alterations. Sam wanted no part of his brother's offer of a custom-tailored cutaway. Pleading time constraints, he bought a black Armani tux off the rack.

In the meantime, Clara was enjoying making plans…most of them. One problem she faced was that the rabbi who'd married Yvonne and Marc had passed on, and the Greenfields' current rabbi had informed her — rather sourly, she thought — that he didn't do "mixed" marriages.

With her usual resourcefulness, Clara found a female rabbi who saw no reason why two people of different faiths should not be married. That took care of Sam's family, and since Melanie was not a church-goer, Clara invited her Presbyterian minister to co-officiate.

Sam would wear a white yarmulke for the occasion, while Melanie would top her coiffure with Clara's glittery tiara and a lacy veil.

"I just *know* I'll trip on the damn train and break my leg," she'd told Sam the night before the wedding.

"Don't worry, I'll catch you," he'd replied. "And let's go to bed early, sweetheart. It's the last night we can make love in sin."

Only family members were present at the wedding, except for Ben's friend, Gordon Getty, who'd graciously agreed to sing a lovely Welsh song. Near the end of the ceremony, Sam stamped on a glass, a traditional Jewish custom. The rabbi blessed them in the name of God, the minister blessed them in the name of Jesus Christ our Lord, everyone hugged and kissed, sipped Dom Perignon, then piled into the limos.

The reception was indeed one of the most glamorous San Francisco had ever seen. More than 500 friends, distant relatives, politicians, and celebrities, Hollywood stars and the *crème* of San Francisco society, gathered to pay respects and enjoy the Stockton bounty.

Clara, of course, had commissioned the city's premiere party planner, Stanlee Gatti, to oversee the décor. With his usual flair, he transformed the Fairmont's Gold Ballroom into a fantasy of pink roses. Thousands of the delicate blooms wound around majestic pillars, embellished the orchestra stand, and formed voluminous centerpieces, all laced with tiny pink lights. Even the waiters wore pink vests.

Gifts of silver Tiffany hearts sat at each woman's place; the men took home sterling cufflinks. The seven-course gourmet dinner was paired with the finest wines and champagne. Couples danced to Abe Battat's 20-piece orchestra, and Steve Silver had sent over three of his *Beach Blanket Babylon* performers to round out the evening.

Clara's only disappointment was the absence of her son, Will. He had regretted both the ceremony and the dinner, saying he'd be out of town, but the rumor was that he was home writing a book — a book about growing up in a privileged family — a tell-it-all, that if rumors were true, could rival the recent earthquake in shaking up the city's elite.

Early Sunday morning, the day after the wedding, Melanie reached a lazy arm across Sam to shut off the alarm.

"It's not the clock, honey," he said, returning her arm to her, "It's the bleeping phone." Making no attempt to hide his annoyance, he grabbed the receiver. "This better be good."

"I'm afraid it is."

Recognizing his executive editor's voice, Sam immediately sat up. "I'm listening."

"The reports are coming fast and furious. Fire in the Oakland Hills. Spreading fast and it's vicious. Temperatures in the high 90s, wind speeds in excess of 65 mph. Firefighters predicting a *major* disaster!"

"Damn it all!" Sam turned to Melanie, now wide awake. "Major fire in the Oakland hills. Would you divorce me if I left you on our first day of being legal?"

"I'd divorce you if you didn't."

"Hold everything, Brady. I'll be right there."

Sam gave his wife a quick kiss, sprang out of bed and headed for the bathroom. With a sigh, Melanie reached for the phone and buzzed Susie Bigelow's private line.

"What now?" a frazzled voice demanded.

"It's me, Melanie. Emergency time?"

"Yeah, but you just got married."

"No problem, Susie."

"OK, the crew's in Oakland. Get your ass over there PDQ."

By night-time, the strong winds had died down to five miles an hour, finally giving firefighters a chance to contain the terrifying blaze. As Melanie reported on the late news, the Oakland Hills Fire would be recorded as the worst in California's history. Later it would be learned that 25 people, including a policeman and a firefighter, had been killed, and over 3,000 homes destroyed, at an estimated loss of more than a billion and a half dollars.

When Melanie walked in her front door that evening, shortly before midnight, her hair was askew, her clothes were covered with ashes, and her feet ached. A message from Sam told her he loved her and not to wait up for him.

Slipping off her coat and shoes, she dropped to the bed and fell fast asleep.

Part 7

The Book

Chapter 58 — 1996

January 8th saw the inauguration of San Francisco's first black mayor, outgoing Assembly Speaker Willie Lewis Brown, Jr.

This was a blow to followers of his predecessor, ex-police chief Frank Jordan, who had helped save the Giants from moving to Florida, and started the badly-needed retrofitting of City Hall.

Jordan's supporters feared — rightfully, as it turned out — that favoritism would soon be rampant.

Late in 1995, the Stockton family, Clara, Betsy, Tim and Yvonne, had all mourned the passing of Lou Ella. After her fourth heart attack, she'd died in her sleep.

Tim had taken the loss badly. Time and a constant flow of Gulf War veterans needing help, however, had lured him back to his profession. Keeping busy, and knowing Lou Ella would have approved, aided the healing process.

In the meantime, Melanie and Sam had settled into their routines. Sam, facing serious problems at the *Herald,* was handling them with increasing skill, and Melanie, a successful news anchor, had found time to give birth to Jimmy, now a lively one-year-old. Life was good for the young Greenfields…then came the bomb.

It exploded in the form of the long-rumored memoir, a history of Will Stockton's life as he saw it — the life of a man who never felt he "belonged" to his rich and prominent family. Titled "Lucky Bastard," a phrase he often heard himself called, the book (penned by a ghost writer, everyone assumed), held little back.

The first few chapters told of Will's early years as a sickly child, son of the great publisher who obviously favored his older son. Will's recollections of his father's put-downs and his mother's loving attempts to stand up to her husband, made for spicy gossip.

The story got better or worse, depending who was reading it. As a lifetime of anger and resentment unrolled, Will recounted how his half-sister Yvonne first met her husband Paul by breaking the rules at the Stage Door Canteen…and how Yvonne introduced her cousin Betsy to a gold-digging drunk she later married and divorced. Marc's infidelities were recorded; where Will got his "facts," no one knew.

Hostility leaped off the pages as Will described how his mother turned on him after his father's death, voting with Tim and Lou Ella to deprive him of his rightful inheritance as the *Herald's* new publisher. Sure, he drank and caroused, but only because his family refused to see that he was "different."

Thanks to a former co-worker at the *Herald*, Will was able to piece together Lou Ella's campaign to entrap the popular Tim Stockton. And though Tim fared comparatively well in the book, Will couldn't resist noting that his half-brother had never earned a living. His inheritance and his late wife's salary paid the bills.

Will even told how his youthful behavior finally got him "evicted" from his mother's house. So at age 22, he moved to an apartment and began writing a daily diary that became the basis for this book.

Then the kicker: nine years later, his mother shot and killed a man she claimed was a burglar. But neither the newspaper reports nor the police files pointed to burglary, and what really happened was never known.

Miraculously, however, Will solved the case, or so he now claimed. According to a former police officer's notarized testimony, the police believed that Clara knew the man and had let him in — and that he'd come there expecting sexual favors, which she refused, so he raped her. Because a rape victim was "disgraced for life" in those days, she'd invented the burglary story.

Of course Will wrote of Katie's reaction — how she'd left the house the next morning, picked up a hippie and moved in with him. Her history of drugs and alcohol was delineated, as well as the long-lasting mother/daughter feud. And since he could find no record of Katie's marriage, her daughter Melanie, his niece, was undoubtedly illegitimate.

The last chapter described how Will finally "came out" to his mother, and confessed that he was living with a male lover. She admitted disappointment that he would produce no grandchildren, but in the same breath, promised to support him in every way.

Not so the rest of the family. Once they learned he was homosexual, he wrote, he knew he'd never rise above being general manager of the family-owned TV station — a prediction that seemed to be coming true.

No one in San Francisco could remember any instance where a member of such a prominent family revealed so many skeletons in a memoir. The literary temblor not only shook up the local community, its aftershocks spread across the country in secondary headlines, with pictures of the glamorous family. Barely a week after publication, "Lucky Bastard" hit *The New York Times* best-seller list.

The book seemed to polarize San Franciscans. Longtime *Herald* critics, competitors, and staunch conservatives were the first to condemn the Stocktons, insisting that such a morally bankrupt family had no right to exert widespread journalistic influence.

Thousands of "well-meaning" citizens shared wait'll-you-hear-this-one tales of encounters with family members. At homes, restaurants, parties, and every imaginable social, political, or charitable event, "the book" was prime chatter.

There were, of course, many irate defenders. Charities that enjoyed the largesse of the multimillion dollar Stockton Foundation, as well as patrons of the arts, came out in force to praise the family's generosity and civic contributions.

Longtime acquaintances, possibly fearful that a similar tell-all might someday thrust them into the same position, were also quick to show loyalty. After all, who didn't have a few skeletons lying around?

Determined to "take the high road," the Stocktons and the Greenfields declined to discuss the book in public, and stayed busy enough to virtually ignore the hoopla. Over Clara's objections, the family lost no time voting to relieve Will of his position at KSTO — but they had no power to relieve him of his 10 shares of stock, or to exclude him from stockholders' meetings.

When the talk finally died down, Clara realized, with a glint of amusement, that her son's mistaken conclusions about the shooting in 1960 had put an end to any speculation there might have been.

What amused her even more, she thought, as she crawled into bed that night, was that Will's sensational sizzler had missed the juiciest scandal of all.

Chapter 59 — 2001

Sam Greenfield was driving to work on a quiet Tuesday, enjoying the dawn and half-listening to the news. Despite all the problems at the paper, he still took pleasure going to his office every day, just as he looked forward to going home to Melanie. She worked mornings now, preferring to spend most of her time with lively six-year-old Jimmy, and their cuddly three-year-old, Kate.

No longer the flippant, self-mocking young man of days past, Sam wore his new maturity well, often reminding himself of his countless reasons to be thankful. The wars, disease and poverty that afflicted the world, as well as the violence, AIDS, and homeless problems in his own city, were realities he faced every day and with more emotional involvement, he realized, than a good journalist should have.

Back in his bachelor days, he'd traveled with Ben on a buying trip to India. They'd seen whole families, some with tiny babies, living on the streets of Bombay — a frightening sight that had made a deep impression, particularly since he and Ben had agreed it could never happen at home.

But it *had* happened, and it *was* happening, and to Sam's deep frustration, no one seemed to be doing much about it. Mayor Willie Brown, in fact, was addressing that exact problem on the radio, when suddenly Sam heard a voice say, "We interrupt this program to bring you a special bulletin."

What followed was an unconfirmed report that a plane had crashed into New York's famous World Trade Center tower.

By the time Sam reached his office, he had a better idea of what had happened. Though facts were sparse, he sensed the news was big — bigger than any news story that had broken in the 12 years he'd been publisher. A phone message that Paul Amory was on his way to the *Herald* underscored his fears.

Though Paul was physically active at 81, and kept in fine shape, he had deliberately let Sam make his own mistakes over the years, and run the paper without interference. The fact that Paul felt his presence might be beneficial in light of the breaking story, gave Sam some idea of its impact — and he was both anxious and grateful. The excitement and electricity in the newsroom was almost tangible.

By noon of September 11th, 2001, the city, the nation, and much of the world were in shock. Sam talked of putting out a special edition, but Paul advised against it. Bay Area residents were already swamped with news of the tragedy from television.

Melanie had called Sam to say she'd be working till five, and very probably into the evening. The nanny had instructions, and Grandma Eevie would look in on the children.

Late that afternoon, drained and exhausted, Sam asked Paul to read over his editorial, *Day of Horror,* for the next edition.

It began, *"What dawned as a warm, sunny Tuesday morning quickly turned into a surreal nightmare, as two hijacked planes crashed into the 110-story World Trade Center towers, causing them to collapse…"*

Paul tightened the prose where needed, and declined Sam's offer to share a byline. Then he asked, "Could we take five minutes?"

"Hell, yes." Sam slid into the chair behind his desk. "Have a seat, then please go home. You've been a tremendous help — but the worst is over."

"In one sense, yes. Now's definitely not a good time, but there is no good time. As you know, the paper's in deep trouble. We saw a 20 percent drop in ad revenue this year. The dot-com bubble burst took a big percentage of our ads, the help-wanteds are down 50 percent, marketing and distribution costs have escalated, and we've been losing millions for almost two years."

"I know." Sam's furrowed brow showed his anxiety. "There's no getting around the L-word, is there."

"We can't avoid layoffs."

"But there's good news, too." Sam's voice perked up. "When our circulation passed the half-million mark, we officially became the 11th largest paper in the country."

"A credit to your leadership. But don't put off doing what has to be done."

"I won't — I can't." Sam came around the desk, hesitated a moment, then embraced his stepfather. "You know, you're the best thing that ever happened to this family — that is, besides my marrying my cousin."

For the next few weeks, the pages of the *Herald* overflowed with tales of the terrorist attack and its worldwide ramifications. New York's Mayor Giuliani warned that the death toll would be in the thousands, while President George W. Bush vowed that America would "lead the world to victory," though no one seemed quite sure who the enemy was.

One morning in November, Sam reluctantly sent email pink slips to his employees. Later in the day, he publicly announced that the *Herald* had made layoffs and offered buyouts to eliminate 200 jobs.

Though rumors had been circulating for months, the publisher's apologetic message did little to soothe the workers. Nothing could alleviate Sam's sense of guilt; it was his fault that so many good people were losing their jobs.

Holding Melanie in his arms that night, he whispered, "This was the worst day of my life."

Chapter 60 — 2005

The American invasion of Iraq in 2003, and the re-election of George W. Bush the following year, polarized the country as never before. Maps showing Republican states as red and Democratic states as blue, launched the two colors as a quick (and oversimplified) way to identify the disputing factions. To no one's surprise, California quickly became "the bluest state in the nation."

Like many families, the Stocktons were of different minds. All except the Picketts — Betsy, Foster, and Tyrone — applauded Mayor Gavin Newsom's daring move in 2004, when he ordered city officials to issue marriage licenses to same-sex couples. His ruling brought national attention, sparking debate across the country, but some say, jeopardizing His Honor's political future.

Despite Will Stockton's mean-spirited memoir, Clara continued to be close to her son, encouraging him to visit when his siblings weren't around. She made it a point to appear in public with him, even inviting him to escort her to the opening of the new de Young Museum in Golden Gate Park. Will was happy to do so, finding the modern structure "cold and stark," while Clara thought it "spectacular."

One evening after work, Sam Greenfield stopped by to see his mother and Paul, at their request. They hugged him warmly and led the way into the library. Once settled on couches, Yvonne asked, "How's my favorite publisher?"

"Tired," he said. "You're looking great, Mom. Is Paul treating you right?"

"Like a princess," she laughed. Paul beamed and filled Sam's wine glass.

"Mmm — thanks. Now suppose you tell me why I'm here. Is anything wrong?"

"Well, yes and no," said Yvonne. "I know you're anxious to get home, honey, so I'll be direct. You're doing a superb job, but as you know, the *Herald* is losing revenue at an alarming rate. It makes no sense, to us, at least, to go on losing millions — your and Melanie's inheritance, too."

"But —"

"Hear me out." Yvonne clasped her hands to hide their trembling. How she hated to hurt her son, but the words had to come from her, not from Paul, where they might be resented. "I know you take great pride in the *Herald*, Sam darling, and I know how hard you've worked. We're so proud of you. But I also know you have a practical side. And we've been approached by a fine gentleman who represents a group of New York investors. They're interested in buying the paper."

Sam gulped. "You're serious?"

"They've made us a serious proposal — in writing. They're offering $550 million for all rights. Our lawyers have talked to their lawyers; we've agreed on the price and some minor concessions. But we can't take it any farther until we know how the family feels about selling."

Sam could barely restrain his anger. "Who *are* these people? What do you know about them?"

"Not nearly enough," said Paul. "I've friends in New York researching them. But as your mother said, we don't want to spend any more time or money on this until we talk to the family. And you're the first one we're asking."

Shocked, Sam sat in silence, trying to digest what he'd just heard, determined to control himself. It would do no good to lash out at his mother.

But he couldn't help feeling betrayed, as if months of plotting and planning had gone on behind his back. It was *his* paper, wasn't it? She and Paul both knew how much it meant to him, how he'd sweated to maintain his grandfather's high standards...

"I'm...surprised," he finally said, hoping his voice wouldn't give away his emotion. "I don't understand why you waited so long to tell me."

"No one was being secretive," said Paul, sensing Sam's hurt. "We simply had to wait until our lawyers confirmed that the offer was legitimate."

Sam nodded. Paul's explanation helped. "Well, frankly, I have no desire to sell the paper. I guess I have more faith in myself than you have in me. I'm convinced I can turn it around so it starts making money again."

"No one's asking you to make a decision now," said Yvonne, feeling his pain. "Just twirl the idea around in your head, look at the pros and cons, talk to Melanie, and see how she feels. We need to do the same. But

I admit, it's tempting to think of shedding all that worry."

"I understand, Mom. You're just trying to do what's best for all of us." Somewhat calmed, but still agitated, Sam rose, kissed his mother's forehead, nodded to Paul, and headed for the door.

That night, he and Melanie talked, discussing all possibilities. There *would* be some advantages to selling, Melanie pointed out, once she got over the shock. She could quit her job, they could take trips with their children, live a year in Paris as she'd always longed to do, and enjoy life and their children, instead of being such workaholics.

But they were also wary. "We can't even think about selling the paper," Sam said, "till we know absolutely everything there is to know about the people who made the offer. We can't have it falling into the wrong hands."

The next day, Yvonne phoned the five other shareholders: her cousin Betsy Kettering Pickett, Clara, Tim, Will, and even Melanie, who, of course, had already heard the news. Yvonne explained the offer fully and promised to get back to them, as soon as she knew more about the prospective buyers.

That afternoon, Paul received a call from a close friend and investigative reporter on the *Times*. The man had access to a source who informed him that the "media conglomerate" interested in buying the *Herald* was financed by a wealthy businessman named Foster Pickett, who, by strange coincidence, happened to be married to Betsy Kettering Pickett, Yvonne's cousin.

Further research, Paul's friend reported, revealed that Pickett was not "clean." Rumors abounded of shady deals and questionable associations. How we made his money was suspicious, and there was talk of connections to New York crime families. He was, in fact, currently under investigation by the FBI.

Hearing the information from a trusted source, Paul began adding up the facts: the buyers' reluctance to give backgrounds of their investors, their anxiety to close the sale as soon as possible, their insistence on having lawyers present at all discussions…gave the strong impression that something about the deal had an odor.

"I never liked that damn Foster Pickett," he told Yvonne, angrily. "If he had any balls, he'd have come to us himself with an offer, instead of trying to hide behind some phony conglomerate. I'm tempted to sue the bastard for fraud."

"That *is* infuriating." Yvonne was puzzled. "But I can't believe that Betsy knows about it, even though we don't see much of each other anymore. She wouldn't try to deceive her own family."

"Are you sure? Didn't you tell me Betsy inherited her mother's 40 percent of the family stock? If she and Foster were to buy the paper for $550 million, 40 percent of that — about $220 million — would go right into their pockets."

"Oh, no! Isn't that dishonest?"

"I don't know. It's up to the seller to do due diligence, and find out all he can about the buyer." Paul exhaled loudly. "There's no way we can go ahead with our plans."

"But the family knows about the offer. What if some still want to sell?"

"I'll talk to them. Once I explain the situation, I doubt we'll have a problem."

For Clara, Tim, Melanie, and Yvonne, Paul was right; they shared his wrath. Will said he liked the idea of getting a chunk of cash for his stock, but he'd "think it over." And cousin Betsy insisted she hadn't known her husband was behind the offer, vehemently denied his "questionable connections" and thought selling the paper was "a great idea."

"There's no getting around it," Paul told Yvonne at breakfast the next day. "We'll have to have a shareholders' meeting and take a vote. But I don't think we need to worry. Clara has 20 percent of the shares, you, Tim and Melanie each have 10, so that makes 50. Even if Will decides to add his 10 shares to Betsy's 40, we'll have a 50/50 vote, and that means no sale. We need a majority to sell."

"That's a relief."

"I'll say." He rose, bent down and kissed his wife's cheek. "I must say, sweetheart — life with you is never dull."

Chapter 61 — 2006

Driving to work on a rainy morning in March, Sam was lost in thought. This was his city…his newspaper…his life. What would the town become if the paper fell into the wrong hands? What would he tell his readers? How could he let that happen? He would, of course, do everything in his power to see that it didn't.

An editorial, he thought. I'll write an editorial about San Francisco, about how it's changed — all the good things and the not-so-good things. If we lose the paper, at least people will know how I feel, how the family feels, how much we all have to be proud of…

He grabbed his recorder and began dictating: "This city — this wonderful town — is constantly evolving. Take downtown. No more S. Greenfield & Company. Business was so bad, the flagship store had to close in 1995. Women are buying online, digging into their closets for 'vintage,' or just not buying.

"Yes, the city's changing…in many good ways. The boundary lines between downtown and South of Market are dissolving. The Ferry Building has brightened the Embarcadero. We've jazzed up Market Street with the Four Seasons Hotel and the Westfield Centre. One Rincon Hill, the town's tallest tower, will reshape our skyline when it opens in 2008.

"Culture and the arts are flourishing. The Opera has a bevy of new supporters, Michael Tilson Thomas keeps leading the Symphony to greater heights, and the Ballet gets rave reviews 'round the globe.

"Parking? Terrible! People are taking cabs and Muni — or walking. Real estate's over the top. A single home on Broadway is selling for $65 million. There's pollution in the bay, the 49ers might move to Santa Clara, and worst of all, there's AIDS — the plague that's claimed 25 *million* lives in the last quarter century.

"Citizens worry about the costly delays of adding a tower to the Bay Bridge. Thanks to politics, it won't be finished before 2013 — that's 11 years of construction, eight more than it took to *build* the bridge!

"And what kind of nutty city wants to spend a gazillion bucks putting a suicide barrier on the Golden Gate Bridge when people are sleeping in doorways?"

Sam set down his recorder, and pulled into the Fifth and Mission Street Garage. He sat for a moment, trying to calm himself, but his thoughts were still racing. He took back the recorder.

"Who's to say what's good or bad for the city — hell, it's *our* city, yours and mine, and we love it unconditionally. Maybe, as Herb Caen used to say, San Francisco is a 'she' — with lots of curves and undulations, and a reputation for naughtiness.

"Writers have struggled for years to capture the magic of this 49 square miles of land, but they'll never stop trying and they'll never be successful...because the true spirit of this city lie in the hearts and souls of its citizens."

Corny, but it's a start, he thought, shutting off his recorder.

The long-awaited meeting took place that afternoon, the only time the participants would all be available. The six Stockton shareholders, Clara, Melanie, Betsy, Tim, Yvonne and Will, plus spouses Sam and Paul — met in the Embarcadero Center offices of Yvonne's attorney.

An elderly man with courtly manners, the barrister welcomed his clients, sat them around his desk and explained what he knew of the offer to buy the *Herald*. On instructions from Paul, he had called Foster Pickett and invited him to the meeting, but Foster had declined with no explanation.

The lawyer then gave his you-all-know-why-you're-here speech, stating that he realized they were very busy people, but perhaps they wanted time for discussion.

Paul was the first to speak. "Since my wife first called all of you a few months ago," he said, "some new facts have come to light. Perhaps most important is that Betsy's husband, Foster Pickett, neglected to inform the family that he's the big investor behind the proposal to buy the *Herald*. That might not be a problem, were he not, reliable sources tell me, part of a much bigger plan by conservative Republicans to take control of all media in California."

"Nonsense," growled Betsy.

"What for?" asked Will. "Aren't the Republicans happy running the country?"

"No, they want to run our bodies, our minds, our voting machines, everything we think, say, and do. Their promise of 'editorial independence' means zero — zilch. They want to destroy our freedoms and erode our civil liberties. They want to keep us from knowing what's going on behind every locked door in Washington."

"It's true," echoed Sam. "Access to information has never been easier, yet we live in an age where government lies and secrecy are the norm."

"Scary," said Tim.

Paul set down his water glass. "Before you get to a vote, I'd like to remind you what's at stake here…"

"Do we have to waste time with that?" interrupted Betsy. "We've all made up our minds."

Paul looked at Yvonne and shrugged. He was only a guest at the meeting. It wasn't his place to hold things up. The lawyer stepped in. If no one objected, he'd be happy to proceed with the voting.

Starting alphabetically, Betsy was asked for her vote. "Yes, on the sale," she said. "It would be a great thing for all of us." Clara, Melanie and Tim voted no, Will said yes, he'd go with Betsy. Yvonne said no, with an angry look at Betsy.

"Then I guess we've a tie," said Tim, relieved. "Where I sit, that means no sale."

"Maybe where you sit, but not where I sit," said Will, so quietly almost no one heard him.

But Tim did. His eyebrows raised. "Something you want to tell us?"

Will smiled. Almost totally bald now, with a neat, white goatee and carrying a cane, he had the fragile look of a man ten years older. "Last year I had my 75th birthday," he said. "Remember my birthday gift, *maman?*"

Clara's face lit with sudden recognition; then she turned pale. "That was to be our secret."

"And up to now, I haven't told a soul. But I think it's time we shared the news of your generosity…and the fact that you gave me the only gift I wanted: the five shares of stock you were going to leave me in your will."

Tim's eyes flashed angrily. "Is that true, Clara?"

She nodded slowly, a tear traveling down her cheek.

"Hold on a minute, everybody calm down," ordered Paul, sensing an imminent explosion. "Let's not race to conclusions. Let's assume, for the moment, that Will hasn't made up his mind…"

"But I have," snapped Will. "I promised Betsy I'd vote with her. It's a done deal."

"Indeed it is," said a defiant voice. "And a good thing, too." All heads turned to Betsy. Gray-haired now, and badly overweight, she had a cold, imperious expression. Yvonne stared at her, stunned. This was a Betsy she'd never known.

"Regardless of my husband's involvement," Betsy continued, "and I assure you I knew nothing about this so-called takeover until Paul called me, I don't share your assumption that the President of the United States is some sort of unfeeling monster. He's by far the most moral, ethical, family and God-worshipping man who's ever occupied the White House."

"If you call a liar and a warmonger moral," said Tim.

"Let her talk," said Paul.

"I don't need to explain my position." Betsy shrugged. "I just want to make very clear that I'm committed to this sale, and Will is, too. Look what happened to this country when the Democrats ran it: drugs all over our schools, sex and violence everywhere you look, people robbing and raping and shooting each other. We're a country gone mad — a country without morals, without spirituality. Without *religion*. You call it free-dom. I call it depravity. And I'm damn well going to do something about it!"

The reaction to her pronouncement was a heavy silence. Paul turned to his brother-in-law. "You and I have never been friends, Will. What you wrote in your book was harmful to all of us. Still — we've never had angry words, we've never sued you for slander, in fact, we've never done much but ignore each other, right?"

He gave Will no chance to answer. "It doesn't need to be that way. We all have more than enough of God's gifts to be thankful for; perhaps we can all forgive each other and be a family again. But first, I have some-thing to say."

Paul's voice and manner were forceful. No one interrupted.

"I have it from an unimpeachable source — actually, a longtime Republican who's appalled at the direction his party has taken — that Mr. Pickett and his group not only hope to gain control of all California media, they have another agenda as well. The reason they're so anxious to mold and shape public opinion is because they're hoping to get an amend-ment passed to change the U.S. Constitution — to allow the President a third term in office."

The room was eerily silent.

"It's not an easy process," Paul continued. "The amendment first has to pass both the House and the Senate by a two-thirds majority. Then it has to be approved by three-fourths of the states."

"But they don't have the votes, do they?" asked Melanie. "The President's approval rating is way down."

"According to today's CBS poll, the President's approval rating has dropped from the 52 percent it was a year ago to 34 percent. I doubt that an amendment would pass. Still, do any of us want to take that chance?"

He turned to Will. "Do you really want another four years of this man in the White House — a man completely opposed to your way of life — and not only opposed to gay people having the right to marry, but opposed to gays having any rights at all?"

"I don't give a flying fig," said Will.

"The hell you don't, Willard Hayes Stockton!" a new voice boomed. Clara was standing up by her seat, short of stature, but a dramatic figure in a red wool suit. Her shock of white hair, perfectly groomed, framed a wrinkled but still gracious face. Her eyes gleamed as she marched over to her son.

"Willard," she demanded, "Have I ever let you down?"

He looked up meekly. "No, *maman.*"

"Have I taken care of you all your life?"

"Yes," he nodded.

"Do you love me?"

"Of course I do."

"Then it's time to do something for me…and for a lot of people. I want you to change your vote, Will. I'm not going to threaten you, I'm not going to desert you if you say no. You're my son and I'll always love you. I've told the family over and over that we've been unfair to you — that you had reasons to be angry at us, but you got all that out of your system and you've grown into a man of strength and character. I'm not sure they believed me, but now's your chance to prove it. You can be a hero to your family rather than a traitor."

She stopped a moment, collected herself, then spoke more calmly. "I'm not asking you to do this for any reason except that it's the *right* thing to do. Won't you please do this, Will? — for me, for yourself, for all of us?"

"Don't listen to her," ordered Betsy. "Be a man! Have some guts, for God's sake!"

Clara glowered. "Do you owe Betsy more loyalty than you owe me?"

That last question seemed to hit its target. Will bowed his head and was silent. Nobody dared move for several minutes. Then he looked up and spoke to the lawyer. "I've changed my mind," he said quietly. "Mark me a 'no' on selling the *Herald*." He paused another moment, then broke into a grin. "And damn it to hell — God save the queens!"

Shouts of joy went up on all sides as Clara and Melanie rushed to embrace him. Sam hugged Paul, and Tim hugged them both. Yvonne sat in her seat and cried. Betsy grabbed her purse and stalked out.

Clara beamed. "Thanks to you, my darling son, we've still got the *Herald*. We've still got our values and our integrity. And I've got my beautiful family together again."

"You're the man of the hour, Will," sniffed Yvonne.

"Someone ought to write a book about these crazy Stocktons," said Paul, laughing with relief. "But then…who the heck is gonna believe it?"

Silence pervaded the upstairs sitting room of the house on Jackson Street, where Melanie had come, at her grandmother's request, for tea and "a chat."

She had listened quietly as Clara spoke, telling of events long buried, of mysteries and memories, of family secrets never before revealed. Stunned, Melanie sat trying to digest all the pieces, struggling to fit them into the jagged puzzle of her life.

Clara's voice broke into her thoughts. "I wanted to tell you about Hart Doyle the day you and Sam first came to see me. I wanted to explain how the romance had gone out of my marriage to James, how I met Hart Doyle, and despite all attempts to avoid him, fell in love with him. We had a brief affair, then I learned I was pregnant with your mom, Katie, and ended the relationship. I promptly seduced Grandpa James so he'd assume the baby was his.

"But I decided not to tell you about Hart that day. The only real reason to tell you would have been, if you'd been afraid to have children. But you assured me you weren't, and now you have darling Jimmy and Kate, and before we know it, they'll be teenagers."

"I'm grateful you told me."

"The story would have gone to the grave with me, Melanie, if you'd married anyone but Sam. But you deserve to know that your real grand-father, Hart Doyle, was a fine man — the kindest, most compassionate, most eloquent man I'd ever met. Your mother was his only child. You and Sam have no blood relationship. You're not even half-cousins."

Melanie nodded in wonderment.

"And the good news is that Will's come back to the fold in a big way. He just rewrote his will, leaving all his shares to Sam. Tim and Yvonne are doing the same thing, and so am I. When we're gone, your darling husband will have 50 percent of the shares in the company, plus your 10 percent — and he'll be able to outvote Betsy and those horrible Picketts."

"That's fantastic! It'll be a great relief for Sam. He'll have to be nice to me, too, since I'll have the swing votes."

"He's always nice to you. He adores you."

"And I adore him." Melanie lowered her voice. "Speaking of that, I don't suppose I should tell anyone that my beautiful, elegant, well-bred grandma had a torrid love affair."

Clara smiled. "My dear, I'm an old, old lady. Nothing I did 65 years ago would cause even a raised eyebrow today. But I hope you and Sam will keep this to yourselves. Tim would be terribly hurt to learn that his best friend, who saved his life at Tarawa, had been my lover."

"The one who'd really be upset," she continued with a twinkle, "is Will, once he realized what a scandal he missed for his book. And I doubt you want to deal with any survivors of the Hogan family."

"You doubt right!" Melanie took a moment to weigh her thoughts.

Clara touched her arm. "I'm a bit nervous…how you feel about all this."

Melanie grinned. "Not to worry for one second, Nonna. As far as I'm concerned, I was born a Stockton, it's my middle name, I'm proud to be a Stockton, and always will be…as long as no one checks my DNA. I'll tell Sam, of course. Then we'll bury it forever."

"That's wise."

Melanie chuckled. "I hope you don't have any more surprises. I didn't know till I read Will's book that I was a bastard. Are you sure Mom and Dad never married?"

"Positive. Jason was your mother's first and last lover."

"I never doubted that. But I begin to understand why she was so different from the rest of the family. She never felt she belonged, and her feeling was right."

"Yes. I enjoy a few tiddlies now and then, but there's never been a hint of alcoholism in either the Hayes or the Stockton family. Hart wasn't alcoholic, but he did like to drink. Fortunately, you seem to have escaped those genes."

"I have Dad's liquor capacity — zilch." Melanie shook her head sadly. "If only Mom were here to share our happiness and enjoy her grandchildren."

"There's a last matter we have to clear up." Clara reached to her side table and drew out a yellowed envelope. "I don't know why I've saved it all these years…maybe for this moment. Take it, please. I've no further use for it."

Melanie's heart beat fast as she took the faded envelope, now remembering her mother's story of how she'd been asked to hide it after the shooting. In the upper left corner Melanie could still read:

Second Lieutenant Hart Doyle, Fleet Post Office, and a row of numbers. Beneath it were the letters "V-MAIL." It was addressed to Mr. Albert Hogan.

Holding her breath, Melanie opened the side flaps and read aloud:

"For Clara, In The Event Of My Death

November 19, 1943 — My Beloved: I'm writing this on my bunk as we prepare to go into combat. If anything should happen to me, Al Hogan will deliver this letter.

By the strange hand of God, in these ungodliest of circumstances, I've become friendly with your stepson Tim, and learned of the birth of your baby daughter — by the timing, I know it has to be our baby daughter.

Dearest Clara, surely you can no longer deny us the happiness we deserve. We're a family now, and we belong together. As soon as I return, I'm coming to claim you and our beautiful child.

It's ironic, but I just recently learned that I'm not even a real Doyle. My mother was the Doyles' upstairs maid who got impregnated one night by the family's inebriated houseguest, a visiting Norwegian publisher. I plan to look him up on my return. My mother died in childbirth, and needless to say, the Doyles kindly reared me as their own.

Should I not return, my darling, I hope you will share this letter with Katherine Marie so she will know her true heritage, and how deeply her father loved her. Should she ever want for anything, show this to the executor of my will. She's entitled to my entire estate.

Take care of yourself, my precious. No one will ever love you as I do. Your devoted,

Hart"

A few seconds passed before Clara spoke. Her voice was soft and sad: "Al Hogan, the man I shot, was Hart's trusted friend. Al knew Katie had no need of Hart's money, so he never delivered the letter. I assume he stored it somewhere and forgot about it. Then times got bad for him, and he remembered it."

"Blackmail?"

"Yes. He didn't break into the house as I told the police. He called

286

that Saturday night. Said he had to see me about an urgent matter relating to Hart Doyle. When he arrived, he showed me the letter and demanded $100,000 for it. That was a large sum in those days. If I didn't pay him, he'd take the letter to the *Examiner*. They'd have a heyday disgracing me, the family, the *Herald,* and even the Doyles' newspaper, the *Clarion,* in a single scoop."

"And the Doyles themselves," said Melanie, "That letter makes me a double bastard! I think it might be in everyone's interest to burn that piece of paper. But please go on."

"Well, I didn't have $100,000 at my fingertips, and trying to get it would have raised a lot of questions. I could have weathered the scandal, but my main fear was for Katie. She had serious emotional problems, and I knew that a shock like that — finding out that her beloved father was not really her father — could have pushed her over the edge."

"Not to mention the public disgrace."

"Exactly. I couldn't do that to the family or to James' memory." She paused a moment, than spoke in a low tone. "But I never *ever* meant to kill Al Hogan. I only wanted to scare him and get rid of him. I told him my diamond necklace was worth more than $100,000, which it was, and I would give it to him. He followed me upstairs. I walked to the dresser, opened the drawer, and that's when I saw the gun."

"What happened?"

"James had put it there years ago. He told me it wasn't loaded — just a 'prop' in case he had to scare off an intruder."

"Go on." Melanie held her breath.

"At first I didn't touch it. I gave Hogan the necklace and asked for the letter. He put the necklace in his pocket, then he said he wanted the money, too."

"The creep!"

"I told him we had a deal; we'd agreed on the trade. He said the necklace was just a bonus and he still demanded the money. I was furious and frightened at the same time. I said I might have some cash in my drawer. I went back to the dresser and grabbed the gun. I pointed it at him and told him to leave the letter, take the necklace and get out.

"He started laughing and daring me to shoot him. When I wouldn't put down the gun, he lunged at me...." Her voice broke as she relived the scene. "In my panic, I pressed the trigger. Imagine my horror when the gun fired! A bullet hit his chest and he fell to the floor. He died instantly."

"You never intended to shoot him."

"Good Lord, no, not for an instant!"

"Why didn't you tell that to the police?"

"How could I tell them what happened without having that whole story come out? I chose to say I shot in self-defense, which was the truth. I was petrified the other facts would be known if we went to court, and what it would do to Katie. So Avery spread around a few generous 'gifts' and the case was history."

Melanie patted her grandmother's trembling hands. "It's all right, Nonna darling. Please don't cry. I knew you never could have killed a man in cold blood. Sam and I love you very much and I can't wait to tell him he didn't marry his cousin. He'll probably think about it for four seconds, then go back to playing computer games with Jimmy."

"Won't he be shocked to learn his grandmother had a lover?"

Melanie laughed. "We always knew you weren't the angelic innocent you pretend to be. Anyway, who cares these days? Don't forget I got married in lily-white, and well, I must confess I wasn't exactly a virgin."

Clara's face relaxed into a smile. "That's hardly front page news, my dear. Shall we have some tea?"